A RUDE AWAKENING

"Bron-Bronwyn?" said Carole, sitting straight up, shaking. Overhead, something shivered and slid across the ceiling. *"Bronwyn!* Wake up!"

"What—?" The Princess opened one eye and reached for her shield.

"Look up there." whispered Carole.

"But there's *nothing* there," Bronwyn yawned. "Certainly nothing that can—YIKES!!" Something had snuck across the ceiling and down the wall and under the bed and up the side to sidle under Bronwyn's shield and *get* them. Silent laughter jeered at her, and unseen fingers tugged at her shift and tweaked her hair and pinched her. Distinctly unpleasant wheezing laughter filled the room and *something* smacked each of them on their backs so hard they fell forward. Much to her shame, Bronwyn felt tears spring to her eyes. The humiliation of it made her angry.

"Very well, spook!" she cried, drawing her sword from under the mattress, "I've felt *your* tender caresses . . . Here are *mine!*" And whacked. And whacked again. And kept on whacking . . .

SONGS FROM THE SEASHELL ARCHIVES, VOLUME 2

BRONWYN'S BANE
THE CHRISTENING QUEST

Elizabeth Ann Scarborough

BANTAM BOOKS
TORONTO · NEW YORK · LONDON · SYDNEY · AUCKLAND

SONGS FROM THE SEASHELL ARCHIVES #2

A Bantam Spectra Book / March 1988

PRINTING HISTORY
BRONWYN'S BANE copyright © 1983 by Elizabeth Ann Scarborough.
THE CHRISTENING QUEST copyright © 1985 by Elizabeth Ann Scarborough.

ISBN 0-553-27009-5

Published simultaneously in the United States and Canada

Bantam Books are published by Bantam Books, a division of Bantam Doubleday Dell Publishing Group, Inc. Its trademark, consisting of the words "Bantam Books" and the portrayal of a rooster, is Registered in U.S. Patent and Trademark Office and in other countries. Marca Registrada. Bantam Books, 666 Fifth Avenue, New York, New York 10103.

PRINTED IN THE UNITED STATES OF AMERICA

O   0 9 8 7 6 5 4 3 2 1

BRONWYN'S BANE

To the memory of Leslie Taylor Wier, with lasting affection, and also to the memory of my beloved cat, Saddleshoes, spiritual father of Ching.

This book is also for my brother, Monte, and for Robert Aranow with love.

The Great Tape is specifically dedicated to Karen H.

Many thanks to Linda Aranow-Brown, Robert Brown and Chris Opland for their services as sounding boards, to Prof. Dean Gottehrer for proofreading, to Nora Young and the late Teeny Fittroon for character ideas, and to Zelma Trafton for the inspiration for the sunken castle.

PREFACE: (FROM THE ARGONIAN ARCHIVES TRANS-
SCRIBED BY SIR CYRIL PERCHINGBIRD FOR
THE ARGONIAN HERALD)

CROWN PRINCESS CURSED AT CHRISTENING!
QUEEN SWOONS AS BEWITCHED
TOY SHOUTS "LIAR" AT HRH BRONWYN

Fort Iceworm, Northern Territories, Argonia: Reign of King
Roari the Red, Year I . . . The Royal Christening of the
firstborn of our King and Queen was marred earlier this year
by the antics of a bewitched christening gift, a jack-in-the-
box that shouted "You're a liar!" at the infant Princess
Bronwyn, cursing her to be one. Queen Amberwine fainted
hysterically but gracefully into the arms of her Lord while
the vocally distraught Royal Heiress was soothed by onlookers.

Experts fear the curse may damage the Princess's ability to
succeed her Royal Father on the Throne and reliable sources say
the King is launching an investigation into the source of the
curse.

CLASSIFIED DECREE: FROM HIS ROYAL MAJESTY
KING ROARI I TO SIR CYRIL PERCHINGBIRD, CHIEF
ARCHIVIST:

"Perchingbird: While We approve of your notion of transcribing
the archives into readable form for the populace against such a
time as the populace shall learn to read, the above article wasn't
exactly what We had in mind. As you know, Our quest to have
the Princess's curse lifted has not been entirely successful,
and must needs be delayed while other matters of State take
precedence. Therefore, in order to prevent undue disrespect
on the part of Our subjects for Our daughter, and to keep
from making life harder than it already is for the poor wee
lass, We and Our Queen have decided that this incident shall
be in no way published abroad until such time as We otherwise declare, and that those persons who have knowledge of
Bronwyn's curse shall keep their big mouths shut about it
around her so she can grow up as normally as possible without being punished and plagued for that which she cannot help.

3

We know We can expect your loyalty in this matter. Roari, Rex.''

(FROM THE ARGONIAN ARCHIVES TRANSCRIBED
BY SIR CYRIL PERCHINGBIRD
FOR *THE ARGONIAN HERALD*)

*GOOD NEWS AND BAD NEWS: QUEEN AMBERWINE WITH
CHILD AFTER MORE
THAN A DECADE AND ABLEMARLE LAUNCHES
INVASION FLEET*

Queenston: Reign of King Roari the Red, Year of the Great War . . . A palace spokesman announced this year that by the Grace of the Mother, our good Queen Amberwine is to bear another child for the greater glory of our realm. The Queen has been elegantly but fruitlessly slender since the birth of Princess Bronwyn, well over a decade ago. Due to Her Majesty's delicate constitution, our Queen's healers have recommended bedrest for her for the duration of her pregnancy. His Majesty is quoted as saying that he doesn't care if the new babe is a boy or a girl, just so it, and the Queen, are healthy.

On the darker side of the national scene, official sources have confirmed that the King announced to his council that we are now officially at war with Ablemarle. A reliable Royal spy has spotted the Ablemarlonian Navy, with King Worthyman the Worthless himself aboard its flagship, headed our way. An unconfirmed report has it that the Ablemarlonians are planning to unleash a new secret weapon to wreak death and destruction among us, may the Mother preserve us. King Roari and the consolidated Argonian Army and Navy, and the three-dragon Air Force, have already set sail to foil the blackhearted aggressors.

During the King's absence and the Queen's indisposition, Her Majesty's half-sister, Lady Wormroost (nee Magdalene Brown) has been appointed Regent by His Majesty. Her Ladyship, a hearth witch from birth and a national heroine (for an account of Lady Maggie's and Earl Colin's rescue of Her Majesty from the Forces of Evil, see *The Herald* back issue dated Year of the Election of King Roari I) was created Honorary Princess by His Majesty some years ago, a title she modestly chooses not

4

to use. Her Lord, Colin Songsmith, Earl Wormroost and President of the Minstrel's Academy Alumni Association, is presently abroad in the countryside, rallying the populace with song and story to the defense of their King and Country. May the Mother grant him speed and success.

FT. ICEWORM

RIVER

AUNT SYBIL'S

TROUTEROUTE

SOUTH HIGHWAY

MOUNTAINS

WIZARD
RASPBERRY'S
EVERCLEAR

R. BLABBERMOUTH

L. DARLINGHAM

ROWAN'S KEEP

GYPSY CAMP

QUEENSTON

BAYSHORE

DRAGON BAY

EVIL ISLAND

THE GULF
OF
GREMLINS

THE EYE
OF THE
NEEDLE

WORM-
ROOST
GLACIER

WORMROOST

WORMHAVEN

MAJESTIC MOUNTAINS

MERMAID'S
ATOLL

OF HORN

THE
SOUTHERN
ARM

N

B. W. DEAN

THE
HORN

ABLEMARLE

ARGONIA

BRAZORIA

FROSTINGDUNG

6

Chapter I

Bronwyn the Bold was still flushed from the heat of battle when the Lord Chamberlain found her in the small courtyard below the eastern wall of the Royal Palace. The courtyard was in ruins. Trees, walls, jousting dummies, the Queen's prize petunia patch, all were gouged, hacked and otherwise dismembered. The Princess knelt beside the wall, her short sword cooling in its sheath, her red carved shield close by her side. Evidently satisfied with the routing she'd dealt her enemies, she bent over the prone forms of her dolls, each of which was blanketed by one of her monogrammed handkerchiefs.

"My lady," the Chamberlain began.

"What *is* it, Uncle Binky?" she demanded in a fair imitation of her father's regal roar. "Can't you see I've mortally wounded casualties on my hands? We need healers and medicine *now*!"

"Yes, my lady," the Chamberlain replied with a tone sober and a face straight from long and difficult practice. "I'll see to it personally, my lady. . . ."

"A simple 'general' will do," Bronwyn said graciously, since she was actually very pleased to have someone to talk to. She hopped to her feet and took the Chamberlain's hand in hers, her action very like that of any normal child except that ordinary little girls didn't tower over adult royal retainers. "What news do you bring from behind our lines?"

"Your lady mother wishes a word with you, madam," the Lord Chamberlain replied.

"She hasn't—?" Bronwyn asked, jiggling his hand excitedly.

"No, madam, she has not. Nor will she deliver the babe for a month yet to come, as the Princess Magdalene has already informed Your Highness." And he clamped his lips tightly shut as if he were afraid she'd steal his teeth.

Bronwyn was quite used to having not only the Lord Chamberlain but everyone else who attended her adopt such attitudes when she tried to question or talk to them, so as usual she continued chattering at him as if he were answering each remark

9

and paying her rapt attention. She supposed it went with her high rank to have everyone so in awe of her presence that they couldn't speak properly out of deference. Later, she decided that his silence was less usual than she'd thought, and smacked of the stoicism of a guard escorting his prisoner to the block—or into direst exile.

Maggie, Lady Wormroost, paced the Royal sick chamber with an anxiety which was in no way relieved by the sound of her niece's big feet galumphing towards her from down the hall. At least this interview would be short, but it wouldn't be easy.

She glanced at the Queen—sleeping, of course, as she should be to conserve her meager strength. Except for the mound of belly drifted over with white satin coverlet, the Queen was more frail than Maggie had ever seen her, her bones sticking out like those of a plucked bird, her skin thinned to a ghost-like translucency, marbled with blue. Maggie loved her elder half-sister and wished there was something she could do for her besides keep her company when she woke and see to it that her chamberpot was kept empty and her bedding spotless.

For though Maggie was officially Regent, she knew only enough about government to know that it was best left in the hands of the few capable ministers the King had appointed to take charge of the war effort on the home front. Oh, she had used her hearth-witchcraft, which allowed her to do all work connected with the home magically, to give a hand at readying the castle and surrounding city for siege. But she hoped the preparations she made, mostly consisting of magically expanding and storing existing food supplies beyond normal winter needs, would be unnecessary.

With any luck at all, King Roari's army would be able to head off Worthyman the Worthless and the Ablemarlonian forces and persuade them of the error of their ways. But it would not be easy. Worthyman was an unscrupulous scoundrel and a wastrel, but in one of his wiser moments he had chosen to squander a large portion of the treasury on a professional standing army of trained soldiers. Immediately thereafter, without bothering to try to forge a trade agreement, he had declared war on King Roari. He used the excuse that his country needed Argonian timber for its ship-building industry, which may have been true since, at his direction, Ablemarle's remaining forest land had been denuded and cultivated. However, the private opinion held by the King, Maggie, and a few others, was that Worthyman was actually hoping to find and eliminate his elder brother, the true

Crown Prince, a focus of frequent Ablemarlonian rebellions even though he preferred to dwell quietly among the Argonian gypsies. Whatever the reasons behind the war, Maggie wished it were over and she and Colin were safe back at Wormroost with their own daughter, Carole.

Which reminded her of her most immediate problem, one which concerned both Carole and Bronwyn. Too bad the King hadn't left her some wise minister to whom she could delegate this sort of domestic crisis, but unfortunately she and the Queen would have to muddle along by themselves.

If only Bronwyn weren't so bloody irritating. With her constant rattling nonsense, she was so provoking that Maggie never seemed to be able to talk to the child without snapping at her, even though she knew what annoyed her most was hardly the poor girl's own fault. Ah, well, Bronwyn was lucky Maggie was only a hearth witch and not a transformer like her Granny Brown or a really wicked witch like child-eating Great-Great-Grandma Elspat, or there were times when Her Royal Highness would have gotten worse than a snapping at. . . .

"The Princess Bronwyn," the Chamberlain announced at the door.

"You think we can't see that for ourselves?" Maggie snapped— damn! The girl was getting to her already. The Chamberlain beat a hasty retreat. Bronwyn gave her a shy smile that was ludicrous in such a strapping girl. Then, with her eyes still on Maggie's, as if anticipating a blow, she tripped sideways to her mother's bedside, stumbling at the last moment to fall across the sleeping Queen. Amberwine gasped and sat up, catching at her daughter's arm. Bronwyn held her mother by the elbow with one hand and with the other hand brushed at her, as if the contact might have dirtied her.

"Leave off, niece. You'll bruise her," Maggie advised as evenly as possible.

Bronwyn sprang away from the bed as if she'd touched the lighted end of a torch.

The frail Queen blinked her wide, green eyes twice and held out her hand to her daughter, who took it timidly. "How good it is to see you, my darling. How are you today?"

"Splendid, Mama. Extraordinary in fact. I've just slain the entire Ablemarlonian army and the leaders have all been hanged in your name."

Maggie groaned and Amberwine, had it been possible for her to have become any paler, could have been said to have done so.

11

"Er—how kind of you, pet. You're such a thoughtful child. Isn't she, Maggie?"

Maggie shook her head and managed a faint, rueful smile. Bronwyn had her mother's eyes and chin, but she was otherwise her father's daughter entirely. A fitting successor to her paternal grandfathers, Rowans the Rambunctious, Rampaging, and Reckless respectively, she would have made King Roari a fine son. Pity. She was a dead loss at the womanly pursuits, and had gone through so many gowns her tiring women had finally given up and allowed her to go about in the simple undergown and armor she preferred. She clinked somewhat now as she perched on the edge of the bed, not quite resting her entire weight upon it, afraid she'd break her mother's bones if she relaxed. She was such a *large* girl—half again as large as either Maggie or Amberwine and uncomfortably aware that she had yet to gain mastery of her body. She knew she could cause irreparable damage to practically anything in the twinkling of an eye. If only she *could* be allowed to puncture something other than her own fingers during her earnest but ultimately painful attempts at needlework, perhaps the child would be good for something despite her—problem.

Amberwine caught Maggie's eye and said to Bronwyn, "Your aunt has a wonderful surprise for you, darling. Don't you, Maggie?"

Maggie felt another stab of guilt as a look of hopefulness and anticipatory pleasure dawned in the girl's eyes, and before it could turn into a full-fledged smile Maggie lost her nerve and tossed the conversational ball back to Amberwine. Sick or not, the Queen was Bronwyn's mother. Let her be the one to break the news. "I think she'd rather you'd tell her, Winnie."

"Tell me what?" Bronwyn demanded in a childish parody of her father's boom.

She was a-wriggle with excitement now.

Winnie shot Maggie an injured look. "Why, that it's been arranged for you to have a nice trip in the country for awhile, dear. To see some of the rest of the kingdom and to meet your cousin Carole. It must be so dull for you shut up in the castle all the time and—"

"But it's not, Mama, really," Bronwyn protested, though, of course, it was.

"There's your duty too, young lady," Maggie said, stepping in before the child got out of hand. "To your mother, your subjects and Argonia. You will need to see more of your realm than the capitol sometime, and there's no time like the present."

12

Bronwyn started to protest, but for once Winnie was firm.

"Besides, I wish it. Maggie and I were such good friends as girls, you and Carole must learn to know and love each other too. I want you to have friends and—oh, darling, don't look like that! You'll have such fun! Tell her about the ice castle and the worm and the animals and the talking river, Maggie."

Maggie began talking very fast, tripping over her own tongue while describing the peculiar sights of Wormroost Manor, before the Princess could start crying or raise some other row that would further upset Winnie. It was unsettling enough to the Queen to be pregnant and bedridden while her husband was at war and her country under attack without worrying about Bronwyn. Not only was the girl a handful to have around at such a crucial time, but if the new reports of the enemy entering the Gulf of Gremlins were true, and by some ill fortune the King's forces could not stop them, the Ablemarlonians might soon be in Queenston Harbor. Bronwyn was Crown Princess and must be kept safe. Winnie was sure that if her daughter knew how potentially perilous the situation was, she would refuse to leave, although it was vital to national security that she do so. Maggie's view was that the girl had to grow up sometime, but then, Maggie wasn't Queen and very glad of it too. So she talked, wishing she had her husband's gift of gab and persuasive musical abilities to help her sound convincing.

Bronwyn interrupted her in mid-sentence, rising from her mother's bedside to stand at attention, her face set in a small painful smile not quite tight enough to control the trembling of her freckled chin. "Thank you for your intriguing tale, my lady aunt. If my Royal Mama commands it, I am sure that I shall greatly enjoy my banis—fostering at your home. If I may be excused, I'll take my leave now and prepare for the journey." And she turned on her heel and left.

Maggie and Amberwine exchanged relieved sighs that Bronwyn had been so tractable for a change. It was a sign of their anxious preoccupation with other matters and the poor state of Amberwine's health that it didn't occur to either of them until much later that Bronwyn's seemingly sensible attitude was more ominous than any fuss she might have made. For the trouble with Bronwyn was that, through no fault of her own, the girl was incapable of telling the truth.

As soon as the Princess clanked down from her coach, the Honorable Carole began getting the idea that having a Serene Highness around the stronghold wasn't going to be the thrilling experience filled with cousinly chumminess she had been led to believe it would be. Since the carrier bird had brought the news of the Royal arrival a month before, Carole had thought of little else. The villagers at Wormroost were all transplants, refugees from another, blighted village. They were all older than her parents and none of them had brought any children with them. Carole's father sang wonderful songs about children at play together, and the village seamstress was fond of telling Carole about learning to stitch while taking in the clothing her older female relatives had outgrown.

Princess Bronwyn was only two years older than Carole, and as a Princess was bound to have some beautiful gowns to hand down to a country cousin. Rumor had it that the Rowans had no magic in their family, so it would be great fun to show Bronwyn the latest refinements in Carole's own little talent. Or so she'd thought.

The metal-girded, wire-haired, red-eyed apparition towering over her didn't look to be in the mood for a magic show, nor did she appear to be at all friendly.

"It is I, Bronwyn the Bold," the Princess announced to no one in particular among the five or six peasants who'd stopped their labor long enough to watch the coach arrive. Three of them, their curiosity apparently satisfied by the introduction, sauntered off again, returning to their work. As if afraid she wasn't being impressive enough, the Princess drew what was for her a short sword, though for Carole it would have been a full-length saber. The Princess was bigger than any man in the village, including Bernard the Guard, Wormroost's military detachment. With a nonchalance obviously planned for effect, Bronwyn sliced the air in two sharp swishes. "I have come on behalf of my father to inspect these, our hintermost provinces. You may genuflect any time now."

Carole didn't know what genuflect meant, but she didn't like the sound of it. Still, she thought maybe Bronwyn only seemed unfriendly because she was tired from the coach ride, so with a patience admirable in a Brown witch, Carole minded her manners and asked, "Would you like to inspect supper first? I think it's about ready."

Bronwyn sheathed her sword with another clattering display, then stopped, staring at Carole suspiciously. Surrounded as the stare was by the Princess's helm and chain mail shirt and the rest of her martial paraphernalia, it was tantamount to a threat. "You have an odd, familiar yet somehow foreign look to you, wench.

14

Are you a spy, perhaps, sent by my father's enemies to poison me? If so . . ."

"Oh, come off it, won't you?" Carole cried, exasperated. "I look familiar because I look like my mother. Well—sort of. I do have my father's nose, Gran says. And of course you know my mother because she's been living at your castle taking care of *your* mother. Come to think of it, if anyone doesn't look like her own mother, it's you. You're nothing like the tapestry of Auntie Amberwine in the guest chamber. You get to sleep there, by the way, and it's the nicest room in the house. You can see the ruins of the ice castle out the back window."

Thinking the girls were leaving, the coachman threw down Bronwyn's trunk, to the top of which was strapped a small shield, and jumped from the driver's seat. He handed a sealed scroll to Carole, and followed the retreating skirts of the most curious of the village wives, now off to her own supper. Carole began stripping the wax from the seal and started after them, only to be jerked back when Bronwyn's metal-fingered hand clamped down on her shoulder.

"Hold, wench," the Princess commanded. "None dare deny the royal resemblance without consequence. Take it back. Say I do so look like Mama."

"I can't do that," Carole said reasonably. "That would be telling a lie and telling lies is wrong."

"Take it back," Bronwyn repeated, biting off each word, her fingers digging more painfully into Carole's skin.

"Hey, stop it!"

Bronwyn looked as if she was about to cry but her voice was hard and angry. "I said take it back, and kneel while you're about it."

"Or what?" Carole demanded. Enough was enough. Cousin or no cousin, the Princess just wasn't a very nice person.

"Or I'll—I'll thrash you, is what," Bronwyn said. Obviously she could, though she'd never thrashed anything but jousting dummies before. Carole was less than half her size and skinny to boot.

"Hmmm . . ." the country girl said. "Will you now?" She didn't seem frightened. In fact, she looked pleased. She was even humming to herself. Perhaps it was her family's battle song? It sounded vaguely military. Yes, definitely a march. Good beat, that. Couldn't keep the feet still. One had at least to mark time to a lively tune like that. Bronwyn loosed her cousin's shoulder to watch amazed as her boots stomped the beat of their own volition. What a march! Why, if father had such a song in

15

the field, his troops would be undefeatable. With a neat about-face, she strutted away from the manor house and from her grinning cousin, hearing the tune in her head long after Carole had ambled back towards the kitchens.

Down the single street of the village she marched, past the blue-white face of the glacier and the half-melted towers of the castle carved from it, through the thin woods and straight towards the river—the talking one, she thought to herself through the one-two beat pounding in her brain. So Aunt Maggie hadn't been telling her children's stories about that after all. She could clearly hear the river saying all sorts of words now, words which became even more easily discernable as she neared the swirling waters. She heard them very clearly indeed as the march swept from her brain when her last step from solid ground plunged her into the chattering flow, which began protesting loudly. As the cold water clamped over her scalp, she belatedly remembered that Cousin Carole was supposed to be a witch in her own right. Evidently it was more than a wild rumor.

"And so, my love," Maggie of Wormroost's letter to her daughter read, "I'm sure you'll try to make Bronwyn feel at home, and will be as tolerant of the little problem she has with what folk here call her 'fanciful ways' as we are tolerant of yours. In her case, there's a curse involved, and she really can't help herself, so I know you'll be fair-minded enough to ignore it. The Mother only knows the child needs friends. I'll write more later. The coachman is loading Bronwyn's trunk now and Winnie's call bell is jangling at me. Be a good girl and give my love to your dad if you see him before I do. Love, Mum."

Carole rerolled the scroll, her smug smile of moments before gone. Curse? Why hadn't anybody said so before? Trust adults to leave out the good stuff! She supposed there was no help for it but to go find the big lout and apologize for marching her all over the countryside, though the exercise was bound to do her good after she'd been sitting in the coach all that while. Not that one could expect Bronwyn to see it that way. For a peace offering, Carole stuck a few biscuits into her pockets before snatching up her cloak and trotting back outdoors. The air got nippy in the evening now. Maybe she should fetch Bronwyn's cloak along too, but she didn't see it when she peeked into the coach. There was the trunk on the ground, though, with the little red shield strapped to it. It might come in handy if Bronwyn was slow to accept apologies.

She set off in the direction the Princess had marched away,

16

but as soon as she came within earshot of the river, she broke into a run. Had the villagers not all gathered at the manor hall for supper, someone would have cried the alarm already.

"Help!" the river screeched, boiling with indignation, "Help! Pollution! Contamination!" Carole's lungs and legs pumped frantically as she sped past all the houses and almost into the water before she could stop herself. It hadn't occurred to her that the silly oaf might fall into the Blabbermouth. And with all that armor . . .

"You—puff—didn't—puff—drown her, d—pant, did you?" she asked, stripping off her boots and balling her cloak between the shield and its strap to keep the garment dry. She thought wildly that if Bronwyn weren't dead, she'd at least be in urgent need of being dried.

"How should I know what the silly thing's done?" the ensorceled river demanded. "Ask downstream. I for one certainly hope not. A bloated, rotting carcass is the last thing I want to take out to sea with me."

"You'd better NOT take her out to sea," Carole said, stepping gingerly into the shallows and wading along the bank. "And don't you dare try to tow me under either."

"I wouldn't dream of it," the river said nastily. But even though it was in a bad mood, the Blabbermouth was at least making sense for a change, which meant a unicorn must have come out of the woods last night and purified it. When she'd gone to draw water for supper yesterday evening, the river was still yammering the gossipy nonsense that composed its usual repertoire. Not only was the river bewitched, it was also haunted by the spirit of the slightly barmy witch who'd drowned herself after listening to the mindless drivel it poured forth in response to the talkative spell she'd placed on it so it would always keep her company. Only after unicorns came to Wormhaven Valley did the river begin to make sense and answer questions, at times with great wisdom, and at other times—well, not with great wisdom.

Having lived near the Blabbermouth's banks all her life, Carole found nothing particularly strange about drawing her water from a talking river, and right now she could see that it had its advantages over less communicative streams.

Burbling at her every step of the way, the river guided her farther downstream than she'd dared to venture before. Not that she wasn't adventurous, but close to the cliffside on which the glacier hung, underbrush grew so thickly along the banks that the river was inaccessible without tangling in a lot of brambles and

17

nettles. Though Father had taken her swimming once or twice in the summer when he wasn't traveling on the King's business or off to some seminar at the Minstrel's Academy (Mother claimed that was a lot of poppycock and just an excuse for him to fool about singing and making up silly songs with other musicians. This seemed unfair to Carole since, as everybody knew, that was what musicians *did*), Mother didn't like her to play in the water. And what Mother didn't like she had ways of preventing Carole from doing.

The waters downstream were far more eager to assist her than those closer to the town. Probably, since they weren't so often exposed to people, they were more entertained by the novelty of having two within them in one afternoon, Carole thought, though she didn't think about it too long since she was intent on trying to keep her footing and on searching. It was hard to see, for in the shadows under the bushes the water was inky black, whereas in the parts that curved away from the cliff and rolled down the middle of the riverbed, the wavelets glittered brightly enough to dazzle her eyes. As if that weren't enough to keep her mind on, she also had to try to pay attention to the river's gurgling instructions.

"This way now. Do hurry. Look out for that hole, there. Clumsy child, aren't you? Try to be more careful in the future. I daresay I can do without another of your sort muddying me up. Look sharp—yes, there, you see, she struck that rock there and made the most dreadful clamor—the rock will never be the same. You can see where a big chunk's knocked off. Ah, yes, here we are. Right around this next bend and—"

"And what?" she demanded, after negotiating the prescribed turn and coming face to face with the cliffside again—and no more river, much less any sign of her cousin. "Hey, that's not fair. Where'd you go?"

"Down here!" the voice bubbled up, seemingly from within the glacier.

"Uh uh," Carole shook her head emphatically and backed off. "You *have* drowned her, haven't you? And now you're trying to get me too!"

"Don't be tedious," the river said. "I think I've made my feelings on that subject perfectly clear. Now then, are you coming or aren't you?"

"I can't just walk into a glacier," she said, a whine creeping into her voice in spite of herself as she eyed the driftwood clogging the immense dirty white base stretching into woods on either side of the river.

18

"No, but you can float," the river replied.

"You ARE trying to drown me!"

"Don't be such a baby. Would I have warned you about the holes and whirlpools if I were trying to drown you? I'm shallow here, except right at the bottom, and I'll sweep you past that. Just keep your head down so you don't bump it on the overhang, and hold onto that thing in your hand so you can keep adrift if you capsize."

"You make it sound easy," she said doubtfully.

"*I* do this all the time," the river replied. "Down with you, now. That's it. Here we go—budge your bottom a bit. You're stuck. There now—WHEEEEE!"

That was all very well for the river to say, Carole thought, panicked, as she first slid downstream. But her fright was soon replaced by elation as she realized that she was not cold and uncomfortable as was quite reasonable to expect in a glacial river in late autumn. In fact, sliding along with the water was tremendous fun. Thrusting Bronwyn's shield inside-up before her, she flopped forward on her stomach and sluiced down into the darkness.

Entrance to the glacier was a shallow slide of water over stone and ice smoothed with centuries of the Blabbermouth's passing. As first her head and then her stomach slid beneath the opening in the ice, Carole closed her eyes for fear she'd strike her head on a rock. She hoped the shield would protect her.

No protection was necessary, however. At the foot of the slide, she knifed straight ahead into a deep pool, stopping abruptly when her momentum deposited her against a squishy, clanking object.

"Mission accomplished," sighed the river. "Get her out now, will you, before she rusts or something?"

Chapter II

The eddy swirling around them giggled and Carole couldn't blame it. High overhead, several huge round holes piercing the roof of the glacial grotto showed a struggling, swearing Bronwyn performing all manner of contortions and gyrations with the portion of her that remained above water. Setting her own feet down, Carole immediately started sinking into a deep layer of mud. With her leg armor on, Bronwyn was unable to kick loose, as Carole herself did only with great difficulty. She swam to Bronwyn, grabbing her arm and tugging.

"Let me be," the Princess said in a mournful and thoroughly frightened voice. "I'm doing perfectly well by myself, thank you." Any idiot could see she wasn't. For that matter, Carole wasn't doing so well either. The pool covered the entire floor of the grotto and its icy rim was little more than a slick, narrow ledge, with nothing to hold onto and no place to pull herself and Bronwyn to dry land if and when she succeeded in unsticking her.

"How do we get out?" Carole asked the river.

"Out? Out? You just got in. How should I know how you get out? You asked me to find your cousin, as if cousins were important! Pshaw! I, for instance, had a cousin once—runny little sort—thought it was the deep blue sea but really, it was scarcely more than a mud puddle—and I'll brook no contradiction on that, let me tell you. I says to this puddle, says I—"

"Oh, no," Carole wailed, and would have stomped her foot under other circumstances.

Bronwyn was sufficiently struck by the hopelessness in her tone to look up from her own predicament.

"The unicorn spell is wearing off," Carole explained. "Now we'll never get out of here. I *knew* this wretched river was trying to drown us both!" She had to shout above the river now, for when it was making no sense it talked constantly and more loudly than when it was sane, and had no manners whatsoever about interrupting others or talking right over them.

"Now what?" Bronwyn managed to howl back with some difficulty, since her struggling was sinking her deeper till by now her chin was half-submerged and her voice almost as distorted as the river's.

Carole dog-paddled around her and finally hollered back— She would have shrugged if she could have managed to do that and keep afloat at the same time—"I don't know. Wait until another unicorn comes to bless the river so it'll tell us how to get out of here or lead the grownups to us, I suppose. Do you think you can hold out?" The last question was more wistful than hopeful.

"Certainly I—blub—can," Bronwyn answered. She had sunk until she could keep her lower lip above water only with consid-

20

erable effort. "Save—glub—yourself, wench. Don't—gurgle—worry about—gulp—me. I'll be—blub—fine."

Remembering Bronwyn's curse, Carole decided that the seemingly valiant disclaimer was, coming from the Princess, a cry for help and a plea not to desert her. As if Carole could have had she been so inclined. The light from the holes overhead was fading and her eyes probed the cavern for a way out or at least an outcropping to hang onto or climb up on. After all, if the river flowed into the grotto, it obviously must go somewhere.

But it was not until she left Bronwyn and paddled around the slippery-sided perimeter that she found the passageway and the odd contraption blocking it. She felt it, rather than saw it, for it was hidden in the shadows. It was a bit like a boat and also something like a bathtub with curved sides, somewhat buckled and smelling of mold, but when she put her hand in the bottom, the wooden surface felt solid and no wetter than her own hand.

"Aha!" She cried triumphantly, and then to Bronwyn: "I think I've found just the thing. Hold on and I'll fetch it over."

"I was—glub—just going for a walk," Bronwyn answered.

Tossing the shield into the decrepit-looking contraption, Carole threw one arm over the edge and tried to kick off. Unfortunately, the rim was too high for her to be able to keep hold and still be able to swim properly. So she flipped onto her back, grabbed the side with her fingertips, and tugged.

The craft—whatever it was—began floating with her, and she was halfway to Bronwyn when she felt a pull corresponding to her own. She tugged harder, but the boat wouldn't budge. Thinking it might have snagged, she raised herself against the ledge. The flapping black horror was upon her before she could dive back into the water.

The thing hissed hideously, like water spilled on a roaring fire or a teakettle gone mad. It smacked her with something soft and yet with great force, so that she felt she was being flogged and smothered by wet draperies. It also punched her shoulder, thighs, cheeks, and back, and barely missed an eye, stabbing at her with what felt like the blunt end of a wooden spoon.

She screamed. Bronwyn screamed. The river babbled madly away and the monster relentlessly stabbed and slapped and hissed. She dove to escape it and kicked toward Bronwyn, only to find the thing at her heels, stabbing, if not hissing, right through the water. Then it was upon her, its weight dragging her down, enveloping her in its draperies—and then it wasn't. She clawed for the surface and saw Bronwyn, mouth underwater but eyes

21

menacing, her sword waving just above the surface of the water, stabbing jerkily now and then at a gigantic black swan.

"Thugs!" the bird hissed. "Thieves! How DARE you?" Carole had never heard a swan speak before, but when you grew up arguing with your water supply, talking animals weren't particularly alarming. Hostile ones were quite another matter.

"How dare WE?" she exploded. "How dare you? I'll have you know I'm trying to save the life of the Crown Princess of Argonia and you're impeding me in the execution of my duties." That sounded very grand and official, she thought. Bernard always said things like that when she wanted him to play with her and he wanted to sleep against the wall, which he claimed to be guarding. "I happen to be the daughter of the Lord of this land, and I'll thank you not to bother us any more."

"And I'll thank you, young lady, to keep your vulgar hands off my chariot."

"I didn't know it was yours. I was only borrowing it to help Bronwyn. I can't just let her drown, can I?"

"I don't see why not," the swan replied. "And anyway, she appears to be doing so regardless of your wishes."

Carole switched to see the top of Bronwyn's forehead and then, helplessly, back to the swan. "It—oh, dear—it's her armor, you see. Don't ask me why a princess wears armor but she does and—"

"A princess? I believe you did mention that before." The hiss simmered down. "Well, now. That's rather different. I myself am of royal blood." The swan's little eyes glittered suddenly as the dying light slanted against them. "You silly girl, if her noble armor is weighing her down, why don't you dive down and remove it from her? Honestly, I think the servant situation must have deteriorated dreadfully since I've put on these feathers!"

Feeling half resentful at being ordered about and half foolish for not thinking of the idea herself, Carole dove. With her new-found facility in and under the water, she had no trouble reaching the leather lacings on Bronwyn's leggings and wristlets, and found despite the darkness and murkiness of the water she could see perfectly well. She tugged, and the sodden leather gave way. Casting the leggings away, she grasped Bronwyn by the ankles, flipped herself onto her back, and pulled Bronwyn's legs free from the armor. Once her feet were loose, the Princess was able to get her mouth above the water, and she and Carole together stripped her of the chain mail and helm, throwing them into the swan's strange boat.

Instead of objecting to this further invasion of her territory, the swan fluttered around them in a maternal sort of way, looking as if she'd like to sprout hands and help them. "The poor dear must be chilled through," she fussed as more of the newly unburdened Bronwyn popped up from the pool. "Quickly now, girl, help your lady into my chariot."

Resenting the way everyone was claiming to be a Princess today apparently just so they could order her about, Carole said, as drily as she could under the circumstances, "You've certainly changed *your* tune," but nevertheless followed the swan's instructions, half dragging, half shoving a noodle-limp and prune-wrinkled Bronwyn into the bathtub-boat. When she saw that the bottom didn't give way beneath the bulky Princess, Carole crawled in after her and wrapped the cloak, only a bit damp around the edges, about her.

The swan, she could see now, was tethered to the peculiar craft by a long strand of something, from which various loops and buckles dangled, rather like an unhorsed sleigh harness. The swan gave an experimental heave and the boat glided smoothly toward her over black satin water.

"Hmm. Yes. Works nicely. I don't seem to have lost my touch," the swan said, preening herself a little.

"Could you pull us out of here?" Carole asked. "Not that it's not nice meeting you, but it's almost supper time and we can't go back the way we came and—"

"I, for one, am perfectly h-happy h-here," Bronwyn said through chattering teeth.

The swan's eyes glittered again and she spoke sternly to Carole. "Your lady says . . ."

"I heard her," Carole replied tightly. But the swan had started to help them only after learning how noble Bronwyn's blood was. It probably wouldn't be smart to reveal the less noble things about the Princess right now. "But, well, she's a great joker, Princess Bronwyn is. Aren't you, cousin?"

"Me? Oh, yes. A very great joker. Why, shortly after I was born, all the court fools quit in protest, so witty were my gooings and cooings. . . ."

"She actually wants to leave as badly as I do," Carole interrupted quickly, "but she's just trying to keep my spirits up, you see. She's far too well-bred to complain of her own accord. But really, we can't possibly stay here."

"Why not? *I* have made this my home for quite some time now."

"But there's nothing for us to eat and nowhere to sleep!" Carole wailed, suddenly overwhelmed with grief at the loss of

23

her dinner, which must be at least cold by now, if not gobbled up by Bernard, who ate anything that didn't try to eat him first.

"*I* eat plants from the bottom of the pond and find them quite succulent," the swan said with a superior air. "Surely you could do the same. But then, oh no, I have forgotten what it was like almost—no, no, of course not, and you have no wings under which to tuck your heads for sleep, poor things. Dear me, it was so *very* long ago. Naturally, you must leave. This place is far too exposed for a delicate creature like the Princess in her featherless state."

"How understanding you are," Bronwyn said, buttering the old bird up.

"That is true," the swan agreed, "However, willing as I am to aid you in quitting this cavern, I fear I shall be unable to do so."

"Why?" both girls wailed at once.

"Because, my dear ladies, the chariot will not pass through the opening and I am bound to the chariot. Were it of a more convenient size, I should have been able to tow it through myself and enjoyed a greater variety of scenery long before now."

"Can't you try?" Carole pleaded. "Oh, please do try. Maybe we can help."

"Very well, but I fear I cannot hold out much hope."

Carole crossed her fingers and wished she knew of a shrinking tune to whistle them through. As it turned out, Bronwyn's natural endowments rather than her cousin's supernatural ones solved the dilemma. What with her armor and her great weight, added to Carole's, the Princess sufficiently lowered the boat in the water so that with only a little maneuvering it squeezed through the opening and shot to the other side.

They felt the swiftness of the river beneath them and heard it far better than they would have wished, but they saw nothing, for they were wrapped in darkness. Neither, however, did they feel any impediments, nor could they feel the walls on either side of them, so they surmised the cave must have broadened again. The glide of the boat, the darkness, and the river's boring monologue, which discouraged conversation, all reminded the girls that it was past their bedtime. Even without the benefit of the wings the swan found so useful, both of them were soon asleep.

Bronwyn was disappointed that no iceworm writhed through the ice to challenge her to battle while they traveled through the mountain. She was sure she could manage to best one, which would make Mama and Papa proud and show Carole that Aunt Maggie and Uncle Colin weren't the only ones who could become legends in their own time for their adroit dispatching of monsters. Though no one had mentioned it, she felt sure the light holes in the grotto were made by worms like the one lying dormant above them in the ice castle.

But they emerged from the tunnel a few hours after they awakened, unthreatened by worms, dragons, trolls, chasms, tricky side passages or even serious inconveniences. Quite an anticlimactic ending for what Bronwyn was beginning to regard as a promisingly perilous adventure. Having survived her terrifying plunge into the river and missing her dinner, she felt pretty cocky about taking on the next danger and was only afraid that none would materialize. No doubt, since the tunnel was so determinedly dull, the best course was the one on which they seemed inevitably set—onward! In the company of a witch cousin and a giant talking swan, surely something at least moderately thrilling would soon occur.

She must be alert as a hawk watching for its prey and miss no detail of the terrain. She must note each nuance in the behavior of her companions and in the character of the countryside. Hmm, yes. She congratulated herself on deducing the approximate time from the straight up position of the brilliant autumn midday sun. Very good, Bronwyn. What else? There was the swan, of course. Much more magnificent than she had first appeared as a black creature wrapped in darkness. She was as big around and as long as the chariot she pulled and her feathers were so shiny that a small perfect rainbow was reflected from each. Her neck was as long as Bronwyn's arm and her beautiful head carried as proudly as a rosebud in first freshness borne on its long stem by a knight to his lady. Being pulled by such a creature was a bit like being attached to the feathered tail of a giant arrow, so swift and sure was her forward propulsion. The river beneath her was cloudy with fine white dirt which gave Bronwyn the feeling of floating on a broad flat stream of potato soup.

Thinking of soup made her wish missing her dinner and her breakfast as well hadn't been the *first* valorous hardship she'd been called upon to endure. One should probably break into these adventurous things gradually, and certainly not on an empty stomach.

The swan's mind was on higher things. "Ah, me—*sun*light," she exclaimed in her slightly accented voice, which was husky and rather sibilant. Spreading her ebony wings, she pulled the chariot into a little circle in the middle of the river, then came to

25

a stop so abrupt that the vessel barely missed her tail. Arching her neck back over her right wing, she asked them soulfully, "Do you know how long it has been since I beheld SUNlight in the fullness of its glory? Many years, my dears, oh many, many years. How blinding is its radiance!"

"Yes," Carole agreed. "Too bad it isn't a bit warmer." Then, not wishing to seem as rude and churlish as her companions seemed to think her, she added, "I suppose it must be very nice for you to be out of that cave, swan, after all that time you said you'd been in there."

"Indeed it is, miss, and a tribute to my hardihood and steadfastness of purpose that I did not perish in the darkness but stayed by my post long after my sisters had turned totally fowl and flown away. I had always been the lead swan, you see, being the eldest, and my harness was more difficult to slip than theirs. Still, they might have tried to help me, silly geese, or at least returned for a visit now and again."

"That was pretty foul," Carole said primly. "But it isn't really nice to say that sort of thing about your sisters."

"*Fowl*, girl, birdlike! And it is not very nice of you, either, since we are lecturing each other on deportment, to address me as 'swan' when I am at least as nobly born as your own lady cousin. However, I shall overlook your boorish lack of courtesy since you have assisted in my deliverance. Perhaps, if you are pleasant, I shall even deign to share with you my secret."

"I'm ever so good at keeping secrets," Bronwyn bragged.

Carole mumbled something to herself, but the swan didn't hear it, since she had already begun to have her say in a voice loud enough to be heard over the river, which was on this side of the mountain no louder or less sensible than the regular sort of river.

"Know then, Princess, that I, like yourself, am a King's daughter. My father was King Niconar Nettletongue of the Nonarable Lands, an unprofitable but fiercely independent kingdom to the south and east of Middle Frostingdung. I am My Serene Highness, Crown Princess of the Nonarable Lands, Duchess of the Frozen Fjords, Marchioness of the Miserable Mires, Anastasia Ilonia Vasilia Gwendolyn Martha Nettletongue, at your service, though actually, you understand, that is only a figure of speaking."

"Your Highness," Bronwyn said civilly.

"Tish, tush, my dear. We Royal colleagues need not be so formal. You may call me by my sobriquet, Anastasia the Alluring."

26

She didn't tell Carole to call her anything, but Carole had a few ideas of her own and barely stifled an impulse to tell the haughty creature she could call *her* Honorable Lady Carole. Although traveling in the company of two beings with such inflated ideas of their own importance as Bronwyn and the swan was probably going to be unbearable, there was no sense in antagonizing the transportation. On the other hand, she wasn't about to sit through what seemed to be another typically boring Argonian story. Bewitched animals, her mother always said (and she should know, she'd met a lot of them in her adventures before she became a mother) never knew when to be quiet and stick to the point of a problem. They always had to regale one with some rambling sob story about how they became bewitched and how totally unfair it all was that someone like them should be turned into a whatever. One would think to listen to them that witches had nothing better to do than to go about harassing innocent bystanders by transforming them into livestock. Carole wasn't about to listen to any of that. Interrupting adroitly, she summarized what she suspected the swan was about to say. "So you and your sisters were turned into swans, huh, and somebody hooked you up to that boat only they left and so did your sisters and you didn't and here you are, right? Wonderful! So are we. So now that we're all here, how do you think we can get back home again, er, Your Highness?"

Bronwyn gave her a murderous glance. Just when things were getting interesting, the witch had to open her big mouth. "My aunt's daughter is far too polite to want to delve into your personal history, Princess Anastasia," she lied in apology.

"The Alluring," the swan amended testily. "Anastasia the Alluring."

"Princess Anastasia the Alluring," Bronwyn said, all in one breath, "I, however, being the heroine of many valiant exploits, have naturally had similar experiences myself. For instance, just before we dropped in on you, I believe my cousin was attempting to turn me into a swan, weren't you, Cousin Carole? Otherwise, I can't think why she would have witched me into the river."

"Well, I'm sorry, I'm sure," Carole said indignantly, "But how was I to know you were under a curse and couldn't tell the truth if it walked up and bit you on the ankle? I thought you were just weird and nasty!"

"Curse?" the Princesses asked together.

"You know—the curse you had put on you when you were a baby."

"Oh, that curse," Bronwyn said, still obviously puzzled.

"You didn't know?" Carole asked. "I'd think your mother would have mentioned a thing like that."

"Oh, no, no, no, my dear young lady. Not necessarily," Anastasia the Alluring put in wisely. "My mother never told me, for instance, of the penchant the women on her side of the family had for turning into swans until I was older than either of you, by which time it was much too late. Families do so dislike discussing the more complicated aspects of one's heritage with one whilst one is still of such tender years, you know, and by the time one is grown, why, more than likely they may have quite, quite forgotten."

"Strikes me as a quite, quite large thing to forget," Carole said skeptically. "But then, Mother didn't tell me about your curse before she sent that letter."

"I haven't got any curse, so just stop saying that!" Bronwyn told her, clasping her sword hilt and sticking out her lower lip.

"Yes, you have, too. You know the royal tax collector? The one that my dad went with to help collect for the war? He did it."

Bronwyn took her hand off her sword and laughed, using the artificial twitter she had learned from the ladies at court. "You misunderstand, cousin. I know the peasants speak of being accursed by a tax collector but—"

"No. I don't mean he cursed you as a tax collector. I mean before, when he was a wizard. He made it so you lie all the time."

"How kindly you put it," Bronwyn said.

"See what I mean? If you could tell the truth you would have told me I wasn't putting it very kindly at all and I—I suppose I'm not, but you're *awfully* hard to talk to, do you know that?"

Bronwyn shrank as far as possible into the chariot. "The servants and courtiers never thought so," she said miserably as she understood for the first time their stiff-lipped silences. "They were always talking to me and playing with me. I had to play war games to scare them away so I could get some privacy once in awhile."

"I'll bet," Carole said, but patted her on the shoulder and slouched down beside her.

The swan craned her head back and fixed Carole with a hard stare. "This tax collector person. What does he look like?"

"I—well, I only saw him once, when he came by for Dad. Mother won't have him around, though I think he's supposed to be related to her. He looks kind of like us, Mum and me, brown eyes and hair and cheekbones that stick out like this,'' she sucked in her own round cheeks. "Why do you ask?"

"Why do I ask? My dear young lady, if I were still in the guise of the gentlewoman I am in truth, I should surely swoon here and now. Your tax-collector-sorcerer is none other than my former master, the Brown Enchanter, Fearchar the Fearsome." Her gaze shifted to Bronwyn, "And you, poor child, are in very grave trouble indeed."

A certain amount of suppressed excitement and self-satisfaction laced her voice, and she next addressed Carole, seeming to relish being able to advise people in a situation she saw as being as grave if not worse than her own. "I think, dear girl, you had best tell us all you know of this matter."

"Naturally, it all makes perfect sense," Bronwyn snapped some time later. "Since my father was so grateful to this hewitch for putting a curse on me that he tracked the man all over Argonia to thank him for his kind christening gift, naturally nothing would do but that the varlet had to be honored with the position of royal tax collector. And I understand perfectly why Father couldn't be bothered to make the wizard remove the spell first."

"Do you?" Carole asked absently, since she'd been trying to think how they would first get back over the mountain to Wormhaven in time for supper. Bronwyn's problem was interesting, but she had, after all, had it most of her life, whereas Carole had never had to go without a meal before and here she was missing three in a row and probably catching her death of cold besides. But Bronwyn and the swan seemed to be waiting for her to say something so she added, "I mean, you don't see, I suppose, do you? Which is just the point. Me neither, but it would be nice if we could figure it out later. This conversation is giving me a headache."

The swan, who had dined more recently than either of her passengers, and who was also accustomed for much of her life to dealing with diplomats and other envoys, had less trouble adapting to Bronwyn's involuntary mode of expression than Carole did. "While you seem to grasp the essence of the situation, my dear Bronwyn, you fail to understand that even had your papa killed my master in an attempt to remove the spell, as I seem to recall he attempted to do, such measures would have been to no avail. That spell was purchased through an agent. I should know, since I took him there and waited while the transaction was completed. One finds out a great many things when one's employer is unsure of the level of one's ability to communicate. I gathered that while my former master thought it a good joke to have your curse related to his own magic talent, which is persuasiveness, the spell was none of his making nor had he the power to remove or alter it in any way."

"Dumb joke," Carole remarked. "Bronwyn didn't even know about it, much less understand it. I don't see the point."

"It was a christening gift, cousin, and meant, we must presume, as all christening gifts are meant," Bronwyn said bitterly. "It was intended to help me grow up to be a better queen. Don't you see how well it's worked? Everyone is so starved for my company because of it that even my own mama and Aunt Maggie banished me here so—so the new baby wouldn't have to always take second place to such a brilliant big sister, I suppose. Can't you imagine what a fine stable government we shall have with all my subjects loving, respecting and trusting me as you do?"

Carole winced. "I see your point," she said glumly. "You think maybe you're supposed to stay here so they can give the baby the crown instead of giving it to you? I understand why you might think so, but Mama and Aunt Winnie wouldn't do that without explaining it to you, I'm sure."

The swan made a rude noise.

"No, they *would* have," Carole insisted. "And anyway, she's not old enough to be queen yet and there's a war on and there could be all kinds of other reasons. Why would Mum make such a point of explaining this curse thing to me if she holds it against Bronwyn? It's just one problem—like—like not being good at drawing or ciphers or something. It's not as if you mean to lie, after all, Bron. I'm sure you're good at other things."

"A very magnanimous viewpoint, but hardly politically pragmatic, dear girl," the swan said, flicking her tail feathers slightly.

Bronwyn thought of all the jousting dummies she'd slain and the battles into which she'd victoriously led her dolls. Surely fate had led her thus far for some grim purpose. "There is but one honorable course for me to take in order to redeem myself," she announced at length. "The reputation of Bronwyn the Bold must be upheld at all costs to prove my worthiness for the throne. Therefore, I must join my father as soon as possible and win glory on the battlefield at his side in order to vindicate myself."

Carole looked pained for a moment, then brightened. "I'm glad to hear you say that. I might have thought it up myself sooner or later but since you mention it, we know it's rubbish."

"Your confidence in me is touching, cousin," Bronwyn said,

but her face lightened a little. At least Carole and the swan were interested enough in her to try to figure out what she meant, even when she wasn't sure herself.

"There is another way, of course," the swan said. The girls looked at her expectantly. "We can attempt to locate this agent person and through her the originator of the curse."

"How?"

"Quite easily. I shall glide to the beach where the two of you will loose me from this harness. Thereupon shall I fly back to Little Darlingham to the home of that so dreadful woman from whom the wizard obtained the curse. I shall make her tell me how to remove it. First, however, I shall stop at your manor, my dear Carole, and request a rescue party come to fetch you."

"Wonderful!" Carole said. "Meanwhile, maybe we can find something to eat."

Chapter III

Carole wasn't the only hungry one in the neighborhood. Bright eyes watched and a stomach that could have been mistaken for a bear growled from within the forest as the girls hopped from the chariot and unhitched Anastasia. The swan had worn the harness for so long that her feathers were rubbed away beneath it, a circumstance that led to a lot of hissing and fussing.

"I suppose that will leave some ghastly calluses on my alabaster skin when I resume my true form," she fretted.

"Maybe you could wear another kind of harness to cover them up—something in gold with emeralds or pearls, maybe—and start a new fashion."

Bronwyn nodded wisely. "Since *I* look so fetching in armor, all the court ladies have affected it recently."

"I think," the swan said shortly, "that there is no time like the present to begin my journey. I shall be gone but a day or two." Then she folded her half-furled wings and asked kindly, "But how thoughtless I am! You children must be very hungry. You'll be famished before your people can fetch you. However will you survive till then?"

31

"We won't even notice starving," Bronwyn promised. "We'll have our minds upon affairs of state. I shall solicit the commoner's viewpoint from Carole."

"Thanks awfully," Carole said.

"There *are* those tasty plants in the bottoms of pools, you know," the swan said. "I could pull some up for you before I go."

"Er—never mind," Carole said, and shrugged. "We can always fish, and there're berries this time of year, bound to be. Oh, and I almost forgot. I've some biscuits in my . . ." She dug into her still damp pockets and extracted a shapeless lump of mush which stuck to her fingers. "Well, they're a bit damp, but we can manage."

"Yes," Bronwyn agreed brightly, though she'd never fished nor eaten berries off the bush and had no idea how anyone could eat such things. "We shall roast them on a spit inside my helmet, as I've done so often when in the field with Father. I know exactly how to do it."

"Don't worry." Carole almost laughed at the puzzled note in Bronwyn's voice. "We'll figure it out. You just fly for help, Your Highness, and never mind us."

"Very well. Stay in this precise place so your people can locate you from my directions."

"We will," Carole promised, regarding ruefully the pasty mess on her hands. "I want to be home for a real supper tomorrow."

The girls watched quietly as the great swan fanned her wings and swept skyward, above the spiring trees, momentarily eclipsing the sun with her body.

But she had no sooner cleared the beach and topped the first line of trees in the forest behind where Bronwyn and Carole stood when something sparkled briefly against the green, and spun upward, like a shooting star in reverse, and Anastasia cried out with a swan's eerie trumpeting. One wing flapping feebly, the other crumpled against her body, she tumbled crazily, plummeting into the woods.

Bronwyn and Carole exchanged a brief startled glance. Then Bronwyn clamped on her helmet, grabbed up her shield and sword, and sprinted into the woods, Carole close on her heels.

They were only just in time to avert a tragedy, though to whom the tragedy would have occurred was far from certain. Anastasia leaned lopsidedly in a small clearing, the hilt of a dagger buried in one shoulder, a ruby ribbon trickling from it. The injured shoulder was the only part of her that was still.

32

Her beak slashed, stabbed, darted, and snaked back to strike again while her good wing whipped up and down, scattering fall leaves and dirt with each beat. She hissed hideously and no wonder. A plumpish, swarthy boy with black hair and a gleefully ravenous expression on his face worried her like a cat teasing an oversized mouse.

He feinted, jabbed, circled her—always avoiding the powerful uninjured wing and grabbing, when he thought he could get away with it, at the knife in the wound.

Bronwyn strode forward and simply pushed the boy off his feet, planting her sword point calmly in his gullet. "Hold knave, or by my grandfather's noble bones I'll spit you as I did the Black Knight when last he trifled with a friend of mine."

The boy didn't know who Bronwyn's grandfather was nor to which black knight she referred, but he did know when he was in trouble.

"Spare me, great lady! Spare this poor hungry gypsy boy. I'll give you a share of the meat. Just don't kill me before I've had my last meal, I beg you. Surely such a magnificent lady as you wouldn't kill a man when his belly's rumbling?"

Bronwyn tried to look fierce, because after all, Anastasia was an ally and one ought to defend one's allies, but then, a person could certainly see the boy's point about eating too. She appealed mutely to Carole. The gypsy caught the look that passed between them and shifted tack.

"Sweet maiden," he said, squirming to try to capture the witch with his large soulful eyes. "You must not allow your friend to slay me. Why, I hold the key to your fortune. Without me, you never will learn of the beautiful hall you shall some day live in nor the handsome stranger who will come into your life—" The stranger he had in mind, actually, was himself. He thought it unwise to mention that if she succumbed to his blandishments he intended to be out of her life as fast as he was in it—though he still hoped to make off with some of that swan first.

Carole gave him a withering look, turned her nose up and knelt beside the swan. She examined the dagger and entrance wound from all angles. Anastasia looked at her so expectantly that she felt compelled to make some comment.

"Stab wound," she said with what she hoped was a certain air of witchy professional proficiency.

Anastasia closed her eyes momentarily, as if relieved. Carole was glad the swan was relieved and wished *she* were. People tended to expect a great deal of witches in difficult situations, even when one hadn't had time to learn everything there was to know about one's own powers, much less one's mother's and grandmother's powers. A person just couldn't help it under such trying circumstances if there were certain deficiencies in one's competence.

Carole was quite adept at dancing things about and could even do some housework more or less magically this way, making threads dance through needles and needles dance through cloth or dishes through dishwater. In that way her magic roughly paralleled her mother's hearthcrafting talent. But Mother hadn't gotten around to showing her what all the powders in her medicine pouch were for, or any of the medicinal arts for which Great-Granny Brown was so well known. Witch from a long line of witches she was, but Carole still couldn't tell mugwort from wolfsbane. She abandoned at once the idea of dancing the knife out of Anastasia's wound when she considered what a mess the blade would made cutting capers in the poor swan's shoulder.

Nevertheless, someone had to do something—and quickly. If only the unicorn's blessing were still fresh in the river water, the water alone would cure anything. Even then, though, they'd still have to get the knife out of the wound.

Suppressing the niggling idea that one reason she hadn't learned the healing arts yet was that she was secretly a trifle squeamish, Carole called to her cousin with all the authority suited to the witch in charge of the case. "Bronwyn, leave that little weasel alone for a moment, won't you, and pull this out of Her Highness. You're stronger than I am and it ought to come out all in one pull so it won't hurt so much."

Bronwyn handed her the sword, still pointed at the boy's throat, and said, "He must not escape. He is doubtlessly an enemy spy sent to kill enchanted royalty."

"What royalty?" the boy demanded, sitting halfway up as the blade retreated during the transfer. He lay down again rather quickly as the blade wobbled back into position against his throat. "I harmed no royalty. Just that swan there. They taste like chicken. Ask anyone."

Bronwyn meanwhile laid down her shield, put both hands on the dagger hilt and pulled. Anastasia gave a long indrawn hiss. She glanced quickly at the blood welling from the dagger hole and flopped her head down, drawing a weary wing over it with one brief willful movement before her entire body toppled over onto her good side.

The gypsy boy laughed a short, nervous laugh. "You have been making sport with me, pretending to be upset and finishing

34

her off yourselves! Ah, well. I am not a greedy man. Are you going to carve or shall I?''

The laugh turned into a cough as Carole pressed forward. ''I will, if you don't belt up.''

The boy's eyes widened with dismay. ''But you are serious! That swan is some kind of friend of yours. Ah, forgive me. It is just my luck that the first drumstick I meet has friends in high places.''

''She's a princess,'' Carole said, and even though she hadn't been particularly impressed with Anastasia's claim, she wanted the boy to be. ''She was going to help us get out of here and even get Bronwyn's curse removed when you butted in.''

''Princess? Bronwyn? Curse? Say, you do not mean—she cannot be—'' He sat up as far as the sword point would permit and squinted at Bronwyn and the swan, then back at Carole, recognition and a wide white smile dawning on his dusky face. He clapped a hand to his forehead. ''What great good fortune to meet together on the same day Bronwyn the Bald-Faced Liar and Magda Brown's witchling! And what luck for you, pretty ladies. For today the stars have smiled upon you and led you if not quite out of the wilderness at least into the protection of Jack the Gypsy.''

Later, leaning back on his elbows and toasting his feet by a cozy fire, Jack rubbed his stomach and sighed. ''How clever you are to whistle the fishes from the river, Lady Carole. Though I practically had to force myself to eat, you understand, so shattered was I to realize I had harmed that wonderful swan-princess. It was only because I was so hungry, you know. Berries alone are not food enough for a man, and my snares have yielded little. Otherwise, I would not have touched your friend. I am very fond of animals. They all like me. Perhaps they know that my own grandfather was once a bear, bewitched into that guise by the same evil man who has cursed the Princess Bronwyn.'' He shrugged. ''For whatever reason, beasts and I understand each other. As I say, they like me. And it is a very good thing for us that fishes like you.''

Carole blushed under his rather self-consciously smoldering gaze. Though he looked a bit younger than she and also as if his recent experience was the only one he had ever had with hunger in his entire life, he was undeniably handsome, with his dark curls and merry grin. She was gratified she had thought of whistling the fish out of the river, where Jack and Bronwyn could catch, kill, and clean them. Jack had a dry tinder box and

35

was an expert firebuilder ("If there's one thing gypsies know about, it's campfires," he'd assured them. They were all soon comfortably full of fish and relatively warm.

"Oh, that's nothing," she said modestly. "Just a little trick I do. And I shouldn't worry too much about Anastasia. She's just sleeping now. I'm sure of it. I don't think the wound is as bad as we thought. Probably the fall just knocked the wind out of her."

"Still," Jack said, "Never will I forgive myself if her injury proves permanent. To think that I struck down the only creature who could lift the curse of Bronwyn the—the so-beautiful Princess Bronwyn—"

"And it doesn't bother you nearly as much that you prevented us from being rescued, I suppose," Bronwyn said. She was not about to be fooled by his flattery now. She'd heard what he called her earlier and besides, it wasn't hard for anyone as familiar with falsehood as she to know one when she heard one.

"Never fear, dear lady. Have I not said luck has smiled upon you and sent you to me? I like you. I take you under my protection. There is nothing more with which to concern yourselves. We have fire, we have fish, we have the great outdoors. . . ."

"We have winter coming," Carole said. He was, after all, only a boy, no matter how nice-looking.

"That should not be troublesome to Master Jack," Bronwyn said sweetly. "He knows everything—who you are, who I am and all of the fond nicknames by which my subjects call me. Surely he knows—"

"Ah, my dear Princess, I see I have offended you!" With the graceful leap of a well-fed housecat who knows on which side its bread is buttered, the boy flowed to his feet and back down on his knee in front of her. "Had your garment a hem I would assuredly kiss it but under the circumstances," he looked significantly at her bare knees between the mid-thigh hem of her undertunic and the top of her sandal laces. "Well, yes, anyway. The name given you by those who have never seen your towering loveliness nor felt the tremendous power of your charming blade came to my tongue only because since I first heard it while listening to my father and grandmother talk at night behind the curtains of our wagon the idea of the beautiful princess whose lies put those of a gypsy to shame has burned in my imagination as one to cherish."

Carole giggled. "Cousin, it sounds to me as if you've met your match."

"Surely not!" Bronwyn replied, blushing till her freckles were joined in a uniform shade of peach.

"And Lady Carole," Jack said, "How can you fail to recognize me? We who played together among the tents of my people when we two were but infants? Your parents and mine fought brave battles together and it is well known among my folk that the only women in Argonia as darkly beautiful as gypsies are the bewitching Brown sorceresses. Who else should I think you are when I know you are no woman of my tribe and yet look enough like me that you could be my cousin as well as the Princess Bronwyn's?"

"Too bad you didn't figure all this out before you knifed Anastasia," Carole said. She remembered her father's songs about those battles Jack spoke of. What the gypsy boy wasn't mentioning was that Carole's folks and his had been on opposite sides in at least one of those battles.

He shrugged. "As you say, it is a little wound. It will surely mend."

"Don't tease, Carole," Bronwyn said. "Think how good it was of Jack to come to these woods specifically with the idea of protecting us and helping us in our quest to end my curse."

Jack waggled a finger, still slick with fish grease, at her. "How alike all you ladies are, even princesses and witches, to think that a prince of the gypsies has no better business than to wait around in the woods to help you. I was here on another matter altogether. . . ."

"Wait a minute," Carole said. "Don't tell me you're royalty too?" She was beginning to feel very left out.

"Oh, yes, dear ladies. My grandmother Xenobia is Queen of the Gypsies and my grandfather is none other than the rightful Crown Prince of Ablemarle, the Prince H. David Worthyman. My father, his heir, is prince of gypsies and Ablemarle both. I am to succeed him, after I—"

"How can it be, *Prince* Jack," Bronwyn asked, suspicion darkening her tone again, "that you are our friend and your grandfather too and he a Prince of Ablemarle when Worthyman the Worthless, Ablemarle's King, is now such a great good friend of my father that my father and his army journey into the Gulf on ships to meet Ablemarle's army half way?"

Jack, not yet used to Bronwyn's phrasing, looked puzzled, but Carole reminded him sternly, "We are at war with Ablemarle, in case you'd forgotten. You're not a spy, are you?"

He laughed with somewhat strained heartiness. "Oh, no, no, no, no, no, dear ladies! My grandfather, I tell you, is the *good,*

37

legitimate prince of Ablemarle, who should be King instead of his worthless brother on the throne. That is why my grandfather is even now fighting at the side of your own papa, Princess, and my father as well. I will go to join them as soon as I have passed to manhood and resumed my rightful position as prince.''

"And when and how does that happen?'' Carole asked, yawning. She was getting bored with these two blowhards.

"Why, it is happening right now, Carole! Even as you look at me, even as I sit here beside you, protecting you from great dangers, I am fulfilling also my obligation to my people, to show them I am worthy of becoming not only a man of our tribe, but prince as well.''

"How convenient.'' Carole yawned again. But Bronwyn's green eyes were big with fascination. She very much enjoyed listening to someone even more full of wild stories than she was.

"It seems to me it must be terrifically hard,'' she said, watching him rub his full belly and settle back again beside the fire.

"Oh, yes, my princess. Yes, indeed. For to gain these honors I must bide here in the wilderness, unaided by my people, and prove my courage and cunning by—er—doing a great deed. Preferably several.'' He chose not to be more specific, in the interests of the picture of himself and his people he wished to present to his illustrious hostesses. Actually, the rules of his manhood test said he was supposed to go into the wilderness unaided and somehow or other make a profit, in gold, on whatever he did. Since this part of the country was relatively uninhabited, there were few purses from which even the most accomplished gypsy could profit, which was what made it such a difficult trial. A future King of the Gypsies was, however, expected to overcome such piddling obstacles.

As if the task wasn't hard enough of itself, Jack had been left with nothing but his clothing, dagger, flint, steel, and tinderbox plus his wits, and his considerable appetite, while his formidable grandmother led his mother and the rest of the tribe south for the winter, promising to return for what was left of him on their way to the eastern coast for the spring smuggling season.

Bronwyn and Jack yammered on about responsibilities to one's people, he making pronouncements, she saying the opposite of what a princess would normally say, followed by Jack trying to figure out what she meant. Carole couldn't think of much to add, so she whistled sticks into piles or danced leaves into pyramids or plaited her hair without touching it, which was tricky. Every

38

so often she rose to see how Anastasia was faring. She was always the same. Sleeping. Head under wing. Bleeding stopped.

As the sun set, the wind rose, and Carole's appetite began plaguing her again. "I'm hungry," she announced.

"And then my mama rides this trick horse in between the wagons, see, and they just leap the campfire. Everyone is always amazed at how easily . . ." Jack was saying.

"Just like my war horse, Hailing Hooves, I'll wager. He can do that, only a lot better," Bronwyn answered.

Carole cleared her throat. "Is anyone else hungry? I think I'll go see about some fish." She had a totally unmagical premonition she was going to get very tired of fish before they got out of this situation unless someone else had some idea how to get food. The idea of singing to a rabbit or a bird and then killing it was distasteful. And she was not only hungry, but cold in spite of her cloak, which she'd reclaimed from Bronwyn. Now that the Princess was dry, she didn't seem to mind the cold any more than Jack did. Carole supposed that was because even though Bronwyn was palace-bred, she was still of frost giant lineage, and who ever heard of a frost giant minding a little chill? And gypsies were used to the wide-open spaces that gave Carole the odd feeling she was emptying out everything that was important about her into them. She wanted her own bed between the walls of her own room with her own pillow and the yellow-bordered brown wool blanket mother had woven just for her.

As she rose to her feet and shook the numbness from one leg, Jack and Bronwyn nodded absently at her and waved, not seeming to hear what she'd said—probably because each of them had had twice as much fish as she before. She slogged back through the bushes to the gravelly river beach and hunkered down beside the water. The river seemed strange now that it just sort of rushed and didn't say anything in particular. Though she thought when she listened closely she could make out a word here and there and even, perhaps, something of a rhythm. But it was only a whisper. Probably the glacier and the mountain filtered out the spell.

It was chilly with no trees to shield her from the wind as she squatted, her skirts whipping about her in the shadow of the great mountain, extending on both sides into the glacier-spiked range. Goose bumps pimpled her arms and she whistled her fishing song slowly—not the jig she'd trilled at lunch but a melancholy air. She usually used the first song when she fished with Dad. He liked that tune. Her talent tickled him, being so much like his own. Mum was always wanting her to learn to do practical things with it like washing dishes and churning butter, but even Mum never turned down a nice mess of fish to fry.

By the end of the first bar, a silvery fish undulated to the top of the milky water, flopped up and onto the bank where it writhed along with her tune. In a short time another did likewise, and another, and she was about to call her lazy companions and demand that if they wanted to share in the catch they'd have to come help kill and dress the dish—when she realized that her tune was not unaccompanied.

A harp? No, a flute—no, perhaps it was a lute, playing the tune way off downstream, so far away that Carole knew no amount of looking or casual strolling away from camp would reveal the musician. Still, she longed to try. She wouldn't be missed surely, the way Bronwyn and Jack were carrying on. As for the fish—

Bronwyn burst out of the woods waving both arms exultingly. Jack walked behind her at a more dignified pace, a grin on his face. "She's asleep! She's asleep!" Bronwyn was shouting. "Carole, come quick! Anastasia is fast asleep."

The music was drowned out in the commotion and Carole scowled at them. "You don't have to yell, do you? Someone else is here and they're playing my song back to me." She cupped her ear, but the music was gone. "You scared them away."

"Well, I'll just go tell Anastasia to wake up again, if that's how you're going to be," Bronwyn huffed.

"What? Anastasia to—oh. Oh! She woke up? Why didn't you say so?"

The three of them turned back towards where Anastasia waited, no longer fainting but sore and silent. Jack was silent now too, and he frowned importantly, as if he was considering a far weightier matter than the preparation of fish. Carole picked up Bronwyn's helmet and headed for the river.

"Where are you going?" he asked gravely.

"I thought Anastasia might like a drink before we turn in."

He shook his head slowly and said portentously, "I would not do that if I were you, Carole. It is not good to go to the river now."

"Not good? What do you mean not good? We've been at the river all day."

Jack lowered his voice and walked towards her slowly, flaring the fingers of both hands dramatically. "That music you hear could be the river men, calling you. They like young girls. They have castles at the bottoms of the rivers and are armed with

40

pitchforks, like angry farmers." He shuddered. The lore about the river men was only hearsay, but angry farmers were a fact of gypsy life.

"Oh, very *well*," Carole said, though she privately thought river men sounded interesting, and that if they had been the ones playing, she'd like to meet them, whatever Jack said. But he sounded serious, though she was sure he was exaggerating because he liked scaring her. Anyway, she was too tired to argue. So she whistled up a pile of leaves for a bed for the three of them and another for cover. Bronwyn and Jack fell quickly asleep and shortly afterwards, she heard Anastasia struggle upright and limp toward the river, and thought the swan must be feeling better if she felt like swimming. Perhaps she'd be well enough to fly again soon.

The music that woke her in the middle of the night wasn't one of her tunes, and it wasn't instrumental. This time she heard a voice—a wonderfully familiar voice, but she couldn't make out just who.

She sat up in a cold mist. The river was pouring it out in thick billows, so that she had trouble picking her way down to the shore. She couldn't see Anastasia, but then, she couldn't see much of anything. All she could do was feel the frosty night air and hear the music cutting across it.

She wanted to call out to whomever was singing and ask them to come closer, and to tell them she was lost, but she was afraid Jack would wake up and scare them away again. The music seemed to come from right down the middle of the river. Perhaps the musicians were camped on a sandbar? Cautiously she waded out, too intent on the music to realize that once her legs were in the water they were no longer cold, that in fact the deeper into the water she got, not only the better could she hear the music but the better she felt all over. It wasn't until she inadvertently stepped in a hole and ducked her head under completely that she found that she could, by some trick of acoustics, hear the music amplified under water. The voice didn't belong to any river man or men. It was her mother's familiar husky voice and she was singing to Carole to come to her, downstream, to meet her. Carole began to swim as she'd never before known she could.

Though still asleep, Bronwyn had been aware when Carole left the leaf pile, leaves rustling the way they do, but had assumed her cousin had only had to avail herself of the privacy of the woods for the usual reasons. It was a dream, not Carole, that actually woke her. The dream was of her mother calling her, singing to her, and though Bronwyn couldn't remember why, the

41

song made her sad and filled her again with the hurt and longing she hadn't been able to speak of at the time of her exile. Sniffling clandestinely, Bronwyn stretched out her hand to touch her shield, and stroked it for comfort, as she always did when she felt bad.

The dream singing faded, and with it the recollection of most of the sadness, though traces of both the feeling and a faint echo of the music lingered. She lay with her cheek pressed against the carved wood of the shield and listened for Carole to return, or maybe to holler that a bear was after her and would Bronwyn be so kind as to get up and save her? The red wood was polished smooth by years of handling, and Bronwyn almost thought she could smell the ale-and-tobacco smell of her father's hands on it. It made her feel close to him, and safe, as it had since she was a baby. The wood was of the rowan, not only her last name but the symbol of her family and anathema to magic. Sort of magic in its own way, really, in that it had the power to repel spells set against it. Too bad she hadn't had it when the sorcerer cursed her—or when Carole marched her into the river, for that matter. She almost fell asleep again holding onto it, still hearing the whispery music and watching the mist weave through the trees.

Jack sat up and rubbed his eyes, scattering the leaves willy-nilly. "Mama?" he asked, in a very young voice, then added something plaintive and muffled in what must have been the gypsy tongue. Before it dawned on Bronwyn that he was not talking to her, he stood up and headed for the river, plowing right through the bushes and not seeming to mind when they slapped his face and soaked him with the touch of their leaves, which were wet with accumulated dew and mist. Bronwyn knew exactly how wet, because of course she had to follow him. Sleepwalking like that, he might do the same thing she'd done, and walk right into the river, in which case they would both get a great deal wetter.

She caught up with him quickly, grabbing him just as his left foot touched the water. When she put her hand on his shoulder to pull him back, he turned and blinked at her.

"See here, my friend, I know it's a wonderful time of night to go wading but—" she got no farther. The rush of water being swished aside from its normal course was immediately followed by Anastasia's black form streaking from the mist. She fluttered toward them awkwardly with one wing only partially extended. Her voice was as shrill as the head chambermaid's after an unfortunate battle Bronwyn had once had with her new bedcurtains.

"Bronwyn! Ah, Bronwyn! Do not try to save her. She went of

42

her own accord—she—she swam. I could do nothing to stop her, to warn her. You must save yourself! Plug your ears! Do not listen to the sirens! Ah, they are terrible, I tell you, terrible. One of them tried even to seduce my old master. No one can—watch the boy!''

While the swan was carrying on, Jack had pulled his sleeve loose from Bronwyn's grip and was wading shin-deep into the river. Glad that she didn't sleep in her armor, Bronwyn waded out after him, and plucked him out again, half carrying him back to shore. He didn't struggle, but looked puzzled. ''What are you doing?'' he asked in a normal voice.

''Sirens!'' Anastasia said. ''They have the girl.''

''But you,'' Bronwyn told him, holding him in her shield arm and indicating his wet trouser legs with a wave of her sword hand, ''are much too clever to be fooled the same way.''

''I am always a fool for a beautiful woman,'' he said, trying to look smoldering again but mostly looking sleepy and making no attempt to extricate himself from her one-armed embrace. ''But if in spite of my warnings, the Lady Carole has fallen for this fish music and even I was taken in by the spell, how did you escape?''

''Overwhelming force of personality and superior intellect,'' she said, nodding meaningfully towards her shield, and dumped him in the boat, climbing in beside him.

For a moment he looked from her to her shield and back again. Then he smiled broadly, ''Ah!'' he said. ''A secret weapon. But of course, my Princess would have a secret weapon.'' He scooted closer to her shield arm. ''Never fear, Your Highness, between your size and that wondrous shield and my cleverness, we shall free Carole from those fish women. And when we have saved Carole, we will make the sirens give us all the sunken treasure they have too.''

''You silly little thug, you have no idea what you're saying!'' Anastasia flapped up beside them. ''They are the most hideously dangerous creatures! You will all be killed and I will not be able to help you at all and—oh, wait!'' She interrupted herself as the boat bobbed off down the river. ''Do wait until I'm healed. I can't even tow you now but—'' But the boat pulled slowly away from her, picking up momentum as the current caught it. The swan found she could swim a little faster. ''Very well, I too shall come. Perhaps the hussies will be afraid to try anything if they see that I am with you, I who know their wicked wiles for the disgraceful tricks they are. Only—wait.'' But the boat was already rounding the next curve. Sighing, Anastasia made a sort of

43

hopping swoop to the center of the river, where the current was strongest. She might become separated from the children, but it was impossible for her to get lost. The sirens could be nowhere but in the sea and into the sea the river was inexorably emptying both her and the little boat.

Chapter IV

As for Carole, she was, with one part of her mind at least, not surprised to see mermaids waiting for her instead of her mother. Though she had felt compelled to investigate the song, she told herself she was more curious than anything and was not as completely taken in by the charm of the music as a mermaid's usual audience was supposed to be.

The sirens, on the other hand, seemed astounded to see her.

They lolled in the shallows just offshore where the river widened into the sea.

"Why, Cordelia, look!" the green-haired one cried, pointing from her seat atop one hump of a half-submerged, silver-spotted sea serpent. "It's a little split-tailed child!"

"And a girl child at that." Her friend, whose hair was light purple, sounded disappointed.

Since the mermaids had stopped singing, Carole was able to swim to shore and greet them while standing on her own two feet. She didn't think they'd drown her, after what Father had told her, but one never knew.

The first mermaid who'd spoken looked just like the one described in Dad's song, as a matter of fact. "Hello," Carole said, not knowing what else to say. "Are there lots of green-haired mermaids or are you Lorelei, the one my father knows?"

"Who's your father?" the purple-haired one asked. "I told you we never should have let that ship go, sister," she added to her green-haired companion. "Those men are carrying tales to their children about how easily duped you were, and now here's one of the little eels come to take advantage of our good nature."

"What do you mean, come to take advantage?" Carole asked. "I was just minding my own business and you called me,

44

sounding like my mother. I knew it was you because my mother's in Queenston and Dad tells all about how you sound like other people in the song he sings about him and Mama rescuing the Queen from the wizard."

"Why, great starfish! Cordelia! Can you believe it? This is Colin Songsmith's little girl! You can stop puffing up like a blowfish. She's practically one of us. Why, I'll bet she came down to the river and told the fish to let us know she was there just so we'd fetch her, didn't you, sweeting? Let's look at you. Hmm, quite the young siren, except for your poor split tail and that dingy-colored hair. Have you schooled yet? And how is your dear papa?"

"Dad's fine. And he's taught me music and Argonian history, and Mum teaches me magical ethics. Princess Pegeen taught me runing and calligraphy when I was just a child."

"But have you *schooled* yet? Oh dear, Cordelia, I don't believe she has."

"Just like these half-breeds to neglect their children's education and then set them loose on us so we'll feel obliged to correct matters. I've a good mind to drown her."

"Don't be such a jellyfish," Lorelei snapped, and dived off the sea serpent to swim protectively in front of Carole. "You saw her swim down the river. Any child of Colin's is mer enough to swim far too well for the likes of us to drown." Carole was very relieved to hear that. Neither of her parents had ever seemed sure how much she had inherited from each of them. Though Dad liked water very much, Mother's aversion to it stemmed from a fear that witches could be melted by too much contact with it, as had once happened to an early Brown ancestress. If Lorelei thought Carole could swim well enough to protect herself against mermaids, then that was good enough for Carole. She walked a little closer to the edge of the shore and sat down cross-legged. Lorelei seemed to be the friendliest, so it was of her Carole asked, "I thought you could only sing ships onto the rocks in the ocean. Why did you sing up the river?"

Lorelei laughed a sparkling laugh and shook back her green hair, then looked up at Carole very closely, the way Great-Granny Brown had started doing after her eyes began to fail. "The fish told us, silly! You surely didn't think you could sing fish out of the river this close to our sea and not have us hear about it?"

"I whistled, actually," Carole said. Lorelei was so pretty. Her eyes were very big and green, even if they might be a little nearsighted, and Carole wished her own hair was that interesting chartreuse color and thick and straight instead of just plain brown and curly. "Would—would you like to hear?"

"Certainly not!" Cordelia said, slapping her tail against the side of the sea serpent. She wasn't as beautiful as Lorelei. Her lavender hair didn't go as well with her fish-belly pale skin and her eyes looked smaller and her mouth tighter. Lorelei didn't wear anything above her shining tail except strategic locks of hair, but Cordelia wrapped a fishnet dripping with seaweed tightly about her shoulders. "We can't have all of our fish committing suicide just so you can show off!"

"I wasn't going to do that one," Carole protested. "I know lots of others."

Lorelei flipped a spray of water back at her colleague. "Go ahead, small fry, don't mind Cordelia. She's just mad because there haven't been any fishing boats around to play with since Brazoria started sending them all to the war. And she's such an old clam I can't talk her into swimming down to the Gulf where all the fun is. I'd love to hear your song. Whistle me something, do."

"Lorelei!" Cordelia snapped.

The green-haired siren surface dived and came up facing her. "We have to know what she can do, don't we?"

"Do we?" Cordelia asked in a tone full of ennui, but she waved her hand that they could continue.

Carole was rather out of the mood to start with, but with Lorelei's smiling encouragement, soon had a wonderful sand castle constructed by whistling the grains of sand into shape. Of course, she had to concentrate fairly hard to keep the doorways from collapsing or the merlons from drying out and falling over the side of the towers, but out of the corner of her eye she could see the sea serpent undulating gently to her tune and even Cordelia seemed impressed.

"I could put sea shell siding on it too," Carole said, "But I guess that *would* be showing off."

"Oh, no, small fry. We need you to show off. As I was telling my dear sister, we have to know what you can do if we're to school you with us. It's going to be hard enough for you with that awful split-tailed birth defect of yours to become a decent siren, but if your other talents are up to it, who knows what—" Suddenly the sea serpent dumped Cordelia unceremoniously into the water and flashed a loop of itself past Carole, up the river channel. A very familiar scream, cursing in a male voice in a guttural foreign language, and Bronwyn's voice crying "By the

46

Rowan!'' her family battle cry, were followed by the returning of the no-longer-empty loop of sea monster.

"Don't worry, Carole!'' Bronwyn cried, "We'll save you!'' Which was nonsense since the monster had looped himself twice, so that an extra coil pinned Jack and Bronwyn together with arms at their sides and Bronwyn couldn't even get her sword free.

"Make him let them go,'' Carole begged Lorelei. "They're friends of mine.''

But Lorelei had dived under when the huge bit of monster had lashed past. Nor was Cordelia in sight. Carole whistled sharply and about a league out to sea, the monster's head snapped up. She began the sand castle song again, easing it into a sedate, relaxed line dance, that caused the beast to uncoil himself and lie out in a line, releasing Jack, Bronwyn, and the boat.

Dragging them ashore, Carole felt unaccountably annoyed. "What are you doing here?'' she asked.

"Saving you,'' Bronwyn said.

"I don't want to be saved. I was just showing my friend Lorelei my magic. She seems to think I could be a pretty good mermaid.''

Offshore, the sea serpent wiggled back into its customary up and down conformation and both mermaids resurfaced, Cordelia resuming her seat on the monster's back with a little scolding pat of her tail against its sides, while Lorelei did a double flip, dived under and surfaced at Carole's feet. "That was wonderful, small fry, the way you made Ollie do what you wanted.'' She peered with her wide, green stare at Jack and Bronwyn, and with less curiosity at Anastasia, who fluttered down beside them. "What are these?'' the mermaid asked. Then, before Carole could answer, pointed at Bronwyn. "That looks familiar.''

"Lorelei,'' Carole said with some pride, though she couldn't have said whether it tickled her more to introduce her cousin the Princess to her new friend the mermaid, or vice versa. "I'd like you to meet Her Highness, Princess Bronwyn Rowan, Crown Princess of Argonia and—er—Jack. The swan is a princess too.''

"Yes, sweeting,'' Lorelei barely acknowledged the last introduction with a bored flip of her hand, whose fingers were delicately webbed. "Aren't they all. Which of you minnows is which, again? You all look alike to me.''

"We are,'' Bronwyn said. "Exactly alike.''

"Er—what she means is we have a common problem,'' Carole explained. "It's really Bronwyn's problem, but you see, it's a patriotic matter.''

47

"Does she have a father too?" Lorelei asked suddenly, studying Bronwyn more closely. "Bigger, but with coral hair?"

Bronwyn looked pleased. "No, actually I'm the first girl in Argonia to be born of a union between a woman and a cinnamon bear."

"Never mind her, Lorelei," Carole practically screamed over her blowhard cousin. "That's part of this problem she has. She's cursed, and Jack and Anastasia the Alluring and I have pledged to help her."

"Isn't that cute?" Lorelei said, but she didn't sound very interested.

"I'd say these rather wreck your plan to school her, don't they, sister dear?" Cordelia asked, indicating the new arrivals with a wave of her hair comb and a voice suspiciously sweet. "They won't survive long at sea."

"No. I suppose not. You wouldn't mind if we drown them, would you, small fry? It'll be quicker and more merciful that way. They'll never feel a thing, but we'll enjoy it enormously."

"I should say not!" Carole said. "I told you they're my friends."

"But if you're to school—oh dear, what are we to do with you? We can't drown you, and we can't just keep letting mortals go all the time. Cordelia is already furious with me about—" She looked up at Bronwyn again. "About that coral-haired giant and that eel of a wizard."

She looked imploringly back to Cordelia, who sighed, adjusted her shawl, and dived off the side of the sea serpent to swim over and have a closer look.

"Oh well," Cordelia said, after her inspection. "She IS talented and there aren't many new ones being hatched. Of course, she'll have to learn to do things properly. But I suppose since we have Ollie, we can let her keep these as pets. We can moor them at the atoll, though I doubt they'll like it."

"You are too charming," Jack said, with a sweeping bow to both mermaids. "But as the Lady Carole has mentioned, we have a mission to perform on behalf of Her Highness. We could not possibly be persuaded from it. . . ."

But Cordelia had already instructed the sea serpent to return to shore, where it caught Bronwyn up in a coil. Lorelei was smiling at Carole and holding out her hand, singing a little song under her breath. It was such a lovely song. And they were both so beautiful. Somehow she knew from that song that schooling was something marvelous, and she felt she must learn what the mermaids wanted her to know. After all, they were part of her lineage just like witches and she already knew witching. She must school. She had to. Just for a little while. Bronwyn's curse had waited all her life. It surely could wait a while longer. Slipping dreamily into the waves, she swam towards Lorelei.

The mermaids' atoll wouldn't have been such a bad place to spend time if not for the weather. There was nowhere for any of the humans to shelter from the squalls that gusted across the barren rock and whipped the gray sea whose pounding waters provided the only scenery from horizon to horizon. Anastasia fared a little better, since the crags of the atoll protectively ringed a central blue pool in which the swan could swim, as she did, gliding relentlessly back and forth, back and forth, every morning as soon as her head was out from under her wing. Her chariot, which she had dragged behind her while she rode the sea serpent to the atoll, was moored on one side of the pool. Bronwyn thought it strange that after so many years of being bound to the chariot the swan didn't gladly abandon it when she had the chance, but she supposed the familiarity coupled with the fact that the boat was now the only thing the swan possessed enhanced Anastasia's proprietary feelings. But chariot or no chariot, the transformed princess was no happier about being stuck on the atoll than Jack or Bronwyn. Though the pool contained fresh water rather than salt unless inadvertently mingled with unusually high waves, it grew none of the plants of which Anastasia was fond, and she was obliged, as were the rest of them, to subsist on seaweed salad.

Carole felt the cold and wet less than the other humans. All she had to do was mimic the mermaids and submerge herself to feel comfortable. Cordelia and Lorelei made sure she was submerged a good deal of the time, often with her feet lashed together to teach her, they said, to swim properly instead of kicking. When she'd tried to talk to Bronwyn and Jack, Cordelia had scolded her. "Split-tails haven't the sense of a piece of driftwood about what's important. You have a great deal to learn to overcome your handicap and be considered even a freakish kind of mermaid. You really must concentrate on your lessons instead of chattering with these others."

Carole had looked for a moment as woebegone as Bronwyn and Jack felt, and Bronwyn had hoped that she would start thinking of some plan to get them off the atoll. Maybe Anastasia would mend enough, in a few days, to fly them to land, one at a time, while the mermaids were showing Carole how to scout for ships or taking her on tours of their past conquests, wrecks sunk far beneath the waves.

But that night the weather was fair and when Carole climbed up on the rocks to be with her friends, the mermaids joined them and Lorelei sang to them all and braided pearls in Carole's hair and the sappy look on her cousin's face told Bronwyn that if she and Jack left now, Carole wouldn't accompany them. Not that Bronwyn cared, the way the stupid little witch was acting, but Aunt Maggie wouldn't like it, and it would be a shame to go through all these perilous adventures and live only to get killed by one's own aunt when one got home.

But as little as Carole seemed to care about her friends' welfare, the mermaids resented them anyway. On another of the nights they spent on the atoll, Lorelei asked teasingly, "Won't you let me drown just the boy? Just to keep my hand in? It's been ever so long since a ship has come along."

Carole had jerked away from Lorelei's comb, giggling, as if she thought the mermaid was joking. "No, silly," she said, using one of Lorelei's pet expressions. "Of course you can't drown him."

Cordelia, stringing pearls onto her fishnet shawl, tapped her tail impatiently against the rock. "There's no *of course* we can't do anything, small fry. This is our territory and you're our guest, and I'll thank you to mind your manners. I've a good mind to drown him myself just to teach you a lesson."

Jack, all the air gone out of him after his first day of seaweed salad and soaking, could only look miserable.

"You do and I won't let you ever catch any ships again!" Carole said. "I'll warn them all away, I swear I will!"

"Hmph," Cordelia said. "Not much chance of that. No ship can resist a siren's song. You know that."

"They can if they can't hear it and they'll be so busy dancing to my tune I promise you they won't hear a thing."

To demonstrate she puckered up and whistled a jig that made the mermaids first pat their hands and slap their tails against the rocks, then dive into the sea and frolic like porpoises, who were diving and frolicking a little further out. Fortunately, the sea serpent was off on some business of his own or he would have been trying to dance too, which would have drenched the island with his waves, making their water too salty to drink.

Jack and Bronwyn shuffled about on the rocks, twirling each other, kicking up gravel and bruising their feet on the stones until one of Bronwyn's feet happened to bump against her shield. Touching it released her from the spell long enough that she could reach down and grab the shield and Jack at the same time. Relief flooded through her as she and Jack collapsed together on the rocks, glad not to have died dancing.

Lorelei surfaced, her cheeks pink with exertion. Both mermaids managed to hoist themselves onto the rocks, though they were still hand-patting and tail-bobbling most alarmingly, while molting iridescent scales onto the rocks as they writhed rhythmically against them.

"Oh, stop," Lorelei panted. "Cordelia, puff, do make her stop. I shall drown of all this air if I must do this any longer."

Cordelia was forced to capitulate and after that, for a time, the mermaids ignored Bronwyn and Jack, though they were rather more severe than before with Carole, insisting that she sing instead of whistle, if she were to be a proper mermaid, and endeavor to learn the bubbling language in which the mermaids spoke to Ollie and the other sea creatures, and master particular songs of calling in those languages.

One day Lorelei undertook to give Carole jigging lessons. This segment of the witch's education afforded Jack in particular considerable diversion, since Lorelei felt compelled to do a lot of demonstrating. Carole couldn't seem to get the hang of it, which was no wonder, since she was not only too young to have the wherewithal to perform the task properly, but was also too strictly brought up to remove her shift, whatever the mermaids did, and so spoiled any small effect she might have been creating. Not even the wet and cold could keep them all from laughing, and that evening dinner was made merrier by the absence of Cordelia.

A moray eel had brought a message from a herd of seals that sounded most urgent, Lorelei explained when she brought the humans their seafood salads, and dear Cordelia had simply had to respond in person. "I know she's an awful old jellyfish at times, but she's very conscientious about her stewardship of these waters."

"Stewardship?" Jack asked, pushing a slimy green strand of seaweed around on the slab of rock in front of him with his dagger. "When you wreck all the boats? That's an odd term for it."

Anastasia stopped gliding in the pool to reprimand him. "I am surprised that even a young hooligan such as yourself would lower himself to speak to these—these . . ."

But Bronwyn, who was glad for a chance to have a general sort of conversation going after almost a week of the swan's silent belligerent swimming, Jack's morbid silence, and the mermaids and Carole addressing each other exclusively, encouraged Lorelei to continue. "I suppose you do have a great chore, knowing which ships are the best ones to sink and keeping the waters clear of the wreckage they so inconsiderately leave behind and so on."

"You're very smart to see that," Lorelei said, pleased. "Most mortals just get stuffy about the drownings, and don't think of the services we perform, livening up the sailors' dreary lives with a little romantic adventure, keeping navies from getting too large, giving the fish a fair chance to fight back—"

"I suppose it's being brought up a Princess," Bronwyn said chattily. "It gives one a larger scope on things."

"Maybe so," Lorelei said. "But I swear, no one would believe the things that go on in these waters unless they swam in them every day. You think Ollie's a monster! You should see some of the abominations that have been growing off the coast of Frostingdung these last few years since the selkies were driven away."

"I'm sure they're no scarier than the beasts I've routinely faced during my many brave exploits," Bronwyn began, but Carole swiftly cut in, as she was annoyingly in the habit of doing.

"Do tell us, Lorelei."

"Some say the seas began to change when Loefwin slew all magic, others say it was not until he brought his Lily Pearl with her mother, Belburga of the pointed teeth and her sister—"

"Belburga?" Anastasia suddenly thrust her head forward. "But how can that be? Surely you are wrong, for there can hardly be two—no, no, not with daughters and pointed teeth. But how confusing! First she is in Little Darlingham selling to my old master the curse which has so cruelly undone Princess Bronwyn, and now you say she is in Frostingdung?"

Bronwyn agreed with the swan. "It's hard to see how she could have moved without consulting you, when you were only under that glacier for a moment."

The swan flipped her head, as if shaking off water, and preened in a quick and finicky fashion.

The mermaid gazed at Bronwyn with new interest. "This curse. It's been mentioned before. What is it?"

"Boils," Bronwyn said, recalling the Lord Chamberlain's affliction, the evolution and resolution of which she used to watch with a sort of nauseated fascination. "I break out in horrible boils whenever anyone lays violent hands on me. Hurts

52

ke the dickens, and of course they're contagious as all get out. ig puffy red ones with white cores that go pop and . . ."

"Ye-ess," Lorelei said, her cheeks almost as green as her yes and hair. "I can see where that might be a disadvantage."

"It's not just the pain, oh no," Bronwyn said, warming to her ubject. "I'm terribly stoic, so though the pain is excruciating, it s nothing compared with the political disadvantage." She waited or Lorelei to ask what that might be, but the mermaid wasn't ising to the bait, so Bronwyn proceeded to enlighten her any- vay. "I mean, you can't imagine how frustrating it is to be rying to build a reputation as a warrior princess, and the first pponent one joins in hand-to-hand combat immediately joins ne in breaking out in big sore spots. Naturally, I can hardly find parring partners any longer. So I simply must get this curse emoved as quickly as possible."

Lorelei touched Carole's arm urgently. "Come along, min- low. I think we should take a midnight dive. I'll show you the ner harp, if you wish, and then maybe we might swim out and ;reet Cordelia coming home. What do you say?"

Carole cast an apologetic look at her friends and turned to dive n after the mermaid.

Jack was shaking with laughter. "Boils! Oh, Princess, that vas wonderful! They will not dare try to drown you now. Maybe ;ince we know that it is to Frostingdung we must go to release you from your curse the fish women will take us there instead, as ;oon as Lady Carole tires of her swimming lessons."

The swan let out a long hiss. "Not very likely. Did you not lear what she said about monsters in the waters? I cannot maginc monstcrs those hussies would fear, but I would not care :o face them. We must find some other way to reach Belburga and lift the curse. I feel I am almost healed enough to draw the two of you in the chariot, but the mer creatures can always send their monster to fetch us, and even if they do not and we reach the shores of Frostingdung, there will be *those* monsters with which to contend. And, pardon me, but it is I who will have my underside exposed to the water. I thank you, no. You must try to find some less dangerous way to alleviate your curse, dear Bronwyn."

"How about the shield?" Jack asked. "Why don't you get it to take the curse off? It protected you from the mermaid magic and let us stop dancing while Carole was still jigging the mermaids about."

"Ah, yes," Bronwyn said, "But those were big spells, not

53

petty little curses like flaws in my personal integrity. My shie
wouldn't waste its power considering such a trifle.''

Anastasia added, ''Besides, a shield would protect one fro
outer danger, and it seems to me that your curse is very li
mine, a part of yourself from which that designed for yo
exterior protection can not defend you.''

Bronwyn only sighed.

Though she'd hinted repeatedly at how interested she was
seeing the underwater instruments which had first called to h
on the river, Carole was too distracted now to pay close attenti
to them. Really, this business of being caught in the middle
two sets of friends who disliked one another was getting e
tremely taxing, more so because the accommodations were not
all what Mother would consider up to par. Though Carole herse
found diving deep into the sea, dancing among bright fis
prying into the cargoes of barnacle-encrusted wrecks, and sin
ing and conversing with sea creatures diverting enough to mak
up for sleeping on jagged rocks and eating nothing but seaweec
she had come to realize that neither Jack nor Bronwyn was ab
to appreciate the adventure's educational qualities.

She'd tried to share. Jack had said something about treasur
and once she had persuaded Lorelei to let her bring some to th
surface to show him, but he had simply held it while asking h
if there weren't some way she could persuade the mermaids t
allow them to leave. When she said there wasn't, he asked if sh
could kill and deliver a fish or two on the sly, when the me
maids weren't watching. But by then she had learned to spea
fish and was more than a little horrified at his suggestion. Killin
river fish had been different. They were stupid and not nearly s
attractive as the varicolored species around the atoll.

''Now I suppose you are wondering how we play these with
out the strings losing their tone in the water,'' Lorelei wa
saying, holding a pearl-encrusted gold harp with her own imag
carved on the body.

''Umm hmm,'' Carole replied automatically. Though the grott
containing the harp and the myriad other valuables the mermaid
had acquired during their ''salvage operations'' was the mos
splendid place Carole had ever seen, with the water-diffuse
moonlight shivering mysteriously through it, she only stayed t
avoid hurting Lorelei's feelings. Cordelia knew more importar
mer lore, and she had explained that mers ruled the sea becaus
they were the original inhabitants of the world and mortal peopl
a dried-out afterthought, an aberration. Since fishermen an
serpent hunters killed sea creatures, mers redressed the balanc

54

by killing the killers. Logical as that sounded, Carole didn't like it. She'd fancied a siren's functions as mainly consisting of swimming, singing, hair-combing and looking fetching. Drowning people had not figured in her plans, but then she had never actually seen Cordelia or Lorelei drown anyone, much less done it herself. She imagined the talk of drowning was just that—talk—the kind of thing people liked to tell to show how fierce and powerful they or their ancestors had been, like Mother going on about Grandma Elspat eating children who came to eat her gingerbread house. Lorelei and Cordelia had surely just been trying to impress her and scare Bronwyn and Jack into behaving. Well, she'd impressed them right back and let them know what she thought of them aiming such shenanigans at *her* friends. She was pretty sure the stories told about mermaids by other people were nothing but jealous lies because the sirens were so beautiful and fascinating. Of course, there *were* all those skeletons at the base of the atoll and the wrecks, but then too, these were stormy waters and the atoll was in an awkward place if one happened to be a ship caught out in a storm.

"Minnow, you're not paying attention to me," Lorelei pouted. "Cordelia will be cross if I don't teach you anything today. I thought you'd want to know about the instruments! A girl can expand her range with them so. We called you with them at first to get your attention, so you'd hear our song." She set the harp down next to a lute made of seashell, a conch horn, and pan pipes made of what looked like the bones of a human hand. The sand swirled up from the bottom when the harp sank into it.

"Lorelei, do you really drown people?" Carole asked, giving the little upward thrust of her shoulders and chest Lorelei and Cordelia had taught her to use to surface instead of kicking her feet, as she'd used to. Lorelei surfaced with her.

"If you'd only be sensible about the boy, I'd be glad to show you, sweeting," Lorelei said in a worried voice. "I'm sorry about the ships but—"

Carole was about to protest that it was quite all right and not to bother on her account when a wave of the eastern sea roiled slightly higher than the rest, then appreciably higher, until she could make out the undulating loops of Ollie wriggling toward them, gray on a lighter gray sky. She heard him calling before she actually saw him, but he was still half a league away before she could make out his message, and then only imperfectly, since she hadn't learned all the sea serpent language yet.

But Lorelei did a delighted backflip and splashed back down again. "Oh, goody! How timely! You see how things work out?

55

Just when we most needed a ship, Cordelia's sighted one.'' He green eyes sparkled in the moonlight as a fond expression crosse her face. ''There, didn't I tell you Cordelia isn't as hard as sh sounds? Instead of wrecking it all by herself, she's saved it for us Quickly now, we're to follow Ollie.''

They met Cordelia just before dawn, the leagues between he and them having been easily spanned by the rhythmic swimming stroke in which the mermaids had tutored Carole.

''I think we'll send Ollie away for this one and wreck the ship on the atoll, just to give your pets a chance to prove their worth minnow,'' Cordelia said slyly, and dismissed the serpent with one of the ululations one used to speak to him. Carole didn' know what Cordelia had in mind that Bronwyn and Jack were supposed to do to prove worth, but somehow she didn't feel i had anything to do with nursing survivors back to health.

While the ship was still a tiny dot in the distance, the mermaids began casting a mist ahead of them. Carole watched with admiration as they sent it skipping across the waves to ensnare the ship. Mist-making was something she hadn't been able to do any better than jiggling, and now she could see why Cordelia had been so put out with her failure. The mist was a disguise for both sirens and for the rocks or sea serpent with which they would wreck the ship.

The sirens sang, and Carole rather reluctantly tried the song with them, but she hadn't yet mastered all of the suggestive intonations that made each listener hear his own particular favorite loved one, so she sort of hummed along with the chorus.

The ship didn't take much persuasion. It was scarcely enveloped by the mist before it was skating back out again, straight for them, its sails billowing against the lightening sky, its hull winking, bigger and bigger, through the fog, until it loomed over them. A beacon shone from the starboard bow, the side facing them, and floating on the mist Carole could see a black and white flag flying from the mast. As the ship drew nearer still, by lying flat and pushing backwards she could make out the design on the banner, and thought it a funny, gruesome sort of thing to put on a flag, a skull and couple of old bones. Wasn't that the sign Great-Granny-Brown used to mark the concoctions she made that were poisonous?

This ship was not responding quite the way Cordelia said they did—it was sliding much too eagerly toward them, too quickly and too close. The idea was that the crew would drop everything as soon as they heard the first strains of the song and listen, neglecting to sail their ship and so leaving it prey to the perils the sirens had in store for them. When drawing a ship to a specific peril, one sang for a while to get everyone's attention, stopped long enough to give the crew a chance to head towards one, then sang again, just so they wouldn't become rational enough to realize the ship was off course. This ship cut through the water as if it knew exactly where it was going. Carole had been back-treading, wallowing in the waves near the stern while Lorelei and Cordelia continued their song and watched the ship's quick progress with self-congratulatory smiles. They seemed to be looking forward to whatever happened next too much to notice what Carole saw as inconsistency between the theory and practice of ship beguilement.

With the vessel alongside the sirens, the deck suddenly swarmed with activity. Something was dropped over the railing. It fanned out, dipped down and scooped up the mermaids.

"EEEK!" Lorelei screamed.

"Ollie!" Cordelia cried more coherently, but by now the sea serpent's leagues-long body would have covered a distance too vast to be spanned by even a siren's unaided voice.

A chorus of laughter rang from the ship and the mist broke, as if dispelled by the laughter.

A net full of white skin, silvery fishtail, and lavender and green hair all tangled together was hauled up. The mermaids shrieked and rough laughter from on deck answered them. The men tugging the net leaned over the railing, and Carole saw their wicked leering faces. One especially evil-looking specimen wore a ragged black eye patch, which doubled rather than halved the nastiness of his leer. He laughed and hooted louder than all the others.

Carole dived, so they wouldn't see her, and surfaced near enough to the hull to get a splinter in her knee while she tried to hear what was being said on board. All she heard was the sound of scuffling, the smack of what sounded like heavy fish against wood and once, with an accompanying yelp, against flesh.

Whether or not turnabout was fair play, in this case it just didn't seem sporting. There were a great many sailors, and rather dreadful ones at that, to judge from the face of the villain she'd seen. For some reason, too, they seemed to have resisted the siren spell. It occurred to Carole that perhaps they were deaf, though who'd be fool enough to hire a shipload of deaf sailors she was too weary to imagine. It wouldn't hurt to test anyway. She whistled a bit of a reel and listened. Feet scuffled back and forth in a non-musical, routine way, the mermaids continued to shriek apparently unheeded except for the odd guffaw here and there. Otherwise it was just slapping waves, creaking timbers and flapping sails. But though she didn't seem to be making much of an impression on the sailors, a rope dangling just over her head was going crazy, whisking back and forth like the tail of a cow during peak fly season in time with her tune. Which gave her an idea.

She dove, surfacing far enough away that she could see the whole ship. The net containing Lorelei and Cordelia now bobbed silently from the prow. The mermaids had stopped shrieking and Carole wondered for a moment if they were dead. An isolated sob persuaded her that they were more likely just too demoralized to maintain a vigorous resistance.

Dawn was breaking by now. In spite of the vast and seemingly unmarked sea around her, Carole thought she could find her way back to the atoll. Though many of the mermaids' best treasures were kept in the grotto at the foot of the atoll, Lorelei and Cordelia were indifferent housekeepers—little caches of jewels and coins, rotting furniture and the wrecks of great ships, were scattered all over the ocean floor like dirty flagons after a party. By diving periodically, she should be able to use these as, well, not landmarks, but points of reference at least. She didn't want to wreck the ship as the mermaids had planned—now that they were in the net and she was in the sea, she found she didn't want to do quite a few of the things they'd discussed, like living the rest of her life in the ocean. Not that she knew exactly what it was she did want to do, but she and the others could figure that out once they'd decided what to do with this stupid ship. If a giant sword-wielding princess complete with curse, a giant black swan with a royal background, a chubby junior gypsy, and a mer-witch in training couldn't extricate themselves and their hostesses from the present situation, perhaps a sea serpent could. If Ollie wasn't already at the atoll, surely one of the underwater instruments would fetch him in short order.

So she sang to the ship, rather than to the crew. But when the vessel tried to take charge of itself, in response to her spell, the helmsman caught on quickly and struggled for control. His flesh and blood hands were stronger than her little song, at this distance, and the ship was a very big piece of material to try to control. It was smaller than Ollie, of course, but then, Ollie was a living creature.

Very well, if they were taking over the rudder, she could find other material aboard that could use some exercise. Spotting a coil of rope, she trilled a loud, but sinuously serpentine measure at it and it responded as Ollie had done to an almost identical

58

song, uncoiling itself and slinking toward the feet of the nearest man.

Another line, likewise responding to her recreational tone, whipped enthusiastically around the helmsman, who squawked, unheeded by his fellows, and fell down. After that, she could once more do as she liked with the ship, and led it like a stray dog back to the atoll.

The look-out in the crow's nest was the first one to look close enough to the ship to see Carole—shortly before he looked far enough from it to see the atoll. Whether or not he was deserting his post by leaping overboard might have been debatable in a naval court-martial, but since his fellows couldn't hear him, it could have been argued that he meant to warn them by example. Two men on the decks below saw him and dove in after him, and two more saw them and followed suit. Another one flew past Carole's nose, dousing her as he crashed into the water, and disappeared.

Jack hailed her from the atoll, waving hugely, and Bronwyn drew her sword. "Aha!" the Princess said, "It seems my cousin has been captured by pirates."

Jack nodded. "What do you suppose she means to do with them?"

Carole was beckoning frantically to them and pointing to the foundering ship, but neither of *them* had mer blood and they weren't about to shed any of the kind they did have trying to swim out and board a potentially hostile pirate ship at that distance.

Another party was less reluctant, however. Ollie's head surfaced from the far side of the atoll, his front-most portion swaying above the fresh water pond only momentarily before he uncoiled himself from around the rocky base of the island and zigzagged towards the ship. As the serpent passed, Bronwyn boarded him, and Jack, not to be outdone, followed suit. Anastasia flapped and fluttered uncertainly and hissed incomprehensible advice.

As the serpent encircled the ship, Carole joined her friends on his back and said, panting, "I think if we're ever going to get out of here, we'd better not let Ollie crush this ship. We have to get the crew to surrender—fast."

"Never fear, cousin," Bronwyn said, "Bronwyn the Bold has boarded many a pirate ship—just let me climb up on the floor and in no time I'll have them all hanging by ropes from those rod things they have strung up there."

"Have at it. But I'd mind the ropes, if I were you. They may

59

still be crawling around a bit. My songs sometimes have a rather more lasting effect than I mean for them to.''

"Er—pardon me for asking this," Jack said politely, "But why are the ropes dancing and the sailors swimming?"

"Because the ropes heard my song, but the sailors didn't. I think the crew is deaf."

"Like Grandpa Worthyman when he puts wax plugs in his ears to drown out Grandma Xenobia," Jack nodded sagely.

"Oh, surely *not,*" Bronwyn agreed, pausing in her climb up loops of serpent to grin down at them.

"It's certainly possible they plugged their ears," Carole said. "More likely, I guess, than that they're all deaf. You'd better check on that while you're capturing the ship."

"Jolly. What if they choose to kill us while we are so kindly trying to increase their listening pleasure?" he asked.

"Why do I have to think of everything?" Carole complained. "Just DO it, before we're boarding a pile of splinters. I have to loose Cordelia and Lorelei."

"MUST you?" Bronwyn called down, just before climbing over the rail.

"I don't think Ollie will mind me if I try to keep him from squashing the ship all by myself."

The two-person boarding party duly boarded with aplomb more dampened, at least on Jack's part, by nervousness than by the actual soaking they'd received from the sea, but they soon took to their task. Only two of the entire crew remained on board: the one-eyed peg-legged villain Carole had spotted and a woman clad in an olive woolen cloak.

The patch-eyed pirate grinned at Jack and Bronwyn as though he'd like to eat them and growled to the woman, "We seem to be boarded, Mistress Rusty. Whatever ye think of me mission, ye'd best 'elp me resist these 'ere buccaneers or they'll be 'avin' the both of us walkin' the plank."

But the lady was already down on one knee, her head bowed, her docile pose broken only by one hand, which reached up to jerk on the pirate's tattered sash. "Nonsense!" she growled back. "If the Princess Bronwyn wants your leaky tub, I suggest you give it to her without further ado. On your knee, my dear scoundrel. Show your future sovereign a little respect."

Carole meanwhile was having difficulties of her own. Using her pidgin version of the sea creatures' language, she persuaded Ollie to refrain from squeezing the ship to smithereens while she freed Cordelia and Lorelei. Scrambling up the serpent's slithery sides, she managed to raise herself to where she was level with the deck and about two arms' length away from the knot. Lorelei and Cordelia were quiet. Perhaps they had fainted. She hoped prolonged separation from water hadn't killed them. But it couldn't have: The waves dashing against the prow could have kept even a fish of the wholly ocean-breathing kind alive.

She wondered how she was going to sing a knot loose, and wished she had remembered to borrow someone's knife, though both Bronwyn and Jack would be needing theirs to fight pirates, she supposed. Then she saw just above her head an abandoned cutlass and grabbing it up, sliced the knot holding the net to the ship, dumping the mermaids over the side and into the sea, where she gratefully joined them.

Chapter V

The pirate shook his head wonderingly. "I been on these seas seven hundred and fifty year, man, genie, and lad, and I never before saw a mermaid—much less two—let go of a single prisoner—much less a shipload—not to mention a young'un she thought she had a claim on."

The ship had left the atoll behind almost two hours ago and now the pirate, who was called Jehan the Fleet, the lady, and Carole, Bronwyn, and Jack sat in the galley with mugs of tea, a plate of salt herring and five loaves of bread, smothered a piece at a time with good mint jam.

Carole shrugged. "Maybe it was because I wasn't a very good mermaid after all."

Jack shook his head and said emphatically, "Oh no, Honorable Lady Carole, you were a wonderful mermaid. They let go the sailors and this ship from gratitude to you, of that I am sure. Did they not give you their flute to reward you?"

Carole fingered the flute—a little whistle actually, made from a single shaft of coral. She was wearing it around her neck, on the same string as her medicine pouch. Lorelei had pressed the instrument on her when Cordelia wasn't looking, "Just in case you should ever need to call us, small fry."

Bronwyn smiled a knowing smile and speared another piece of

61

salt herring, saying to Jehan and the lady as she did so, "You mustn't make too much of it, you know. Saving your ship was nothing for Cousin Carole. She's Queen of the Sirens. They'll do anything she tells them. They recognized her superior magic and leadership qualities right off and insisted she stay around to rule them with us to advise her. Upset as they were about my boils, they simply couldn't be parted from us. Needed someone like Carole to organize them. Wishy-washy lot, left to themselves." Mercifully, she filled her mouth with food and had to chew instead of talk.

Carole made a face at her and grabbed the jam pot as it slid past her to the lowest part of the tilting table. Separating Lorelei and Cordelia from the sailors was one of the hardest things she had ever tried to do, partly because the mermaids had been so angry and so glad to get their hands on their tormenters, and partly because Carole was just plain puckered out from whistling ships about. She'd scarcely had so much as a tweet left to dance the mermaids from their prey. By the time she'd saved the sailors, she knew for sure that bubbly Lorelei and cantankerous Cordelia did indeed drown seamen for fun and profit, as they'd been telling her all along. Only out of gratitude to her for preventing their permanent change of occupation to ships' figureheads had they released the ship and crew. Jack had been right about that. She'd also threatened to dance them on the ends of their tails for all eternity if they didn't.

But it was nice to have the others appreciate her. Bronwyn's lie had at least elevated Carole to Queen of *something*, which was equivalent and even a little above Bronwyn's own royal status and that of Anastasia and Jack.

And if the mermaids had proved to be not so good as they were beautiful, neither was Jehan the Fleet so bad as he was ugly. He and the lady in the green cloak, Mistress Raspberry, were both old friends of the King's, which was how the lady had recognized Bronwyn. Jehan didn't see as well as his companion due to the injury that had cost him his eye and which was why, Carole supposed, he sported that awful squinting leer. He'd told them he had captured Lorelei and Cordelia with the aim of turning them loose on the combined Ablemarlonian and Brazorian navies.

"Me jolly roger is just for old times' sake, ye understand," he said. "I was in the international import-export business before I turned genie and just had a mind to try it out again, before I got to the war."

"I too would like to go a—pirating," Jack told him, "But I am pledged to help my Princess end her curse." He regarded his

62

Princess adoringly from the corner of his eye. Such a regal person, his Bronwyn. How nobly she ate with both competent hands, her fine appetite befitting her imposing figure. How safe he had felt behind her when they'd boarded the boat—truly, this was the sort of woman worthy of his protection. Hungry as he had thought he was while choking down seaweed salads, he could manage only eight slices of bread and a few sedate sips of tea while Bronwyn polished off three times that amount.

Carole suddenly could scarcely eat another bite for yawning. The swimming she had done in the week past had honed her down, sharpened and darkened her till she felt like a blade of her former self, but the effort of moving the ship and battling the mermaids had drained her.

"So," the elegant Mistress Raspberry said to Bronwyn, licking a bit of jam from the edge of her mouth with a rather pointed tongue which disappeared quickly between her lips. "You've finally decided to do something about that curse, Your Highness. What's this about boils? You're a liar, aren't you? That's what it says in the archives. I know. Sir Cyril Perchingbird asked my advice about them when last I was in Queenston. Oh, yes, I see. You were lying about the boils. Mother, what a bore for you, you poor child! I can certainly understand why you'd undertake a quest to do something about it. But I do think your timing is a bit off. I mean, really, dear, there is a war on and all. Shouldn't you wait until your father's around to help you?"

"My father can't be bothered with silly things like curses," Bronwyn said.

"I think she means, ma'am, that he has tried," Jack said, checking Bronwyn's eyes to make sure he was on the right track, "and it has become too important, too urgent, to wait. Besides, the Princess feels it is her curse, not His Majesty's."

"Yes," Carole said, yawning gustily and leaning back in her chair, cradling the back of her head with her hands. She did remember to brace her feet firmly against the shifting deck while she reclined, so as not to be thrown to the floor when the ship rolled. Her companions and the galley kept disappearing beyond her heavy eyelids, but she continued to try to explain, somewhat mumblingly, to Jehan and the lady, "See, when the King tried to cure the curse, he went after the tax collector, only then the tax collector *wasn't* a tax collector, and Bernard says he's really my mother's uncle which is why he's a wizard and looks like us. Except, it wasn't him—I mean, it wasn't the wizard tax collector who made up Bronwyn's curse even though he put it on her, because Anastasia says it was a witch named Belburga."

"Ogress," the lady corrected softly.

"Ma'am?" Carole undrooped her eyelids to see the lady looking at her with a sort of wry wistfulness, like a cat wanting to sit on two laps at once.

"Yes, ogress. Belburga is an ogress." The wry wistful smile turned to one full of sharply pointed teeth that matched the lady's ears and virtually everything else about her. "I should know. She's my mother. We have the same mouth."

"Oh, bother!" Bronwyn said. "We've fallen into the hands of the enemy." She dutifully lifted the magic shield but caught it on the edge of the table, which upset the tea mugs and sent them sliding down the starbound-tilting table, and crashing to the floor. Her pronouncement was lost amidst a lot of wiping up.

"Hardly," Mistress Raspberry said when the drips were mopped. "Mother and I aren't close—obviously, since she's been in Frostingdung since she abandoned me to go there when I was only fourteen."

"But that's terrible!" Carole mumbled, her eyes slitting open again in what would have ordinarily been, had she not been so sleepy, wide-eyed sympathy. "Jus' terrible."

"Not really. Actually, it was one of the high points of my life. When she abandoned me, my father finally decided to raise me himself. And he's a much better parent—and had a lot more to teach me. He's a great wizard, you know. A friend of your father's, Your Highness, though you may have never met him. We live in the woods, and Father almost never leaves home—except for such dire emergencies as the war."

"But if your father is a good man, why did he marry an ogress?" Jack asked. "They are very bad, are they not? They eat people, I think my grandmother said."

"Well—perhaps the old, pure-blooded ones once did. But like practically everyone else in Argonia, ogres and ogresses interbred, mostly with giants and wizards and witches of ill repute at first. Eventually some, like my mother, took to social climbing and mingled their blood with that of a better class of people. As is often true of the more deadly species, ogres have always had a certain crude fatal charm. Mother, in her youth, was apparently more charming than most. And she doesn't eat people, you understand. She just sort of nips at them until they feel thoroughly shredded." She smiled a sardonic, pointed smile. "At which time she chews them up and spits them out. The phrase 'to eat one's heart out' might have been coined in recognition of my mother."

64

"No one with any sense would be fooled by somebody like that!" Bronwyn said.

Mistress Raspberry looked at her pityingly. "Perhaps no one with any sense, my dear, but several men with other outstanding qualities certainly were. As I've mentioned, my own father is quite a powerful, prominent wizard. My younger sister, Daisy-Esmeralda, was sired by a he-nymph who did have the sense to turn himself into a tree to escape the mess he'd gotten himself into. Daisy's had a fondness for growing things and animals since she was a tyke, as a consequence. And Mother always encouraged my elder sister, Lily-Pearl, to be very superior about the fact that *her* father was a prince, albeit a minor one. Lily used to drive us all crazy with her white dresses and rose-petal-and-milk baths, which Mother insisted she take every day to ready her for the day when her prince would come. Fortunately for us all that scheme worked. Poor Loefwin was dazed from a near-mortal wound at the time and had recently undergone what amounted to an unusual religious experience. He never stood a chance. Though I rather pitied him, I didn't particularly care for some of his ideas, and when I heard Mother and Lily-Pearl discussing how we would all go live with him in Frostingdung, where Lily would be Queen, I ran and hid. Mother was in such a hurry to leave she didn't look for me very hard, and I haven't seen any of them from that day to this."

"And no great loss that is, I'd say, Mistress," Jehan put in.

"Perhaps not. But still, my friend, one misses one's family. Daisy particularly was quite a decent sort. I've often thought she'd have been much happier if she'd hidden with me and come along to live with Father. He's elvish himself and as dotty about animals as she is. Besides, I'm hoping to persuade Lily-Pearl to use her influence with King Loefwin to get him to join into the war on Argonia's side. I received word from one of my father's—er—envoys—that Ablemarle has been trying to bring pressure to bear on Frostingdung to side against us."

"Do you always hop aboard the nearest pirate ship when you want to attend family reunions or propose political alliances?" Bronwyn asked.

"Not exactly," Mistress Raspberry replied amiably. "Jehan once served me in his former capacity as a genie. After I liberated him and obtained my wishes we remained friends. Why not? Naturally, when he expressed a desire to resume his maritime career, I saw no reason to avoid indulging my wish to see my family again."

Jehan grinned rapaciously and said through a mouth full of

fish, bread, and jam. "That's how I knew to stuff me ears, y'know, against them sirens. From me geniein' days. You'd be surprised what a lad can pick up bobbin' about in the sea in a bit of crockery."

Two days later, the look-out spotted the first of the monsters. "She blows!" he cried, and everyone swarmed onto the deck to see what blew.

"Off the port bow, Cap'n," the mate told Jehan, pointing.

"What is it, sir?" the bosun asked. "I can't make it out."

"The poor creature," Mistress Raspberry said more softly than any of them had heard her speak before. "It isn't blowing. It's bleeding."

And it was. Blood gushed upwards from the fin on top of its head, and also from the stubby tentacles sprouting from every part of its body. It was spotted black and white, like a killer whale, and was twice as large, though unnaturally large, as if it had swollen.

"Well, I never," Jehan breathed. But he did again, and frequently, all that afternoon. No one went below after the first sighting, but stayed on deck to watch as more of the mutilated creatures surfaced briefly and disappeared again beneath the waves. "'Tis a mortal shame, that is," Jehan said, nodding towards one of the surfacing things. "But all the same, I hope all the really big'uns has died of whatever it is afflicts 'em." He squinted expectantly down at the deck beneath his feet, as if waiting for a tentacled back to burst through the boards, and thereafter, everyone else cast an occasional apprehensive glance downward too.

Towards late afternoon their vigil was relieved by another kind of sighting.

"Land ho!" the lookout cried. "Frostingdung dead ahead!"

Jack, Bronwyn and Carole exchanged quick glances. The deformed sea animals had to be some of Lorelei's monsters. Were there worse yet to come? Creatures fearsome enough to make even a siren shudder?

Jehan apparently thought so. "Lower the jolly roger, bosun," he ordered. "If the sea beasts looks that bad, I don't want to think what the people are nowadays."

The people looked perfectly normal to Bronwyn, even slightly better than average at first, so tired was she of seeing the same faces and hearing the same voices day after day on shipboard. And the land looked beautiful. Stable, stationary, stretching up a swelling hill topped by a squat square castle, not a wave in sight from the shore inland as far as the eye could see, except for the river off to the right, and she wouldn't look at that. Once she set foot on the beautiful gritty ground, it didn't shift, wiggle, squirm, bounce, slide, or do anything but lie there.

Jehan's fears about leaving them seemed baseless. The port town where they landed appeared quite ordinary, except that it was cleaner and neater than the few coastal fishing villages Bronwyn had seen. Everything shone with whitewash and the people walked purposefully through the narrow streets. Nets fenced shore from sea along the waterfront. Reassured that no one was going to eat his passengers as soon as the ship disgorged them, Jehan sent them ashore in the long boat, towing Anastasia's chariot upon which the swan had situated herself like a chicken brooding a singular egg.

Once the four people had been handed ashore, the sailors jumped back into their boat and rowed for the ship as if their lives depended on it, and perhaps they did, for moments later a brisk wind bellied the sails and bore the ship away again, which was fine with Bronwyn.

Mistress Raspberry pointed to a series of mortared stones half drifted with sand at the base of one of the cottages. "King Loefwin's work, those ruins, I'll wager," she told them. "Outer Frostingdung was Sulskeria, before the conquests."

"What a learned young woman you are," Anastasia said approvingly, spreading her feathers to dry in the sun. She too was glad to be out of the salt water. It was certain to have damaged her once-excellent human complexion.

Mistress Raspberry smiled at her. "Not too learned to be amazed to understand you without conversing in Pan-elvin. Odd that I never heard that the Dark Pilgrim's swans could speak."

"There are situations where it is best to remain silent," Anastasia replied. "And then too, we were ensorceled to obey our master without question by the wizard who sold us to Brown, and that was after we had already changed to swans— but never mind, for it is a complicated matter and of no current importance."

"No current advantage in speaking of it either," Mistress Raspberry said hastily and in a low voice as a man bearing a large blacksmith's hammer approached them. "We must be careful here. From what I've heard, magic is forbidden in Frostingdung. Comforting sort of rule, isn't it?"

"I should say so!" Bronwyn said, for though she had no magic herself, she couldn't imagine what life would be like

67

without people who had, so that one could, if absolutely necessary, do things only possible by magic, such as talking to animals, getting places quickly and changing inappropriate items into more suitable ones. Of course, magic *had* caused her trouble from time to time—well, all the time, if one counted the curse—but just the same she felt it was needed and liked having it available.

Mistress Raspberry greeted the hammer-bearing villager with a quick nod, which he returned. Smiles apparently weren't customary here, judging from the faces of the other passersby. Even if they had been, with a set of teeth like Mistress Raspberry's, a nod was a more civil expression. "Tell me, my good man," she said, slowly and distinctly, "which road does one take to reach the capital, if you please?"

"I couldn't tell you, I'm sure. Never been there myself. Never have. Never will. Never want to," the man replied. He spoke in a language very similar to Argonian, except that he tended to stress the second syllables of words rather than the first, and his accent had a hard sound to it. He stalked past, edging away from their party a little, as if afraid they'd soil his hammer.

"Helpful chap," Bronwyn said.

Another man strolled by and Mistress Raspberry repeated her question, receiving an even less courteous reply than she had from the first man, despite her offer to pay the newcomer well for his assistance.

The third man she asked didn't even bother to answer. "Well, *really*," she said.

"I've a good mind to give them dancing lessons," Carole said, her eyes narrowing dangerously.

"Not here. We'd be jailed at the very least for breaking their silly rule. If we must resort to that, it'd be safer if I inquired of the animals, though I dislike the idea of entering my sister's adopted country on a diplomatic mission only to break a law of the realm first thing."

"I don't see that it matters," Carole said. "It's a stupid law, and besides, the way these people act, no one will ever know we're here anyway."

"Perhaps someone more used to meeting strangers would have better luck," Jack said winningly. "Give me the money you would have wasted on that smith, great lady, and *I* will learn the way to the capital."

"My sword thirsts to assist you," Bronwyn volunteered. Her sword had absolutely no feelings one way or the other in the matter. She, however, hated to let the one person who had been consistently friendly to her out of her sight. One never knew when Carole would decide to dunk one in something liquid, or when Anastasia would fly into a royal swanly conniption. And Mistress Raspberry was cool and dry, though she *had* maintained an air of respect for Bronwyn's rank and person, which was more than the Princess could say for some people.

"No, my dear Highness," Jack replied. "You must stay here. This task calls for expert skulking in true gypsy fashion and your most impressive height ill suits you for it." He swaggered off, hesitated, and returned for a moment, adding confidentially, "however, since this town is even more strange to me than usual and I have not my tribe to back me up, you might ask your sword for me to stay thirsty, and if you hear me shout—"

She nodded, and he was off with a flutter of faded tatters and a flash of dirty heels.

"For being so vastly ignored, I somehow feel dreadfully conspicuous," Mistress Raspberry remarked, setting her valise on the ground and plopping down beside it right there on the beach. Bronwyn and Carole followed her example. Within the next quarter of an hour, three women passed by them on the way from one little whitewashed house to another equally unprepossessing one on the opposite side of the village.

"Well," Bronwyn said. "We can't blame them for being so chatty, I suppose. This *is* a frightfully busy and exciting city." She even looked longingly after the pirate ship, now faded to a bump on the horizon.

"Yes," Carole said, watching how the few people who came in and out of houses had all sorts of business with one another until they passed near the strangers, whereupon they grew tense and silent, their backbones visibly stiffening. "Isn't it?"

"For a fishing village," Mistress Raspberry remarked, "they don't seem to be doing a great deal of fishing. See there, most of the boats are upended, and look," she said and reached out to pull a silken gray strand of cobweb loose from one of the fish nets, "these nets are dry. They look as if they've been hung about for ornament and haven't seen a fish in years."

"So they're not only snobbish, they're also lazy," Carole said. "So what?"

"Nothing, I suppose, except that I wonder if they eat seaweed, like your aquatic friends, Carole. I don't see any gardens or animals or anything else to eat here, do you?"

"It's a holiday," Bronwyn said, "And they've all given up eating and speaking to outsiders to honor one of their gods."

Another woman bustled by, and with one look at Carole's

brown rags, Mistress Raspberry's pointed ears, and Bronwyn's battle gear, fled. Carole expected her to make a sign against the evil eye and thought her own party might well do the same. This village didn't feel right, somehow. Though she'd thought at first these people looked just like any others, on closer observation she saw that they didn't: they were much less attractive than the average Argonian. Every single person here seemed to be squatty, even the tall ones, and frowning. They possessed back sloping foreheads, protruding noses, retreating chins, and more hair in their eyebrows than on their heads. But as she waited, she saw that several people who did not come near the beach were slightly better-looking. These people were either quite elderly or very young and wore golden bracelets which, even at a distance, she could see bore pretty scrolled designs. "Now look, those are nice. Perhaps they don't fish here any more, but just make those bracelets to sell. I wish I had some money. Those are the prettiest things I've seen in this whole dumb village."

She heard a chuckle behind her and turned. A small, wrinkle-faced creature with youthful freckles across her nose, withered cheeks and a catlike, triangular chin, stretched out a hand to stroke Anastasia's feathers. The swan, usually not one to encourage familiarity, seemed oddly inclined to accept the gesture. The hag held out her other arm to Carole. One of the bracelets clasped the crone's bony wrist above her heavily veined and knotted hands. Though the patches on her dirty dress were neatly sewn, there was certainly nothing from her bare feet to her raggedly cropped hair to indicate sufficient affluence to purchase such a trinket.

"You can have mine, missy," she said, her voice oddly young and melodious. "Free, tee hee, but it'll cost you." She jabbed her finger sharply at Carole as if to point out the jest and tittered again. At least she was easily amused, Carole thought sourly.

"That's nice of you, but you're not making any sense at all, you know," she informed the hag with a little frown of disapproval, just so the poor old thing would know that at least one person around here was in touch with what was what.

"Oh, am I not? Tis a slave bracelet, missy! And I'd give it to you freely but it would cost you your freedom, it would! Hee hee! Do you get it now?" Behind her, a growl and a bark and a small dog, some sort of terrier perhaps, popped from between her knees to give Anastasia a piece of his mind. Mistress Raspberry said something quickly in a strange tongue which made the woman look sharply about her, hushing the dog and the lady at

70

the same time. "Speak the Tongue, do you, madam? Shouldn't do that hereabouts, or you'll get arrested for practicing magic and win one of these bangles for your very own, if you live to wear it."

"Don't be ridiculous. I performed no magic. The Tongue, as you call it, is only a language."

"Ah, you know that and I know that but—" Up what passed for a street in the village Jack came, followed by several burly men. "I'd best go. You too, if you know—" but they were not to know whatever it was she would have told them. One of the men called to her and she hobbled quickly away, her aged legs covering an amazing amount of territory in a short time.

Mistress Raspberry rose to meet the men accompanying Jack, her brush of foxy hair and olive cloak spreading with the salt wind. The men were well dressed in a fabric which looked like fine linen, their clothing simply cut but sturdily made. The hand of one of them was clasped around the back of Jack's neck, as if the man intended to pinch his captive's head off. Bronwyn and Carole stood up too. Bronwyn stepped a little in front of Mistress Raspberry, her shield covering the three of them and her hand on the hilt of her sword.

"No loitering," the middle man said, half-shouting, and flinging his arms seaward, as if to physically push them all back into it.

"You needn't shout," Mistress Raspberry said testily. "I can hear and understand you quite clearly."

He looked surprised and doubtful and glanced back at his friends, who regarded the lady and her companions as if expecting them to start drilling themselves into the ground at any minute. "Well," he said, "if you can understand me, understand this. Just pop yourselves into that little boat of yours and go back same as you came."

"I beg your pardon," Mistress Raspberry said in a tone which said plainly that she did no such thing, "but I doubt my sister, your Queen Lily-Pearl, would share your distaste for my society."

"Empress," the man on the right said, licking his lips.

"Eh?" asked the third man, the one who held Jack.

"Empress. Lily-Pearl's Empress now, not Queen. Emperor Loefwin invested her last year, remember?"

"I'm delighted to hear it," Mistress Raspberry said.

The middle man was not convinced. "Anybody can come in off the sea and claim to be related to the Crown. The Empress *has* a sister."

"Aye, and a mother too," the lip-licker said ruefully.

"I've seen them both myself. The Empress's sister is not one to go joyriding on foreign sailing ships. She's a Princess, married to Prince Loefrig. . . ."

"I'm so pleased for her," Mistress Raspberry said.

"And she doesn't have pointy ears."

"Well, then, since you're such an intimate of my family, and recall my sister's physical characteristics in such detail, perhaps you can also recall," Mistress Raspberry smiled her saw-blade smile, "if she has pointed teeth."

While the bold one in the middle was busy being nonplussed, his lip-licking companion nodded several times. "Yes, well, that proves it, Murdo. She's got the teeth. Yes sir, she's . . ."

The third let go of Jack's neck. "Proves she's good solid ogre stock, at least," he conceded.

The lip-licker nodded. "Pointed teeth are a sure sign. They say Loefwin's grandfather, King Gawdauful the Goblin, was married to a woman whose teeth were so pointed she bit her lip once and bled to death."

"I—er—we, that is, seem to have made a mistake, Madam," Murdo said. "You appear to be, after all, at least a suitable sort of person to set foot on our shores. But we three are guardians here while the young Lord is at court with his men, and we have to be careful, you see. If you are related to the Imperial Family, I trust you'll speak of our diligence to the Empress, and not hold our questioning you against us?"

She inclined her head graciously, but the gold flecks in her eyes sparkled.

"But then," Murdo continued, "I suppose we'll know soon enough if you're who you claim, won't we? Your sister will be expecting you, and no doubt will send soldiers for you."

"No doubt she would if she'd known I was coming, but I'd planned my visit to be a surprise. I had no idea these shores were so—hospitable."

"Nice of you to notice," the lip-licker said, his eyes darting from her to her companions, lingering rather longingly on the fluff-feathered, beady-eyed Anastasia. "Maybe you'd tell us what a nice lady like you is doing in the company of these ragamuffins? Have you brought the contents of your dungeons to share with your sisters for sporting purposes?"

Bronwyn answered, "Keep a civil tongue in your head, foreigner. Can't you see when you're outnumbered? *I* just happen to be Her Ladyship's woman at arms, Wyndy the Warrior, and these two are Her Ladyship's personal midgets and chief advisers.

They are," she said significantly, "five hundred years old, collectively."

"Hmph," Murdo said. "They'd have to be practicing magic to live to that age."

"Not at all," Mistress Raspberry said coolly, to Bronwyn's astonishment. "A difference in diet, climate, the sort of work one does, can often produce radical changes in life span and stature. Just because such long lives aren't customary here . . ."

"Here now," the one who had held Jack said. "Who's saying they aren't? Why, our folk live as long as any midgets—"

Murdo gave him a withering glance. "Pringle, watch what you say. It's not like anything smacking so of magic is a thing to be proud of. What about the bird?" he asked Mistress Raspberry. "I suppose you'll be telling us it's your lord and master."

"Certainly not," Mistress Raspberry replied, and added with a lack of veracity worthy of Bronwyn, "She is my steed, presently lamed. I presume you have adequate mews for her. If not, a stable will have to suffice, though I assume gentlefolk hereabouts ride swans just as they do elsewhere?"

Murdo said nothing but jerked his head back, indicating that the other men should step aside with him, which they did, the three of them talking in low voices and casting glances towards the strangers from time to time. The glances weren't exactly hostile, but they weren't exactly friendly either. The ones they gave Anastasia were more covetous than anything else, Jack thought.

"Why, of all people, did you have to fetch *them*?" Carole asked him.

He shrugged and hung his head. He was disgraced. He was unfit to lead his people, now or ever. It seemed he could not even skulk properly. "Forgive me," he said sadly—but charmingly. It was always wise to be charming when seeking forgiveness. "The pub of this town is also headquarters for these constable people."

They'd seized him the minute he walked in the door, which he had to do since there were no windows on that building, just white wash. They'd demanded to know where he came from and what he was doing there. That was when he'd led them back to Mistress Raspberry and the security of Bronwyn's sword.

73

Chapter VI

The inn was neither a busy nor a merry place, and after the strangers had been served their supper, Jack knew why. They'd been fed a bowl of gray-white goo with black speckles, a basically bland flavor, and a bitter aftertaste. The food was served to them by Murdo's wife, a woman no less well-dressed and no more attractive than her husband. If wolverines had suddenly lost their fur, stood on their hind legs and donned clothing, Jack thought, they would have looked a lot like Murdo's people. The children were just as bad, all seven of them, the eldest looking a year or two younger than Jack, the youngest a baby passed back and forth like an oversized ball between its brothers and sisters. They were as clean as their parents, but snarled at each other constantly and took turns pinching and whining at their mother.

When the meal was over, Mistress Raspberry dug into her dress pocket and extracted a piece of gold. "This ought to cover it," she said, trying to hand it to the woman.

Goody Murdo examined it as if it might be dirty. "Oh, I doubt that, milady," she said. Though she hadn't been told of Mistress Raspberry's claim to kinship with the Frostingdungian Empress, she treated her with the deference due to her silk-embroidered, lace-trimmed woolen gown and to the topaz brooch clasping her cloak.

"What? That's enough gold to pay for two good horses and some left for a loaf besides."

"Maybe where you come from, madam," the lady said, wiping her hands on the underside of her spotless apron. "But here we pay in iron." Her husband shot her an unfathomable look and she added quickly and with a generosity that hardly seemed typical of these people, "But I'm sure once you've been able to trade for our local currency, you'll pay up. You could sell that nice bird you have to raise money, and have enough cash to get by for a while and to buy bracelets for your slaves.

Them coins you have would do nice to coat slave bracelets," she added approvingly.

"Yes, we met an old woman who said she was a slave and showed us her golden bracelet. But why do your slaves wear such expensive jewelry?"

"Mercy, milady, gold isn't that pricey here in Frostingdung. Iron's the thing, has to be, considering. We get both from our mines, and for a long time the slaves wore bare iron. But the Empress, when she was just a Princess, said what this country needed was a bit of sprucing up, and ordered all the iron bracelets dipped in gold. It does have a nicer shine to it, and one can make the bracelets a bit lighter, and save money, by coating them. Which old lady would it have been that you met, milady?"

"Oh, very old, with a d—"

"Glitha. That will be enough," Murdo said. "Our guests will be too tired for your chatter. They'll be staying here tonight. You should show them to bed. The lady sleeps in the big room, the two women servants in the next, the manservant in the smallest."

Goody Murdo looked dismayed and Mistress Raspberry said, "We shouldn't like to put you out. We're quite accustomed to rough living and could share space on your floor. If you and your family usually sleep here . . ."

"Mercy, milady," the woman replied, stopping halfway to the door. "We wouldn't think of sleeping here. We have our own cottage, with proper iron bindings and—" Another look from her husband silenced her.

"Your Ladyship needn't worry about us," Murdo said. "We mind our own business and it would go well for you to do the same."

Lady Carole and Princess Bronwyn were already yawning, and retired gratefully into the room assigned them. Lacking Jack's natural instinct for intrigue, they seemed not to notice the ominous undercurrents in Murdo's civil, if not friendly, behavior. The man reminded Jack of a local lord who had invited the gypsies to perform in a village of his specifically to take blame for the failure of the crops that year. Fortunately, some of the tribe had arrived late and spotted townsmen building a gallows, and his people had escaped in time. Now he noticed immediately the wooden bar which could be shoved across his door from the outside. There was no lock on the inside, so it was obviously meant to keep the occupant in, not to keep intruders out. But a good gypsy prided himself on being catlike—it was impossible to keep him out where he wished to go in and it was equally impossible to keep him in where he wished to go out. If Jack had not been so busy figuring how he could escape he would have been insulted. After all, how did these people know he was not what he seemed to be? He might very well not be planning a late visit to the castle in order to relieve the premises of some of the gold this country found so useless. But such a barrier as the bar would give him no trouble. He still had his dagger.

The room was simply but comfortably furnished with a bed covered by a worn blue blanket. Under the bed was a woven reed rug dyed brown and also an earthenware chamberpot. There was in addition a washstand with a basin and pitcher.

He lay down and covered himself with the blanket, and pretended to sleep. A short time later, the bar thunked down into the fastenings on his door, and he crept up to it, listening.

A debate was in progress.

"But what if she'th who she says?" a familiar squeaky voice he recognized as belonging to one of his first Frostingdungian acquaintances said. "We'll all be executed!"

"She can't be. Does she look like an Empress's sister to you?"

"Well, no, except for the teeth."

"Any ogress has them. She's an adventuress, I tell you, and this time she's ventured too far. Anyway, it's not the likes of us that's hurting her. We're just feeding her and putting her up with the best we have available, as is our duty. No one could do better than that. If she gets damaged, it's no more than's happened to us and ours many a time, is it?"

"Oooh, but Oswy!" Goody Murdo's voice interjected. "The Empress's sister! Shouldn't we . . .?"

"How can you forget what happened to your own son and Cressida Pringle? It's all very well to make things look nice for the Empress, but looking nice is not government. It's about time the nobles realized what the rest of us are up against out here. Imagine that young drunkard taking all the soldiers with him when he went to the capital, leaving us with no protection. And us the chief port of Frostingdung! Besides, if she does turn out to be the Empress's sister, who knows she's here except her and us and that tin-toting giantess and those two dark brats of hers?" His laugh was unjovial.

"You don't think they're really five hundred year old midgets?"

"If they are, they have come to the wrong place if they want to live to be five hundred and one. Hurry now, curfew's going to sound any minute and we've knives to sharpen yet tonight so we can see to the bird first thing in the morning."

With grunts and scrapings of benches, squalling from the children and a smack here and there, the people left the hall, and the silence crept back in. It was punctured a moment later by an eerie blast from a deep-voice horn. Jack took that to be curfew.

With an expertness that thrilled him, he stuck his dagger blade into the space between door and frame, pushed up until the blade met the hard wooden bar, and up further until the bar was parallel with the door. He pushed again and let himself out. The inn was dark, but the faint smell of burning lamp oil still hung in the room. He presumed Mistress Raspberry and Bronwyn and Carole were locked in their rooms as he was supposed to be, and with a bow to chivalry briefly considered unbolting them. He held his breath until the ungypsyish urge passed. Bronwyn was better armed than he, Carole possessed magic and he had little doubt that Mistress Raspberry too was the possessor of certain arcane, and in this society, illegal assets. All of those ladies were far better equipped to take care of themselves, should they need to, than he.

Whatever danger Murdo hinted at didn't seem to be direct or immediate, and probably the man only considered Jack's companions as vulnerable to it because he thought of them as women and children. Hah!

The other reason Jack hesitated to touch the doors of his companions was for fear of waking them. The thought crossed his mind that they might not approve of his foraging plans for the evening. He would be back in a few hours, much enriched, and at that time he would waken them and tell them of the conversation he had overheard and together they would take pains to see to it that they and the Princess Anastasia remained whole and mobile enough to repair to the capital.

His conscience thus cleared, he ventured through the inn, out the front door—unbolted, which seemed more than a little strange—and into the road between the inn and its stable.

The stable was lit. Since Anastasia was probably not staying up reading, and would have been unable to light a candle even had their hosts been kind enough to provide her with one, he had to assume someone else was in the stable. A groom? Perhaps. At any rate, it would be a good idea to practice one's somewhat rusty skulking skills again to determine who the person was and assure oneself of the Princess Anastasia's safety before one set off on one's own adventure. It occurred to him that if he could free her from the stable, she could stand guard outside the doors of Mistress Raspberry and Carole and Princess Bronwyn, unlocking the chambers if necessary, further freeing him mentally and physically to pursue his own interests.

A moon of useful fullness lit the night. By it, Jack saw that for people who valued iron so highly, the Frostingdungians used it liberally. The stable was banded in three places with strips of iron, one near the roof, one near the ground and one running all the way around the middle and across the door. As he drew close enough to notice this detail, he also heard an odd cackling and singing, and once a sharp bark.

"Do you mind terribly?" the voice of the Princess Anastasia asked. "I am trying to obtain my so-necessary beauty rest."

He peeked through a gap between the double doors of the stable. The light he had seen from the door of the inn was a candle which lit the startled face of the little old woman he had seen hobbling away from his friends when he and the constabulary arrived. She peered curiously upward for a moment, shuddered slightly, and wagged her head from side to side, asking the splatter-coated tan and brown dog at her feet, "Can a body grow the opposite of deaf, Dragon? Or am I as addled as they say and hearing things in my dotage? Never mind. Shall we wing us another song? Or will you dance instead? Let's have a dance, shall we? Up now, laddie. Up, I say."

"And *I* say, Cease. That is a royal decree!" Anastasia hissed from on high. Though Jack couldn't see her, he assumed she'd flown into the loft.

"Shhh, Dragon. Be still." The old lady held up her hand and glanced around, furtively. The dog whined and she reached down absently and patted it, her eyes still searching the room. Finally, hunching her shoulders together as if expecting to take a knife between them, she hitched up her skirts and began climbing a rickety ladder.

Jack, who had the greatest respect for old ladies, since his grandmother could still out-lie and out-fight every man in the tribe, tugged open the door and let himself inside. He meant to tell the woman not to trouble herself, that he would talk to Anastasia. But suddenly the dog flew at him, yapping and snapping furiously.

He stared silently at the animal, mesmerizing it with his hypnotic gypsy eyes, commanding it silently to be silent. It naturally obeyed, and he spoke soothingly to it in his native tongue. The dog sat down and cocked its head to one side, as if trying to think what exactly Jack could be saying and regretting it had never completely mastered the gypsy language. Then it thumped its tail and whined. He advanced upon it, still staring at it, holding out his hand and talking to it. It rose, wagging, to lick his palm.

The woman turned around on the ladder. "Eh?" she asked, and then, seeing Jack, called to the dog. "Are you daft, Dragon? You ain't supposed to lick 'im. You're supposed to bite 'im. Kill!" The dog continued to lick Jack's palm. The crone half-fell down the ladder, and hobbled toward Jack, muttering, "If you want a thing done right . . ."

"Do not blame your dog, Grandmother," Jack said pleasantly. "I am irresistible to all animals."

"Yes," Anastasia called down. "If they attempt to resist him, he has ways of enforcing his charm. I should know."

The old lady stopped in her tracks and looked from Jack to the loft, then leaned forward and jerked her thumb upward, cocking her head inquisitively while eying Jack. He smiled and shrugged.

"That is only the Princess Anastasia having her little joke with you, old one."

"The Princess who?" the old lady asked.

"The swan. She is the Princess Anastasia. You must have seen her today on the beach, before you ran away."

Anastasia swept down upon them, glared haughtily at the old woman and seemed to find upon landing that her ruffled feathers took considerable preening to smooth.

"Ah, the swan!" the old slave said. "She *would* be a princess, wouldn't she?" She waggled a finger under Anastasia's beak. "You see here, my beauty, if you're a fine lady you'd best change yourself back to your real self if you wish to live. Folk around here are meat-starved and—"

Suddenly a long wavering cry pierced the night. The crone's chin snapped up to hug her upper lip and her head trembled a little, as if she were making a conscious effort not to look around her.

"What's that?" Jack asked.

She waited until the cry died away before answering, then said with a sly smile, "That? Why, that be one of the reasons folk here are meat-hungry. But mind me, beauty, you'd do well to change to your real self again."

"My dear woman, this has *been* my real self for the last two decades, and I shall tolerate no impertinence to my person in this guise or any other."

"The old one only gives you warning, Your Highness," Jack told her. "Those men who have housed us are indeed hungry ones."

79

"You're the witch's boy, then, are you?" the crone asked, watching him keenly. "Did Murdo send you here to sleep?"

"No. We are all roomed at the inn but—"

"Are you?" She giggled again, but now he heard that it was not from amusement that she laughed, but nervousness. "Oh, that Murdo thinks he's a sly dog, but you be slier, eh, lad? Saw your doom," she said, exaggerating the word by booming the o's comically but he still didn't feel she was amused. "And escaped it, did you?"

"I did unlock the door and decide to—er, have a look about," Jack admitted. "But as to doom—" he shrugged. "As soon as I have completed my errands tonight, I shall accompany my friends away from here. But I think first the Princess Anastasia should join them."

"Oh, I shouldn't think so!" the old woman replied, still giggling but also in earnest. She whispered from between cupped hands, but loudly enough to be heard in the inn. "Curfew's blown, you know."

"My dear grandmother, I am a gypsy and not of your people. Your curfew does not concern me."

"That's talkin' daft, boy." She waggled a finger at him, but stopped whispering to say in a suddenly sober tone, "Curfew concerns everyone."

"Why are you here then?" He pointed to her bracelet. "Even if you are a slave, they surely do not require that you sleep in the stable."

"They'd do worse than that if my master'd stand for it," she said. "An ill-bred, ill-tempered, and ugly lot they are. But no, I come to the stable to be with Dragon. He's the last dog in Suleskeria, and master says he's mine to keep. But the housekeeper won't let me keep him at the castle. Also—I'm afraid if I'm not here to leave with him in the morning, Murdo and the other Dungies'll eat him, or feed him to *them* just to spite the master and me."

"Feed him to whom?" Anastasia asked.

The old lady pointed her chin towards the door. "Them. What's outside now. What would get you if you was where Murdo thinks you are, boy, and what will get your fine lady friends, I fear."

Jack had left the door open a crack when he entered. As the woman pointed to the door, she spotted the opening and sprang forward, crying, "Fool! You've killed us all."

Though Jack didn't know why she was so upset, he sprinted ahead of her to shut it and thereby apologize for his unwitting laxness. As he touched the wood, the moonlight caught briefly something curdled and red, and finger-long teeth shot from the redness and snapped at his face. He slammed the door, and heard a splintering and the cry again, and collapsed against the inside of the door before suddenly springing up again to search for a bolt.

"Ain't one," the crone said. "But with the door closed, the iron'll keep 'em out."

"I begin to understand the currency system here," he said, mopping his abruptly moist brow. "Where did that come from?"

"If you could see it, from the sea," she said. "The nets stop most of them. They're terrible afraid of the nets. But if you couldn't see it, 'twas a hidebehind. They can't be seen or heard, mostly. You just feel 'em. Till they get you, that is. Come," she said, and crooked a gnarled finger at him, leading him through an empty horse stall. She searched the wall with her fingertips for a moment, then told him, "When I says look, look quick. They'll find the hole in a thrice if we leave it open that long."

With her thumb and forefinger she grasped a protrusion and pulled forth a knot from its hole. "Look!" she said, and shoved him at the hole. Jack looked.

The night was filled with horrors. Not all were as bad as the thing at the door, or the one the lookout had spotted from shipboard, but misshapen creatures of all description waddled forth on flippers and fins, bloody tentacles and legs. Most hung outside the nets which formed a sort of sea wall. But aside from the sea creatures, there were others.

Several of them sailed in the air.

"What are the flying things?" he asked.

"Fliers," she said. "They sting."

They were as large as bats and the moon glinted off spear-like projections from their noses.

"I hope they kill you at once," Jack said, shivering.

"They don't kill you at all," she said. "You kill yourself. The sting is powerful itchy. I've seen grown men flay the hides from themselves with their nails before their friends could tie 'em up. Even tied up, they'll die from trying to scratch if you don't soak 'em in oil." She giggled again.

The moon glinted clearly on the whitewashed walls of the inn across the way. The thatch on the roof crawled. It wavered and faded and folded back into place, rippling the moonlight. Unconsciously, he stepped back and made horns of his fingers. The woman shoved him back and put her own eye to the knot.

81

"Ah, the hidebehinds are at work. I hope you weren't over fond of the lassies."

"I—what?" Something about that blinking roof was worse than all of the sea-born horrors he could see plainly.

"You'll not be seeing them again if the hidebehinds get them. And they will, in that building. No iron, you know."

"Bron—Bronwyn," Carole sat straight up, shaking. Overhead, something shivered and paced across the ceiling. "Bron*wyn!* Wake up."

"Wha—" the Princess opened one eye and reached for her shield. The girls shared a narrow bed and Carole had to lie half on top of her cousin to get any room at all. This had not especially bothered Bronwyn. Carole wasn't very big and didn't move around much, but this jouncing up and down and yelling in the middle of the night had to stop. "What a wunnerful time to wake up," she mumbled, hoisting the shield across both of them.

"Look up there."

"Where?"

"There!"

"What is it? I can see everything very clearly." It was pitch dark.

"I don't know. You can't really *see* anything—but you can sort of follow the tracks with your finger." She demonstrated, arching her finger to trace an invisible line above them.

"But there's nothing there," Bronwyn yawned. "Certainly nothing that can scare—YiiiIIIKES!!" Something had snuck around, and without seeing anything they both knew it had come across the ceiling and down the wall and under the bed and up the side to sneak in under Bronwyn's shield and *grab* them. Bronwyn was on her feet in no time, whirling with the effort to keep her shield in front of her. Silent laughter jeered at her, and unseen fingers tugged at her shift and tweaked her hair and pinched her. Carole, without realizing she had done so, had rolled out of bed to cringe at her cousin's feet. Had Bronwyn been wearing her armor, it would have rattled like a kettle full of stones, her knees and elbows shook so. Solid foes she was prepared to fight, and even those with magical powers—but ones who ducked out of sight just when you thought you were about to face them, who attacked from the rear, who taunted the corners of your eyes and writhed quickly across your vision, solid enough to pinch but too fleeting to see, these were enough to daunt the bravest warrior.

"C—Carole, do—do y-y-y-y-you k-know any gggggggghost songs?" Bronwyn asked, and yelped as a hank of her hair was pulled hard.

"Shh," Carole said. She'd grown quiet once she realized what was going on, and had become too frightened to speak, but while she was being quiet her excellent mer ears picked up the whispers swirling around, accompanying the unseen bodies.

Bronwyn hushed, all but the sound of her hair bristling, her teeth chattering, and the goosebumps swelling on her skin like the boils she'd described to the mermaids. She heard only those sounds, and the hammering of her heart. Then she too heard a sort of windy sighing.

Distinctly unpleasant wheezing laughter filled the room and something smacked each of them on their backs so hard they fell forward. Much to her shame, Bronwyn felt tears spring to her eyes. The humiliation of it made her angry.

"Very well, gentle spook!" she cried, and drew her sword from under the mattress, where she'd kept it handy during the night, "I've felt your tender caresses. Here are mine!" And whacked, and kept on whacking. The sword whistled above Carole's head, and that was how Carole found her own whistle again.

" 'Never fear, Princess,' " Anastasia mocked, " 'I am a big strong gypsy man. I will protect you.' What nonsense!" She flew at Jack, fanning her wing derisively in his face. "What conceit! While you sneak around trying to steal things, you desert your companions. For SHAME, young man! For shame."

"But Your Swanliness, I thought you needed protection more than they! That is why I came here first."

"You thought! Your thought was to get what goods you could and leave. Do not forget, my boy, I have had dealings with your sort before."

"Have you now, my beauty?" The old woman asked, cackling slightly. "And what are they like, all the same? Isn't that a pretty thought?" Her bright eyes leapt from one to the other. "That's what the Dungies said about my folk—that we were all alike. Oh, but we're not. We're not."

The hag seemed to slip from sanity to senility and back again but her eyes gloated like those of Jack's aunts when they conned ignorant peasants out of their silver by pretending to be even more ignorant peasants.

Anastasia looked somewhat abashed and finished lamely, "Nevertheless, you should not have left those poor ladies alone."

"One of those poor ladies," he pointed out, "is armed to the teeth and the other two, as you very well know, are witches which is more than can be said of you or me."

"*Are* they?" the little woman asked. "Witches, you say? Real witches?" She rubbed her hands together happily and the dog butted them with his nose for attention.

"Carole is a witch of a certainty. Mistress Raspberry is a witch I only suppose, but she is an ogress in fact." He grinned and pointed to his own teeth.

"Tsk tsk. Such lovely illegal young ladies to get put in the inn. If my lord were here, 'twould never have happened so, but he ain't and I fear their powers won't help much with hidebehinds."

"Are they in more danger in the inn than we are here?" Anastasia asked.

"Oh, aye. No iron on the inn. Old building, only original one left from before the wars. No, they won't last long in there."

"But this is simply dreadful!" Anastasia exclaimed, glaring at the old woman as if it were all her fault, glaring so fiercely, in fact, that the dog growled at her. "Do you mean to tell me that those young people are trapped in that building with all of those abominable creatures and we can do nothing to assist them?"

"Not by sitting weeping you can't, no indeed," the woman said.

"And by sitting here and not weeping?" Jack asked angrily, furious at the hag for mocking him. "Do you suggest, old one, that I would not do all in my power to aid the Princess?"

"Would you now?"

"Of a certainty."

"Very well, then, come along," she said, leading them to the stable door. "But I'd pick up that shovel there if I was you. There's iron at the tip. And you might drape yon bridle across the swan. There's iron in the rings and the bit. Won't protect you full, but 'tis better than naught."

The inn was barely ten cart-lengths from the stable, but the journey to it was one of the longest runs Jack had ever taken in his life, and his had not been without a few frantic sprints. Far worse than angry farmers, indignant villagers, bloodthirsty mobs or infuriated wizards were the mewling things milling through the darkened streets or buzzing perilously close above his head. He ran with his blood beating through his limbs, as if he were escaping and yet realizing that at the end of his run he would still be far from safe inside the invaded inn. It looked naked and vulnerable, now that he knew the significance of its lack of iron banding. Beyond the building, seaward, a thousand glowing orbs

84

glared at him from behind the sea net and the monsters waved their tentacles in the moonlight and their sad gills heaved and their misshapen bodies surged against the sea net.

Anastasia reached the inn first, but had to fend off monsters with her wings while she waited for the others to pull the door open for her. The old woman brought up the rear, mumbling and cursing under her breath and swatting at monsters with her braceleted arm.

Inside, the inn was convulsed with the noise of pounding blows and the very walls seemed to keen. Too late! Jack thought, running for the door to Bronwyn's room, though he did pause, thinking that if he was indeed too late, surely his friends would not wish him to open the door and loose the creatures of their destruction upon himself.

But even as he paused the door boomed outward, thudding, splintering, and finally bursting asunder. He fell backwards before—Bronwyn.

"Bloody thing was wide open," she called back inside, and flipped up the bar as if it were a mere latch hook. She tore it loose as an afterthought, and handed it to Carole, who stepped through the door behind her. Inside, the room looked empty, but seemed to Jack to sway rhythmically.

"But my Princess, you are safe!" he cried, launching himself at her, aiming poorly, and ending up clutching her knees.

"Rather!" she said. "I see they got you, did they?"

"I—er—escaped them with fast footwork and the use of my agile wit," he said modestly.

Carole, still humming with a small mirthless smile on her face, took in Jack, the swan, the old woman and her dog with one glance and stepped behind Bronwyn to the adjoining room. Mistress Raspberry had had no protection, and Carole could only hope that her own magic songs had somehow attracted or distracted the lady's would-be assailants. She lifted the bar and tugged, and Bronwyn and Jack stopped talking to peer over her shoulder.

Mistress Raspberry knelt in the middle of her bed, which she had pushed back from the rolled-up rug. Under the rug, a trap door was laid back against the floor to reveal a yawning square of blackness.

Unlike the room Carole and Bronwyn had shared, Mistress Raspberry's chamber did not pulse with dancing waves. Instead, the darkness in the hole quivered slightly, and the lady strained forward, her pointed ear tips twitching, her tongue licking across her pointed teeth.

Bronwyn shook her head. "Poor thing, cowering in fear of her life."

Mistress Raspberry looked up at them, the slight glaze leaving her eyes as she smiled a sliver of a smile and flopped the trap door back down over the hole.

"Insubstantial," she said, smacking her lips, "I appreciated the song, my dear. It allowed me to isolate one. Next time I shall be able to obtain its essence."

The dog yapped and bounced like a mop gone mad and Jack absently picked it up and stroked it quiet again. The old lady looked past him to the wavering energy in the room Bronwyn and Carole had vacated. "Out! Out! Back to the stable or they'll have us yet."

"But will they want us?" Jack said, more than a little proud of how his friends had acquitted themselves.

Mistress Raspberry grabbed her cloak and valise and pushed past him toward the door. "When in a strange place, my dear boy," she said, "never argue with native customs."

They curled up in the cleanest corner of the stable and waited for dawn.

Jack grumbled, "We could probably have slept in the beds. We beat the creatures, after all, and even a wolf pack will retreat when beaten."

The old woman tittered. "Ah, but that's no wolf pack, that's not. The night things return and return and wear you down with returning till they swallow you up—or worse. Ask Murdo, if you don't believe old Teeny."

"What I'd like to ask old Teeny is what's so funny," Carole said. "Those horrible things nearly got us and you act like they're court jesters."

Jack, more used to the old woman's rather black sense of humor by now, didn't take it so personally. "What I would like to know is what those monsters are, and where they came from."

"That's just the sort of animals they have around here, Jack," Bronwyn said. "Instead of bunnies or house cats or something. Didn't you notice how well-matched the dear things were in temperament to the people? Am I right, Dame Teeny, or am I right?"

"Right, dearie, and wrong as well. For it's true enough that there ain't many of the other kind of beast left, except for the few horses that were protected and a dog or two who escaped." She held the dog against her cheek for a moment and stroked his

86

fur with her knotted fingers, and when she looked up again, her eyes blinked in the feeble candlelight. "They—them things out there—ate up most of the natural animals, along with a great many people—ours, for we weren't banded then, and the Dungies." Her titter made a momentary feeble comeback. "There were no monsters at all before the invasions, save the natural beasts—bears, dragons, deer, serpents, seals, otters, whales, unicorns and the like. Gone now, all gone. Stung to death by the fliers gone mad when their masters died on the Day of Disenchantment, changed to them wretched things that has to crawl out of the sea to feed since when Loefwin threw all potions into the river."

"Did the Loefwin make the monsters then?" Carole asked impatiently. "Why would he do that if the monsters killed all the animals and some of his own people?"

"Charming family your sister married into, eh?" Bronwyn remarked out of the side of her mouth to Mistress Raspberry.

"Anyway," Carole continued, "how could Loefwin make monsters? That would take magic and he doesn't allow that."

The old lady snorted. "He don't allow magic on account of he can't do it himself. But my folk could, once. Greatest magicians in all the seven lands was Suleskerians. Selkie blood among us, from the seal-people, you know, and elvin on the other side. Not like the Dungies—they be half man, half goblin, with a touch of ogre." To Mistress Raspberry she said, "No offense, dearie, but that's why it is we're so much comelier." She fluffed her snarled tufts of gray hair.

"Then it was your own people who made the monsters?" Carole asked. "I wouldn't be so proud of that, if I were you. Comely is as comely does."

Teeny glared at her. "It was the war done it. I told you."

"Oh, yes," Bronwyn said. "The war. She did say so, Carole, and I think that explains it."

Carole shushed her impatiently, but Bronwyn continued placatingly to the old woman. "My cousin is a very kind and peaceful person, Dame Teeny. She doesn't understand about war like us veterans."

"I just don't understand why anyone would make such horrid things that would turn back on themselves, for war or any other purpose," Carole said slowly and distinctly, from between gritted teeth.

"They wasn't so bad to begin with," Teeny replied. "The fliers started out as weapons—they was made up in Bintnar, what's West Frostingdung now. While the wizards that made

87

them was alive, they obeyed and hurt naught but what they were aimed at. They went wild, you might say, when all their masters was killed on the Day of Disenchantment. And I suppose you could actually say Loefwin was responsible for making them things as crawls out of the sea. When the selkies sought to aid my folk during the invasion, Loefwin seeded the waves with that which he used to destroy the Six Kings and the Great Mages on the Day. And when his men raided the studies and the laboratories of our great ones, he had them throw the potions and sacred books into the rivers and the sea. And all of the sea beasts and the selkies that didn't escape got changed into them things that come ashore of a night to feed on us. What they used to eat died, I suppose, from the magic in the water. That's why we don't eat fish here no more.''

"And those—those ghosts,'' Bronwyn's spine crawled again at the memory. "They are the ghosts of your dead? Or are they perhaps enemy dead, made by your magic to haunt the premises in perpetuity?''

Teeny tittered again. "Not ghosts exactly, dearie. You might say more of a last will and testament. When the Dungies invaded us, we were already beat before we got started, you understand. Any mage strong enough to withstand them they'd killed by treachery on the Day of Disenchantment. The wizardry we had left was feeble indeed, but we thought if we hid some of the few half-decent magicians we had left in caves and cellars they could fight the Dungies from underground. Didn't work. Dungies found 'em and guarded the holes with iron till they died of starvation. But when the moans stopped and the bones was took away, the Dungies stopped guarding. That's when the hidebehinds come out.'' She made crawling motions with her fingers along the fur of the dog's back. "And GOT everybody. Leastways everybody not wearing iron already, which wasn't so many as you'd think. Dungies are mad for iron, and come well supplied with it to fight us.'' She looked ruefully down at the band glowing in the feeble light against the wrinkled skin of her arm.

"But if it was your people who made the hidebehinds, why do they hurt everyone? Why don't they just take vengeance on your enemies?'' Carole asked.

Teeny shrugged. "Once a spear's been thrown, does it turn away if a friend gets in front of it instead of a foe? Their makers are dead and they're invisible and outlawed to boot. What do they know of loyalty?'' She chuckled again. "But the way things stand for my folk, these bracelets they use to control us also protect us, not that life's a great joy any more. The Dungies have more to lose."

"Stupid of Loefwin not to polish off his enemies cleanly or make peace with them," Mistress Raspberry said, rising to her feet and stretching. "Seems to me that the way he did it, your people are a great deal more trouble to him dead than they were alive."

"Aye." The old lady grinned, and chuckled again. "He must feel it so, too. He's tried to pretend it never happened, since he's come back from Argonia with Herself. He's cleaned up the streets, cleaned up the houses, cleaned up the history. But he has not cleaned up the hidebehinds yet, nor the other horrors, for all of trying to pretend he's all of a sudden not a goblin. And he still refuses to permit the most innocent magic, or any talk of it. But he don't know everything."

"You mean you still practice?" Carole asked.

"Oh, not I. Not I. Not with this bauble on me. But Dragon and me, we talk. And we notice things the Emperor doesn't see. There's magic at work in Frostingdung makes our old kind look tame."

"We'll keep that in mind," Mistress Raspberry said. "But what we need now is a mundane means of leaving this dreary place."

"You must leave with us, Dame Teeny," Bronwyn said. "I will pull the bond from your arm and slay any who would seek to enslave you again."

"Are you daft?" Teeny said, beating Bronwyn's companions to it. "I told you, this bauble of mine protects me." Bronwyn looked properly rebuffed and the old woman put a soothing hand on her arm. "Not that you don't mean well, lass, but I'm too old to go traveling, and there's Dragon to think of. My master's not so bad, as masters go. He's young, is Gilles. I've known him from babyhood, when he was born to my lady after she give up her honor to keep company with the Dungie general who took our castle." She chuckled. "Babe looked like a Dungie when he was born, and my lady was alive with her magic unrestrained by iron. Nowadays, though, them as remember, and some of the Dungies do, might mistake him for our late lord. Not a popular lord, my Gilles. But the best master in Suleskeria and," she grinned a gap-toothed grin, "quite mad. The others can't stand him. So I'll bide here, thank you, I'll just bide here."

"Well, I rather think we shouldn't," Mistress Raspberry said. By now the candle flame was little more than a glimmer in a puddle of wax, but light strong enough to see each other in a gray sort of way was filtering into the stable. "Can you direct us to the capital?"

"Anyone could," Teeny said, sounding surprised. "Go straight upriver for two days and veer right where the channel splits. You can't miss it."

CHAPTER VII

"When you stop for the night," Teeny told them, "you'll come upon two dwellings. The first is large and comfortable-looking. Pass it by. The second is small and humble, of iron-banded logs. Stay there."

"Are the people who run the first one evil and likely to slay us?" Carole asked.

"No, but they overcharge and the food is bad. The second is a wayside for—I suppose you could still call them fishermen. It's kept provisioned and people are known to leave it alive in the morning."

Before they dealt with the problem of where to stay, they had to get there, and for a time it looked as if that would prove impossible. They had little trouble vacating the stable before the villagers arose after the growing light dispersed the monsters. The chariot was where they'd left it, intact and apparently unmolested, and they towed it to the river. They pushed it half into the water, but when they were ready to hitch Anastasia to it, the swan flatly refused.

"There are far too many of you and besides, *I* saw what crawled out of the sea last night. Do you think I would sink so low as to swim among them? I prefer to fly."

"What if we row? Would that help?" Carole asked.

"It might help *you*, my dear, but it couldn't possibly make the slightest difference to me. I shall be in the sky."

"Anyone would think you'd been turned into a chicken instead of a swan," Carole said. "But if you'll swim, I'll swim. That way there won't be so many in the boat and you can't say I'm not taking the same chances you are."

"I am not taking any chances."

The conch shell blew the all-clear, and behind them, the town began to wake.

Jack mentioned in a casual way the conversation he had overheard in the inn, when Murdo proposed that the men go after a certain bird at dawn with sharpened knives. Jack also mentioned how he had risked his own life to warn the bird in question. Was this how she repaid him, by risking his life again, and the lives of their friends? If this was how royalty acted, he was glad he was only a poor gypsy.

Several villagers left their houses and began walking toward them.

"On second thought, Carole, your suggestion has considerable practical merit," the swan said hastily, adding to Bronwyn, "well, what are you waiting for? Do you think I can pull that silly harness on with my pinfeathers?"

Bronwyn sat on one side of the water-worthy chariot, Jack and Mistress Raspberry balancing her weight on the other side.

"Well done," Mistress Raspberry whispered out the side of her mouth to Jack. "You can be quite persuasive."

He shrugged. "It is only that I have this way with animals."

"Do you speak with them often?" she asked, surprised to find that she had something in common with a grubby male of Jack's tender years.

"Only the usual things—jump, whoa, giddyup, down, roll over, sit. Though the Princess Anastasia is naturally a special case."

"How dreary! Why have you never bothered to learn to speak with them properly?"

"It is beneath a man to speak to beasts who cannot speak a proper human tongue," he said, folding his arms across his chest and looking extremely superior. "How is a man to retain control if he lowers himself to saying bow-wow or bubble-bubble like those ridiculous fish women talking to their snake?"

"Very well then, if you have that sort of an attitude, I certainly won't press you to learn Pan-elvin. I had thought it might amuse you. My father and I converse regularly with all sorts of animals—his closest companion, in fact, other than myself, is a raven named Jack and I must tell you that that other Jack once held the same reservations about communicating with humans as you do about speaking with non-humans. I can't say that I blame him. Personally, I often find the society of animals a tremendous improvement over that of certain so-called people."

"*You* converse with animals? Like the fish women?"

91

"Certainly. But I can converse with any sort of animal, not just sea creatures. I've even been known to change into one or more species occasionally, though I can't do it as easily as my father. I was trying to determine the best way of changing into one of those hidebehind things when you interrupted me at the inn."

"Oh. I thought you were trying to eat them."

"Both father and I are almost strictly vegetarian by dietary preference," she said primly.

Jack was fascinated, but his pride warred with his curiosity. He glanced at Bronwyn. She lay with her head over the side of the boat, her mouth open, sleeping. Carole and the swan stroked ahead of them. Who was to know? "Surely a fine lady such as yourself would let not the natural pride of a poor and ignorant but promising boy keep you from teaching him a skill he should know to be a better man? It is your duty as an adult to force me to learn such things. Very well, I submit myself."

The day rolled on. Bronwyn woke only long enough to complain of hunger. Carole swam, also complaining of hunger. Even Anastasia complained of hunger, since, as she said, she wasn't likely to dive for plants in this sort of place, even if she were not occupied with the business of transporting passengers. Mistress Raspberry and Jack joined the complaints in a companionable way, but Jack was so interested in his lessons he could almost forget he was hungry.

At least Carole and Anastasia were not troubled by water monsters, a fact with which they comforted each other. Whatever malformed fish or other undesirables lurked in the river stayed decently covered by the water and made no attempt to accost them.

They passed the first place Teeny had mentioned in mid-afternoon.

"She didn't say we couldn't stop there for lunch," Carole said longingly. "She only said not to stay the night."

"She did say the prices were high, however, and I have only gold, which I do not intend to squander despite the local preference for iron," Mistress Raspberry replied. "The cottage she recommended can't be far."

It wasn't.

No palace had ever looked finer than the iron-banded hovel. Inside were two beds of straw with real blankets, and food—cakes, stale but hearty, dried fruit, nuts, and some of the gray-white porridge congealed in a pot over the hearth. They didn't touch the pot or the porridge. There was not, they noted grate-fully, any sign of a trap door.

Bronwyn, who was tired of sleeping, said she would stand watch, though there was nowhere to watch from, since the door would have to be closed to keep out hidebehinds and other creatures and the hut had no windows.

Anastasia tucked her head under her wing and fell asleep immediately and Carole, exhausted after a night of magic and a day of swimming, was also soon asleep. Mistress Raspberry fiddled with a few items in her valise, and made some notes in a book, before curling up with her cloak for a pillow and settling down beside Carole. Jack was still repeating his lessons in the language that would make him the greatest trainer of trick horses and the most magnificent dancing partner of bears ever known to his tribe when he too drifted off.

The woods seemed quiet, compared to the village, and even Bronwyn was lulled to sleep by the peacefulness.

At dawn, after cramming as much as they could carry into their pockets, the five of them pulled the boat back out into the river. Jack stepped in something and slipped, sliding halfway into the river.

The something was red and of the consistency of mashed potatoes, except for the odd bone here and there. Jack jumped back, dropping his end of the chariot.

"Wha—what's that?" Carole asked, gagging.

"An animal of some sort," Mistress Raspberry said, poking it with the pointed tip of a fingernail and rolling it over. "Indistin-guishable, unfortunately."

"Too bad," Bronwyn said, making a sweeping gesture up and down the banks of the river, which were littered with similar gruesome remains, as was the river water. "There don't seem to be any more."

But the smashed shapes were too formless for the travelers to tell what they might have once been, except that they had been alive and animal in nature—some had bits of fur, some a recog-nizable eye or limb. Mistress Raspberry's companions disap-pointed her by vetoing her desire to inspect the grisly debris more closely.

"They are dead, my dear," Anastasia said. "What they were when living I would rather not know if I am to spend my day swimming among them."

"All the presence of these things proves really," Bronwyn said, "is that it was every bit as safe out here in the woods last night as it seemed. We were much safer than in the village."

Anastasia and Carole were pleasantly surprised later in the morning to learn that they would no longer have to dodge mangled flotsam. Two boats floated towards them, downstream, a net strung between them. The boats were of royal blue, bearing the red and gold crest of Loefwin Patebreaker, a crowned skull with a sword cleaving it.

The men in the boats wore handsome livery and demanded that the chariot and swimmers leave the river until the boats had passed. As the net swept by, Bronwyn saw that it was clogged with red shapes.

"Tidy lot," Mistress Raspberry remarked, as she climbed back into the chariot beside Jack.

They reached the capital in late afternoon, after passing through a forest followed by a strip of charred earth bordering the outer walls of the city.

The walls were fortified, but apparently not against people. No one questioned them when they dragged their boat out of the river and onto the bank. A barred iron gate separated the river inside the city walls from the river outside.

The city was a new one, built around the river. One channel flowed through it, between the stubby iron-banded houses and business establishments. The smaller, right-hand channel was dammed up to feed the moat surrounding the shining castle.

The castle's silver and gold shingles mirrored the rose of the setting sun. "But it's so beautiful!" Carole wailed. "I can't go in there like this. I'm dripping wet."

"They don't seem to be very free about allowing through traffic anyway," Mistress Raspberry remarked. The drawbridge was raised, making a forbiddingly blank wall between the two guard towers.

"Do you suppose we need an appointment?" Anastasia asked. If they did, they appeared to be late. All around them shops were closing and people were locking themselves inside their houses.

"We probably only have to call to get them to let us in," Bronwyn said.

"That will be none too soon for me," Jack said. "My belly would very much appreciate a hot meal."

"Shouldn't be any problem," Bronwyn said blithely. "Why, Mistress Raspberry's mother, now that she's had time to think it over, will no doubt just give me the countercurse, once she sees I'm a friend of her daughter's, and we can all go home again. After all, she hasn't anything against me personally."

"Remember, *you* said that," Carole reminded her grimly.

"I'm rather afraid it won't be that easy," Mistress Raspberry

94

said. "Mother doesn't conduct her affairs with regards to person-
alities. You shall be very fortunate, Bronwyn, if she can be
persuaded that some advantage will accrue to her if she lifts your
curse."

"I'll give her an advantage," Bronwyn growled, grasping her
sword hilt.

"Remember, my Princess, the ogress is Mistress Rusty's
mother," Jack said, subtly showing the others who was really
the familiar friend of the Empress's sister, and worthy to call her
by her nickname.

"Sorry," Bronwyn said unrepentantly. The only thing she
was sorry for was that Belburga was her friend's mother.

"I must admit I've felt the same way at times," Mistress
Raspberry said, "But perhaps she's mellowed. I hope so, for the
sake of all concerned. Right now I just wish she'd answer the
door."

"Maybe if we all yell at once, the guards will hear us," Jack
suggested. The five of them agreed on what to yell, counted to
three and bellowed, "Hello, the castle!"

Nothing happened.

"It's getting very late," Carole said, noting the ruby hue of
the sky, mirrored by the moat. "Look at the sunset. If we're out
much later, it will get dark and the monsters will get us. Perhaps
I should swim the moat and tell the guards we're here."

"Yes," Bronwyn agreed. "You may have to tap on their
helmets to get their attention. They seem to have put wax in their
ears like Jehan's pirates."

"Or maybe they have all gone inside to eat their suppers and
go to bed," Jack said, a little tremulously. "If I were a soldier in
this country, I should not like guarding things after dark."

Except for its red color, the moat looked a great deal cleaner
than the river. Carole jumped in, feet first—and scrambled, dripping, back up on the bank again as the water boiled furiously and
the redness in the water gathered itself together into a great flat
ribbon as long and wide as Ollie the sea serpent. The ribbon had
a head, also flat, but peeled in two thin layers at the front to
form a mouth. Its eyes hung from two little stalks. The head
hovered halfway between the travelers and the gate.

Mistress Raspberry addressed the beast in Pan-elvin. "Kindly
let us pass," she commanded. "We have business with the
Empress."

"Not until you've followed proper procedure. Have you been
summoned? If so, have you the proper forms and identification?
Also, it is my duty to inform you that you are in violation of

Statute 7.21 which prohibits humans from addressing beasts and subsection D which specifies that humans are not to converse with great tapeworms.''

"I beg your pardon. We are Argonians, and not familiar with all of your statutes, however, I'm positive that the Empress, who is my sister—''

"Have you verification to that effect?'' the worm asked.

"Will dental records do?'' she asked, baring her teeth.

"No. We need proper positive identification. You should have filled out forms 670 and 1083, had them processed and already paid the appropriate tributes and fees before approaching the castle.''

As it spoke, the worm folded and pleated itself until what would have been coils on a round worm formed sharp-edged tangles and snarls as high as the banks of the moat. Its head thrust forward and leveled nose to nose with Mistress Raspberry's.

"Don't be so stuffy, my good beast. I am the daughter of Belburga, and sister to the Empress. You have only to inquire within. Now kindly let us pass.''

"It is not my function to inquire within. That is the function of the herald. It is my function to prevent intrusions into the castle by persons not pursuing proper channels and therefore not crossing the drawbridge.'' With each additional word, its body fan folded against the existing tangle to build a thin but complex construction of flat red worm halfway up the castle gate.

"All right,'' Mistress Raspberry said angrily, jerking open her valise and pulling forth her big book and pen, the tip of which she stabbed angrily into an ink bottle somewhere in the depths of the bag. "That's quite enough out of you. What is your name and who is your immediate superior?''

"I am the Great Tape, guardian beast of the official government of Greater Frostingdung housed within this fortress and I answer to no one and you'd better believe it,'' the Tape said with a vicious snap that sent another tier of tangled red edges and surfaces as high as the battlements.

Carole took advantage of the beast's preoccupation with Mistress Raspberry to edge around and enter the water nearest the tail, which the worm had withdrawn from around the castle so that it could use its entire length to build a parchment-thin edifice obstructing the entrance. She was sure she could swim around the creature.

But before she'd swum a stroke, the tail untangled and whipped around her, flattening her arms against her sides and squeezing. "Stop! That hurts,'' she cried. "Help!''

Bronwyn drew her sword.

"Cut right through it, Princess," Jack urged, but Mistress Raspberry said, "No! That's er—not very diplomatic. Carole, can't you hum your way out?"

"I'm sure that's going to be easy for her to do while she's being squeezed to death," Bronwyn fumed, but Carole tried.

The worm only squeezed harder, and Mistress Raspberry and Jack heard it say, "In addition to trespassing forbidden waters, you are now in violation of Statute—"

"Tape" a voice called from above. "You naughty, *wicked* Tape, you! Cease that at once! Now, I say. Put that child down!"

Though the voice was high and sweet and spoke softly in Argonian rather than Pan-elvin or Frostingdungian, the worm obeyed at once. "You know very well," the voice scolded, "that you're not permitted to dispose of people without prior approval."

"Daisy?" Mistress Raspberry scanned the battlements above the monster, who rapidly released Carole and began to straighten itself out. A plump matron with long curling blond hair waved down at them from the crenelations, and on being hailed, stopped waving, stared hard at Mistress Raspberry, and waved harder and more excitedly.

"Rusty? Oh, can it really be? Rusty, is it truly you?"

"Your worm didn't think so," Mistress Raspberry called gaily in return. She was also waving madly.

"Oh! But this is wonderful! Oh, Rusty, darling, I'm so very sorry—do forgive the Tape. It's marvelously efficient at its job of confounding and confusing folk and keeping them at bay, but I'm afraid it's not very bright or discriminating. I'll be down to let you in this very instant!"

"Everything is under control now," Mistress Raspberry said, turning to the others, who were dragging a gasping Carole from the moat. "That woman is my younger sister, Daisy-Esmeralda."

The drawbridge thudded down onto its landing on their side of the bank and Daisy crossed to meet them.

The two sisters embraced, but when Mistress Raspberry started across the bridge, Daisy halted her with a raised hand. "There's something I must settle first. Tape, do you hear me?" It raised its head enough so that its eye stalks were above the water. It looked thoroughly cowed. "These good people are not only legitimate guests, but this woman is my very own sister. I want you to apologize, and show them how happy we are to have them here at Giltrose Palace."

The eye stalks waved from side to side for a moment, as if embarrassed or undecided, then a great length of the beast folded itself along the splintery boards of the drawbridge, laying a red strip from end to end. At Daisy-Esmeralda's insistence, the visitors used the proffered portion of the worm's anatomy as a walkway. With the eyestalks watching them balefully, their trot across the bridge was gingerly in the extreme.

They passed under a toothy portcullis and into an exquisite garden, walled all around with gold and silver shingles. From an inner courtyard a woman with hair that vied with the shingles for sheer brilliance rushed to meet them. "Daisy-Esmeralda, a pox on you for worrying me so! The Prince has been calling for you and it's almost curf—Ruby-Rose!" Without missing a beat she ran toward Mistress Raspberry with outstretched arms. So smooth was her transition and so pretty her surprise that Bronwyn could have sworn she'd known they were there all along and was only pretending to just notice them. Had she been watching while the beast menaced them as well? "Ruby-Rose, my lost darling! What an appalling dress that is! Must be your father's taste. And your hair hasn't been styled in months, by the look of it. We'll have to do something about that before the feast, but don't worry, Mother will have you up to snuff in no time. Are you married yet? Good! There are many more suitable young men here in Frostingdung, and we're so much better connected now. You've picked an excellent time to come home and mend the broken heart of your loving mother."

As soon as the woman identified herself, Bronwyn's hand tightened on her sword and she began to stride forward purposefully to confront the ogress who had so callously ruined her life, but Mistress Raspberry pulled her back and muttered, "Wait. My mother can be a dangerous sort, Your Highness. She must be dealt with properly. If you want your curse lifted, stay back, be patient, and leave her to me."

In a louder voice she said, "I didn't leave *you*, Mother, if you'll recall," and embraced the woman even more gingerly than she had walked across the back of the moat monster.

"No," the woman said, giving her daughter's companions looks that made the Tape seem an amiable fellow. "As I can see, you were spirited away by evil companions."

"I wouldn't say that," Mistress Raspberry said, amusement edging the exasperation in her voice. "I'd like to present Her Royal Highness Bronwyn Amberwine Magdalena Rowan, Crown Princess of Argonia, Prince Jacopo Worthyman, scion of a no-madic subculture and in indirect line for the throne of Ablemarle,

98

and the Honorable Lady Carole Maud Songsmith Brown, daughter of Magdalene, Honorary Princess of Argonia, and the Earl of Wormroost." She cast an apologetic look at Anastasia, "And that only includes *some* of the noble members of my party."

The swan looked away, pretending disinterest, as they entered a room the size of a ballroom, which was planted with flowers and had an ornamental fountain. Anastasia flew into the fountain and proceded to glide serenely around in it as if she were part of the original decor.

"Charmed, I'm sure," Mistress Raspberry's mother said in a gratingly nasal voice as flat as the Great Tape.

"So are we all," Bronwyn said sourly, only her curse allowing her to respond with unfelt courtesy. She glared fiercely at the rude woman's back, which she had continued to show them throughout the introduction. Even if Belburga hadn't been responsible for her curse, Bronwyn would have disliked the woman. She was brassy, common, loud, rude, and furthermore had the nerve to produce the impression that she considered none of the rest of them quite up to her standards. She no doubt found wicked, curse-throwing wizards more to her taste.

"Lily-Pearl and the Emperor will just be delighted to see you, darling," the woman babbled on in her grinding monotone. "There's a feast tonight. I'll see to it that you and your friends are provided with proper attire and—"

"Fine, Mother. I have business I must discuss with the Emperor, and I'm afraid you and Princess Bronwyn and I need to have a little talk, too. Something about some assistance you once rendered to a certain sorcerer."

"You know me, Ruby-Rose, darling, always ready and willing to help anyone in need. I've always said—"

And she went on at length to repeat what she'd always said, until she and Mistress Raspberry retired to a sitting room off the hall and Daisy-Esmeralda had a servant conduct the rest of the party to guest rooms.

The banquet hall was outlandishly sumptuous. Not even King Roari's great hall at Queenston Castle surpassed it—but then, Bronwyn recalled with no small degree of self-righteousness, her father expended his strength in the defense and administration of his own people, not in the oppression and exaction of tribute from others.

Thousands of torches flared between opulent, jewel-toned tapestries, the table blazed with tapers, which blazed again in the gems encrusting the gowns, headgear and ornaments of the

99

revelers. The floor was inlaid with mosaics, not covered with rushes in the usual fashion, and brilliant cut flowers of hues rivaling those in the attire of the assembled nobles filled every spare corner. Elsewhere on the walls and around the room shields and armor were burnished to a high luster and proudly displayed.

"You won't recognize Lily-Pearl," Daisy said to her sister.

"I barely recognize anyone, myself included," Rusty replied, surveying her traveling companions with a bemused look. They stood at the entrance to the banquet hall, waiting for the herald to announce them. She herself wore bronze-trimmed gossamer green, a fairly conservative choice considering it had arrived at her room through her mother's instigation. Daisy, whose new round shape lent a certain solidity that had not been present in the flitting half-dryad maiden she had been when last Rusty saw her, looked very like her namesake, clothed as she was all in bright yellow, with brown velvet lining and trim. Even the overlay of melancholy in her expression, no doubt caused by the lack of any animals in this kingdom save monsters like the Tape, became her.

Jack was resplendent in red satin britches and an orange tunic. "I picked them myself," he admitted with a lowering of his curling lashes which was supposed to denote modesty. Carole's pink gown with garnet-colored trim became her well, but the whole party paled before the splendor of Bronwyn.

Belburga's snobbery had apparently gotten the best of her ogress instincts, and she had clothed her most illustrious guest in raiment she deemed appropriate to the station of a Crown Princess. Bronwyn's gown was deep purple, embroidered with gold and silver peacocks with amythests and aquamarines in their tails. A little cap which looked like another peacock tail and which was also set with aquamarines and amythests was pinned firmly to the Princess's wild red hair. One hardly noticed the hasty addition of aqua silk at the hem, starting at Bronwyn's knees, and at the sleeve, midway up her forearm, to lengthen the dress sufficiently to fit her. The total effect was stunning, and marred only by Bronwyn's insistence on carrying her shield along to the feast. Fortunately, the shield was only a small round buckler, easily concealed by the voluminous sleeves.

"Nice of you to have a feast in our honor," she said chattily to Daisy-Esmeralda.

"I only wish it were in your honor," Daisy said, sounding worried. "I'm not at all sure Loefwin is doing the right thing by making a fuss over Gilles Kilgilles."

100

"Would that be Lord Gilles?" Carole asked. "Which one is he? We met a friend of his on our way here."

Daisy looked surprised but answered, "He's that chap over there with the pale hair and the face half in his wine cup. Oh, dear, I do wish Loefwin hadn't made my husband sit next to the man! The poor darling is simply green about all this already."

The herald announced them then and they filed in, and took their places at the table. Frostingdungian custom seated the men on one side of the table, the women on the other. The Empress, a white-haired wight in a white gown evidently inspired by a winding sheet, sat opposite her husband. Daisy-Esmeralda, next to her, sat opposite her own spouse, Prince Loefrig, who was more widely constructed than Loefwin and balder, with a broad nose and slitty eyes and a mouth that seemed to run from ear to ear. Yet there was considerable family resemblance, and Bronwyn remembered she had heard that Loefwin was one of a set of triplets. Mistress Raspberry was seated on Daisy's other side, opposite Lord Gilles, which gave her something much nicer to look at than either of her sisters. Gilles Kilgilles might be mad, and he was most certainly already quite far into his cups, but he was strikingly handsome, especially among the Frostingdungians. Not as handsome as Bronwyn's father, of course, but his sleek cap of spun silver hair was striking, his eyes were the blue of a glacial lake, and his movements, drunken or not, were fluid and graceful. Mistress Raspberry seemed to be carefully avoiding looking at him, but Carole, opposite Jack, gaped frankly, so that Bronwyn wondered how her cousin intended to eat with her mouth seemingly permanently open.

Bronwyn faced a swarthy man with pitted dark skin, an athlete's figure, piercing dark eyes and rather greasy-looking dark hair. His dress was a conservative, natural-colored linen, tastefully embellished with gold ornaments. "Duke Docho Droughtsea, Your Highness," Daisy offered helpfully. "One of Loefwin's chief advisers and the architect of this castle and city."

Bronwyn didn't fancy the man herself, but then, she didn't need any chief advisers, having already received more unsolicited advice in the last two weeks than she had ever had in her life.

"I understand you're a swordswoman, Milady," the man said conversationally, while chewing on the entrée, which was undercooked and cold by the time it got to the table. Loefwin apparently tried to make up in dining accouterments what he lacked in menu. Gold plates were all very well, but she would have preferred hot mutton.

101

"Who, me?" she asked. "Who could have told you a thing like that?"

"Your young friend," he said and nodded to Jack, "mentioned it when I—er—made his acquaintance near the treasure room earlier this evening, and Dame Belburga was kind enough to tell me something of your family history."

"Imagine that," she said noncommittally, so she didn't have to lie and deny what a splendid fighting woman she was.

"I thought perhaps tomorrow, if you have the time, I might be able to interest you in a contest."

"Oh, I'm sure I won't have the time to indulge in that sort of thing," she said eagerly.

"Pity. I didn't mean sword against sword, you know. I wanted to demonstrate to you the native weapon of my coun—region."

"Oh?"

He pulled from his pocket two pitted copper cones on a braided leather thong, which was looped midway between the weights and knotted. Bronwyn wondered fleetingly why the weights weren't iron, like everything else in Frostingdung.

"Behold the Bintnarangian senyaty."

"I can see it must make an excellent hacking and gouging weapon," she said politely.

He laughed. "Milady has a charming sense of humor!"

"Milady would prefer to have the pepper. Would you pass it please?" She hoped he'd pass the salt as well, since that was what she really wanted.

The pepper, as well as the salt, were in the custody of the Emperor, who obligingly passed them along, interrupting himself in the middle of a heated discussion about his proposed reforms. When he noticed to whom he was passing condiments, he decided to try to enlist reinforcements for his argument.

"What do you think, Princess Bronwyn? Your father's King of quite a large country and it's known to contain monsters as well as other—"

"Watch it, brother," Loefrig said. "I want to remind you there are ladies present."

"Just so happens all the ladies within earshot are from a country where they have lots of you-know-what. Shouldn't think they'd mind," the Emperor said, but turned a little red in the face anyway.

"I wish someone would say what we're supposed to be too delicate to hear," Mistress Raspberry commented.

"Now, Ruby-Rose," her mother began.

"Magic, milady," Lord Gilles obliged, rising and falling in

102

one swoop of a bow. "Magic, wizardry, sorcery, charlatanism, hocus-pocus, spooky stuff."

Prince Loefrig turned on his dinner companion so quickly he nearly knocked his chair over. "Sir! I'll thank you to mind your tongue! My wife is present and I'll not have her insulted by such langu—urgit!" he finished with a croak. As he'd been ranting, his skin had taken on a wet, bumpy appearance, and instead of reddening, as angry people are usually wont to do, he greened. Bronwyn was reminded of Lorelei but Daisy-Esmeralda was reminded of something else altogether.

"Urgit!" he said again and his wife scrambled across the table to kiss him full on the lips.

"There, there, darling, you mustn't take on so. I'm not the least offended. I know the mention of you-know-what upsets you, but that's no reason to turn now, is it, in front of all our guests? After all, if it hadn't been for you-know-what, you and I would never have learned to love one another, now would we?"

She repeated her kiss several times, and gradually his skin drained back to white. "Urg—sorry, darling. Sorry, Your Imperial Majesty, old man. You know I've just got a bit of a thing about that. But you, Kilgilles, should still learn to watch your mouth!"

"Now, now, old Froggy, let's not be so hasty," the Emperor said soothingly, "I want to hear Gilles' opinions on a few things. His district's one of the worst off. What do you think, eh, Gilles?"

"Think, my liege?"

"About my little idea. Don't you think that if we screened them well enough, we could let a few of the natives doff the bracelet, at least part of the time, buy their way free in exchange for growing crops, breeding cattle. I swear we've tried with our own folk, but we Frostingdungians are miners and warriors. We can't seem to make a thing grow except porridge vine and more of these damned hidebehind things! How's a person supposed to run a country when no one has access to anyone else as soon as it gets a bit dark?"

"I'm sure I don't know, my liege. I wouldn't want to be in your shoes." Gilles smiled a charming and almost genuinely sympathetic smile.

"Well, I need your help, my boy. As you can probably taste." Loefwin glared at his food and stabbed the table with his knife. "While we're at it, let's free some chefs too. A person should be able to get used to this sort of thing, but my gut doesn't seem to know that."

103

"Release some of those savages?" Loefrig protested. "Brother, you don't know them like I do. As soon as you take their bracelets off they'll be up to their old tricks—"

"I think you underestimate the thoroughness of Frostingdung's victory," Gilles argued. "The leadership of the six client kingdoms was utterly destroyed on the Day. The Emperor represents the only alternative any of us have to chaos and another war, which no one is prepared for. If one chose properly from among the slaves—"

"And I say a slave is a slave for a very good reason and ought to remain a slave. They're savage inferior people. Why, the merest contact with one of them has maimed me for life—would have been much worse if not for Daisy. Not to mention our sainted brother Loefric, who never has had the heart to return to the bosom of his family since he made the ultimate sacrifice on the Day. You were born afterwards, boy. You don't know what you're talking about."

"No doubt you're—" he hiccoughed delicately, cupping long elegant fingers to his mouth, "right."

"Well, if this isn't the gloomiest party!" the washed-out Empress exclaimed in a tone as genuine as the high red color on her mother's cheeks. "Loefwin, you do know how to spoil a feast with your talk of slaves and other nasty topics."

"Sorry, dearest. Someone has to run the country sometime, you know."

"Yes, but not during festivities. Where are the musicians? Let's have some dancing. Aren't you just dying for Ruby-Rose to show us the latest steps from Queenston?"

"Just dying," he agreed.

"Milord Gilles, since my husband is feeling so gloomy this evening, perhaps you'll—?" She rose and extended her hand across the table. He looked at the hand as if wondering whether he was supposed to leap across or crawl under the table to claim it, and decided to bow low and kiss the hand and walk around the table before leading the Empress to the floor.

"Well, Princess Bronwyn." Loefwin turned to her, smiling. "A couple of warriors like us ought to be able to fake hand-to-hand combat if we can't actually dance, now, oughtn't we? And I'd like to ask you a thing or two about the extent of your father's holdings. You stand to inherit don't you? Meet you at the end of this damned table."

Belburga's eyebrow shot up to her hairline as her son-in-law and Bronwyn joined the other dancers. As Droughtsea approached to claim her, Mistress Raspberry gave her mother an

104

innocent smile. "Did you mention Lily-Pearl and Loefwin had been spatting lately? Love's like that, I suppose. If one brings no dowry but beauty and lineage to a marriage, one can only expect—" But she didn't finish, swept away on the fine linen arm of the Duke.

"The nerve of that girl!" Belburga said. Carole listened with great interest. "Why, that hulking giantess is nothing but a child."

"A titled, *landed* child, I'm afraid," Daisy-Esmeralda answered.

"Your sister always was a wretched little troublemaker," Belburga snapped, and flounced from the table.

"I believe I'll retire, my love," Prince Loefrig said hastily. "Brother has more affairs of state to discuss with me tomorrow, and I'll need my sleep if I'm going to be up to Milord Kilgilles. Are you coming?"

"Can you forgive me, darling? Rusty and I have so much catching up to do and we've scarcely had a moment to ourselves."

"Of course."

With professional curiosity, Carole leaned over and asked Daisy, "Excuse me, was I mistaken or did your husband almost turn into a frog there for a moment?"

"Yes, I'm afraid he did," Daisy admitted. "So kind of you not to say anything in front of him. He's terribly sensitive about it. Shortly after Loefwin left on the trip to Argonia where we all met, my husband was leading an expeditionary force in Negelia to make sure all the minor magicians had been rounded up— they, I don't know how to explain this to you, Carole dear, but they seemed to feel at the time that that was the proper way to handle their affairs and I'm afraid—"

"We heard," Carole said. "Go on."

"The long and the short of it is that he found a magician—a witch, actually, and before they could round her up she managed to change him into a frog. Animals being as scarce as they are, one of his men put Loefrig in his pocket and returned with him here, thinking to fry him up for the Emperor—the men in the expeditionary force had no idea what had become of their Prince, of course. They thought he'd been taken by hidebehinds, I'm sure. But Loefrig divined the intentions of his former servant and hopped out of the pocket at the crucial moment, and lived in the fountain in the entrance hall where your darling swan is now. I suppose Rusty must have told you that I have always loved animals, and I missed all my little friends from our tower in

Little Darlingham ever so much, and one day after we arrived, when I was sitting by the fountain crying—''

"I know!" Carole said. "He showed himself to you, and you took pity on him and kissed him—''

"Actually, it was more like he took pity on me and allowed me to kiss him. I was simply dying for an animal to cuddle by then," Daisy confided.

"And he turned into a handsome—''

"A Prince at any rate. The only problem is, I'm of dryad heritage, and not a princess, so the counterspell didn't work as well when I administered it as it would with a real princess. I have to kiss him again rather frequently or he has a tendency to revert.''

"You mean—turn back into a—?" Carole made a face.

"I'm afraid so," Daisy said resignedly.

"Ugh!" Carole said.

"Rather," Daisy sighed. "Though sometimes I almost prefer it. I get so tired of humans and at least if Loefrig's in a froggish temper it's a nice change for me from the Tape's company. I am so very glad you've come and brought Rusty.''

By that time Jack had finished demolishing all of the halfway edibles he could find remaining on the table, and approached Daisy with his most flourishing bow, and together they joined the dance.

If one could call it that. If there was anything Frostingdungians did worse than cooking, Carole thought, it was making music. The problem wasn't just that it was foreign music either—her father knew several foreign songs and she usually found them intriguing, if not as danceable as Argonian ones. Nor did the fault lie in the skill of the musicians, who played competently enough, though they didn't seem particularly interested in what they were doing. They might as well have been scrubbing pots or cutting grain for all the joy they displayed in their tunes. Which was perfectly understandable. This was something Carole had never thought to hear—boring music.

And all of the dancers looked as bored as the musicians sounded, even when the dance bestowed them each upon different partners than those with whom they'd begun. Bronwyn was with Droughtsea now, and Mistress Raspberry with Lord Gilles. They made a strange-looking couple, and Carole could see that though Mistress Raspberry tried to be gay in her brittle fashion, Jenny's young lord was hard to cheer up. He looked sad and worried and perhaps a little frightened—maybe mad, but Carole wasn't sure. She had a feeling after the people of Frostingdung

106

got to know her and the people she'd been traveling with, the Dungies would think all of the Argonians madder than Lord Gilles.

While she was thinking and watching the dancers, she started humming, just a little. She didn't exactly mean to practice magic. Still, merely humming a few suggestions to the musicians, purely musical, as one artist to another, couldn't possibly count as magic. So she added a little harmony here and a glissando there, this tiny embellishment and that, gaining confidence and inspiration as she went along until her humming blended in with the new and improved music.

It sounded much better. By the end of the dance everyone had a sheen of perspiration on his or her face. "I say, I don't remember that one going exactly that way, do you, darling?" the Empress asked the Emperor, with whom she was now partnered.

"Never gave it much thought, dear," he said. "Believe I'm getting tired after all, and the game wardens are coming tomorrow to make their weekly reports. What say we—"

"Oh, very well," the Empress replied crossly.

Many of the courtiers followed the Imperial pair from the room, but the musicians played another dance for those remaining, and Carole helped on that one too. Mistress Raspberry flushed as red as her name and she danced again in Lord Gilles' arms, and Gilles laughed and smiled throughout most of the song, and seemed to be joking with her.

But as the last strains died away, and Mistress Raspberry trotted dutifully off with Daisy-Esmeralda, the beautiful young baron looked over the heads of the dancers to meet Carole's wistful gaze with a shrewdly appraising one. He sauntered over to her, poured himself another draught, drained it, and leaned against the table, folding his arms across his chest and regarding her with a perplexed expression on his face.

When everyone had left the room except the servants clearing the tables he said in a low tone, "Little tricks like that can earn you a new piece of jewelry here, Miss."

"Who? Me?" Carole looked innocently around her. "You're mistaken, sir. I was just sitting here enjoying the music."

"Hmmm, so I noticed. And since that's normally quite impossible, I immediately deduced you were the culprit."

"Not bad for a mad man," she said. He might be beautiful but he took a lot on himself.

"I see my reputation precedes me. No need to be so sharp, Miss. Your secret's safe with me. I'm widely known as a halfbreed witch-lover anyway, though up till now at least I don't believe I've ever had the pleasure.''

"But isn't Teeny a witch really, without her bracelet?" Carole asked innocently.

"Teeny Fittroon? Might have been. She was bound when I was born. No way of telling now."

"Won't her magic come back if the King lets you take off the bracelet?"

"Not much chance of that." He slumped down in a chair and filled and drained his cup twice more, mopping his mouth with a gesture less graceful than previous ones. "Loefwin's not the same man who conquered the Six since he got religion or whatever it was he got in Argonia, besides that female hidebehind he's married to. But Droughtsea and Loefrig are the same. They're not likely to let any bracelets be removed, even if the whole country starves to death."

"If the people are slaves, can't they be forced to grow things?"

"Certainly they can. My father, Gory Kilgilles, did just that. The vine that makes out pasty porridge is tended by slaves. But that won't help bring back the meat animals and fish."

"You must have some meat," Carole said. "We had roast tonight."

He laughed, and though his laugh was full and deep instead of old and tremulous, he reminded her of Teeny. "Yes, what did you think of our roast beast? Loefwin's game wardens catch that particular form of crawler by setting out traps each night baited with part of one from the previous night. Originally, a slave was used for bait, but Loefwin doesn't care for that practice any longer. People in my region do the same with the sea creatures. When those aren't available, we eat the gruel."

"I suppose you get used to it," she said doubtfully. Marta, the seamstress at Wormroost, was fond of saying that, but then, Marta had never eaten the Frostingdungian gruel.

"Not unless you've never had better. I have. Food has gotten shorter and worse every year of my life." He started to say something else, but abruptly his face and entire bearing changed. Most of the candles and torches in the room had by now been discreetly doused, and as Carole watched, she could almost see another person slide over Gilles' head like a garment. His eyes narrowed and lengthened, his skull broadened, his body straightened and became less drink-riddled and resigned and more stern and forbidding. He shifted his position to the left, and addressed the space he had formerly occupied.

"You sniveling whelp! When I think of the indignities your

108

mother endured at the hands of that goblin in order to produce a sorry specimen like you, I could weep. Sobbing for our supper, are we, with our people in iron and our realm in ruins? How would you like to eat dirt for all eternity?''

"Wait!" Carole said, searching the face for some trace of the original Gilles. Frostingdungians might call this madness but any witch worth her salt knew the supernatural when she saw it. This wasn't madness, this was either haunting or possession. "Just who are you and what makes you think you can just barge in on our conversation like that?''

"I'm his father," the new entity informed her coldly. She found she was rather surprised it was aware of her presence. She'd always thought that hauntings/possessions were more or less personal matters between the haunter and its host, so to speak. "Who are you?''

Before she could answer, the man shifted in his seat again and became Gilles once more. "She's a witch, old man, a real unbanded potent witch. And you're not my father and furthermore if you want either of us to survive, you'd better not even let me hear you think such a thing. Don't you realize we're in Loefwin's castle?''

He switched positions again and the caul of his father's personality slipped back across his features. The ghost wasn't the least bit interested in its geographical location. "Witch, eh? And with your powers intact. Won't be for long, around here.''

Gilles shifted back to himself again. "I was just telling her some of the problems the country has been having and how Loefwin is trying to solve them. I'm trying to persuade him to unband the slaves, to help solve the food shortage.''

"The country! What do you mean the country! Seven countries is what we are, and Frostingdung the lowliest of all. Suleskeria, Bintnar, even the Nonarable Lands, all of us had enough to eat when there were fish left in the sea and our people had the power and skill to coax the plants from the earth and the beasts were allowed to breed—Dungies never understood that you can't separate magic from production. Goblins rape the earth of metals it doesn't replace. You can't do that with food, or you starve. So now they're starving and I say, let them!'' As the ghost spoke, it became more and more distraught, its cultured voice grew louder, and it ground Gilles' teeth angrily.

Carole watched, both fascinated and apprehensive, waiting for the young nobleman to turn into himself again, when she heard another noise.

"Hsst! Lady Carole!" Jack hailed her.

"Who's that?" the ghost asked, whirling to face Jack. "Another witch?"

"No, that's Jack. He's a gypsy."

"Certainly is. What about that creature you were dancing with earlier, whelp?"

"That's Mistress Raspberry," Carole answered, not willing to watch the switch again. "She's an ogress and—also a little bit of a magician, I think."

The ghost chuckled. "So, Loefwin's inviting magicians back to his court, is he? Could be he's found he needs 'em."

Jack heard the chuckle and rushed forward. Gilles shifted position and answered his specter, "I'm trying to convince the Emperor of just that, if you don't queer the deal for me first."

"You! All you ever do is wallow in your brew," the ghost said from the left again. Jack, who had at first clasped Carole's arm, dropped his hand and stared first at Gilles and company and then at her.

"Come, Carole. It is not good for you to be in this dark hall with Teeny's crazy lord. No offense, crazy Lord," he said quickly. "But you also should be in bed. Old Teeny would wish it," he added lamely.

"An excellent idea," the real Gilles said, rising. "We can continue this discussion in my room, old man."

"Bah!" the ghost replied, but was then silent.

CHAPTER VIII

Bronwyn hadn't really been avoiding the Duke of Droughtsea when he found her, but neither had she been seeking him out. She'd actually been waiting for Mistress Raspberry, who had asked Bronwyn to meet her in the west courtyard after breakfast. Breakfast being a great deal like dinner, she'd decided to skip it despite her hunger. She arrived in the courtyard early in hopes of getting in a bit of practice with her sword.

After the ogress lifted her curse, she intended to go directly to the Front and lend her father a helping hand. No doubt he had everything under control, of course. He was the world's greatest warrior. But she still wanted to prove she was the world's second greatest. It probably wouldn't be enough just to have the curse off. She'd probably have to convince a few people they needed to believe her when she said something, and Father always said there was nothing like a good sword to make a believer out of someone. She tried a few experimental thrusts, pretending to quarter a few Ablemarlonian generals. When she tired of that, she thought she might find good new offensive and defensive maneuvers for dealing with monsters tactically useful in this terrain, and set out to devise some. With the Great Tape in mind, she ferociously minced a hapless clothesline which happened to be hanging in the wrong place at the right time. Recalling the fliers, she hacked several large chunks out of the sky, but she was beginning to get bored when the Duke came along.

"Your Highness! So you've decided to honor me with a duel after all," he said with a flourishing bow.

"I've been waiting for some time," she said, panting from teaching the sky a lesson.

"Then by all means," he said, drawing his weapon from a pocket, "Let's begin."

Droughtsea felt in no way imperiled by this oversized child. Even if Loefwin mistook her for a grown woman, he did not. He'd had it out of the gypsy boy that the Princess was large because of lineage, and a fighter only because she so designated herself. She was unblooded, whereas the Duke was very bloody indeed.

For a time they circled each other, Bronwyn feinting once or twice. She had practiced against veterans before, for though her father was her favorite sparring partner, he seldom had time to spare and often sent some general who was waiting for an audience to school his daughter in battle. She had always had the feeling these men weren't taking her seriously and did not fight hard against her for fear of injuring the royal heiress. She'd done her best to challenge them, and had few qualms about her ability to match her sword with sword or lance, but the unconventional weapon wielded by the Duke was another matter.

After her second feint, he fell back, and set his weapon in motion, the right-hand weight twirling in the direction of the sun, the left-hand weight twirling in opposition to it. Bronwyn became so interested in watching the things flip around that she almost didn't see when he loosed it.

He had thrown for her neck, which wasn't sportsmanlike at all, but she hopped backwards. Consequently on its downward fall, after failing to meet with her throat, the senyaty found her feet instead and wrapped securely around them, tripping her.

She fell back with her sword still raised and her shield covering her. She wasted a precious moment thinking how to untangle the senyaty without destroying it before she glanced up and saw the Duke advancing on her with his sword drawn and realized he had every intention of destroying her, whatever she did to his weapon. Her reflexes were well-trained enough, but her confusion delayed her almost too long. She was still thinking about untangling her feet, and had her blade engaged with the leather strip, when his sword came crashing towards her head.

She threw up her shield, and his sword shattered against it at the same moment hers severed the leather binding her feet. Before she could raise her weapon to press her own offensive, he sprang upon her, another senyaty in his hands, wrapped it around her neck and pulled so tightly that most of her strength fled with her breath.

Why was he doing this? Didn't he like redheads or was it tall girls he hated? Of all the Argonian party, Bronwyn had the least magic. If he was of a magic-hating people, why pick on her? No doubt he realized her natural valor would cause her to fly to the defense of her companions if he attacked them first, so he was getting her out of the way before proceeding to his real target. She wanted to ask him if she was right, but all she could say was, "Ack," as he jerked her around in front of him and pulled harder on the leather thongs. Her sword arm was powerless to reach him.

She fell backwards, her height helping her fall heavily to knock him down. The cords loosened and she ripped them off, though her fingers felt lifeless. Her sword had clattered to the ground in the tussle and now both she and the Duke jumped for it.

"Ah, Droughtsea, helping our lovely young guest get some wholesome exercise, I see," someone said, and both Bronwyn and the Duke abandoned the sword to turn sweating, discolored faces to the Emperor. Mistress Raspberry and Lord Gilles stood on either side of him and Rusty lifted a thin eyebrow at the sight of Bronwyn's disarray. "Kind of you to entertain her—but don't be so rough, my dear fellow. We don't want to damage her—heh heh."

Before either Droughtsea or Bronwyn could reply, a young page ran into the courtyard, slowing to a more sedate pace when he saw Loefwin. "Your pardon, Sire, but you asked to be informed when the gamekeepers had assembled. They await your pleasure." Spotting the Duke, he also bowed to him, looking a bit leery of addressing the man, Bronwyn thought. "Milord, His Highness Prince Loefrig asks you to attend him in his bath."

The Duke bowed hastily and retreated and Bronwyn rose, accepting the Emperor's proffered hand and examining her skinned knees on the way up.

The Emperor looked after him for a moment and Bronwyn thought she saw a glint of suspicion in Loefwin's deepset eyes, but if it was there, he masked it almost at once with a genial smile. "Mustn't keep the gamekeepers waiting, must I? But, Princess Bronwyn, I would like to have a word with you after court. While talking with Sister Ruby-Rose and Kilgilles here, it occurred to me that perhaps we might come to some arrangement of mutual satisfaction with Argonia concerning your war and our food shortage. I should like your opinion."

Before Bronwyn could reply, Mistress Raspberry gasped with a motherly concern which was totally uncharacteristic. "Why, Princess Bronwyn, dear, you've bloodied your knee! That will never do. Come along, and we'll ask my mother to help us fix it."

The Emperor fled the moment the tone turned to such womanly matters, and Rusty said under her breath, "We mustn't risk your curse botching this conference. Let's talk to Mother right now about curing you."

Belburga was at her dressing table when they reached her chambers. She looked surprised enough to see Rusty but she looked absolutely amazed to see Bronwyn. "But—my dear, what an unexpected pleasure," she said, quickly recovering her composure. She waved a rough pot in the direction of Bronwyn's knees. "Whatever have you done to yourself?"

"You know very well the Princess can't give you a straight answer, Mother, but it's my belief that she was attacked by the Duke of Droughtsea. His sword was lying broken on the ground when we arrived. I believe," she continued, looking straight into her mother's eyes, "that someone must have put him up to it. But Bronwyn won't be able to bear witness against him so that we can clear the matter up unless you remove the curse you put on her."

Belburga was coy. "Curse? But, Ruby-Rose, my darling girl, your journey must have worn you out to the point of distraction. A curse is a form of magic. I have no magic."

"Haven't you?"

Belburga carefully avoided her daughter's eyes and Rusty sighed. "Well, that's a pity, I suppose, since it will be difficult to punish Droughtsea. But on the other hand, I'm sure the Emperor won't let anything happen to Bronwyn once I tell him

113

my suspicions. He has plans that would make her demise extremely inconvenient, to say the least.'' She turned to Bronwyn, who was beginning to wonder who the cursed one was around here anyway, and said in a world-weary way, ''Bronwyn dear, I'm afraid there's no way to let the Emperor know your true feelings on the matter he was discussing with you. I know you're quite young still but—''

''But what?'' Belburga's predatory eyes pounced on each of them in turn. ''What's that soft-headed son-in-law of mine up to now? Is he planning to betray my Lily-Pearl?''

''Oh, no, Mother, I wouldn't put it so harshly. But he is getting on towards middle age and you know how men are then, and Bronwyn has a substantial inheritance and in her present condition is unable to rule alone. What could be more natural than that King Roari would seek an alliance—''

''But the Emperor is a married man and she's scarcely potty trained! Besides, Loefwin hardly knows the Rowans—''

''Loefwin knows that Argonia still has food. And wives have been set aside—or worse—before, for political reasons. Why make such a fuss? I'm sure he'll provide for Lily-Pearl—and you, of course, though you won't want to live in the palace since it would be too awkward under the circumstances.''

''Yes,'' Bronwyn said, ''Don't worry, ma'am, I'd see to it that you and the Empress got your gruel twice a day and a nice piece of monster now and then. And when I'm done with a gown, why, just think, it'll make one for each of you!''

''Wait—let me think.'' Belburga put her finger to her chin and cocked her head in what was supposed to be a pensive gesture. ''Not that I have personally ever done anything so vulgar as you suggest, but perhaps, just perhaps, I remember something from my genteel education that might be of use to the poor girl.''

''I'd be ever so glad for any crumb of wisdom you could share, ma'am,'' Bronwyn said as demurely as she could.

''You shall certainly have it,'' Belburga replied in a sweet voice that was still buying time, accompanied by a smile full of daggered teeth. ''How sad for you to be the object of such a sordid political barter.''

''Pity you couldn't have been so solicitous when you provided the sorcerer with the curse that got her into this mess.'' Rusty smiled an equally toothy smile.

Dame Belburga saw from her daughter's expression that she'd better move smartly along to her next tactic, and she sank to a brocaded couch which had formerly held only a bit of embroidery in ivory hoops. The ogress passed her bent wrist across her

114

spit-curl-adorned brow. "But, precious, what would you have had Mother do? That wretched wizard and his bandits were all about us. What help was there except her wits for a poor but still attractive widow with three beautiful, vulnerable daughters? I was forced to do his bidding to save our honor. Ruby-Rose, you'll simply never know the sacrifices Mother has made for you."

"Well, Mama, now you can make one or two more and I do promise this time to be properly grateful if only you'll get a move on. Loefwin isn't Emperor because of his patience, you know. And I'll promise you this too: the sooner you help us, the sooner we'll be out of your hair."

"I'm glad YOU are promising, dear," Belburga said with a spiteful jab at Bronwyn, "or I wouldn't believe a word of it. How does it feel, Miss Princess, you with your palace and your pretty mama and rich papa to know you're such a deceitful person no one can possibly ever care for you, any more than they're likely to believe you when you tell them the curse is lifted?"

"Fine," Bronwyn said, wishing she could run the woman through.

"Bronwyn might well ask you how it feels to be one of the reasons people might wish to stamp out magic in Argonia as they've done here," Rusty told her mother.

"As they think they've done here," Belburga spat back.

"You're not the only one who can get nasty, Mama," Rusty said quietly. "I've developed certain—talents—of my own under Father's tutelage."

"That weakling wouldn't teach you anything really potent."

"Wouldn't he?" Rusty laughed Belburga's own laugh and Bronwyn stared at her, startled. "No, he wouldn't teach me how to use power against you, but then, he needn't. I'm your daughter too, after all. Are you interested in my career, Mama? I've learned some of Father's skill with disguises, you see, except that I do it differently, quicker and more convincingly and—and I can turn into things that aren't very nice, Mama. But I can do more than Father because I can also turn other people into things that aren't very nice. How would you like to wake up looking like one of the sea monsters, Mama, or—oh, maybe have the head of one of those bat things staring at you in that lovely dressing table mirror one morning? You never know."

"Very WELL. You don't need to give yourself airs, my girl. They're most unbecoming. You never were the sweet child your sisters were. That's why I left you."

"The curse, Mama."

"I don't have it. She'll have to consult the firm from which I purchased it and—"

"Firm?"

"Certainly. I met their representative at one of my family reunions. I've traded with them ever since."

"And where is this firm located?" Rusty sounded increasingly skeptical.

"Not here, of course. There's no magic here, as I keep trying to tell you."

"Where?"

"I couldn't say. You don't think I go to Miragenia every time I want some teensy little ensorcelment, do you? Not on your life, darling daughter. I always just put in an order and they send them by return courier."

"What's Miragenia?" Bronwyn asked.

"A country," Belburga said. "It's where I always send the orders."

"This is all very interesting, Mother," Rusty said. "But what we need to know is who exactly is personally responsible for Bronwyn's curse."

"Goodness, dear, do you think Mother knows everything? I haven't the foggiest idea. You and all these scruffy children will simply have to go to Miragenia and find out who's responsible, won't you, if you ever want Miss Priss here to come clean?"

"Have I ever told you, Mother, what a thoroughly unpleasant woman you are?"

"Why, no, darling. I didn't know you cared. But really, though I must admit you've never been my particular favorite, I must say that of all of you girls, you seem to be the one who takes after me the most."

Rusty ignored the last remark. "You'll have to arrange transportation to this Miragenia place, Mother."

"I? Arrange the matter with my son-in-law. He would be glad to help her get to Miragenia if only so he could find it himself."

"You mean he can't find it? Where is it?" Rusty was rapidly losing whatever patience she had once possessed.

"Across the border somewhere. But it's a magical country and Loefwin doesn't believe in it so he couldn't find it—he conquered all the ones he did believe in."

"Is it close then?" Bronwyn asked.

"There are a few mountains and a bit of a desert but that should give you no problem, a great big girl like you. It's the fliers and the hidebehinds that will do *you* in. Now then, why don't you get started and leave me alone? I've been more than cooperative.''

"You've been more than evasive," Rusty countered. "But I suppose if you're not to be cured, Bronwyn, you're not. Loefwin will be glad of that at any rate.''

Belburga had momentarily forgotten that aspect of her daughter's argument. "Very well. You've made your point and as both Loefwin and Droughtsea are incompetent fools, I suppose there's no other way. But if I give Her Highness here the seven-league boots so she can go to Miragenia, you must promise to trouble me no further about the matter. I don't want to see you, her, or those other grubby urchins ever again or I will expose you to Loefwin for the cheap witch you are if it ruins us all.''

Bronwyn had been traveling alone half a day when she remembered the advantages of having companions. Carole might get cross, but her magic had provided the fish. Rusty had raided the kitchen while her mother was fetching the boots, but a crock of porridge was hardly enough to satisfy the appetite worked up by seven-league walking. Bronwyn had eaten all of it within the first two hours. She missed Jack sorely too, and wondered what he would think of her just taking off like this, without him. Rusty hadn't given her the chance to say goodbye—she was afraid her mother would change her mind if Bronwyn wasn't ready when the ogress returned with the boots.

Walking in the boots was a chore all by itself. Bronwyn was used to being tall, but it was alarming how each step picked her up off the ground, carried her over seven leagues of Frostingdungian forest or barren foothills, and set her down again, sometimes rather jarringly, since she couldn't see through the trees to where she was setting her feet down. She kept to the uninhabited lands for fear of stepping on someone and crushing them.

The boots were Argonian of course, of elvin manufacture. Belburga had gotten them from the bandit who had deprived Loefwin of them. Where the Emperor had acquired the boots and why hc, who claimed to despise magic, had possessed them, the ogress hadn't bothered to explain. The upshot was that the boots had been left with her, since the bandit who had taken them was a werewolf and had no need of such things. When Loefwin had spirited Lily-Pearl's mother and sister away with him as well as Lily-Pearl, Belburga had somehow felt the boots might come in handy. She said she now wished she'd thrown them in the moat, but the Tape couldn't be trusted not to carry tales.

But Bronwyn was glad Belburga hadn't tossed the boots, cramped and uncomfortable as they were. They took her very quickly across Loefwin's miserable domain. So quickly, in fact that she created her own wind. Mistress Raspberry had fortunately remembered that winter was on its way, and had loaned Bronwyn the olive cloak, for which the Princess was now profoundly grateful. Soon the wind she made by her swift passage was joined by a rising north wind, and the clouds conspired to form a solid white ceiling overhead.

At least the snowflakes seemed to discourage the flying monsters, and maybe the others as well. This was more than mildly fortunate, since Bronwyn had had to leave her shield behind so it wouldn't counteract the spell in the boots. She hadn't liked doing that, but then, she didn't like the thought of being a liar the rest of her life either. But when night fell and she kept jogging along, far too excited and also too cold to sleep, she was unmolested.

By the time she reached the foothills it was morning. Both the hills and the mountains beyond were covered on the Frostingdungian side with a light coating of snow that indeed made them look exactly like frosted dung heaps. But one more step took her to the other side, where the mountains were clear and the cloud cover lifted to reveal sky of an unexpectedly harsh hot blue and leagues of stony hills followed by leagues more of rock and sand. Bronwyn stepped out onto the sand and suddenly felt she could not possibly take another step. The swift change from cold to heat wearied her more than her march. Hoping that being free from the Frostingdungian forests meant she was also free from the denizens of Frostingdungian forests, she flung herself onto the sand and fell into an exhausted sleep.

She dreamed home wasn't there any more—that the palace, the city, the shipyards, were all just empty shore with nothing but the wind-tossed waves touching a weed-grown rocky beach. She saw herself running, looking for anyone, but she couldn't seem to find her parents or Uncle Binky or Jack or Aunt Maggie. Once, though, when she called and called, she heard a laugh behind her and turned to see Docho Droughtsea snapping the thongs of his senyaty between his fists.

The dream was so upsetting she woke early. She was sweating beneath the wool cloak, and she ached all over, but she was very glad to be awake for all that—until she looked around her, and began to wonder if she were truly awake after all.

Her sword was still buckled to her side and the boots felt welded to the skin of her swollen feet. But the entire landscape had changed. No mountains, no foothills, no rocks—just sand.

118

She wasn't even sure in which direction the mountains lay. She stretched her legs and instantly was transported, horizontally, many sand dunes from where she woke up. What in the Mother's name, she wondered, then realized that she must have been really running, or at least moving her feet, in her dream, and that the boots had carried her forward just as if they'd been flat on the ground.

She was terribly thirsty too, and when she tried to stand she found it was more than she could bear. "There's no one around out here," she told herself. "It will be perfectly safe to remove the boots while I rub my feet and let the swelling go down."

And though the sand was as hot as a dragon's breath, the easing of her toes made it bearable. It felt so good, in fact, that she thought she might just go back to sleep again, with the boots tucked safely under her head instead of on her feet where they could hurt her and wander off with her when she wasn't looking. So she slept. When she woke she was understandably vexed. Even when she wasn't wearing the boots, the stupid scenery wouldn't stay put!

Docho Droughtsea listened with his usual sangfroid to the ogress's rantings. He didn't mind listening to her. He found her most attractive when she was being her natural, undiluted self.

"Imbecile!" she shrieked. "Because of your incompetence I've been humiliated and disgraced by my own ingrate child! Do you realize you have made me disclose an important business connection, not to mention that in doing so I have very nearly been exposed to that namby-pamby Loefwin as a trafficker in magic?"

"Tsk, tsk," the Duke said without any sympathy whatsoever. "I don't see what you're complaining about. You're not the only one who knows about Miragenia—your daughter would have found out sooner or later. And who knows when, or in what condition the Argonian giantess will return from there?" He yawned deeply and sprawled beside her on the brocaded couch where she had remained, ostensibly half fainting with shock and dismay, since he'd first answered her summons. "Besides, you won't need to worry about who Loefwin fancies soon. You'd better keep that washed-out witch he's married to now out of sight for awhile."

"Why, whatever do you mean?" she asked, scooting over to make room for him and batting her spiky lashes flirtatiously. He really did prefer her in a temper.

"I was just wondering whether it really made any difference to you which of your daughters was Empress?"

"You surely don't mean that poor frog Daisy's married to is planning—?"

Droughtsea nodded. "With my help. We agreed a pragmatic woman of your talents might be of great use right now. Though, if you choose to remain loyal to Loefwin—"

"That milksop! Not very likely. But where, my dear Duke, do you come in?" She arched her neck in what she hoped was a winning manner, and several of her wrinkles smoothed themselves obligingly.

"I expedite matters, you might say, dear lady. Like yourself, I have certain unsuspected talents—" He frowned. "I have one less since I broke my sword on Her Highness's shield this afternoon. That sword had special—er—properties. It will cost you dearly to replace that, madam—since I attempted to do away with the girl at your bidding. I have nothing against her myself. She'll make an excellent hostage in fact."

"Ah! Yes, I do recall Ruby-Rose mentioning that your sword shattered—be wary, Docho darling," she said, and he noted with amusement that their intimacy was growing by leaps and bounds. "My daughter may be a snip but she knows magic when she sees it. I hardly think it discreet of you to wield a sword of power in her presence."

He rose and bowed. "I wasn't wielding it so much as breaking it, actually, but I'll heed your warning. *And* put your troublesome daughter where she can do us no harm."

"And those other awkward brats as well. I don't care if you feed them all to Daisy's monster."

"Consider the matter attended to," he said, reassuringly if vaguely. He had neither the time nor the inclination to discuss with her the plans he already had for the Argonians, but in this magic-poor place, he had no intention of unnecessarily wasting all that talent.

Carole sat on the edge of the fountain and fumed while Anastasia zoomed around the statue of the octopus spouting water into the pool. The nerve of Bronwyn to just run off without them after they'd come all this way to help her. If Rusty hadn't been considerate enough to tell them what had happened they'd have both been beside themselves with worry.

Not only that, but it was incredibly dreary in this gloomy castle. How she ever could have thought it beautiful was beyond her. Guards stood at practically every doorway, forbidding a person to go anywhere. You couldn't go out into the city because you had to get across the drawbridge and past the officious Tape to do that. And now it was blowing snow outdoors and too cold to make expeditions to ajoining buildings inviting. Without even a tasty dinner to look forward to, it was almost too much to be borne. The only useful thing she could think of to do was sit here and keep Anastasia company so someone didn't snatch the swan up and eat her. Carole had to admit, if she hadn't known Anastasia's true identity, the bird would have looked tempting by now.

Jack entered from a side corridor, not the one leading to the great hall or the wing in which their party had been quartered. He looked disconsolate and somewhat unfinished, as if he needed someone tall looming over him to complete his appearance. He carried Bronwyn's shield hooked over his left wrist, and held it on his lap as he sat down beside Carole.

She patted him awkwardly on the shoulder. "Rotten trick, wasn't it?" she asked in a comradely fashion, then added reasonably, as much to herself as to him, "Of course, I'm sure Rusty wouldn't have sent her off if it wasn't fairly safe, and one could hardly expect even Bronwyn to walk to that Miragenia place in seven-league boots while carrying us piggyback. It just seems pretty poor that she didn't bother to say goodbye."

Jack asked irritably, "Why do you dwell on these matters when I know as much of them as you do? You insult me. Bronwyn's absence troubles me not in the least. Do you think I suffer from the want of one woman, however glorious?" He made a derisive noise to show that he did not, then let his shoulders sink and nodded slightly, "But it is true that I am worried."

Anastasia stopped circling to glare at him, hissing, "Since you have just made it abundantly clear that your concern is not centered on Bronwyn, are you going to inform us of its topic or is it time for riddles?"

"I will tell you," Jack said with dignity. "For unless I am wrong about my suspicions, I am right."

"That makes sense," Carole said.

"I mean to say, if there is one thing a gypsy knows about, it is deception and alas, this time it is I, the gypsy, who have been deceived."

"You? No!" Carole said encouragingly.

"Me, yes," he acknowledged soberly. "The Duke of Droughtsea said to me last evening before dinner when I was making a little tour of the castle (strictly to acquaint myself with its structure, you understand, in order that I would not become lost) that I must leave a certain tower room at once, because it was the

121

treasure room and I, a stranger, was not allowed so close. So naturally today I went back to the same room when I was sure he was occupied with Rusty's ugly mama. It is nothing but a bathing chamber! A servant was cleaning it and left the door open. I could see inside most clearly. No jewels, no monies, no valuables of any sort. Very disappointing. Not only, you understand, because there was no treasure after all but also because,'' he looked very offended at this point, "a nobleman thought he could get away with telling an untruth to a gypsy.''

"Well, I could have told you he isn't a very trustworthy person,'' Carole said. "He looks mean. I've thought so all along: And Rusty told me after lunch today that she thinks he tried to kill Bronwyn. That was one reason Rusty made her mother help Bronwyn leave for that magic country so quickly.''

"Yes, but killing is one thing. Lying about a bathing chamber is something different. He can have no reason to lie about such a thing.''

"I don't think old Docho needs a reason to be sneaky and rotten,'' Carole said, tossing the top of a decapitated flower into the pool. The flowers weren't even real. They were made of some kind of cloth.

Anastasia craned her neck over the edge of the fountain and asked, hissing as viciously as Carole had ever heard her hiss, "Docho? Is this Docho a Bintnarangian mercenary?''

"Oh, I don't think so,'' Carole said. "He's a Duke—the Duke of Droughtsea, I believe. But as we've been saying, he is not a very savory type.''

"Ah, if only I could have been spared this! It can be no other, and if he is here, all is lost. Oh, Carole, Carole, why did you not tell me of this sooner?''

"Sorry. If I'd known you wanted a guest list, I suppose I could have asked Daisy.''

"You never tell me anything! It is because I am a swan, is it not? The unenchanted are always so inconsiderate! So unkind! Whenever you have another of your own sort with whom to consult, you neglect entirely to keep me informed.''

"You're getting sidetracked—and loud,'' Carole warned her in a low voice.

Jack didn't help. "It is hard to remember you are more than a mere animal,'' he admitted.

"Docho the mercenary is part of the reason I am an animal,'' she said with tragic dignity. She stroked a couple of feathers on her back, as if considering whether to tell them more, and then

122

added, "He is also the one who sold my sisters and me into captivity."

Bronwyn had heard of shifting sands, but this was ridiculous. The vast white-crowned mountains ahead of her were not made from sand, nor was the brilliant city with its ornate arches and spires and multi-colored onion-shaped domes a sand castle. Even more to the point, the broad gleaming band reflecting the city in its green depths was certainly water. If it wasn't, she'd drink it anyway.

She didn't don the boots again, for the city was much closer than seven leagues, she was sure, so she scrunched her toes up and crabbed painfully across the hot sand for some distance. The morning sun reached the middle of the sky and dipped down again to torment her eyes, so that she sometimes couldn't look at the city or the water for the blast of brightness surrounding them. Surely her eyes were being scorched out of her head. To prevent that, she looked down at the sand instead of ahead, which was a good thing. Had she put her bare foot down in the spot for which it was headed she would have stepped on the snake.

The snake didn't seem worried about it. It didn't coil or hiss or rattle or anything like that. It raised its bright green head and flicked its forked tongue a couple of times and said in good Argonian, "Bless me, if it isn't a little girl giant! On your way to the city, are you?"

Talking swans were one thing, and she almost understood about the moat monster, now that it had been explained to her by Carole, Mistress Raspberry, Jack and Daisy-Esmeralda. But this talking snake was not possible. Actually, she wasn't sure any snake was possible. She'd seen Ollie, of course, and the Tape, and the dragons, who were supposed to be related, and also the snow under which the ice worm was supposed to sleep. But a little green snake, this size? What was it, a monster's version of a Little Person?

Whatever it was, it seemed to be expecting her to answer, so she said, "No, I'm just out for a stroll, taking in the desert air so to speak. Brisk today, isn't it?" She congratulated herself on the cordiality of her reply. Before her recent experiences, she probably would have told the snake she'd come to conquer the place single-handed and the snake would have bitten her and that would have been that.

The snake seemed to appreciate her attitude. "Sorry if I seem curious," it said. "But we don't get too many visitors out here."

"Are you from there?" She pointed to the city.

"Oh, yes. I was sunning on the wall and saw you coming and thought I'd just come out for a slither and see what you wanted. What was it again?" the serpent asked slyly.

"Oh, nothing," Bronwyn said, digging a little hole in the sand with her toe.

"Well, maybe so, but people seldom come out all this way just because they're in the neighborhood. In fact, not everyone sees the city. A person has to have legitimate business here or they never find it."

"Is that so?" Bronwyn asked, thinking that for a snake, this creature knew a great deal.

"It is. Why don't you wear your boots?"

"One never knows when one might want to go wading," she said, "so I thought I'd be prepared." It was a lie, but not a bad one, she decided. Sometimes her curse accidentally made good suggestions. The snake had evidently decided to take its slither beside her, probably to keep her under surveillance. When she finally stepped into the wide river, feeling the pleasant coolness slide like silk over her burning feet, the snake laced its way into the water ahead of her, keeping just in front of her shins.

"You're not poisonous or anything, are you?" she asked it, still worried that it might just be looking for the right moment, from its point of view, to bite her.

"Seldom," it replied, "And I assure you my intentions are honorable. I thought you might like a guide to show you through the city—to take you wherever your business must be conducted. Miragenia is an unusual place and you might easily stray."

"How can I stray when I don't want to go to any special place?" she asked. The snake didn't dignify that lie with a reply, which might have meant it was catching on to her curse. She couldn't be sure. So she asked, "Do all the animals here talk?"

"Certainly. Except a few of the very stupid ones, mostly imports from elsewhere. I was remarking to Mizmir just the other day—"

"Mizmir?"

"A dromedary of my acquaintance. This water does feel nice, doesn't it? Though not as lovely as your average sunny wall—"

"Naturally not," Bronwyn agreed. By now her entire body was absolutely awash with pleasure and she managed to stoop down a little and make the water come to her waist. Even getting her curse removed seemed poor enticement to leave the sweet wet river for the elaborate but stifling confinement of the city.

"So congenial to meet a person with the discernment to share my views on the subject," the snake said. "But I don't know if the wall is wide enough for you to have a nice stretch. The dust in the streets is lovely too, though. Follow me." It writhed ashore. Its conviction that its services as a guide were indispensible seemed to be catching, for Bronwyn found herself following it, telling herself regretfully she could come back and wade when she wasn't a liar anymore. A ruler had to expect to make some sacrifices.

But her skin burned and what had been wet dried instantly as she followed the snake to the gate.

"Since you had nothing particular in mind," the serpent offered, "Perhaps you'd care to see the marketplace."

"Perhaps," Bronwyn said eagerly. Maybe the snake had second sight. She cursed her curse for not allowing her to tell the helpful creature exactly where she wanted to go, but it seemed to be taking her in the right direction. Belburga had said a firm was responsible for the curse. A marketplace should be an excellent place to find a firm.

The snake ss'd itself importantly ahead of her for one or two paces, then said, "If I continue to slither in the marketplace, I shall no doubt be trodden upon and damaged. Have you a pocket in your gown?"

Carry a snake in her pocket? What a revolting idea! But it had been a nice enough creature so far, much nicer than some of the people she had just left, and if it had wanted to bite her, it had had plenty of opportunity before now. Truly, it would be most ungrateful to offend the little thing, so with goose pimples and ripples of low grade horror along her spine, she let it slide up her arm and into her breast pocket, near her heart. If it hit her there, at least she'd die quickly.

The snake sensed her discomfort under such intimate circumstances as it had not been able to earlier, and quickly reassured her. "I was only being cautious before. I'm not in the least poisonous. As it may have occurred to you, now that you know me better, I am a magic snake. I don't say that to impress you. Everything in Miragenia is magic. And everybody."

"Everybody?" She found that curious. In Argonia there were some magic things and some people who could practice magic, like Carole and Aunt Maggie. But by and large, everyone was fairly ordinary, though not so ordinary as in Frostingdung, where everything was ploddingly, unattractively ordinary—except the monsters, of course. Miragenia promised an interesting change.

The promise was more than fulfilled. The marketplace was unlike anything she'd ever seen in her life. In Argonia, everyone

125

appeared to be normal enough, though there were hints of the dwarfish, elvish, giantish or whatever about many of the folk and they often dressed in odd and elaborate costumes and talked strangely—though not, now that she came to think about it, more strangely than she did. Rarely would she see someone obviously magic—a tiny Little Person, a mer or a dragon. Most of those sorts of magical people and beasts required a special environment or were for other reasons unsuitable to appear in court.

But here nothing looked even remotely ordinary. For one thing, the people who looked like regular people had the irregular habit of floating about on various colored mists which covered them from the hems of the outrageous looking robes they wore on down, giving them the appearance of being footless. Also, animals walked on hind legs and people on all fours and some horses wore the heads of people and some people wore the heads of animals. Many of these beasts and people and combinations of the two (or more) also seemed either less opaque or more sparkly than was common anywhere Bronwyn had ever visited.

Not only that but a great many animals she had never previously encountered roamed the streets. One small hairy one which was vaguely man-shaped with a pushed-in, ugly-endearing face wrapped from forehead to crown with an orange bandage walked by on its hands while juggling orange fruit with its feet and waving a banner with its tail.

"What's that?" Bronwyn asked.

"Just the usual juggling monkey," the snake replied. "And not a very good one at that. He dropped an orange during the last full moon and his agents have not profited by him since."

"That *is* a shame," Bronwyn said, having no idea why such an animal would need an agent or how the agent would profit by him.

Other animals even stranger than the monkey passed them on the narrow, crowded streets of the market, which fairly exploded with noise and colorful cloths and pots and strings of things hanging and strong musky and flowery scents that made Bronwyn feel a little faint, in combination with the heat and the dust and the general unfamiliarity of everything. The snake pointed out several dromedaries, which were uglier than a Frostingdungian on a bad day. The beasts were very tall, with long faces more like that of a moose than a horse, had dun-colored coats and were cursed with pathetically humped backs. Their agents, if that's who the people fussing with them were, tried to disguise this with fancy blankets woven in gaudy geometric patterns and hung with bells and tassels everywhere a bell or a tassle could possibly be hung. One of the dromedaries carried a small pavilion on its back, and before the snake could warn her, Bronwyn, curious, pulled aside the curtain hanging from the structure's pointed roof, which was just about eye level for someone of her height. A pair of angry black eyes flashed out at her from amid billows of pleated gauze.

"You mustn't do things like that," the snake hissed from her pocket. "Come, let's go to the main market."

"In my country, snakes like you are executed for nagging princesses of the royal line," Bronwyn said.

But no matter how many stalls and tiny shops they passed, the snake wouldn't let Bronwyn watch the men lying on spikes or climbing ropes into thin air or have any other fun. It kept urging her forward to the marketplace, though she could have sworn half a barefooted league before he allowed her to halt that they had been *in* the marketplace all along.

Finally, when they stood before a shop three stalls wide and jammed with carpets, baskets, bottles and lamps of all descriptions, the snake suggested they stop, which she was glad to do. Spicy cooking smells wafted from doorways all around and it was all Bronwyn could do to keep from drooling all over the snake's head. Some of the smells were coming from the shop in front of them, and Bronwyn hoped the man who sat weaving in the doorway would think about knocking off work pretty soon and offer them something.

He seemed completely absorbed in his work, though, shifting back and forth to balance the pattern of carefully tied knots in carmine, azure and gold teardrop shapes. He had the rug about half woven, and since he was weaving on a large frame instead of the horizontal loom the weavers at Queenston usually used, his work was by now above his head, so that to reach the next row he would need to stretch a little higher. But as he reached, the rug upon which he was sitting obligingly lifted from the ground and floated a thumb's-length or so above it so the man didn't have to exert himself quite so much.

Bronwyn clapped her hands, delighted. "Oh, that's just what I need! I can never reach anything."

The man, who had a white beard and wore a blue bandage on his head with a blue jewel where it wrapped in front, turned to them. "May the Profit increase," he said politely, and waited for her to speak. Before she could, the snake crawled out of her pocket, down her arm and plopped onto the ground beside the man, who said, "Ah, Mirza, you return. Then this must be she."

127

"She is. But first, by the Profit, would you be so kind as to bring your unworthy servant his basket."

The old man bowed. "Hearing and obeying," he said, and turned away completely from his weaving, whereupon the rug on which he sat dumped him unceremoniously on the ground.

He picked himself up and ducked into the shop.

"That rug is fit only for weaving," the snake told her. "As soon as he tries to do anything else on it, it dumps him. Rebellious, unprofitable item."

The old man reappeared carrying a narrow-mouthed, bowl-shaped basket. He lay the basket on its side on the ground and the snake crawled inside, whereupon the old man set the basket upright, produced a flute from his robes and began tootling a weird tune that Bronwyn was sure would have made Carole very happy.

As the old man played, the snake undulated upright out of the basket, stretching up and up to three times its original length. While stretching, it broadened, broader in some areas than in others until at last it was as large as the old man. Then it misted all over, and when the mist solidified, Bronwyn saw that the snake was a tall bearded man and the mist was his robe. He stepped out of the basket, tripping slightly as his right foot finished forming before he quite had it free. "Blast!" he said. "Really, Uncle, we must get a larger magic basket for this trick."

"We will," the old man promised. "But you know how the overhead eats me alive. And magic baskets have gone up fantastically since the drought took the best reeds—"

"I know, I know," the nephew-snake, Mirza, replied, then bowed low to Bronwyn, making a wrist-twisting, finger-waving motion with his right hand from forehead to chest to waist as he bowed. "Great Lady, the firm of Mukbar, Mashkent, and Mirza Magicks greets you in the name of the Profit and with great enthusiasm. We have long awaited your coming."

Prince Loefrig soaked in his bath and entertained third thoughts to go with the second thoughts he had had for some time now about Droughtsea's plan for the palace coup. Using monsters seemed so repulsive. Old Fwin didn't really deserve that, even if he had gone a bit soft since his marriage.

"But how else can Your Highness hope to achieve your destiny?" the Duke had argued. "The army is his, and always has been. Nothing less than presenting your assumption of the throne to them as a fait accompli will save you from being

128

deposed before you've had a chance to mend the mess your brother has made of this realm.''

The man was right, of course. Even in this idiocy about freeing slaves, the army would support Loefwin, who had commanded it in its conquest of the Six. Everyone remembered the conquest. What no one remembered was the part Loefrig and Loefric, poor Loefric, had played, which was the greater, the more important part. While His Current Majesty had been living it up in the rape and pillage department, Loefrig had been learning the administration of the country from their father, whose health had been slipping even then. And Fric, poor Fric, had already sacrificed himself, had already played the greatest part of all in the coming of the new social order, and had vanished into self-imposed exile.

But Loefwin, when he came home with the bride Loefrig had been too busy being the real power behind the throne to acquire, and Fric was past caring about, forgot *their* part in his victories, forgot *them* entirely. He was intent only on making over the seven nations into one that would run *his* way.

So maybe monsters weren't too extreme. Still, Loefrig wished they didn't have to enter the palace through his bath. Despite the Duke's promise that there wouldn't be many, Loefrig didn't want *any* monsters or hidebehinds either, for that matter, crawling into the castle through his bath. But it couldn't be helped. Loefwin had insisted the castle be built without a cellar or dungeon, and the doors couldn't be opened without at once alerting the guards, who would take Loefwin's side. At least the guards could not obtain reinforcements—the Tape, Droughtsea's Bintnarangian pet who had so brightened Daisy's days and lent an air of sanctity and efficiency to what government Loefwin managed to do, would see to the castle's outer security. It was not really that bad a plan.

And there was a brighter side to the entire affair, besides being crowned Emperor and seeing Daisy crowned Empress. Droughtsea had promised that while no harm would come to Daisy's mother and sister, they would be taken by the monsters far, far away, where Loefrig would never have to listen to Belburga's frog jokes again. And surely, once he was Emperor, he could have the Duke build him a new bath. Smiling a faintly green smile at the thought, he rang for a slave to dry and oil him.

"I am much too well-bred to intrude in the affairs of others, ordinarily," Anastasia assured them. "But in this case, with Docho the mercenary and the Anarchy of Miragenia both occur-

129

ring within such close proximity to charges of mine, I feel I must share my own experiences of that man and that country with you.''

Carole was not reluctant to hear the swan's story. It couldn't possibly be any worse than the rest of the day. ''Go ahead,'' she said. ''Tell us how you got your curse. Maybe I'll get one myself. The Mother knows they seem to be fashionable these days.''

''It is not, strictly speaking, a curse,'' the swan informed her with great dignity. ''It is more accurately a hereditary protective spell. You see, the women in my family have always been the *most* beautiful, *most* desirable women in any realm anywhere. For that reason, Kings of the Nonarable Lands have always chosen their Queens from among my mother's people. With such great beauty, we are of course the objects of the lusts and dishonorable intentions of many men.

''My great-great-great-great grandmother, Athractisha by name, was no less lovely than the rest of us, and very wise and learned, and also rather impatient with the foibles of men. They were always asking her if they didn't know her from somewhere, which of course, they did, since she was queen at the time.

''Since the King was often away on business, and the Queen found her admirers sometimes alarmingly aggressive when her husband was gone, she devised a potion which could transform her into a swan. As a swan she would not only not be bothered by the lecherous, but could also escape them at will.

''It came to pass that the King was away at battle for her sake—one of the most ardent barons had gotten out of hand and His Majesty was undertaking the correction of the man's manners, forcibly. The Queen awaited, pregnant with anticipation for her lord's safe return and also pregnant with child.

''But the unruly baron was a treacherous fellow, and instead of staying with his armies in the field, he divided his forces, leaving half to hold the King at bay and half to besiege the castle.''

''Clever fellow,'' Jack said, rubbing his hands together and leaning forward with shining eyes.

''A cad,'' Anastasia said, tossing her head disdainfully. ''He threatened to set flame to the village beyond the castle walls and murder the peasants unless my poor relative would deliver herself into his wicked clutches. It happened that the kingdom was very short on peasants that year, what with previous wars and a famine and several bad bouts with a fatal influenza. Besides, the Queen was far too kind to allow her subjects to suffer. But she was also far too fastidious to allow herself to be ravished by her overzealous suitor—and there was the child to think of too. So she decided to try out her potion. She turned herself into a swan and flew from the top of the keep to her husband's side.

"Unfortunately, the enemy archers took it upon themselves to use her for target practice and she sustained mortal wounds which caused her to deliver her daughter prematurely and die— beautifully, of course—at her lord's feet. As she breathed her last, she regained the form of the lovely lady she had been and he recognized her and in his grief won the battle and went home and slew his enemy and had all the archers in both armies put to death. The ability of our army to raise bowmen has suffered accordingly from that day, to the best of my knowledge, to this."

"Did she pass on the potion to the girl?" Carole asked. "Because if you have some of it, I could get Granny Brown to analyze it and—"

"Of course she would not have passed it on, you silly girl. Did I not just say that she was dead? The child grew up and married outside the royal family and had many children, but only two girls. One lived happily ever after and the other, Gwendolyn the Gorgeous, encountered more or less the same situation as her grandmother. When under pressure from potential despoilers, Gwendolyn too turned into a swan, but did so spontaneously, without the help of the potion. Unlike her grandmother, she remained unharmed and married her true love while she was still in swan form. As soon as they were married, and she safely under his wing, so to speak, she reverted to her rightful self and they lived happily ever after."

"And the same thing happened to you?" Carole asked, lying down beside the pool. "All except the happily ever after part, I mean. I guess we just haven't gotten that far."

"Not quite the same thing," Anastasia replied. "In my generation, the spell seems to be more eager and actually rather presumptuously possessive. It did not wait until actual danger was upon us before effecting the transformation. One minute we were combing our hair and the next, you might say—zip—we were flying. ·Not that I was in an entirely rational state at the time of the transformation, you understand.

"My father had seen to it that the seven of us were in a state of distraction from worry, so far had he built up in our minds the bestiality and loathsomeness of the most persistent of my suitors. I was frantic that I would have to marry this so-unsuitable person, and my sisters, who were all younger, were terrified lest I

131

refuse him and he choose one of them instead. My father, now that I think of it, seems to have been primarily concerned that he not be called upon to produce dowries for seven daughters he would as soon have at home bringing his slippers and playing backgammon with him.

"He seems to have forgotten about the spell, or perhaps he never knew of it. He was not of the old line of Kings, you understand, and knew little of our mother's history. Indeed, I had known as little as he until shortly after my sixteenth birthday, when Mother told me all and gasped her last, victim to a fatal, romantic, and nonwasting disease.

"Father kept putting the fear of this fellow into my heart, and I in turn transmitted it to my sisters, along with the lore our mother had imparted to me. When my suitor finally entered our gates, we stood watching from the battlements. He was wearing armor, which was not a bad idea, considering my father's state of mind at the time, and when he raised his visor, we girls were all so overwrought that we could stand it no longer: most maidens would have swooned under similar circumstances—we flew."

"*All* of you?" Jack asked.

"We always did everything together," Anastasia said. "But now, you will ask, and this is where that nefarious mercenary steals into the picture, why did not the seven princesses wait until the undesirable prince had gone and return to their father and their natural forms? Because, I will answer, among the troops the Prince brought with him was Docho the Bintnarangian."

The swan paused and said with emphasis on each word, "He is not what he appears to be. He followed us, though we flew and he was on horseback. You may figure that one out for yourselves, but whatever master he claims to serve now, you may believe me that magic is no more against his principles than war. While we slept, he cast a net around us, and compelled us by some other warlock's wiles to transport him across the sands to the Anarchy of Miragenia, where all are merchants and magicians and any magic may be had for a price. There he sold us to a broker, who in turn sold us, with the spell that compelled us to remain beasts of burden, to a wizard who later lost us in a wager to the Brown Enchanter. Had I but known that Bronwyn's spell came from Miragenia, I would have insisted that she give up her quest."

"Why?" Jack asked. "Just because you had a bad experience with them—"

"I do not care to argue the point," the swan said loftily, "but I can assure you that in any dealings between a Miragenian

132

merchant and a second party, it is the Miragenian merchant who will profit.''

Between his worry about Bronwyn and the Duke and the flavor of the gruel or rather the lack of it, Jack could hardly eat a thing at supper. He wasn't alone. Carole picked up a spoonful of gruel, looked at it, and dribbled it back down into the bowl. Neither of them participated in the conversation around them, which mostly centered on the hunting party the Imperial Game Wardens had arranged for the Emperor the next morning.

Jack was almost relieved to be able to return to his room, although he didn't feel like sleeping. If only there was something he could do besides wait. If only there was even something enticing to snack upon while waiting.

Of course, there was one thing a gypsy could always do inside the house of wealthy people, which was to find some way to avail himself of some of their wealth.

Since Duke Docho had lied to him about the location of the treasure room, Jack decided now would be a good time to find where it *was* located. Also, he would investigate other places in the castle where he knew riches were to be found. All of those golden plates from which Locfwin's court ate its ghastly food would bring a nice price in Argonia. If he could sneak into the room of the nobles who had stumbled drunkenly to bed, he might be able to relieve them of some of their gem-studded clothing as well, although he thought he should not actually take anything tonight. No, that would not do, for where would he hide his loot? He had no idea how long he and Carole would be compelled to wait in this gloomy place for the return of Bronwyn. But a man could learn things while he was waiting.

When curfew had blown and the normal noise of the castle stilled, Jack stepped into the corridor. From each side of the long hall, the flames of torches saluted each other, their shadows standing guard behind them. What were these Frostingdungians, anyway? Babies who were afraid of the dark and had to have lights burning in the halls all night? Well, why not? With its beasts visible and invisible, Frostingdung was an excellent place to encourage such fears. Certainly the lights would make it easier for visiting gypsies to scout around, though they would make hiding difficult, if he had need to hide. He was not such a fool as to imagine the people within the castle were all or even mostly friendly towards him and his friends. Not at all. As a matter of fact—he ducked quickly back inside the room and picked up Bronwyn's shield before ducking out again—the buckler would be a reassuring item to have at hand. Surely it would protect him as it did Bronwyn, and even if it did not, it would make an excellent platter should he be able to pilfer a half-edible snack while auditing the kitchen.

He walked unmolested down the corridor, a vague sense of unease, of wrongness, causing him to keep the shield firmly in front of him. Perhaps the novelty of doing his reconnaissance in the full light of the torches accounted for his nervousness, but at any rate, he thought he would first make for the kitchen, and then if anyone should surprise him, he would have a good excuse to be abroad.

The kitchen was beyond the great hall, in back of it. Unlike the corridors, the great hall was lit with only three torches and one candle in its death throes. But the light was sufficient for Jack to see that he was to be foiled before he started. The place was inhabited.

Carole woke all at once, fully alert and listening. Her chest was tight with alarm and she felt as if her hair stood straight up, like antennae on some bug or the whiskers on a cat, quivering to pick up a hint of the danger that had awakened her.

For it was danger, she was sure of that. She'd heard a smothered scream in her sleep, and had dreamed it was a fox. But when her eyes flew open and she lay tense and waiting upon her bed, no trace of the scream lingered in her mind or in the air. She tried to will herself to relax.

But she felt too tightly tuned, as if she'd snap apart if she just lay there absorbing the tension. She jumped out of bed, hugging herself and dancing on the cold stone floor a little as she fumbled for her tunic. That was when she heard the second sound, a soft scraping, a faint susurration.

She ran to the door and pulled it open and looked down the corridor. A wisp of something rounded the corner at the end of the brightly lit hall, several doors down from her room. The wisp disappeared in the direction of Anastasia's fountain. The other turn led to the great hall, and now she definitely heard noises from there too. She didn't really want to investigate, but she didn't want to be murdered in her bed either. She thought she'd better wake Jack. That way at least there'd be two of them to get into trouble. It felt funny out here, weird. Maybe weird feelings weren't supposed to bother witches, but she was still a girl. And besides, anybody would be scared. Even Dad. Even *Mama*.

So she set her shoulders and walked in the direction of Jack's room, which was straight ahead and to the left. She thought she'd much rather have Bronwyn along, with her sword and shield and big, sheltering lump of a body, but Jack would have to do.

She took two more steps. They didn't take her as far as she expected. In fact, she wasn't moving at all. It was as if someone had grabbed the tail of her gown and was pulling her back. She took two more steps and stayed in the same place. I must be dreaming, she thought. All right then, I'll dream my way back to bed. Effortlessly, she turned and reentered her room, which was, after the brightness in the hall, suddenly alive with darkness. Her bed was tucked impossibly far back in the shadows, and seemed to be waiting for her, a baited trap. Whatever was in the halls was no dream, she was sure now. Law against magic or no law against magic, that hallway was under a spell.

She opened the door again and stepped out, this time trying to go the other way. Ten paces without leaving the threshold of her room annoyed and frustrated her sufficiently to cause her to jump around and try to run in the direction of Jack's room again. No luck. She felt like screaming, but the scream stuck in her throat and she swore softly instead, using a wicked blasphemy for which Mama would have washed her mouth out.

She stood shivering, not entirely with cold, and tried to think what to do. She hated being herded back to that bed, to the Mother only knew what slimy, creepy, reaching things that might be waiting to kill her in terrible ways like gouging out her eyes and dismembering her or—stop that, she told herself. You're just making it worse. But repulsive creatures wreaking painful and messy mutilations on her helpless body kept flashing before her eyes and she could not talk herself into going back to that room and getting into that shadow-shrouded bed. But on the other hand, one could hardly stay here all night. She tried to cry out again, not a curse or a scream, just a rather strangled call. "Jack? Jack? Ca—can you hear me?" There was no answer.

Vaguely she remembered Daisy telling Rusty when the four of them had first arrived that they would have the wing pretty much to themselves, since only two other guests would be staying there. Rusty's room was between Carole's and Jack's. Odd that Rusty hadn't heard the commotion and come out to investigate herself. Carole hadn't especially wanted to awaken her, since grown-ups tended to pooh-pooh the kind of feelings Carole had now, but recalling the toothy look on Rusty's face as she'd stared down into the hole full of hidebehinds, Carole decided that for an adult, the lady might not make a bad ally after all.

But calling Rusty's name produced no better results than calling Jack's.

Well, maybe her calling had fooled whatever was restraining her into thinking she'd given up. She charged towards Jack's room again, and again swore roundly as she stayed within the frame of her own door. The swearing felt so good she repeated it, nothing terribly blasphemous this time. "Damn, damn, double damn, triple damn. Damn!" It formed a sort of syncopated rhythm, and she repeated it several times, then dropped the words and hummed it. It had a galloping sound to it. She kept humming and tried once more to get past her own door, skipping to the sound as if she were playing horse, pretending to gallop. Still in the doorway. Damn, again! Surely her magic was as strong as this dumb spell. If she could dance a sea serpent and a full-rigged ship around on the sea, she ought to be able to dance her way past a piddling illegal spell. But she tried again with no better results and stopped, catching her breath and blowing out of her nose like the horse she was imitating. Once more, she thought, and I'll give up. I'll go back and get murdered, I guess.

She closed her eyes this time, and hummed her oath, and galloped forward, humming. Something rustled again, down the hall, and she thought she heard a squawk. Her eyes flew open. Nothing moved at the distant end of the hallway, but the end was about a forearm's length less distant than it had been before.

"Eh? You, is it? Does your mother know you're out, lad?" Gilles Kilgilles roused himself to ask. He was leaning heavily on one elbow planted in a puddle of wine on the table. His right cheek dripped transparent pink where it had lain in the puddle during the nap Jack had just interrupted. His Lordship appeared as well-lubricated as he had on the previous night.

"I very much doubt that she does, great lord, since she is many leagues across the sea. But I can assure you she would approve."

"Would she? Oh, well then. Glad to hear that." His elbow slid a fraction farther across the table and he sat up straighter, shaking his head and wiping the wine from his cheek.

"Why are you here so late, Your Lordship?"

"Midnight snack," the man answered, righting his overturned cup, and raising it to his lips. Withdrawing it he stared at it in distaste before turning it upside down again. "Damn poor wine these days," he said. "Worse than the other food. Doesn't last at all."

136

From the door by which Jack had entered they heard a faint scuffling.

"Big rats for such a new castle," he said conversationally, sliding cautiously onto the bench beside the crazy lord.

"Very big indeed," Kilgilles said with a wryness that was absolutely sane. "Man-size, I'd say."

"You suspect evil doings of other men even here in the Emperor's court?" Jack asked with his most boyish innocence. Kilgilles nodded. "But you are an important nobleman. If you suspect evil doings, why do you not investigate?"

Milord Kilgilles smiled. "If a man investigated every evil doing in this country, he wouldn't have time to eat—which wouldn't be a great loss nowadays—sleep, or drink."

"Speaking of eating," Jack said, "do you know by any chance where the fruit is stored?" But before the man could answer, a soft shush-shush noise whispered up the hallway, and he felt the strangest urge to leap to his feet and imitate the sound. But it stopped. "Did you hear that?" he asked.

Kilgilles deliberately turned his head and stared the opposite way. "Hear what?"

The noise started again, six beats worth. "That," Jack whispered, clutching Bronwyn's shield to him.

"Boy, I hear nothing and neither do you. I am here to win Loefwin's ear and help him turn this magic-forsaken Empire into a place at least habitable for all of us. I can't risk it by getting involved in palace intrigues or with things that go bump in the night."

"But, Great Lord, if these noises are unlawful, is it not correct for you to order them to desist in the Emperor's name?" He held out the shield, helpfully. "I have here the spell-breaking shield of Princess Bronwyn. If you hold it before us, no unlawful witch spells can get us, I think."

"You have an overabundance of imagination, boy. It is as foolish to fear magic spells in the palace of the Emperor of Greater Frostingdung as it is to fear attacks from sea serpents in trees."

The shush-shushing shush-shushed closer. The thud of Jack's heart in his ears measured its approach, and far off he heard a groan and a faint squawk.

Then, to his amazement, Gilles jumped to his feet and cried in a voice older and deeper than his own, "Coward! I should disown you!"

Kilgilles sat back down again and sighed, in his own voice. "Oh, how I wish you would," then jumped back up again and

137

commanded with a firmness that left no room for dispute, "You have been offered a thing of power as an ally. Seek out the disturbance, or I vow on your mother's head, you will never sleep or eat after sundown again."

The sternness went out of the voice, the steel out of the body, and Kilgilles dipped his head in Jack's direction and held out his hand to accept the shield. "It seems I am at your service."

"Whatever you say, Crazy Lord," Jack said, his eyes rolling a little, in spite of himself.

They crept cautiously down the hall toward the juncture of the corridors leading to the guest wing and the entrance chamber containing the fountain. Gilles seemed brave enough once you got him going. He strode boldly ahead, the shield before him, and Jack held on to the tail of his tunic so as not to be out of range of the shield's protection.

They stopped and surveyed all three halls. The darkest area was behind them, Jack noted with relief. He was even more relieved to hear Kilgilles burst into unmaniacal laughter, and as the young lord pointed down the hall toward the guest chambers, Jack peered around the man's middle to see what amused him.

"What's so funny?" Carole demanded. She looked like a demon, her brown eyes wide and staring, her hair coming out of its braids and her borrowed nightdress tangling around her legs. Her forehead gleamed with perspiration and she was panting, as if she'd run a great distance, but she made no attempt to come closer to them.

"Nothing, my lady. It is only that we are so pleased to see you instead of—" He started towards her, and Jack bravely stepped out from behind him and stopped, unable to move any farther.

"Hey!" he cried.

"I was just going to warn you not to come here," Carole said. "Now we'll all be caught. There's a spell on this hall. I was trying to dance my way out of it."

"Nonsense," Gilles said, still striding forward. "Here, take my hand. You're just frightened."

"Take my hand too, Great Lord," Jack said, "And we can all leave. Do you not see? There is a spell upon this hall, as Carole says. But Princess Bronwyn's shield protects you."

"Eh?" He looked at both immobile children and asked suspiciously, "This isn't a game you two are playing with me, is it?"

"Give me the shield and see for yourself," Carole suggested.

He handed it to her, and walked in place for a moment before he reached for the shield again. "Curious. Well, I suppose if we're to make any progress, we'll have to walk with the shield in front, touching each other, like the chap with the goose and all the children trailing behind that Teeny Fittroon used to tell me about. But you know, I still don't understand how a spell could get in here. There are iron bands all around and—''

This time the noise was not muffled. Anastasia squawked and trumpeted, and the terrified pounding of her wings rushed at them from the entrance hall, along with her human voice crying, "Help! I am being assassinated!"

They grabbed onto each other awkwardly, and charged forward in ragged unison. Their close formation made them vulnerable, despite the shield, a disadvantage that didn't occur to them until Anastasia squawked another warning.

She was perched atop the fountain, her wings fanning furiously. Bristling, snake-armed creatures surrounded the pool and the water boiled with invisibles. "Jack! Carole! Run, my friends! They have taken Lady Rusty and I am as good as slain! Save yourselves! The door! The door!" Abruptly, invisible forms obscured her.

Jack, attempting to follow her advice, forgot the spell of the guest hallway and flung himself around. No magic stood between him and freedom, just the iron-bolted door. He grappled with the lock and heard Carole scream and Gilles swear and with the eyes any gypsy worthy of being pursued by the law carries in the back of his head, he saw the monsters turn from Anastasia to attack her friends. The lock gave and he heaved, and fell sprawling into the snow. Before he could scramble to his feet, something like a bear with pincers for paws and a bad case of mange and something else like a boar with scales and a lion's mane fell upon him.

"Welcome to the Anarchy of Miragenia," the former snake said with a self-congratulatory smirk at having fooled her. As a man, he was tall and dark and had a hawk's nose and a rabbit's eyes. He had made a far handsomer snake.

"Well, that's more like it," Bronwyn said. "Do you give all your visitors such a pretty escort?"

"Your pardon, great lady, may you live forever," the man with the basket said. "But may I speak freely?"

"I should say not!" Bronwyn replied. But the man was well aware of her curse, as he ought to be, since he was, she was now certain, one of the people responsible for it.

"Thank you. Know then, that even were it not for your noble birth, lofty stature and astounding beauty, we should have sent

139

an escort to guide you to us. For if we have provided you with a curse, you have likewise provided us with one.''

''Me?'' Bronwyn asked, very pleased with the idea of her cursing someone else. ''Well, yes, actually, I do have these secret powers—''

The serpentine Mirza bowed again, ''What my uncle means to say, great lady, is that you curse us in that you are obviously a dissatisfied customer—''

His uncle directed a cuff in the general direction of the lower wrappings of the nephew's head bandage. ''Fool! It is not for you to interpret to our guest what I say. Have you such a short memory that you fail to recall that it is not she who is the customer? She is rather—'' He paused, pulling his stringy beard while puzzling over how to express himself. Then, fanning his hands outward in a gesture that requested acceptance of the inevitable realities, he said, ''You are, dear lady, in a manner of speaking, returned faulty merchandise. We at Mukbar, Mashkent and Mirza Magicks are proud of our long and illustrious reputation, and the quality of our work is guaranteed. That is how we have managed to maintain our success for fifteen centuries. We should have been devastated had you chosen to go to one of the gouging purveyors of shoddy goods who unfortunately are able to exist in this, our noble Anarchy, as well as honest merchants like ourselves. We wished to help you personally with your problem and thereby back up our product. That is why Mirza donned his alternate guise and provided you with an escort who could charm and amuse you, while steering you safely past those dishonest sellers of items of no worth.''

''Do you understand now, great lady?'' Mirza asked.

''Perfectly,'' Bronwyn said. ''I suppose now you will send me back for retooling or whatever the proper procedure is for dealing with faulty merchandise? Perhaps you can replace me with a changeling and my parents won't know the difference.''

''Your Highness jests,'' the old man said. ''As you well know, there is nothing wrong with Your Highness but an insignificant curse, purchased from my incompetent nephew a decade and some years ago by an old customer of ours. The fault lies not with you but with the curse. When this imbecile had it created, he neglected to include the specifications for release from the spell. The inclusion of such a release is, as any performer of card tricks knows, implicit in the structure of the central spell. Most magic items must be limited to three uses, likewise the term of service of a djinn. Other spells revert with a kiss, the last stroke of midnight, or during the dark or the full of the moon. It is essential to have these clauses," the old man said, looking pointedly at Mirza, who attempted to look shamefaced. "Otherwise the power is endlessly drained by obsolete spells. The omission of the formula is a sin before the makers of magicks and a serious commercial error—and reduces the longevity and durability of the spell. You understand, we are men of manifest integrity and commercial dignity in this house or we would not admit this to you."

"I'm thrilled to hear it," she said drily, a tone which was not at all difficult to achieve since she was so thirsty her tongue felt like a pillow stuffed with straw.

"We naturally are prepared to do whatever we can to remedy the matter," Mirza said.

"Please don't trouble yourselves," she said, though inside she was desperate to ask what they meant—"prepared to do what we can." What did that mean? If they hadn't made the curse right to begin with, could they just take it back and fix it? Somehow Mirza's tone didn't promise quite that much. What then? Was she stuck with leaving as she'd come? Had she braved the perils of the desert and seven-league blisters just to go home lying again? They couldn't do that! It couldn't be true. She wanted to demand answers, but they had cursed her too well.

"Never mind about me," she said bravely, "You needn't feel obligated on my account. And don't worry about your reputation. I'd never say a word."

She would, but no one would believe her—she knew she wouldn't be able to resist trying to tell people about the monkey and the snake and the dromedaries, but she also knew that everyone would laugh at such tales. She couldn't even tell Jack and Carole about Miragenia so they'd know what it was truly like, with its dust and heat and perfumes and cooking smells and the way the sounds all blended into a roar in one's ears and the colors that all shifted to a blur in front of one's eyes till one's gorge rose, hot and acrid at the back of the tongue, and the special Miragenia spell that made the world start whirling and the ground rise up to meet—

"Catch her, son of a she-donkey!" the uncle cried, springing forward himself as Bronwyn crumpled to the ground.

"Surely she will crush me if I do," the nephew protested, and indeed, already he was too late for the Princess lay as peacefully at their feet as if she were in her own bed.

"Unconscious giantesses on the threshold are bad for business," the uncle said.

"But it would be one way out of our dilemma if she were to

die," Mirza pointed out. Not that he would have dreamed of harming the girl, but if she should conveniently choose to pass into genteel nonexistence rather than cause them further problems, surely her demise would be to the Profit of all. On the other hand, she was a pleasant child and would be a woman worth trading one's entire harem to possess when she was grown. They had seen the sand blowing hotly in her wake all night long as she marched toward them, even in her sleep, and her lies were most entertaining and charming. Perhaps if she could not be cured, she might consider the possibility of becoming a merchant? In her present state, she possessed excellent potential.

"Is it not odd," he asked aloud, "that a nobly born girl should travel so far alone and girded for battle? Is this a custom of her country, Uncle?"

Uncle Mashkent shook his head, and walked from one end of the girl to the other, as if pondering how to lift her without rupturing himself. "It comes to me that she travels thus to protect herself from those who would slay her because she is accursed, and also because she is of a warrior line. What was it she called herself when we observed her in the pool when first the ship landed the four wayfarers in Suleskeria? Wind—"

"Wyndy," he said. "She said she was Wyndy the Warrior. But that was not the name I gave the gremlin when I charmed him into the magic box."

"There were one or two other important things you failed to give that gremlin, and no wonder. If you cannot remember the true name of the Princess Bronwyn Rowan even after you have contributed to what most certainly will be her ultimate destruction, how can you expect your minion to do so? This Wyndy is obviously a diminutive, a nickname. Now stop distracting me with your ignorance and help me roll her onto the weaving carpet, so that we may remove her from the heat of the sun."

"Yes," Mirza agreed, sighing as he pulled Bronwyn to one side while Uncle Mashkent tucked the carpet under her as far as it would go. This was the standard procedure for transporting unconscious ladies in carpets, and Mirza scarcely had to think as he assisted, though the lady's size made the transfer to the rug somewhat more awkward than usual. "It is too hot for our little Wyndy, I fear. Perhaps a seedcake and sherbet by the pool—"

Uncle dropped the girl's feet and stared at him. "What did you say, inept one?"

"I but commented on the heat of the day and suggested refreshments might—"

"No. You said hot, wind and seed. Very significant words—

very portentous. Ah well, it is said that true wisdom flows from the mouth of simpletons and now I believe it, though I too knew there was a sound business reason for appeasing this one beyond our usual policy. She is the one! She has come at last! Our Profit is assured!''

"What—?'' Mirza was baffled, but his uncle motioned him impatiently to pick up the carpet at Bronwyn's head and straighten it, which he did. They led the girl-laden rug inside the shop, where it knocked over several copper pots and unrolled a bolt of cloth suitable for making cloaks of darkness. Mirza opened the door in the back of the shop that led to his uncle's home, and they carried her through the doorway from the dim crowded store into a yard full of birds and flowers and a clear, still pool of water the color of the finest turquoise stone. With a reverence usually reserved for strings of cash, Uncle Mashkent bade the rug to settle down with its burden.

Facing his nephew with a satisfied smile he said, "Do these words mean anything to you, foolish one, or do they not?

" 'When the hot winds of war stride across the desert and blow away the seeds of disenchantment, then shall prosperity come to the tent of Mashkent.' "

"Uncle, you've been using oracles again!'' Mirza scolded, wagging his finger at the old man over Bronwyn's body. "That practice is only to their profit, you know, and not to ours.''

"Not in this case, boy, not in this case.'' Mashkent clapped his hands imperiously and a hireling scuttled forth, bowing with the prescribed humility—ten gold pieces a year's worth of humility, to be exact. For fifteen, one purchased a hireling who would do a full genuflection at each encounter, but Mashkent considered this a waste of money. "Revive the lady and amuse her.''

"Amuse her, great one? What is—er—her pleasure?''

"How am I to know? We've just met. But she is an illustrious personage. Show her my nightingales, show her the—show her the pool. That's it. Let her select a vision from the pool, and put it on account for her. Perhaps in that way we shall learn her price.''

"Her price?'' Mirza was baffled. "Uncle, didn't you say we had to give her a remedy? What is this talk of price?''

"Come,'' Mashkent said, and smiled into his beard.

143

Chapter IX

"So good of you to come," Docho Droughtsea said as the three new captives were indelicately unloaded into the cavern beneath Prince Loefric's private bathtub. "I suppose you're wondering why I've asked you all here—"

"Spare us the rhetoric, please, Milord," Rusty said. She sat, apparently unhurt, with her back against a dripping river wall.

"*I* was wondering, Your Grace," Jack said sincerely. He always wondered about things like being attacked in the middle of the night by monsters in supposedly monster-proof castles.

"I thought you would be. I've had you brought here to offer you a unique business opportunity." He clasped his hands behind his back and tried to pace the water-slick floor of the cavern. A pair of torches wedged in cracks in the glitter-speckled rock walls showed a narrow spring bubbling along the length of one wall. It was fed by the waterfalls, ranging from rivulet to stream-size, which wandered down the walls like stragglers late to a meeting. Droughtsea looked appropriately sinister, his face lengthened and shadowed by the upslanting light, so that the outthrusting shelf of his brow veiled his eyes, except for an occasional flash of reflected light. The monsters huddled well away from the torches, and muttered and snarled among themselves as Docho talked. They seemed to be afraid of him.

"Business opportunity? Is that a new euphemism for being unlawfully imprisoned, Your Grace?" Kilgilles asked. His sword had been taken from him, but Jack noticed the shield was propped against his knee, its device too deep in shadow to be read.

"Always leaping to conclusions, you Suleskerians," the Duke chided. "*I* wasn't going to discuss this with you until afterwards. It was your decision to leave your rooms and go wandering despite the deterrent spell I had cast on the corridors to and from the bedrooms to prevent just such interruptions. How did you get past my spell anyway?"

Carole carefully avoided looking at the shield, which Jack saw that she too had noticed. "I broke the enchantment with a spell of my own. We heard noises—"

"Hmm. I'll remember next time to bring a pall of silence with me. Thank you, young lady. You're already proving my instinct to keep you intact was a wise one, despite Dame Belburga's protests to the contrary."

"Mother!" Rusty spat. "So she's behind all this!"

"No, no, Milady. Far from it. Oh, not that *she* doesn't think she's behind it, but what she thinks is of little consequence. In reality, she is a small part of the plan, as you are and as is Prince Loefrig. You see, after a long and fruitful career as a soldier in the employ of various magnates, I have decided that I am wasting my talent working for others. I have decided to branch out, to use my many talents to go into business for myself. I am, after all, the grandson of a Miragenian djinn, and I trust I do not flatter myself to think that I have inherited the Miragenian genius for administration and the intricacies of commerce."

"Is that where you got your spell?" Mistress Raspberry asked. "From Miragenia?"

"Originally, yes. In the course of my service to the Frosting-dungian Princes, I was called upon to perform a task which has regrettably alienated me from my Miragenian contacts, but fortunately I have a modest backlog of merchandise I acquired in trade with that remarkable land prior to the divergence of our interests. But enough about me. I'm sure you're anxious to know what is in store for you in this dynamic new venture."

"Yes, pray do tell us," Mistress Raspberry said. "We're simply—you must pardon the expression—dying to know."

"Do not fear, my poppet." The Duke smiled. "You won't be harmed unless you prove unreasonable, and I'm sure you, as Belburga's daughter, are far too bright for that. Of course, you can't really begin work until after the preliminaries have been taken care of. While Loefwin remains alive and in power, I cannot afford to trust you not to sell out to him and betray me—naturally you would. I'd do the same thing in your place. But tomorrow night—no, tonight, I suppose it is!" He clasped his hands together happily. "So close! Tonight, when the Prince and his hunting party are slain by my servants outside the castle gates, I shall put Loefrig on the throne, with myself as his chief adviser, for the time being at least. At that time it will be in your best interests and mine for us to join forces. Until then, I'm afraid, you must consider yourselves not imprisoned exactly, but under detention."

"Aren't you risking quite a lot by telling us all this ahead of time?'' Kilgilles asked. ''What if we escaped and took this plan of yours to Loefwin?''

''In another hour or two that will be impossible, since Loefwin, his personal bodyguard, and the game wardens will scamper off on a merry hunt, far from the confines of this palace. Besides, why should you wish to betray me? You three,'' he said and indicated Jack, Rusty, and Carole, ''are Argonians, and uninvolved in our political fortunes. While I can understand that you, Milady,'' he said and nodded to Rusty, ''might have some personal feelings connected with the Empress, I assure you that both she and your mother will be perfectly safe. The delightful Princess Daisy-Esmeralda will replace her. I should think your own fortunes under such circumstances will change very little. As for you, Kilgilles, if rumor about you is true, and I don't see how it can be otherwise, you have every reason to despise Loefwin and to wish to aid me in establishing my new regime, where with the help of our esteemed foreign colleagues magic will once again flourish within our borders.''

''I beg your pardon, Your Elegance,'' Jack said deferentially, ''but as one man of the world to another, I must ask what is to be our reward for aiding you?''

''I knew I could count on you to understand, my boy, from the first time I found you lurking outside the door to the bath. Your people are known for their astuteness. Do you know there is a theory that gypsies are merely a nomadic tribe of Miragenians?''

''I am flattered,'' Jack said, pulling his forelock humbly. ''But I still wish to know about the rewards.''

''Titles for all of you, of course,'' the Duke said, ''and lands—and good marriages for the ladies, along with optimum conditions to practice your various versions of the Craft, and numerous subjects available for experimentation so that you may develop innovations particularly suited to the Frostingdungian Empire.''

''I should like to be a count,'' Jack said. ''It is my favorite title.''

''Done,'' the Duke said, ''as soon as you've earned it. Well then, I trust we all understand each other? My associates here will keep you company. Sorry I can't allow you any light, but they rather dislike it, as you can see, and until Loefwin is defeated, you understand—''

''Perfectly,'' Mistress Raspberry said.

''I have a question,'' Carole said tightly. ''The Princess Anastasia—what have you done with her?''

''The Princess—oh, the swan. I haven't done anything with

146

her, but I suppose by now she's probably hanging, developing her flavor to the fullest for the victory banquet night after next. I am so weary of roast monster, aren't you?"

Consciousness swam back to Bronwyn, a consciousness full of silvery tinkling, and cool wetness on her forehead and across her eyes, rich flowery perfumes and something cool and deliciously sweet dripping between her lips. She sat up, and the silken towel sopped in pale wine slipped from her brow, and was deftly caught by a large man with black skin and eyes and a bald head and golden ear hoops. He wore only billowing crimson trousers ending in the mist so favored as footwear by many of the Miragenians she had seen. After catching the towel, he bowed three times saying, "Ah, a great bargain it is to see you healed, illustrious lady. Welcome to the dingy and dog-dirty hovel of my master." He indicated the opulent gardens, the splashing fountains of perfumed, many-colored waters, the brilliant peacocks strutting and complaining, the mosaic tiles set in intricate patterns of intertwined blues, grays, and greens in the pathways and walls and interlaced with golden tracery. "Would it please you to eat some tasteless morsel of an inferior brand from my master's table?"

"I don't know if I could force another thing down," Bronwyn said, her dry mouth starting to water again at the thought. "But try me."

"Ah! Low sales resistance! An excellent quality in a foreign-born lady." He clapped his massive hands and four beautiful maidens of diverse coloring and costume so scanty that they made the mermaids look modest, tripped out bearing silken cushions and trays of sweetened fruits and cakes and a jug of pastel-colored drink which Bronwyn immediately seized. She wondered for about two heartbeats if she endangered her chances of leaving the city again by eating here. She'd heard of people visiting faery kin in their own country, or the underworld, wherever that was, and not being able to return home once they'd accepted food. Looking at and smelling the succulent tidbits, she decided that she didn't care. If anyone tried to stop her, she'd fight her way out. She ate the contents of four platters by herself and then reclined on the cushions, staring at the sky, while two of the servant girls fanned her. "This *is* a miserable hovel, isn't it?" she asked the djinn servant. "I don't know how you stand it—what's that?" she pointed overhead as a creature flew gracefully across the open sky above the courtyard.

"What does it look like, high-born?" the servant said.

"I'm sure I couldn't say," she said haughtily. It was obviously the most beautiful stallion in the world, as golden as the sun and borne aloft on a pair of golden feathered wings each a little longer than the horse's body.

"I mean no offense, high-born, but the creature is in its present form a flying horse, one of a race peculiar to our blessed Anarchy, and a source of great wonder and Profit to many of our citizens, my master included. However, if you wish it to be some other animal, I can easily arrange that it—"

"Don't bother," Bronwyn said quickly.

"But you must let me do something to amuse you—it is my master's bidding that you be amused. Perhaps the pool?"

"I don't need a bath," Bronwyn said. She definitely did and looked longingly at the bright water, hoping he'd insist. If ten of those girls loaned her an extra costume each, she might manage to make an acceptable change of apparel out of the various bits.

"You misunderstand me, oh highly valued one. The pool has the power to show to you in living color and two-dimensional sound any person in any time you wish to observe them. In this pool did my masters watch your approach. This great marvel can take place before your very eyes for a very small sum, and is a bargain at twice the price."

She wanted to say she hardly thought she could afford the marvel if it were free, but her curse wouldn't permit her to be so honest, which was just as well. She looked longingly into the pool. It *would* be marvelous to know how her father was faring at war. He'd probably already sent the Ablemarlonians home to lick their wounds, but she would like to see the final battle, even if she couldn't actually participate and show him what a dauntless warrior she was. If the war was already won, there'd be no need to recruit the Frostingdungians as allies, either, which suited Bronwyn fine. She didn't trust any of them.

But her wistful reflections had already activated the Pool's magic, and as the mirrored surface ruffled and calmed an image began to form.

She shot a guilty glance at the servant, but he was nodding and smiling in a benevolent way and waved a ripple-fingered wave at the pool. "Indulge yourself, dear lady. For you, my master has made a special deal, an unprecedented introductory offer to the wares of his firm. Your credit is excellent."

She didn't need further encouragement. From the clamor arising from the pool and the flashes of light shooting across its surface, she knew before she looked that the war wasn't over yet. How nice that she could hear what was happening as well as

148

see it! No doubt someone would soon say, "If only we had the Princess Bronwyn here, the day would be won!" But neither her father nor anyone in what was left of his army was discussing her. They weren't even fighting.

Instead, they seemed to have decided to go swimming in a thunderstorm. Her father, eyes red, face streaming with water, hair and beard plastered against his skull, clung to a timber bobbing madly in a churning sea. His normal ruddiness had drained away and his face was the yellow-white of a fish's belly. His chest heaved as he twisted and kicked, trying to maneuver his bit of wood around to his starboard side where a general Bronwyn recognized was unsuccessfully battling the waves. All around him other men on makeshift rafts tried to save themselves and drowning comrades. Her father stopped kicking long enough to throw back his head and scream at the sky, and at first she thought he'd been grabbed by something, but when he kept kicking she decided he was shouting orders. She couldn't hear him for the claps of thunder that kept exploding across the pool, rupturing the images momentarily with each clap.

After each clap a burst of lightning flashed, always from the same direction, and momentarily lit up the black seas and boiling clouds. During one such flash she saw *Queenston's Pride,* a magnificent new battleship her mother had christened just before it sailed. The lightning illuminated the ship in all its splendor for an instant, during which Bronwyn wondered why it hadn't taken its sails down in the face of such a storm. Then the bolt connected with the top of the mainmast, turning the mainsail into a sail of fire. In seconds, the ship was diving for the bottom of the sea.

Bronwyn was about ready to dive into the pool to help when three flares in the opposite direction from that which generated the lightning blazed across the pool and the Royal Argonian Airforce, the dragons Grimley, Grizel, and Grippledice, swooped into view, their multicolored scales undulating along their sinuous bodies like banners as they flew into the unequal fray. Abruptly, their flames were extinguished and Bronwyn bit back a cry, but the next flash of lightning showed that the dragons were unharmed and had stopped flaming voluntarily to permit them to scoop their countrymen from the sea without boiling them in the process. The great Grimley's claws gripped her father around the middle and as the dragon hoisted him aloft, Bronwyn saw what lay below them.

She thought at first the pool was malfunctioning, showing her a double image. The right side of the water showed the scene she had been watching—the destruction of the Argonian army and navy, storm clouds, lightning, men drowned and drowning, a small island around which much of the wreckage had collected and toward which some of the men were making their way. But the left side of the image showed glittering waters only slightly disturbed by the turbulence adjoining them, which seemed to be crashing most of its fury in the opposite direction, a cloudless blue sky cheerfully ornamented with a bright sun shining benignly down upon the Ablemarlonian fleet. Her father struggled to yell something to Grimley, and the dragon activated his flame and swept across the bow of the flagship as near as he dared, which was still out of range. Apparently Grimley didn't want to risk damaging his royal cargo, even when under orders. But his pass across the ship showed Bronwyn the source of the unusual weather the area seemed to be having.

Among the men who stood on the bow of the flagship was one dressed in tight red britches, wine-colored boots, and a tunic shaded from gold to rose and decorated with gold lightning flashes and silver stormclouds. The plume in the small red cap on his white hair was a rich yellow. The total effect would have been ridiculous, for he was far too old and much too ugly to carry off such finery, except for the goose-egg-sized ruby ring he aimed deliberately at the dragon and the King. A bolt of lightning jumped from the ring, narrowly missing the rapidly ascending Grimley, and sizzled into the water over on the stormy side of the pool.

A burly man with a head of dark curly hair ringed by a gold circlet patted the gaudy wizard on the back. As if he had anything to be proud of, tampering with the weather the Mother deemed it wise to send Her children! What if they melted the glaciers or froze the mountain passes prematurely? No one in Argonia would stand a prayer of a chance! Of all the rotten tricks, using a wizard with weather-controlling power to win a war. Her father would never have done that, even had Argonia had a magician with such power. It was unnatural and dangerous to tamper with something that belonged to everyone as the weather did.

The wizard shot another bolt after Grimley, and by its light she saw Grizel and Grippledice returning for more passengers. Grimley, flaming back in retaliation, veered off toward the island to deposit his burden.

Before she could see if the dragon's flame hit its mark or not, another missile plunked into the pool, this time from above rather than within it, fragmenting the picture into a thousand circular wavelets and settling in a brown lump at the bottom. Bronwyn looked up and saw twenty of the flying horses gallop airily past and beside her, the djinn swore in what she presumed was his native language and ordered one of the girls to clean the pool.

"Your pardon, illustrious one. Such indignities are the consequences of having airborne livestock."

Bronwyn wasn't listening. The image in the pool was a trick, wasn't it? It was wrong. Her father couldn't actually be *losing*—he was the best warrior in the whole world, and the handsomest, bravest, strongest, smartest King. Nobody who stooped so low as to cheat and use weather magic to wage war could beat someone like that, could they? What could the palace be like with that curly-headed king occupying the throne, using her father's room, putting his shield where the Rowan one belonged? Would he pace at night as her father did, patrolling the passages, his footsteps ringing off the paving stones to echo through the silent passages while he thought through some knotty problem? Bronwyn sometimes joined her father when he did that. She never felt that she had to talk then, and he seldom spoke but she knew he was glad she was there. What if she went home and found home wasn't there anymore—that her father was killed with all his soldiers and even the dragons. Would the palace be left standing, or Queenston? Surely even the Ablemarlonians wouldn't be so mean as to kill Mother and the new baby—Aunt Maggie wouldn't let them. Maybe they'd kill Aunt Maggie too but—nah, they'd never get past Aunt Maggie. Would they? Bronwyn focused again on the horses flying above her and wished fiercely she had one to ride home or into the battle. Before she could pick a single one to wish for, the horses skimming the extreme south end of the courtyard suddenly began rearing and stampeded back the way they came.

"Dolts! Dunderheads!" a familiar voice said. "Do not think to impede *me*! After what I have been through today, you are no more than overgrown horseflies!"

Anastasia batted at the horses with her wings as if they were exactly what she said, then circled the courtyard like a hawk. Bronwyn jumped up and began waving wildly. The bird spotted her and exclaimed. "Bronwyn! Whatever are you doing down there, my dear? I have been flying since last evening looking for you all across this dreary stretch of sand. You are simply the only one who has any sense at all and you must come back immediately and help me rescue the others."

151

The swan swooped down, making a perfect landing in the pool. Mashkent's servants discreetly vanished.

Bronwyn couldn't think how to tell the swan about the pool or the battle or to let her know that they needed to go home right away, even if it meant keeping the curse.

Anastasia wouldn't have heard what she was saying anyway. She was trumpeting insistently before she hit the ground. "Come now, we must fly to the aid of our comrades immediately. Time is of the essence! Why, I myself barely escaped with my life from an entire army of monsters, and then only because that brave little gypsy lad opened the door and endangered himself to distract my persecutors from me."

"But—"

"But me no buts, my dear child. Have I not said the situation is grave? Lady Rusty was the first to be seized, and now Carole, Jack and that handsome young madman have joined them. All have been spirited away and I fear greatly for their safety. Naturally I came to you," the swan said, fixing Bronwyn with a beady and disapproving stare. "I flew through snow and braved more monsters to reach this place where I was first bound in servitude and hoped never to see again to reach you, Bronwyn. I really think you might show more interest and enthusiasm."

The djinn servant popped out from behind an arch and bowed three times to Bronwyn again. "Is this beast annoying you, high born? Shall I have it cooked?"

"Try it," Anastasia hissed. "Bronwyn, you have fallen under the influence of cheats, liars, and profit-mongers. I urge you to fly with me now. If you will not, then I must return alone, to try to seek the help of the Emperor, though it means exposing myself as an enchanted creature."

Bronwyn looked longingly again at the horses, then sighed deeply, pulled on the seven-league boots, which had been newly polished by one of the servant girls, and started for the door. It was no good trying to go back home without the others, anyway, even if it weren't her duty as a representative of their government to protect them, which it was. While she tried to think of brave things to say about how she would rush off single-handed to rescue her father and save Argonia, she knew with a sudden sick certainty that there was nothing she could do alone and unaided that would be of any importance.

She was so distracted that she forgot the special properties of seven-league boots. She never saw the door at all, but stepped over the courtyard and six and a half leagues of desert before Anastasia could leave the ground. "Wait!" the swan cried, almost in unison with Mashkent and Mirza, who dangled a charm between them.

But all the merchants saw was her shadow and all they felt was the wind of her passing, and that of the great black bird in her wake. Mirza wrung his hands. "She's gone!"

The djinn wafted through the shop and out into the street, bowing the required number of bows in front of Mashkent, who fumed at him. "Fool! Bad buy! You were charged with her entertainment and you've allowed her to vanish, still an unsatisfied and uncommitted customer! Did I not say she was special?" But as the older man lifted his hand to strike the djinn on his bald black head, the servant drifted back, shaking a beringed finger at his employer.

"A cuff will cost you extra, oh master." Mashkent thriftily withdrew his hand, and the djinn continued, grinning through his strong white teeth, "I report the successful completion of my commission, master. I know what it is the illustrious lady desires and thereby that with which she can be purchased." And as he explained, Mashkent's disgruntlement was transformed to joy.

"Hasten, oh nephew," he said to Mirza when the djinn had revealed his knowledge and received a fat bonus in return. "We have but to make a few preparations to complete this transaction Profitably!"

Anastasia flapped furiously toward Bronwyn while the Princess dug her magic toes in the sand and waited. "I beg your pardon," Bronwyn said through teeth she was studiously not grinding with impatience. "Perhaps my impression that we are in a hurry was mistaken."

"We *are* in a hurry, Bronwyn dear, but you can hardly expect me to fly seven leagues in the length of time it takes you to take one step. I fear you shall have to go on without me, and even then we may not be in time. I overheard the Mercenary giving instructions to his creatures relative to some wickedness he has planned for tonight. Flying the very shortest possible way, it still took me most of the night and half the day to reach you."

Bronwyn shrugged, only half listening. "It didn't take me nearly that long."

"Did it not?" the swan asked, then, with a flash of inspiration. "I mean to say, did it? How did you go? Oh, never mind. You are unable to explain, I realize. However, since my flight is so much slower than your boots, and it took me the same length of time to arrive at Miragenia as it took you, I must conclude

153

that we did not pursue the same route. Perhaps if you could carry me along with you I could direct you—"

The image of herself carrying a swan who was half as large as she jolted Bronwyn out of her preoccupied state. "No problem," she said drily. "You can perch on my finger like a budgie."

"Yes, I see your point. Well, I need not actually ride upon you, just so I am attached to your person so the magic of the boots will work on me as well as you. Much as I loathe being harnessed to anyone again, perhaps we can make a lead for you out of your bodice lacings."

With fingers fumbling in haste, Bronwyn untied the leather lacing that held her gown close to her chest and tied one end around her wrist and the other around Anastasia's neck, allowing her gown to flow loosely around her calves. Then with a high heart she stepped forward, and heard a gagging behind, and quickly backstepped to retrieve a strangling Anastasia.

"Perhaps around my legs as well as my neck," the swan suggested when she had regained her breath. But even at this, Anastasia lagged so far behind that the lacing cut cruelly.

"I can tell already we're saving time," Bronwyn growled.

"I know," Anastasia said. "And the deaths of our dear friends will be on our heads. Wait! Our heads! Oh, Bronwyn, that is the answer. Bronwyn, stand still a moment."

And before Bronwyn could ask a confusing question or try to move, Anastasia had flown up and anchored her webbed feet in Bronwyn's hair.

"Ouch!" the Princess cried, bracing her neck. "You're light as a feather."

"Wait. Bear up," the swan said, and began to fan her wings in a way that relieved both the pressure and the heat of the day. "Now then, if you turn a bit to your right, I think you'll find there is a short cut across the desert."

Bronwyn set off again, and this time both she and the swan found their traveling arrangements bearable. Anastasia's wings raised such a wind that Bronwyn found she was propelled forward at double time, like a ship under sail.

For a time after Droughtsea left, while the memory of torchlight in Carole's eyes dimmed and the noise of Loefrig's specious bathtub scraping back into place faded to be replaced by the thump of her own heart in her ears, no one said or did anything. She felt only the chill of the icy sweat from the cavern wall seeping into the back of her tunic, and heard little but an occasional cough, the subdued muttering growls of the monsters, the spring whispering past, and the conspiratorial drip on one side of the cavern answered by a stealthy drip-drop on the other side. Then, abruptly, a long exasperated sigh.

"Well, *really*," Mistress Raspberry said in a voice so expressive that Carole could almost see her rolling her eyes. "What an absolute unmitigated ass that man is!"

"I don't know about that," Kilgilles' voice said. "Perhaps he's right. Perhaps this coup of his will work out for the best. Things could be worse, after all. At least he seems to mean us no harm."

"Do be serious. You surely can't propose that we concur with his idiotic plans and act as pawns for him in his overthrow of the current government?"

"It seems to me matters have been taken out of our hands, which is just as well. I don't see what you're making such a fuss about. I confess I'm rather disappointed in your naive clinging to the status quo, particularly when it isn't *your* status quo. I had thought you a more logical, intelligent woman than that. This isn't Argonia after all and I don't see what possible difference who sits on the Frostingdungian throne can make to you."

"It can make considerable difference since, as you would know had you been listening with the intelligence you question in me, Droughtsea plans to keep us in Frostingdung to aid him. Quite aside from that, there's the alliance to consider. Argonia needs help—"

"And is just as likely to get it from Droughtsea as from Loefwin. Droughtsea is a professional soldier. He enjoys war and its profits. If your King can guarantee him these, your alliance should be in no jeopardy. If you think Loefwin will aid you simply out of the goodness of his heart, think again. My father, Baron Kilgilles—" Here he paused and his voice roughened and deepened to interrupt him. "Your mother's rapist, puppy. Kilgilles was your mother's rapist. *I* am your father."

The voice changed back, not bothering to reply to its counterpart. "My father served Loefwin from before the time I was born until he died, but I've never been unaware of Loefwin's cruelty, of his lack of foresight in destroying what he sought to conquer, in obliterating what he couldn't control, or of his brutal oppression of the native peoples of the six conquered nations. Droughtsea has been his man until now, and I for one am content to allow that the less than valorous deeds the fellow has committed have been for Loefwin's sake, and not of his own volition. The man is intelligent, professional, and knows the value of a sound economy. Not particularly likable, but one needn't like

155

one's ruler to serve him. And at least Droughtsea admits the existence of and is willing to make use of magic to rehabilitate the country." His voice had risen gradually as he became more and more excited by his own argument. As his volume increased, so did the growls and snarls beyond him.

"Shh," Mistress Raspberry said. "You're upsetting the monsters." When both Gilles and the monsters had subsided, she continued in a quiet voice harder to hear than a whisper.

"Has it occurred to you that he may conclude that the use of magic, both his and ours, is legitimate in his hands but no one else's? Men of power do tend to be snobbish in that regard. At least Loefwin's rules applied across the board, though the man you represent as his professional and trusted servant has chosen to disobey those rules." Carole heard the beginnings of a protest from Kilgilles but Mistress Raspberry cut smoothly through. "Not that I find your cynicism less than understandable in view of your circumstances. I simply do not share it. I have reasons of my own to believe that Loefwin has undergone a sincere reformation of personality and truly means to improve the conditions in this country. You see, I happen to know why he has, as several of your countrymen have so astutely put it, 'softened' since his return from Argonia. I was all but on the scene of the event which changed him."

"Truly? Madam, you amaze me." Kilgilles obviously was trying to sound unamazed, but wasn't quite succeeding.

"I'd have spoken before now but the event is connected with something of a state secret. But I suppose that the secret really only concerns what came later—not the bit about Loefwin—so perhaps I won't be betraying a trust by mentioning this. When Loefwin was gravely wounded in a battle not far from my girlhood home, he was healed by a treatment of unicorn-blessed water, which, it seems, has the property—or was found to have on other subjects treated rather later—I'm traveling dangerously near to what I mustn't tell—of curing shall we say spiritual wounds and maladies as it cures physical ones."

Carole, who had been listening with intense personal interest, piped up, "That's true. My mother told me—she has a unicorn friend she sees sometimes. He watches over our river, or has one of his family do it. He's—well, if Loefwin was cured by Moonshine, I say he's all right and I wish if you grown-ups are going to run things you'd think of a way to spring us from this hole so we can help him."

"A plan," Jack added, his voice trembling with cold, "which is safe for defenseless children and will guarantee success."

"You don't want much, do you?" Mistress Raspberry asked. She sounded amused, and Carole thought that next she was going to say something like 'but I happen to have just such a plan.' Instead she said, "I'm afraid I'll have to disappoint you. I've never been kept anywhere against my will before. I was rather relying on your experience in this instance, and on yours, Carole. I may have some small contribution, but right now I'm tired, both of arguing and from lack of sleep. Since we are in a currently impossible situation, my only suggestion is that we wait until our host deprives us of at least a portion of our opposition, and until then, that we replenish our strength with slumber."

She proceeded to demonstrate by refusing to say another word. Her plan was, if not immediately helpful, at least easy to follow, and for an undeterminable number of hours Carole followed it, despite the noises of the monsters, which would have given her nightmares except that she was too tired to dream.

A sudden light, a rasping followed by shuffling paws and a gamey smell woke her. She sat up, disoriented, stiff, and sore from being curled into a tight ball. Both her hands and feet were numb. The light shone from above, where Droughtsea knelt over the hole with a torch, beckoning to the shuffling beasts, which were beginning to climb a ladder. He waggled his fingers cheerfully at his prisoners, and withdrew the light as the first beast neared the top. When the last fork-tailed and spike-humped back cleared the lip of the hole, there was a brief groaning sound and more scuffling overhead, and Droughtsea reappeared to pull up the ladder again. As he started to replace the tub across the opening, Jack jumped to his feet.

"Your Grace, wait! If you go forth into battle against the Emperor, will you not require our help as well as that of those unreliable animals?"

"I think not, young Count," Droughtsea answered. He was in the high good humor of a dog that knows it has a carcass waiting in the woods. "But I hardly need to worry about guarding my flank from my own people. I'm understaffed as it is. Your zeal will have plenty of opportunity to be tested later. Meanwhile, you won't be lonely. I've left you several companions, though you may not be able to see them," and with that he swung the tub over the hole again dousing the light.

"W—where are they?" Jack asked, sitting down again and scooting as far back as he could.

Carole felt for him in the dark, and edged over to him, ostensibly to comfort him but also because she could use his

157

body heat to warm herself. "Buck up, Jack. I can handle a few hidebehinds if they get rowdy. And we have the shield. They can't get past that either. If only we had a light—"

"But we do!" he said, patting himself, and with a slight clacking sound withdrawing something from his clothing. "My tinder and flint—"

"Isn't it wonderful what naps will do for children?" Mistress Raspberry asked. "I was quite sure you'd think of something."

"But we haven't really," Carole said. "We can control the hidebehinds if we have to but we've no way to escape from here."

"Haven't we? I wonder why Droughtsea bothers to post a guard on us if we couldn't escape otherwise."

"Is it really a guard?" Kilgilles asked. "I got the impression he was just billeting his extra troops down here until they—and we—were wanted."

"Perhaps. But that little stream may lead us out of the cavern. It's worth a try, wouldn't you say? Come on now, why don't you have a go, Carole? There's a good girl."

Wishing Rusty wouldn't treat her quite so much like a child when she was using her talent to save them from very adult dangers, Carole began whistling a jig, but had to stop almost immediately. Since she didn't know where the hidebehinds were, she couldn't focus on them, so the jig affected everyone but herself, and the others were slipping and sliding on the wet floor. When she stopped, she felt the hidebehinds closing in, menacing her from every side. They not only didn't like to dance, they also didn't like to see their charges hopping so energetically around the cavern.

"This is never going to work," she moaned.

"Wait," Jack said. "Crazy lord, you have the shield. It will protect us from Carole's magic." Everyone scrambled frantically in the dark and when the scrambling stopped Jack said, "We are ready now, Carole."

"Good. When I start again, could you try to light your tinder?"

"I have a bit of candle. I—I had planned to go exploring," he said.

"Wonderful. Just light that as soon as I start."

She whistled again, and after a few moments of the scraping of flint against tinder and heartfelt cursing on Jack's part, the tinder caught and Jack lit the candle. It made a poor feeble light but it was heartening to be able to see. She waddled forward, pigeon-toed, as she did when she wanted to be careful walking across ice. She slipped anyway, grabbing at someone's leg and jerking herself to a stop that almost knocked the whistle out of her. The effort chased some of the chill that made her feel as if an icicle had been rammed down her spine. Standing in front of her friends, with their warm breath at her back, she could still barely manage to look where she was whistling. The invisibles didn't so much hide from her as repel her eyes, as if they were always just about to materialize into something so unbearably ugly, so terrifyingly gruesome, that she wouldn't be able to look when the change came. Much of the energy she needed for her magic was consumed in shrinking from a touch that wasn't forthcoming but was threateningly close. Not knowing what would happen when the things did touch her made her all the more afraid. What did hidebehinds do to their victims after they made them disappear? Torture them? No one had said. As she whistled, the small portion of cavern illuminated by Jack's flame smudged and wavered, not randomly, as the hot air of a flame does, but in time with her music.

"Gotcha," she said, and stopped, knowing the music should hold them for several minutes after she quit whistling, since they were animate beings. Cups and rocks and other objects with no movement of their own ceased moving when she ceased a song, but animate objects were held a little longer.

She heard a rustling behind her and Rusty whispered, "Never mind me. Keep them occupied," and darted out into the light, her gown shimmering with pale luminosity. Carole, afraid the spell would wear off just as Rusty reached her quarry, refused to watch until she heard a cry, and her head turned in spite of herself. Rusty was half gobbled by darkness. Carole winced, and began whistling again. Gilles and Jack started forward, but a slim hand popped out of nowhere and waved them back. Suddenly they heard a great whoosh, like the air going out of one of the silken balloons Carole's parents inflated on holidays, and Rusty reemerged into the light, her teeth bared and jaws slightly parted.

Reaching up, she pulled at a space between her upper and lower teeth. "There now," she said, her lips relaxing over her teeth as if she'd just removed a chunk of meat from between them. "I've never fancied attending battles without being properly dressed for the occasion. I'll have some disguises from this hidebehind sample whipped up in a jiffy and then we'll see if we can get out the way the Duke's associates got in."

They had to follow close by the banks of the stream to avoid getting lost or taking a wrong turn, and even then, no one could be sure the stream wasn't branching. Jack's tinder, with nothing

159

substantial to feed on, kept going out. The cave floor slanted sharply downhill too, and the spring tumbled into occasional waterfalls, spraying droplets across the stone floor and making the footing even trickier. Carole longed to dash forward, running as fast as she could, but instead she practically had to crawl, fearing always that something would fall on her from above or catch her from behind.

They were perhaps under the outer bailey, by her reckoning, when Jack suddenly flew into the spring and vanished—all but one leg, which they only knew existed because he kicked out with it and in the process kicked Kilgilles, who had the presence of mind to grab. This awkward rescue was sufficient to cause the thing Jack later claimed had grabbed him first to release him. It was also almost sufficient to drown him, but finally, with Kilgilles' assistance and a great deal of advice from the others, he turned right side up again and sloshed back onto the cabin floor. He was unharmed, but the candle was extinguished, and the tinderbox soaked beyond redemption.

Later, they heard a rushing sound, a thump and the thud of feet over their heads, but not until they rounded another down-tilting curve and saw the faint light filtering into the cavern through iron bars did they spot the batlike creatures with the spear-shaped proboscises hanging overhead. Carole saw perhaps two hundred of them.

"Fliers," Jack whispered. "They itch you to death."

"Not if they're in here and we're out there, they don't," Rusty told him. With the light, they made their way quickly to the iron gates, and looked out—across the broad expanse of the moat, filled with the red snarl of the Great Tape.

"Now what?" Carole asked woefully.

But before anyone could answer, from far back in the cave they heard the first unmistakable rasp of the tub being pulled away from the hole.

Jack dashed back the way they'd come, but Mistress Raspberry grabbed his arm. "Before we return, we must prepare ourselves. I've made magical disguises for us from the essence of the hidebehind. Everyone take one of these invisible pellets and swallow it," and she held out little pieces of air to them. Jack stuck his in his mouth and disappeared. Mistress Raspberry did likewise. However Gilles took the pill with no visible—or rather, invisible—effect.

"Give me the shield," Carole said, tugging at it. "That's what's holding you up." He didn't stop to ask questions but took

160

her word for it, handing the shield to her, and winking out of sight as the others had done.

Carole shoved the arm strap over her wrist and plunged forward, feeling suddenly alone, though she could still hear the patter of her friends' feet ahead of her. She slipped her pellet into her medicine bag. She harbored a distrust of Rusty's spell, and didn't want to risk not being able to turn visible again. If worse came to worst, she'd take it, of course, but for now, she thought it best to trust the protective powers of the shield and the mobilizing powers of her own two feet and run like mad back up the slippery, slanting floor.

Though the space beneath the hole was empty when she arrived several bruises and a wild dash later, light still poured into the cavern from above. The ladder had been lowered again, and at the top of it hunkered a chunky form, greenish in the torchlight—Loefrig. He gave a triumphant croak when he saw her. "Aha! There you are, my gurik—girl. Where are the others?" But before she could answer he seemed to fling himself forward into the hole, hurtling past her into the stream.

Chapter X

Bronwyn missed the capital of Greater Frostingdung, stepping over it and back three times before she had the presence of mind to stumble backwards at an angle and take half a step and hop the other foot down with the first. This expedient threw her off balance and she landed rolling in the courtyard. Anastasia had disengaged herself from the Princess after the first miss and had flown the last seven leagues to the palace. Now she flapped above the Princess, hissing, "For mercy's sake, Your Highness, take off those blasted boots."

Bronwyn, only too glad to obey, sat tugging at them in the middle of the courtyard when something snagged on her foot and swore, then said in a voice very like Jack's, "Ah, my Princess, I knew you would return to save us!"

"I'll do no such thing!" she snapped, looking vainly around for him. She was already half wild with frustration and the overwhelming desire to rise and wield her sword where it most needed wielding, dispensing with this minor local dispute which had had the gall to involve her friends so she and they could move smartly along to the *real* war at home.

"The boots, boy—er—wherever you may be. Help your lady remove her seven-league boots or she will not be long for this country."

Bronwyn stuck out her feet, though she still saw neither Jack nor anyone else. She was startled, therefore, though not at all displeased when the boots were sucked from her feet as if by the wind.

"Excellent," Anastasia said. "I take it, young man, that you have some reasonable explanation for not showing yourself."

"It is my hidebehind disguise," Jack's voice said from the direction of Bronwyn's throbbing feet. "Mistress Raspberry made it. Is it not clever?"

But just then Carole stumbled out of the castle and ran toward them. "Bronwyn! You're back. The Mother be praised! I was trying to rouse someone in the palace to help us, but Droughtsea's put a sleeping spell on everybody, from the look of them. We'll have to lower the drawbridge ourselves."

"That's not important," Bronwyn told her, "Wait till you hear—"

A gargling scream rent the night. "Never mind. We have to hurry. Come on! Droughtsea and Loefrig have locked the Emperor and his men outside the palace and sicced monsters on them. We may be too late already."

Bronwyn rose, digging her fingertips into her ears and wiggling them to try to stop the popping caused by the up-and-down movement of the boots. When the background roaring in her ears ceased, she could hear more clearly the scuffle emanating from the battlements.

The few sword-bearing men-at-arms outlined in the night sky above the ramparts all had their backs to the courtyard, and though they seemed engrossed in whatever was taking place in or across the moat, they did not seem to be embroiled in warfare, or even particularly upset over anything. They rather looked as if they were enjoying themselves.

Assorted screams, cries, and bestial shrieks were suddenly interrupted by Emperor Loefwin's angry voice. "Dammit, what sort of moat monster are you, anyway, Tape? I'm the Emperor! This is MY palace! You're supposed to be protecting *me*. Let me in now! I command it!"

The Tape responded with a high-pitched squeal. Bronwyn

162

had no doubt it was citing some regulation contradictory to the Emperor's interests.

"The drawbridge, Carole!" Rusty's voice cried from the ramparts. "Lower the drawbridge! They're being slaughtered down there."

Carole tore the shield from her arm and tossed it to Bronwyn and ran, and Bronwyn, still trying to decide what was happening, scrambled to her feet and ran after her.

Rusty's voice had been heard by others as well, and several of the soldiers detached themselves from the wall and clattered down the stairs.

The pulley to hoist the drawbridge was beside the portcullis and Carole threw herself upon it, feeling in the darkness for the handholds by which it could be operated.

The door to the guard tower banged open and a half dozen men, their naked swords drawn, rushed into the courtyard. Bronwyn stood between them and her cousin.

"Your luck is ill this night, villains," she said. "For you have crossed Bronwyn the Bold. Prepare to die." And so saying she slashed—and felt a thrill and shock when her blade connected with another, and yet another, as she fought the six of them back to the wall, her steel ringing on theirs.

However, the first time her sword bit into flesh, nearly severing a man's arm, she found she had to scream her battle cry to keep from getting sick, and also to keep from watching his blood spurt. She knew that if she gave in to that sort of morbid fascination, her own blood would very rapidly join his on the ground. She tried not to think that what she was dealing her foe could very well be dealt to her—and might have already been dealt to her father.

A man on her right lunged at her with a broken spear and tripped, nearly impaling himself. He was saved by one of his comrades, who also tripped and fell against him, knocking him aside. Bronwyn thought at first they were simply very clumsy enemies, but when they all started tripping and tumbling, and when their fellows clattering from the battlements to aid them started falling down the stairs and over each other, she knew her invisible allies had come to her assistance.

Carole was still struggling with the pulley, and Bronwyn leaped over the jumbled bodies of three guards. Pushing Carole aside, Bronwyn grasped the wheel and turned hard, and it gave at once under her weight. As Bronwyn looked up, the bridge crashed down in front of her, braining what appeared to be a two-headed bear that had been about to tear the face from one of Loefwin's game wardens.

Of the hunting party, only the Emperor had been mounted, and his horse now lay bleeding in the snow. Monsters and men alike staggered, still locked in combat, across the drawbridge, while the Tape snarled itself into ever higher and more indignant tangles. Bronwyn charged the cluster of beasts surrounding Loefwin and they broke apart to face her. She cut into them with less chagrin than she had felt attacking her human foe, and congratulated herself on becoming a hardened veteran so quickly. Then Loefwin beheaded two monsters with one swipe of his sword and she abruptly turned away and searched for opponents who weren't inclined to bleed so alarmingly.

Invisible ribbons threaded through the melee, confusing the efforts of both sides. Bronwyn ignored them to slash a wolf-faced, five-armed boar savaging a game warden. But no sooner had she slain the beast than the man it had been attacking vanished, all except his sword arm, which hacked ineffectively and seemingly independently. Rusty's disembodied voice cried, "Release him, fiend!" and something gave a windy scream before the man popped back into sight.

When the next monster Bronwyn tried to engage pranced four paces back, four forward, and chased its forked tail three times in succession, and the half-griffin to its right bowed and repeated its movements, she sensed Carole's fine choreography at work. Soon she too could hear the tune but she didn't find it inspiring to her own sore feet. Carole was evidently learning to discriminate between the musical tastes of people and those of monsters, though some of the Emperor's goblinesque vassals twinkled their toes as they dashed about dispatching foes.

Bronwyn almost wished her cousin had not been so readily able to bring the situation under control, but glory must be given over to expedience under the circumstances. Sometimes even a natural-born leader had to control her lust for battle when the good of the common cause was at stake. Therefore, she didn't begrudge Carole the full use of her awesome power to turn the tide of the battle with unsporting speed. Stepping over several bodies of various persuasions, she helped Loefwin, who had been driven to his knees, rise.

Loefwin slew a couple of monsters himself, and the misshapen beasts danced but also raked and snapped, and stank as if they'd already been dead several years. Under Carole's spell, the creatures were dancing themselves to exhaustion, and were so vulnerable to the harvesting blades of the King's men that Bronwyn almost began to feel sorry for them.

Carole stopped whistling for a moment, and two of the monsters, apparently either less sensitive to music or more terrified than the others, broke and ran, waddling and howling back across the bridge. The Tape's long thin head nipped up from the moat and gobbled one of them whole. It made an unsightly bulge in the moat monster's sleek form. The other galloped through the deserted streets between the blocky, whitewashed, iron-banded houses to the outer gate. No guards manned the outer wall that Bronwyn could see, and apparently the great doors had been left unbolted, for the creature flung itself against them and they gave, releasing it into the night.

"Perhaps," Loefwin said thoughtfully, pausing before he brought his iron blade across the bulky neck of a half-bull, "we should spare these things. They're useful for meat, after all. The men who allowed them entrance are another—"

A bat-winged horror swept down upon the Emperor, stabbing with its needle nose. The Emperor's trained reflexes saved him, and he rolled aside, whereupon the flier buried its nose in the monster's neck.

Bronwyn wheeled, her shield knocking aside the nose of another just in time. She looked up. A black cloud of the fliers hung against the moon for a brief flash, dispersed, and rained agony on the exposed party beneath it, stinging man and monster alike. Bronwyn had to dodge and twist, contorting herself until she felt like a rag to keep the shield in front of her. Some of the men began bolting for the guard tower—others fell, scratching themselves so hard they drew bloody circles in the snow.

Carole switched tunes and shrilled a retreat as she dashed for the tower. The monsters, released from their previous dance, fled back across the drawbridge. Only the men remained and Bronwyn slung one of the fallen ones under each arm to lug them to safety. They scratched and writhed so pitifully that she found it impossible to carry them, so she punched each of them in the head. They straightened right out, and she delivered them and returned to the courtyard for others.

Loefwin also carried wounded from the field. The screaming, crying, moaning, and swearing were so loud that Bronwyn wondered whether the sleeping spell was sufficient to keep the denizens of the palace in their beds. And why hadn't the people in the village surrounding the castle sought to aid their Emperor? No doubt everyone knew when they were well off, and felt curiosity an unaffordable luxury.

The fliers reformed, blotting out the moon again, their spear-like stingers aimed at Loefwin and Bronwyn. Bronwyn shouted to the Emperor, who had his fist raised to knock out the victim he was trying to transport. At her shout, the Emperor looked up, and his passenger's elbow caught him under the chin, knocking him backwards into the snow.

The other bodies, which had been levitating of their own accord, dropped like rocks and Jack, Rusty, and Gilles Kilgilles appeared, racing for the fallen Loefwin. Before they could reach him, however, something flew over them so fast it blew their hair into their eyes, and the bandy-legged, green form of Loefrig hopped down beside his brother and began dragging him towards the tower.

The fliers stormed down upon them, one striking Gilles, another hitting the frog-man broadside, not neglecting to pierce him on the way. Bronwyn threw herself across Jack and Loefwin, her shield on top of them all, deflecting fliers as they charged. Gilles' cries and Loefrig's pitiful croakings made Bronwyn feel like crying too but she resisted. What sort of warrior cried in the middle of a battle? Her sort, she realized, as the tears flowed while she did her best to protect her remaining friends. She had no idea where Mistress Raspberry was, until she heard a flier scream and caught a glimpse of the lady crouched under an ornamental bench. Her pointed tongue daintily licked in a feather. But even if she changed herself into a flier, Rusty alone couldn't hope to defeat the entire flock.

The fliers regrouped for another attack, but this time when they dispersed, it was to fall leadenly to the ground, burning as they fell, till they lay like dead coals in the snow.

A clod of brown fell beside one of them, and Bronwyn looked up, wonderingly. The piece of sky they had formerly occupied was now filled with flying horses. In a thrice, these were herded to a landing in the courtyard by Mirza, Mashkent, and the black djinn with the gold earrings. Bronwyn disengaged herself from Jack and the Emperor so Loefwin could rise to greet his deliverers. Mirza and Mashkent dismounted and made their sweeping, ripple-fingered bows, not to Loefwin, but to her.

"About time you got here," she said, not ungratefully.

"We trust our arrival will be deemed Profitable to all," Mashkent replied.

Bronwyn felt oddly invigorated by the battle, perhaps another legacy from her warlike frost giant ancestors. She had been victorious in her first fray! With that behind her, almost anything seemed possible. Now she followed her father's teachings and did as he said any good warrior would do, ignoring her own compelling need to find out what the Miragenians and their flying horses were doing here and concentrating instead on evacuating the wounded from the field.

Those injured by the ordinary run of monsters or by weapons were cleaned and bandaged, while Gilles, Loefrig, and several others were mittened and restrained to keep them from flaying themselves and immersed in Loefrig's all-too-familiar bathtub for the night to soak in oil. Four men had been attacked by hidebehinds, and two of them were missing in action. One simply could no longer see his left arm, though the visible end didn't bleed and the juncture was smooth as glass and he could furthermore still feel the arm. The fourth had a see-throughish spot in his middle, and kept glancing glumly down at it. A change of shirt did a great deal to restore his spirits, the new shirt covering the transparent wound where the cloth of the old shirt had simply disappeared with the man's flesh and bone. Everyone reassured him that he was very lucky to be holding up as well as he was, considering.

The Miragenians had spread cushions and carpets around the fountain, along with trays of viands and sweetmeats and assorted nectars. Assuring Loefwin that the bill for this after-the-battle catering service would be absorbed by the firm's diplomatic relations department, Mashkent bowed to Bronwyn.

She was rather reluctantly having her feet salved and massaged by Carole, who had been enjoying herself, acting as infirmaress to the soldiers, but had decided, since she didn't want to miss what the exotic strangers had to say, that Bronwyn needed her ministrations more at the moment.

Mirza kept bowing unctuously to Loefwin as his uncle said smoothly to the company at large and to Loefwin and Bronwyn in particular, his glance bouncing back and forth between them, "Great Emperor, Illustrious Lady, please forgive our intrusion into your affairs. But when our esteemed guest left our company so precipitously, giving us no opportunity to complete the transaction we had begun, we were of course devastated. Upon questioning the servant who was placed at the Princess's disposal, we learned that the poor child had witnessed the destruction of her father's ships and the dispersion of his army into the sea at the hands of his enemies."

Carole gasped and Jack's eyes widened with alarm. He glanced at Bronwyn, who nodded sadly, but looked up sharply again when the merchant continued.

"Ah, yes," the merchant said, with hands and eyes cast helplessly ceilingward, "The Ablemarlonians unleashed their secret weapon—a renegade wizard formerly in the employ of one of our competitors, a powerful man, but without business sense. The indiscriminate changing of climatic conditions sows havoc and upsets the source of the power to the Profit of none. Under the circumstances, we naturally understand the Princess's untimely departure. Her filial devotion speaks so well for her, we could not but extend ourselves to offer aid.

"Therefore, we saw fit to consult with our senior partner and founder, Mukbar the Magnificent, may his Profit increase. With his consent, our firm has unanimously and magnanimously decided that, in view of the desperation of the situation, the lady's valorous nature evidenced by the deeds on behalf of her host, her high birth, her breathtaking beauty—"

"Her rightful claim against your company?" Carole suggested suspiciously, paying no attention to the barefooted kick from Bronwyn, whose foot was still in her lap. Bronwyn might be taken in but *she* wasn't. The news about the war was catastrophic, but she somehow felt the merchants were determined to profit by it rather than use it as an opportunity for a good deed. These people were related to Droughtsea, however distantly, and she for one didn't trust them. They might have even tricked Bronwyn with a pool that showed illusions instead of reality, just to upset her so they could cheat her.

Mashkent overrode the interruption, but hastened to the point. "It seems we can make a deal. As you have seen, we have by happy chance brought to this land our fine flying steeds, a wondrous crossbreed between the giant golden eagle and the hornless unicorn, a beast of marvelous properties, the most miraculous of which are swiftness and ferocity in battle." He turned to Bronwyn. "We are prepared to give you a chance to have your curse lifted entirely—not merely a partial clearing, you understand, but a 100% guaranteed bona fide cure *and* the use of these incomparable steeds to fly your allies here to the aid of your father. All of this we propose to let you have for the price of an insignificant boon we think you may be able to perform for us."

"Now?"

He nodded.

"Oh fine!" she wailed. "I have lots of time to go running errands." She wanted those horses badly, but what would be the point of having them if she had to delay flying to her father's assistance while she performed boons?

Loefwin touched her arm urgently. "My dear Bronwyn, don't distress yourself. If there is anything within my power that can be done to aid you, consider it yours."

Bronwyn shot him a grateful look, though in truth she had no idea how or if he might help.

Mashkent was continuing. "Now, now, my dear Princess, rest assured that we value the expediting of your mission above all things, may our dinars decrease if we do not, but this task of which I speak is urgent, under the circumstance, though it is but a small matter."

"Why is it just this one thing?" Jack asked suspiciously. "And if it is of such small value, why is it so urgent? Why can she not perform it later?"

"She may perform it later if she deems speed of more importance than supplying steeds to her allies." Mashkent bowed to Loefwin and coughed delicately into his fist. "However, either she must perform the boon at once or we can provide horses only to her and her original companions. If she elects to do our bidding later, and is still able to do so, we would even be prepared to accept alternative payment."

Mirza beamed. "Yes, a bit of Argonian real estate would be a fortunate acquisition, say, half the kingdom, or perhaps your first-born child. The promise of some such trifle would be perfectly adequate to induce us to consider letting you have the flying horses, but the curse would still be upon you, although if you could spare us half your kingdom *and* your first-born on account, we—"

"What's the boon?" Bronwyn asked flatly.

"It's nothing! So inconsequential I hate to mention it—" Mashkent fanned his brown hand dismissingly.

"A trifle, as my Uncle has said—" Mirza tried to look as if he were embarrassed to be a party to the solicitation of such a small favor.

Jack said to Carole from behind his hand, "Sounds to me as if these merchants have a worse dose of Bronwyn's curse than she does."

Mirza added, "In truth, we would never have bothered to come all this way to offer you so much for so little except that my uncle's third concubine is pregnant and has a craving for these things."

"*What* things?" Bronwyn demanded from between gritted teeth.

Mirza's hands fluttered helplessly, as if they were trapped moths. "Oh—only one thing. A—um—it's a pomegranate, actually."

169

"Is that all?" Bronwyn asked with puzzled relief. "What's a pomegranate?"

"It's nothing—a snack craved by my spoiled darling," Mashkent put in. "A little red fruit, hardened and filled with seeds. That is all. Nothing dangerous. BUT, remember what you receive in exchange—the use of the steeds for you and your allies, the safety of your kingdom, the respect of your father and your subjects, your veracity established for all time, AND as an extra added bonus, we'll agree to grant you use of the charm we've prepared to provide temporary relief from your curse at no extra charge."

"Are there any dark mysterious strangers in your plan or long journeys over water?" Jack asked with narrowing eyes, naming the old standby phony gypsy fortunes.

"What?"

"Just wondering," Jack grumbled. He too was remembering Droughtsea's description of these men. The rebel Duke's claim that they might represent the stationary forerunners of his people seemed more likely than he had first thought. Probably the Miragenians had cheated his own folk out of house and home, which was no doubt what had set gypsies roaming in the first place.

"Is this some guessing game," Carole asked, "or do we get to know where this stupid fruit grows so Bronwyn can pick you one and we can use your precious horses to win the war before both our allies and our enemies die of old age?"

"It cannot simply be picked!" Mirza protested indignantly. "Naturally, as you would expect in view of the inducements offered for it, the pomegranate of which we speak is a rather special one—"

Loefwin, who had spent the last few minutes in consultation with the Chief Game Warden, returned his attention to Bronwyn and the merchants. "Pomegranate?" he asked sharply, his voice sounding as if he thought they had said 'dragon' or 'hurricane' instead of simply 'pomegranate.' "What's all this?"

Both merchants gave him long, enigmatic looks from under their turbans and his eyes widened and he shook his head in a palsied fashion. "Oh, I say. You can't mean *that* pomegranate. See here, that's no sort of thing to send a child in after. I'll go myself, or send one of my men—"

"Your Duke of Droughtsea, perhaps?" Mirza suggested, sounding unlike either his jovial serpentine self or a bumbling apprentice merchant. He sounded bitter and menacing. "It would be unprofitable to allow you our steeds while you possess or could possess the pomegranate."

"I—er—see your point. And I admit that business was a bad move. In fact, I deeply regret it and assure you—"

"As you assured the Mages and Kings of the Six that they were to have a relaxing feast?" Mashkent asked. "No, Your Imperial Highness. Forgive this unavoidable, and I trust you will agree, understandable, breach of your hospitality, but I must tell you that your word in regard to such matters lacks value with us."

Mistress Raspberry spoke for the first time. "Besides, Your Highness, will you not need to gather an army if you're to ally with Argonia?"

"How fortunate I was to marry into a family where there are so many women ready to remind me of my responsibilities!" Loefwin growled. "Yes, I'll have to gather an army. And I'll help Rowan with magic steeds or without. I just don't like—"

But Bronwyn didn't wait to hear what he disliked. She had made up her mind. Her father must have those horses—all of them, *with* Loefwin's army on their backs. She faced Mashkent and said firmly, "I wouldn't go after the nasty old fruit for all the—"

"For the sake of the Profit, give her the blasted charm!" Mashkent cried.

Mirza fumbled in the sleeves of his robe and brought forth a nondescript copperish chain with a blue-green leather-wrapped stone dangling from it. With one of his ceremonious bows, he proffered it to Bronwyn. "Pray pass your buckler to your squire," he instructed, as she turned the bracelet over in her hand, "and place this charm upon your wrist. It will enable you to speak the truth without your accustomed cumbersome circumlocutions."

Bronwyn did as she was instructed, but wished they'd come up with something less likely to be in the way. Something like the slave bracelets would have been more functional. But the charm had the desired effect.

"Only direct me, good merchants," she began, but before she could finish saying what she meant for the first time in her life, Jack interrupted.

"Hold a moment," he ordered, laying an irritatingly protective hand on her arm and addressing the merchants sternly. "What is the catch?"

"Catch? Who is this louse-ridden lackey to speak to me of catches? Milady, control your minion!"

Loefwin looked as if he wanted to speak, but before he could Carole chimed in. "Watch who you're calling a minion, peddler.

171

Where Bronwyn goes, we go. She may not know much about magic, but I do. I got very high marks in magical ethics—well, the theory anyway, and I know as well as you do that there's a price to every spell, a cure for every ill, an ill in every cure, or it simply doesn't work. So it's only fair that you tell us—what *is* it with this pomegranate? And while you're explaining, why will we need to fetch it for you before she can be cured if this bracelet allows her to tell the truth anyway?''

Mashkent spread his hands on his knees to signify defeat. "Very well, so the bracelet grants her only the first three minutes of speaking the truth and then it is powerless. Is that so terrible? At least while wearing it she can give her word. Once she fetches the fruit, she will need no charm. As for the pomegranate, I am sure His Imperial Highness can enlighten you with far more authority than I. He was the one who loosed its powers. We merely want it returned to us and to Miragenia for—'' and he was joined by Mirza as they both intoned, "the Profit of all.''

Loefwin, who had seemed eager to speak before, shifted uncomfortably under the accusing stares of the merchants and the curiosity of his guests. For a moment all was silent except for the ripples Anastasia made as she glided back and forth in the fountain pool, calming herself with her own movement. Loefwin cleared his throat and began awkwardly, "Wasn't me that did it—not exactly. It was my Fric's idea, actually—Fric's my other brother. You haven't met him yet, Princess, but he's the one who has the pomegranate now, and he's the one who thought of it to begin with and organized the feast. I wasn't even there. All I had to do with it was paying for Droughtsea's services and directing the clean up operation afterward.''

"Clean up of what?'' Anastasia hissed suddenly, poking her head over the edge of the pool so her bill was right beside his ear.

He jumped, looked to see who was speaking, and shook his head as if to say he'd now seen everything, before answering. "Cleaning up after Fric used the pomegranate on the charlat—mages—running the six countries that surrounded Frostingdung with their hocus-pocus and necromancy since I was a lad. When I first decided to unite these lands into a single, strong country under one competent, central authority—namely me, though my father held the Frostingdung throne at the time, I knew the first thing I had to do was counter the unfair advantages the kings of those other countries had over us honest normal Frostingdungian men. Fric—he's the triplet you haven't met—said he knew these fellows.'' He flipped a thumb at the

Miragenians. "He said they had a little plant could do the trick and that old Docho, who's one of them, could get it for us for the right price."

Mashkent snorted so lustily his nose-hairs waved like banners. "Do you think one of us would have done such a deed for a price so small we would be obliged to serve as vassal to another man? The one you call Droughtsea is an outcast and a poor bargainer. Not to mention a thief of the property of others, who commits foul deeds not for Profit but merely for love of mischief." His voice and expression suggested that a person operating from such perverse motivation was capable of anything.

"As I was saying," Loefwin continued, glaring haughtily at the merchant. "Fric told me what I needed was one of those pomegranate things. Well, I believed him, a bit, but I figured what I needed was an army, so I left the nasty stuff to Fric. He's always been good at it. He had the banquet for all the Mages, Kings, wazirs and other fakers and gave each of 'em some of the fruit for dessert. After that lambs to the slaughter wasn't in it for easy—he killed them right there while they were wondering where their abracadabras went. Me and the army mopped up the rest. Iron swords and iron bracelets will do a lot to subdue minor magickers."

"But if the pomegranate was eaten, how's Bronwyn supposed to get it back?" Carole asked.

Mashkent replied, "It is a different pomegranate, of course. A new one grown from a single seed of the original—only one plant grows each twenty-one years."

"How do you know Fric didn't destroy all the seeds? How do you know this new plant exists?" Loefwin asked belligerently.

"We have seen it in the pool of visions, whereby the Princess saw the fate of her father. With that pool we may see all that is and has been," Mashkent said.

"Hmph," Carole said. "My Great Aunt Sybil can do *that*, and she only needs a crystal, not a whole pool."

"It is not a rare magic," Mashkent said humbly, "but it is one of great utility. It enabled us to see that the pomegranate is still within the castle of the Emperor's brother."

"And we want it," Mirza said. "So the brother of the Emperor will not some day choose to employ it against Miragenia."

"We must have it for the Profit of all," the uncle reiterated piously.

"I must say, despite all the mumbo-jumbo, I agree that it's a very good idea. Old Fric isn't what he used to be, and I daresay a dangerous morsel like that would be safer in less unpredictable hands," Loefwin said. "But I still don't see sending children for it. Why not go yourselves if you don't trust me? I'll give you my seal to show Fric—"

The merchants looked at each other nervously and Mashkent said, "What? Risk the liquidation of our chief assets when this excellent young lady needs to earn the price of her steeds? That would be not only ungenerous of us, but foolish as well."

From beyond the doors a highpitched whinnying sounded, and the merchants jumped to their feet and ran out into the courtyard.

The black djinn writhed in the snow, his eyes popping and his chest heaving frantically as he tried to dig the thongs of one of Droughtsea's senyaties from the flesh of his neck. A winged stallion soared above the walls and over the town. Droughtsea and Belburga clung tightly to his back.

"So much for the Duke and his palace coup," Rusty said. "I hope Mama's not afraid of heights."

The Miragenians finally agreed that Bronwyn, Carole, and Jack could ride the flying horses to Loefric's domain, as long as they dismounted and released the animals at the border of Western Frostingdung and walked to the castle from there. Once the children were on their way, the Emperor would use the horses to gather the army. Warning that they would be overseeing the use of their valuable property from the pool of visions, the merchants loaded their injured servant between them and flew away.

Bronwyn and her companions were mounted and ready by first light, after the shortest possible delay to provision themselves, for the merchants had warned that they must eat or drink nothing that came from Loefric's castle. Jack and Carole rode double on one of the horses, while Bronwyn rode another and Anastasia flew herself alongside.

The trip took most of the day, and had all the gay holiday air of a forced march, what with Bronwyn staring grimly ahead, Anastasia anxiously circling beyond the others in private little scouting forays, and Carole alternately making crabby, pessimistic comments and nodding in the saddle. None of them had had the time or inclination for sleep.

Jack supposed he too ought to act very serious and try to worry. Both his father and grandfather were with King Roari. But they were gypsies; they had been in tight spots before, and wet ones too, for that matter. Were they in his place now, they would not be worrying about him when they could do nothing— they would instead be enjoying a thrilling ride on the back of a magnificent beast. Never had he traveled so far so fast and on

174

such a beautiful animal! If he couldn't somehow contrive to take one of them back to his tribe with him, perhaps he could arrange to breed one to a gypsy mount—the foal of such a union ought to be worth enough to earn the gold required to fulfill his manhood test. He was uncomfortably aware that time was growing short. How sad it would be to help save the kingdom only to remain a perpetual boy.

By late afternoon the sun disappeared, fading into a sky of blank, colorless uniformity. Soon the forest thinned to a few trees and those dwindled to shrubs, then those too vanished into a vast gray expanse of parched wasteland.

Anastasia flew with her head angled downward, her sharp eye scanning the empty landscape. Just when Jack had convinced himself she was merely looking for something to eat, she descended from the sky in a dizzyingly swift spiral, as if she had suddenly grown too heavy to stay aloft. The horses followed suit, landing in a somewhat less abrupt manner, and the children dismounted.

"What is it?" Carole asked the swan, who stared incredulously into the gray land beyond.

"It is—it is as I feared. We are now in what is left of my own dear home, the Nonarable Lands."

"That can't be so," Bronwyn protested. "The Emperor distinctly said that this was where we would find West Frostingdung."

"Nevertheless these are the Nonarable Lands, more nonarable than ever, but I would know them anywhere. Ours must have been the first Kingdom to succumb to conquest, if Loefric implemented his fiendish plot from here. Poor Father! I knew someday our inability to raise archers would be the end of us."

"Well, wherever we are, I suggest that we find the Prince and the castle and get indoors before the hidebehinds and monsters come out for the night." Carole shivered.

"I think there is nothing so vigorous as a monster in this land," Jack said, regarding the surrounding featureless aridity sadly. "There is no cover to conceal anything."

They dismounted and slapped the horses on the rumps, sending the steeds winging back to their masters, and set out on foot.

Anastasia flew alongside them over what looked to be flat land, but what felt to the walkers as if it was one long upward slope. "Who would think all this gray, weedy gravel once was a garden of quicksand and bog, a home for the insect swarms, a haven for the playful serpent and slothful alligator?" the swan mourned. "Oh, my kingdom, what have they done to you?"

Whatever it was, it wasn't pleasant. The walking was vile.

Small stones, just big enough to make the footing difficult and cause rock bruises, littered the ground. The sluggish sky bestirred itself now and began to boil, lashing out with a bitter cold wind that whipped through the few stickery weeds thrusting through the gravel and stung the travelers' eyes with cold and flying dust, snapping right through the fine cloaks they'd borrowed at Loefwin's palace.

When they came upon a deep scummy pool that looked as if it had been sitting there since before Loefwin's war, Anastasia landed in the wind-rippled water, which sloshed up and down, leaving, when it receded, an unsightly green-brown ring around her sleek blackness. Her wings she kept folded fastidiously up over her back. "Is this all that is left of my lovely river?" she asked softly, and said to her friends, "Once there flowed a great river right here, where we are walking. It fed the swamps. No wonder they have vanished."

"It has been many years since you saw your home," Jack said kindly. "Perhaps this is not it. Perhaps you are mistaken."

"No—I knew we were bound for my father's lands from Loefwin's directions. But never did I dream of this devastation. How I wish I'd followed my heart and fled in the opposite direction! The unspeakable wretches, that they should despoil my country so." And without waiting for them to catch up, she flew away.

But they had only to walk a few paces beyond the pool before they topped a rise, and saw that a path stretched up to meet them. On first sight, it seemed to be made of broad stones, once white, now dirtied and stained to a slightly paler gray than the surrounding gravel. When Carole paused for a rest and sat on one of them, she found it even more rounded than she had thought. Since it wasn't very comfortable, she reached down with her hand to rearrange it. It wouldn't budge. Squatting, she pried it up with her fingers. Her hand slipped—under the rock, so she thought—but when she gave a long pull to loosen it she found she'd run her fingers through the eye sockets of a skull.

A rustle of wings announced Anastasia's return. Carole quickly shoved the skull back into its niche. After all, it might be a relative.

The swan had scouted ahead. "I confess I grow almost as curious as I am distressed," she said. "The central keep is right there, though shorter than I remember. But the rest of the castle is *not* there. I cannot think where it might have gone."

They soon saw what she meant, and discovered the solution. The keep was centered in the customary fashion on a man-

176

made mound, and had suffered less from what appeared to be a cataclysmic settling than had the rest of the castle. All that remained above ground of the outlying structures were the toothy merlons and the tops of some of the towers. Since these were as unrelentingly gray as the landscape, they had escaped Anastasia's notice when she'd first flown over them. A wide ditch outlined the perimeters, but contained not the slightest drop of moisture. The path of skulls led straight through it to the door of the keep.

"The old place has certainly gone downhill," Anastasia said with a pathetic attempt at levity. Carole glared at her, and wished the creature would stop dwelling so tiresomely on how painful it was to return home and find it ruined. While it couldn't be easy for the swan to face such changes, she could at least have the good grace to do so in silence. Carole for one didn't want to think about the subject and she certainly didn't want to hear any more bad jokes about it.

Jack, hearing the catch in the swan's voice and watching Bronwyn's suddenly stricken face and Carole's angry one, found that Argonia was not so distant as he had earlier felt. While a gypsy had no permanent home to return to, he had a sudden vision of himself flying his flying horse all over his native countryside looking for his people and finding them nowhere, their campfires dead for good. But again, he could do nothing about that now. As protector of these helpless females, it behooved him to think instead of their welfare and of the task at hand. "Your Highness," he said kindly to Anastasia, "perhaps it would be a good thing for you if you returned to the palace—"

"And risk being stung to death by fliers again?" the swan said and sniffed. "No, thank you."

"But see what this brother of the Emperor's has done to your castle! I would not like to think what he would do to one of the people who used to live in it, and in your present form you could hardly defend yourself. You cannot handle weapons or maneuver well in a closed space and we—we might not be able to help you."

She was silent for a moment, then said tiredly, "Oh, very well. I suppose procuring that so-unfortunate fruit must be the first priority and my presence might well be a detriment. I shall wait at the pool and if monsters of either the landlocked or flying sort attempt to trifle with me, woe betide them. Besides, I can always dive. Surely nothing can be alive in that water." She started to take off, but turned back for a moment. "Before I go, pluck out one of my feathers. If you need me, burn the feather and I shall come immediately."

Jack did so and she flew away.

Bronwyn had unsheathed her sword. Now, using the hilt, she pounded on the top portion of the door, which had sunk halfway into the gray and gravelly earth.

Jack was not perhaps quite ready for so *much* action, so quickly. Making the sign against the evil eye, he ducked back behind Carole.

"Oh, really," the witch said reproachfully. When Bronwyn's knock failed to bring a response, and the big Princess retreated a step with a puzzled, helpless expression on her face, Carole strode boldly forward and knocked smartly, three times. On the third knock the door gaped open on creaky iron hinges, one of which broke, and the cracked oaken slab skewed crazily aside, falling half off its frame to land inside the keep with a whoosh and a bang and a gust of musty, unclean-smelling air. Clouds of gray dirt billowed up and they all broke into fits of sneezing.

When they had recovered, Jack asked, "Do you think we should go ahead and enter?"

"I don't see why not. He mustn't mind visitors too much if he doesn't even have a proper front door," Carole said tartly. "Maybe he isn't even home—"

"It does have that lived-in look," Bronwyn, who had removed her bracelet at the beginning of the journey to conserve its power, agreed.

Another icy blast of wind cut across them, and this time it carried the first pellets of a hail storm. They ducked into the keep, stumbling on the sunken steps. Jack and Bronwyn pushed the door to and shoved it back into place as much as they could.

Inside it was dark, and outside the wind had taken up whistling, the hailstones rattling a fast tattoo against the walls. A long anguished baying echoed through the building. It seemed to come from beneath them, and Jack could have sworn the floor shuddered with the vibrations.

"Did you hear that?" Carole asked.

"Hear what?" Bronwyn asked through determinedly clenched teeth. "That was nothing."

"A werewolf, at least," Jack whimpered. "We have been sent to our doom."

"Nonsense," Carole said, shaking herself. "Besides, there is iron

178

on the door. We're p-perfectly safe. Do you have that new tinderbox we got from Loefwin's kitchen?"

"But of course."

"Try to kindle a flame then, and perhaps Bronwyn can find a torch. There should still be one on the wall somewhere."

Bronwyn edged back towards the door and followed along the wall with her hands. She took only two steps before barking her shins on something sharp, and several objects clattered, banged and rolled across the floor causing her to trip and flail about a great deal before she was able to regain her balance. But while she was flailing, her fingertips scraped across something that at least felt like a torch, so she grabbed, and when she had regained her equilibrium, held it out for Jack to light.

It blossomed with a light more comforting than the sun, at least for a moment, though it cast disfiguring shadows over everyone's features. Jack made a face and said, "Oooh ha ha," in a mock frightening voice, but then realized he really was frightened and making matters worse so he shut up.

As soon as his eyes adjusted to the light, however, he let out a low whistle. The torchlight, dim as it was, sparkled off the facets of thousands of gems embedded in mountains of treasure heaped all over the room. Gradually he could define the outlines of jeweled chairs, tables, dishes, chests, cabinets, clothing, weapons, armor, and all sorts of other articles stuffed into the room in careless piles.

"Anastasia would just love the way her family silver is being treated," Bronwyn said in what was supposed to be a light tone.

"It is very messy," Jack agreed, and began stuffing his pockets from the nearest pile. "I will just tidy up a bit."

Carole stopped his arm in mid-filch. "If the Emperor's brother is still living here, we aren't going to charm the pomegranate out of him by stealing from him."

"Do you really think anyone would notice?" Jack asked, but sullenly began replacing the gems and coins. He could always retrieve them *after* the pomegranate was secured.

The clatter the jewels made sliding back into heaps masked for a moment the slow tread rising a lumbering step at a time towards them. Jack froze, listening.

The steps faltered at what seemed to be a given point, like a doorway or a staircase landing. Labored breathing rasped through the room, louder than the hail. Then, with agonizing slowness, the steps stumped closer.

The man that finally faced them was not in the least formidable, except perhaps that he was formidably depressing. Not the sort one would invite to court, or even to a party. He was bent, sour-faced, and unsanitary-looking in the extreme. His clothing, which might once have been as rich as the garments jumbled around the room, was torn, stained, and so dirty its color was grayed into nonexistence. The tarnished metallic band with the empty jewel settings that trimmed a ripped sleeve dangled to the top of one of many rents in smelly old hose that sagged down his spindly legs. He had a yellowed filthy beard half knotted into a kerchief tied around his head. His watery eyes blinked repeatedly in the light of the torch while he smacked wrinkled lips over sunken gums.

"Bloody bones!" this apparition cursed in a muffled voice, "What're you? Not that I care. You're where you've no call to be. I'm calling the hounds."

"No, sir, don't do that," Carole pleaded with all the little-girl sweetness she could muster.

"Why not?" he asked, though he didn't sound interested in the answer.

"Because," Jack said. "Because we come from the Emperor—"

"Yes," Bronwyn said. "We've been sent to board with Prince Loefric. We're from the Empress's Orphan's Aid Benevolent Society. We were chosen as the most benevolent orphans available to fill positions as his wards."

"Were you now? You call that benevolent, banging about in the darkness, bothering a man? Can't imagine what we'd use orphans for, benevolent or otherwise, except dogfood. Hounds do tend to languish on a steady diet of snake and rat."

Carole began to get the feeling that this was not a nice old man, but one had to try, after all. "Please, sir, may we see Prince Loefric?"

The old man held his arms out, dropped them to his sides, turned his back, held his arms out again, and dropped them back again. "That's all of 'im there is. Now you've seen 'im. Get out."

Bronwyn drew herself up to her full regal giantess stature. She had been afraid from the first that, despite a conspicuous lack of family resemblance, this man was Loefwin's long-lost triplet himself and not a servant. Had he been a servant, he would have been hanged on his own bell-rope long ago, judging from the condition of the keep. To Jack and Carole she said, "How shortsighted of us, friends, not to have recognized the Prince at

180

once by his splendid hospitality, for which he is so well known throughout the realm. I understand his last dinner party made history."

"Did it?" the codger asked. "I'll bet it did! Now, get out, if you don't want to be served the same fare!"

"But it's hailing outside—" Carole protested, and they were all quiet so he could hear the hailstones and the wind and take pity on them.

Instead he took pity on himself. "I'm too worn out to treat with brats this night. Come along if you must." And he led them through the labyrinth of loot, picking his way back to a massive table, piled almost as high as the rest of the room with filthy golden and silver dishes caked with moldy messes. Without asking permission, Bronwyn lit four more torches from her own, and felt some satisfaction in watching Loefric cringe from the light. Then she joined Jack and Carole, who sat on the floor with their backs to a rolled tapestry.

Loefric glared at them. "Ah yes, children. One of the best of many reasons I decided not to return to the outside world. Same as ever, aren't you, brats? Snot-nosed, greedy, and noisy." Bronwyn wanted to point out that hers was not the nose that was dripping, but refrained and let him rant on. "Probably come to rob me, have you? Well, you'll find nothing of interest here. Nothing. Just the dogs and me—and all this trash."

"But these are *lovely* things," Carole said indignantly, fully justifying with her acquisitive gaze the Prince's estimation of her as greedy.

"Bah! Not one chair or bed gives comfort to these brittle bones nor rest to this aching head. Not one shirt or pair of pants is easy to wear or fits properly. No, most of them are for looks only. Can't use them or they break or tear. Worthless." And he spat at a priceless inlaid urn.

"You mentioned you have dogs," Jack said, trying for a less controversial topic. "They must be good company for you. Do you hunt with them?"

The old man wheezed with such lung-searing bitterness he started coughing and had to wait until his breath returned to ask, "Hunt where? Hunt what? Shall I hunt the weeds around the keep or shall I venture into the Disenchanted Forest and hunt things that hunt me more skillfully than I can hope to hunt them? How did you come to be here without seeing that there's nothing, nothing at all, to hunt? All dried up, withered away, given up and gone. Give us another year or so and we'll be gone too."

181

"If it's so bad, why do you stay? Why don't you go back to court?" Carole asked.

"What? Back to that madhouse? That'd be even worse. Oh, it used to be jolly, when the three of us were trying to see who could be King, you know, but there was never any question, no really, but that it would be Loefwin. And frankly, he can have it. What's the good of all that so-called power? You tell people what to do and have fatiguing fights with them trying to get them to do it, and when they don't you kill them and they still won't do it, so what's the point? I was going to be a great magistrate, run the legal branch. That was the deal Fwin and I made when I gave the dinner party. Now I ask you, how's a man supposed to make a career of the law once he's done in every wrong-doer and potential wrong-doer on the continent in one evening? Frankly, I rather miss all those chaps, tossing their balls of power around the room, raising the dead, that sort of thing. Entertaining, at least. But we couldn't have it, you see, them carrying on with something they had and we didn't. It wouldn't do. We had to fix it so nobody had as much as we did, so that no one was more interesting than we were—" He blinked around the shambles of a room, and spat again at the hapless urn. "We succeeded."

No one said anything for a moment and pretty soon he stirred himself again and said, "So. If you've come to keep me up all night with your childish prattle, you might at least tell me why I've been invaded. Or do orphans commonly wear fur-lined cloaks these days?"

Bronwyn had a fantastic tale ready but Carole cut in quickly, deciding forthrightness was the proper approach. "The pomegranate. We've come for the pomegranate. Your brother, the Emperor, said we might have it and you were to give it to us."

"What do you want with that? Going to a potluck supper, are you?" he asked with a barking laugh ending in another fit of agonized wheezing.

Bronwyn wasn't about to put her bracelet back on and waste some of its precious power to tell the old miscreant anything concerning the war or the bargain with the Miragenians. She felt sure if Loefric knew how much depended on the pomegranate, he'd not only refuse to help them, but would probably do something beastly that would make everything worse. Quickly she said, "It is for my sake that we seek the pomegranate, sir. Because I am cursed to tell only the truth, no matter to whom or of what I speak. I'm told only a smidgen of the pomegranate

182

rubbed judiciously into the scalp over the truth centers of the brain daily for a fortnight will relieve me of the onerous burden that is mine.''

He sucked in his lips and said, "Hmph. I'd rather hear that my brother is intending to plant an orchard, but since he isn't, I suppose your reason is as good as any. But make no mistake, that pomegranate and this keep are mine, not Fwin's. I stole 'em fair and square. High point of my career, as a matter of fact. This garbage is all I have to show for it and I don't mean to have you mucking it about, raising dust and making a lot of ruckus for nothing.'' The mention of dust set him wheezing again. When the seizure passed, he appeared more composed, though his torch-lit complexion had faded from gray-yellow to paste-white and his voice quavered more than before, so that it barely emerged in a sly whisper when he said, "I'll have to sleep on it. You whelps can't just barge into a man's keep and rush him about so.''

That seemed fair enough, especially since the guests were at least as much in need of sleep as their host, and what with the storm and the dark there seemed little that could be done immediately anyway. Still, as Jack was later fond of saying, had their mission been less urgent and had it not been hailing outdoors he would gladly have refilled his pockets and bade the creepy old chap farewell. He had thought from the beginning that this entire pomegranate business was fishier than Carole's ancestry.

So the children made the best of things. They polished off some of the bread and cheese they had brought with them, though it was hard to remember one's appetite in an atmosphere so stinkingly filthy and cold. The fumes from the torchlight hung in the stale air, making their eyes burn and their throats sting. Hail struck the roof and the sound ricocheted off the stone walls as loudly as the roar of an avalanche. The wind shrieked ear-splitting banshee cries and circled the keep, like a hungry monster looking for a way in.

The prince sat in his chair and ignored them while he slurped at gruel that must have been cold since the torches provided the only fire. Carole, who'd been drilled in manners, especially to those who were her elders or who outranked her, no matter how rank they were, offered him a share of her food. He declined everything by ignoring it, except for her entire loaf of bread, which he snatched up and began using to sop his gruel, which predictably dribbled into his beard in a disgusting manner. After that, he pushed his bowl toward the other dishes, and fell asleep slouched in his chair.

The children made themselves as comfortable as possible on the floor and the last thing Jack heard was Bronwyn saying, "It's all very well for him to talk of sleep, but as for me, I shan't sleep a wink," and her lusty snores.

CHAPTER XI

"What do you think you're doing?" Loefric's voice crackled. Carole jumped straight up, scattering a cask of jewels and bumping her head on the outthrust leg of a throne.

"J-just l-looking around."

Jack and Bronwyn, who were also looking, stopped and came to stand beside Carole.

"Did I say you could look yet?" They exchanged nervous, guilty glances and he grunted in a satisfied way. "Well, you can't. Not till I'm finished with you. You brats always think you can get something for nothing."

"But the Emperor *said*—" Carole began indignantly.

"And *I* said what he says doesn't count. But never mind. I'm going to let you have the damned thing, and welcome to it, if you can find it. I've got no use for it, but I don't rightly recall where it is and I've no intention of wasting my valuable time searching. And I'm not going to have you mucking about in here, raising dust and making noise for nothing either." He let his breath out along with the spurt of vitality that had been animating him. After grumbling to himself he glanced irritably around the room. It was lighter than it had been at night thanks to the hail, which had enlarged a hole in the roof. Wan sunlight peeked timidly through. "I suppose if you have to look, you have to look, but I'll not have you messing the place up and breaking things. You, girl," he aimed a spray of spittle at Carole and she stepped back, crunching fine craftsmanship under her heels. "You think all this trash is so wonderful, you can clean it up as you go. Polish everything, put it in its proper place. It'll partly pay me back for putting you up. Besides," he said and smirked toothlessly, "you'll never get downstairs to look through the rest of the castle if you don't. And no dilly-dallying, you understand. I'm tired of this mess you brats made. Everything must be cleaned and put away by sunset whether you find the fruit or not, or out you go. Now then, get started. I have to go below and pull the garden and beat the dogs, but remember, sunset.''

He shuffled off, his footsteps retreating and descending beyond the bejewelled junk.

"Sunset!" Carole wailed after him, "But how can I—" He had gone by then and she turned indignantly to the others. "Well of all the nerve. After he's spent probably most of his life *making* this mess, he blames us and wants ME to clean it up by sunset!''

"But is it not as well that we find the pomegranate as quickly as possible so we may return in time to aid the King?" Jack asked soothingly. "I for one intend to diminish this pile with great dispatch." This time, when he filled his pockets, no one objected.

Unfortunately, if all three of them had filled every pocket of every garment, it would still not have been enough to make the mountains of treasure seem one bit smaller. Now by the watery light from the hole in the roof, they could see that riches did indeed fill every nook and cranny of the room, almost to the ceiling, and only the narrowest of pathways allowed access to the door. Even if the pathway were filled, it could hold perhaps only one thin layer from the top of the heaps, and they couldn't reach the top of the heaps yet.

If there was anything gypsies knew as much about as traveling, animals, and stealing, it was moving things, and Jack, after a perfunctory inspection of the situation, announced, "It is hopeless. There is absolutely no way we can do this. I guess you will simply have to do without the pomegranate, my Princess.''

"Where's Anastasia's feather?" she asked.

He searched his pockets and found the feather crumpled between an emerald necklace and a carnelian-studded gold belt.

She took it and picked her way back to the door. They lit it indoors, to keep the wind from dousing the spark Jack made, then Bronwyn rushed outside with it.

A thin greasy smoke spiraled into the gray sky. As the flame burned down the quill to Bronwyn's fingers, Anastasia swooped to earth.

"Ah, you have completed your task quickly," she said. "I must confess I am glad. A tarn is not a desirable abode during a hailstorm. It is beginning to ice around the rim. I shall be most pleased not to have to spend another night there.''

"Well," Bronwyn began, unsure of how to proceed.

Carole helped her. "We're in a pickle, Anastasia the Alluring. It seems the Prince has been a very sloppy tenant in your ancestral mansion. He has oodles of simply scrumptious treasures all in that one room and they're all jumbled together and there's no way in the world to put them in order, but if we don't do it by sundown he's going to kick us out without giving us the pomegranate. He *says* he doesn't know where it is, but I think he's just being mean. That place is hopeless!''

"Hmm," the swan said, preening in a quick picky way that meant she was thinking hard. "Perhaps not.''

"But you should *see* it!" Carole insisted.

"I have no doubt the accursed man is an atrocious house-keeper. However, your plight is not entirely desperate if you can locate my hope chest. You may use it to hold the extraneous furnishings.''

"There are," Carole said, "a *lot* of things.''

"My dear child, my hope chest is capable of holding a *lot* of things. My entire dowry was to be contained within it, including a castle, stable, mews, and all the accouterments.''

"Oh," Carole said. "You mean it was magic.''

"Is," the swan affirmed, arching her neck imperiously.

"Still, do you think? I mean, that fruit took all the magic out of the people and—and from the looks of it, from everything else.''

"My hope chest was not in the habit of devouring fruit," the swan said. "I very much doubt it made contact with the disastrous stuff.''

"Well, then, all we have to do is find it. Which will be at least as easy as finding the pomegranate.''

"I suppose it is back to work, then," Jack said in a mournful voice, and took several deep breaths of crisp cold air to fortify himself against the miasma of the keep.

Bronwyn started dutifully to lift the broken door aside again when Anastasia said, "Perhaps Carole could use her craft in this matter.''

"A giant with a shovel using HIS craft would be more like it," Jack said.

"Possibly so, but I feel that my chest, being a hope chest, will respond to magic in a spirit of fellowship, whereas it may remain hidden from more mundane attempts to locate it.''

186

So, with Bronwyn at the door to haul things into the open, Jack scrambled agilely up the mounds, scuffing gilt and dislodging gems and handing piece after piece of priceless whatever down to Carole, who in turn handed everything out to Bronwyn.

The wind stopped blowing and the sun grew warm enough that soon all of them were perspiring. Anastasia rested beside Bronwyn, and remarked occasionally on the origin of a piece with a comment or two about previous owners. The chest was not, of course, on the top layer, although a lute of rare woods and broken strings, tapestries of silken and gold thread with mouseholes chewed in the fabric, a cradle with a stained spot on its velvet mattress as a legacy from a previous occupant, and no end of jeweled casks, small throne chairs and other lighter-weight trifles, were. In time, the piles outside grew so high that they too were developing a top layer. Anastasia excused herself when she saw her mother's jewelry case containing a delicate crystal crown spring open and spill its cargo onto the rocky ground.

"Have another feather," the swan said before she left, "and call me if you need me again. It is more than I can bear to see my kingdom's wealth treated like pillage." And with that she winged back to her refuge.

As the morning wore on, Bronwyn and Jack grumbled as they hauled, lifted, dragged, and pushed, enduring the imprints of gem facets on their hides and splinters of rare woods in their hands, but Carole, confident she could meet her deadline with the help of Anastasia's chest and her own magic, wanted to inspect each beautiful object. A jeweled box that she would have deemed the most wondrous thing she had ever seen paled in comparison with a gold scapular with intricate tracery, and that was nothing compared to a carved throne with butterflies whose sapphire eyes and enameled wings were so lifelike she expected them to fly away.

Bronwyn glared furiously at her when she took the time to remove the necklaces and bracelets she had piled onto her neck and arms and replaced them with others, but Carole ignored her. The jewels probably did slow her down, since the beads and chains around her neck kept getting caught when she lifted things and the rings and bracelets cut into her flesh when she carried something heavy. Still, they were no more cumbersome than the lumps in Jack's clothing that changed his outline to resemble that of a craggy boulder, and she liked them. In answer to Bronwyn's exasperated glare, Carole took extra care admiring the next handful of baubles Jack flung down at her. A ring with a stone as large as a goose's egg was among the other trinkets, and Carole put it on a finger that bore only three other rings and spread her fingers to see how it looked.

"For pity's sake, Carole—" Bronwyn began and Jack, still standing on the pile, turned to frown down at them.

"I would think, Carole, that if you care more about jewels than about finding the pomegranate, you would at least pick something pretty. That is not a jewel of quality."

"Of course I care about the pomegranate," she said defensively, rubbing the ring on her skirt before holding it out again. "But a person can only work so fast. Anyway, I think those merchants tricked Bronwyn with their silly pool, just to get us to do as they want. We can't be losing the war! Why, King Roari is probably—oh, dear. I guess he's not at that."

The ring must have belonged to one of Loefric's dinner guests, for it certainly was no ordinary ornament. Perhaps its power responded to being on the hand of a real magician again, Carole thought, or perhaps polishing it against her skirt activated it, but for whatever reason the cloudiness which had marred the stone cleared, and myriad shapes and colors shifted across its facets, forming miniature, seemingly living, images, people clustered tightly together on a small island in the midst of a pounding sea. Prominent among these was a bedraggled redhaired giant, hunched over a half-drenched campfire, several of his equally bedraggled lieutenants surrounding him.

Jack jumped nimbly down from the pile. He followed Carole's gaze into the ring, and expressions of dismay and relief washed across his face in succession. "There, on the King's left. That is my father. And that one, like the great gray bear, that is my grandfather. They do not look at all well, but they do seem to be in one piece."

Bronwyn was too overcome at seeing her own father to remark on the fact that Jack's grandfather looked startlingly like Worthyman the Worthless, the King she had seen standing on the bow of the flagship beside the weather wizard. She half reached out to touch the ring, then drew her hand away as within it, Roari Rowan rose quickly, his back to them, his stiff posture and the slight turning of his head indicating that he was watching the sky. Boiling black clouds were ripped apart by lightning bolts. Soon a massive crimson and gold dragon flew low in towards the back of the island, behind the group around the fire. The men moved aside to reveal two other dragons huddled together. The big red dragon, Grimley, dropped to a landing and huddled protectively over his mate, who was already huddled

188

over their half-grown get, the dragonet, Grippledice. No sooner had the dragon left the sky than a bolt of lightning homed in on one of the men standing on the outskirts of the island and struck him down. Grimley raised himself wearily and shot a retaliatory flame back. Though the surface of the ring was too small to show how far the flame extended, it seemed to Bronwyn that the dragon's range of fire was less than usual and that the flame had faded somewhat. As the image of the dragon-fire died, so did the rest of the scene, and the stone looked as it had before, a dull gray rock set incongruously in fancy fretwork.

"Get it back!" Jack said. "Rub the stone again, Carole."

She tried, but the ring stayed dull. "Maybe it only had enough power for just one sighting," she said, flicking her fingernail against the gem in a futile attempt to revive it. "When Aunt Sybil gives a person a magic mirror, you can only use it three times. Probably this already got used twice. I'll just take it home and—" She had been going to say that she would take it home and see if her aunt could recharge it for her, but, as if one of the lightning bolts had jumped out of the ring to strike her, she suddenly realized that the scene she had just seen was the continuation of Bronwyn's vision—Bronwyn's *true* vision, since for two magic things to show related false visions to two different people was virtually impossible. If they failed to find the pomegranate—but why be morbid? Someone around here had to show some initiative. Stripping off her finery while she talked she said, "Great flying fur fish, Bronwyn, why didn't you tell us about this?"

"Well, I s-suppose I must have wanted to s-spare you!" Bronwyn sputtered with exasperation. Great flying fur fish, indeed! Why didn't Carole listen when someone *did* tell her something?

"You shouldn't have, you know. We have an important task to perform here. Now, if you two will be so kind as to step out of the way, perhaps I can make enough of a path for that hope chest of Anastasia's to surface."

Slow as the going had seemed to Bronwyn, the three of them had nevertheless managed to cart outdoors a great quantity of the contents of the keep, though an even greater quantity still remained, it was true.

Carole hummed, using only one strain of melody at a time, parting aisles in the begemmed heaps as a peasant mother uses a single finger to part a child's hair, searching for beasties. The valuables moved slowly at first, but as the tune moved faster the

189

treasures shifted accordingly. The light was so thin and shadow-pocked now that she could see very little, despite the additional space the morning's work had provided.

Now seemed as good a time as any to try to call to the chest. A wedding march seemed appropriate, and she hummed one. At first there was no response, and then, very faintly, there was a tiny clattering from a far corner, near the rolled end of a tapestry half-hidden under the curtains of an upended bed. She raised her voice and a small chest, not much larger than Bronwyn's buckler, thumped around the corner of the tapestry. She sighed partially with relief and partially with weariness, for if she hadn't extended herself physically earlier, she felt she'd more than made up for it once she started using her magic. Never did she recall needing so much energy to exercise her talent! Bumbling over to the box, she unlatched the lid. It was empty except for some miniature furniture, too tiny for any doll's house, in the bottom. But this had to be it. Her hum would not have called anything else. To make sure, she hummed at the tapestry. It raised itself on end and unrolled, feeding a corner of itself into the box and rapidly shrinking to handkerchief size, then to the size of a hole in the mesh of the finest lace.

"Found it," she called through the junk and carried the chest to the door, meanwhile calling to the other objects. From the largest to the smallest, they rose into the air, minuetted or reeled, each according to its nature, across the room, and threaded themselves into the bottomless space inside the little hope chest.

All afternoon Carole hummed and filled the box. Bronwyn and Jack first looked on with wonder, but at last grew bored and began to play stones-scissors-and-paper together, using real gemstones, leaving her, this time, to do all the work.

By the time she had magicked into the hope chest everything she didn't wish to use in furnishing the room, and had sent a battalion of velvet polishing rags—remnants of unsalvageable garments—jigging vigorously over each piece remaining, the day had grown short.

She wearily surveyed the results. A swan-shaped four-poster bed filled one corner, a tapestry with fewer mouseholes than most she had uncovered hung on the wall, Loefric's worn throne and three of the more comfortable-looking chairs surrounded the freshly dusted table. She hadn't washed his repulsive dishes but had stashed them in the hope chest and replaced them with freshly wiped ones from the piles, storing them in a cabinet

190

opposite the table. Enough chests, chairs, shields and bits of armor were located about to give the room a suitably rich look. Unfortunately, if the pomegranate had been hidden in any of the items she had either stored or used to furnish the room, she had overlooked it.

Bronwyn saw her worried look and patted her shoulder, having completely forgiven her her earlier lapse. Carole *had* cared after all, she simply hadn't truly been aware of the situation. "Don't fret, cousin. As soon as the Prince sees what a bang-up job you've done, I'm sure he'll hand over the pomegranate immediately and send us off to Argonia with his blessings."

Jack snorted. "More likely the charming Prince will accuse us of stealing the items he cannot see," he said with an air of wounded dignity not entirely appropriate to one whose pockets were so perilously and feloniously full.

"Nonsense," Carole said, collapsing into a chair, "I'll simply tell him they're in storage, which is perfectly true."

When Loefric disinterred himself from the depths some time later, he hardly seemed to notice any difference. He was busy nursing his hand. All he said, when he deigned to notice, was "Hmph. I could have sworn there was more trash here than this."

"Not at all, sir," Bronwyn said with a smile. "It just needed a woman's touch."

"Is that so?" Loefric demanded, and shook his torn and bloody hand at her. "I just had a woman's touch—right here. The bitch nearly took off my hand. I can tell you, I gave her more than a touch of my boot for her trouble, that I did. Worthless hound. Just because I kicked that pup of hers back downstairs where it belonged. What does she suppose a master is for?"

"Not for kicking her puppy, apparently," Jack said, his eyes flashing with indignation not directed at the dogs.

"Damned dogs don't know their place," Loefric muttered, but he seemed to be enjoying being angry, for his watery eyes lit up in their dim fashion and he didn't stop grouching to himself all through the preparation and consumption of his gruel. He didn't even notice that the task had been facilitated for him by Carole's labors.

When he finished, he gazed accusingly at his hand and asked them with what he apparently thought was a crafty air, "So, did you find your precious pomegranate?"

Bronwyn started to say that they had, but had remained around the keep for love of its wholesome, invigorating atmosphere and in anticipation of his stimulating companionship, but thought better of it. She might convince him she could tell nothing but the truth while telling many lies, but a whopper of that magnitude would never pass.

Jack and Carole shook their heads.

Any hope they might have cherished that the old wretch would simply hand them the fruit in exchange for services rendered was squelched by the titter with which he greeted their admission of failure.

"Well, then, perhaps you need help," he said sweetly. "You, young man. You seem to be an animal lover. Perhaps you could gain the aid of my hunting hounds in helping you hunt for your quarry, eh? They should be glad of the chance. They haven't hunted anything but vermin in years. Besides," he added not-so-sweetly, "you'll need to get past them to search the second level, won't you? That's settled then. I'm going to take a little nap before supper, so see that you don't wake me up with your screams while you're getting acquainted. And boy?"

"Yes, old man?" Jack managed to reply, though he was staring with gruesome fascination at the bits of bone and tendon protruding from the jagged tear in Loefric's hand.

"Have a fine time digging through the dogshit while you're looking for the pomegranate. Seems to me the kind of job that should suit you." And with that the noble prince's chin dropped to his chest and he slept, smiling to himself.

The light and warmth of the day were fading and a little snow had begun sifting through the hole in the roof by that time, but clearly another consultation with Anastasia was in order. So out they all went, Bronwyn lighting the new swan feather from her torch. In a short time they heard wings beating back the wind and in another moment Anastasia was among them.

The swan fluffed her feathers and twitched them energetically, shaking out the snowflakes. The children pulled their new cloaks tightly around them and everybody huddled close together for warmth.

"Well?" the swan asked. "How have you fared? Was my hope chest of service to you?"

"Oh Princess, it was," Jack said. "But not quite enough, since we failed to find the pomegranate. Now both we and the King will be lost unless you can think of some way we can keep from being devoured by the old goblin's hounds when we go below to search among them for the accursed fruit."

Anastasia preened for a moment. "Below, that would be—let

192

me think, now—ah yes, the upper level of the addition to the additions to the keep, now sunken, as they are, to form a second level, or a top subterranean level."

"Which means there is another level below?" Jack asked, feeling rather sunken himself. So. If he survived the dogs, he would have to brave yet another dimension of the Prince's reprehensible idea of housekeeping. How ghastly! Perhaps the dogs could be induced to swallow him up in one relatively painless gulp.

"If it is still intact," Anastasia said, answering his question. "The stables used to be just West of the keep, in what was the central courtyard, and the kennels were on the other side. What a degenerate knave that man must be to house dogs where the bedchambers once were!"

"Stables and kennels? I wonder what became of all the animals," Carole said.

"They perished of being overfed," Bronwyn told her.

"Not likely around raisin-face," Jack remarked. "But that gives me an idea. If we feed the hounds, they will know we are friendly and—"

"What do you propose we feed them?" Carole asked.

"Bread and cheese," Bronwyn said dismally. "Hounds are very fond of bread and cheese. They also like onions very much."

"No, Bronwyn," Jack said glumly. "Dogs do not like onions. They like meat. And bone."

"I should be able to find that easily enough," Anastasia said nonchalantly.

"You can? Where? How?" The other three were all ears.

"I shall simply fly to the woods and gather some of the bits and pieces from the monsters' maraudings. I believe they prey on each other."

"Well," Carole said, "Monsters don't make the best meat I've ever eaten, but it's no doubt an improvement on rat and snake."

"Will one of you provide me with a garment which has pockets or something to wrap my findings in so I may carry them conveniently?"

"Bronwyn or Carole will have to do that," Jack said. "I can't give you mine. My pockets are all full."

"You'd best keep them thus," Bronwyn agreed. "Those hounds will want the stones you carry to add roughage to their meal when they gobble you up in two bites. And I shan't protect you, either."

193

"Oh, *Bron*wyn."

Anastasia returned with her gory baggage a short time later and Jack distributed the bones throughout his pockets, dislodging as few of his treasures as possible. Then bidding the swan farewell, the trio marched purposefully past Loefric, their footsteps vindictively loud. The only sign the old man gave of noticing was to twitch one grizzled eyebrow and mutter, as if in sleep, "Lotta animal lovers around here."

Bronwyn preceded the other two, her shield in front of her and sword drawn beneath her cloak.

Jack held the torch in one hand and a bone in the other and tried to remember every animal training trick he had ever learned, and also the Pan-elvin Mistress Raspberry had been teaching him.

Carole trailed behind him, rubbing her eyes and shuffling a little. Jack feared they could not count on her to teach dogs to dance, if necessary. She seemed completely spent.

Down and down they went, until the stairs ended in a tunnel, crudely supported by posts made from small trees, their bark still intact. The yapping and howling began before they were halfway through the low corridor, which was fit only for trolls. Jack wondered if Loefric had built it himself or if the dogs had simply dug it out. It could not have been part of the original structure. But he kept his speculation to himself. Ahead of him, Bronwyn was taut as a drawn bowstring. Again he thought what a fine shield her tall figure made. It was perhaps not glorious for him to walk behind his chosen love, but then, someone had to hold the torch, did he not?

Yapping, howling, baying, and growling filled the tunnel and rang through their ears, and the clicking of claws on stone, click, click, click, click—a multitudinous mob of clicking, picking up speed as it increased in volume, prancing, trotting, and finally charging toward them.

Bronwyn's sword, now naked, trembled in the torchlight which, as a matter of fact, also trembled. "N-nice doggie?" she greeted the first glittering pair of red eyes to charge them.

"RRRRR-RIP!" the dog said, which, if Jack remembered his Pan-elvin, and was interpreting it correctly, meant, euphemistically speaking, "Stop patronizing me!" and also, "Prepare to die like the two-legged insect you are," or something to that effect.

"We—we are friends," Jack said in Pan-elvin, and hurriedly tossed his first bone among them. It served its purpose of

194

delaying their immediate demise, becoming a literal bone of contention among the pack, which had gathered in a fire-eyed, shadow-backed snarling solidarity that had every intention of eating them.

"So are we—man's best friend," growled the lead dog around a mouth full of the bone it had succeeded in winning from the others. "Man—hah! He doesn't deserve a best friend."

"That is not entirely fair," Jack argued—but diplomatically. Very diplomatically. "Everybody needs friends. I have the Princess here, and the witch, and you have your—" he interrupted himself hurriedly to toss another bone, "pack. And we come bringing you gifts."

"Gifts? Nah! You were throwing things at us! You aren't trying to claim you knew they were tasty, are you?"

"But of course," Jack said, trying to look longingly companionable as he fixed the dog with his most melting wide-eyed gaze. "I am very fond of bones myself. But these I chose to share with you, because—"

"Yip! Yip! Grr-yip!" A small furry missile hurtled beyond the pack leader and clamped tiny teeth into Jack's trouser leg, which it began to worry with puppyish abandon. The pup was promptly followed by three others of roughly the same size, all yipping and growling fiercely and earnestly gnawing the cloth of his pants. Jack took a deep breath and started to bend his knees in a careful stoop. He wanted to pull the pups off and pet them into a gentler frame of mind, for he was afraid their innocent aggressiveness might start a trend.

Bronwyn glanced from him to the little dogs and back again, her sword poised, but he shook his head imperceptibly. From behind the lead dog, a bitch slunk forward, her lips writhing back from her bared yellow teeth, snarling, "I'll tear his throat out."

The leader stepped back, acknowledging her claim.

One of the pups, still yipping happily, bounded from Jack to the bitch, squirmed and wagged around her for a moment, and frolicked back to Jack's ankles. Quietly, Jack relieved his pockets of several more bones, letting them drop to his feet. The puppies pounced on them.

Withdrawing another bone, Jack held it out to the bitch. "For you, my beauty," he said coaxingly.

She strained her head forward, sniffing. "What's that?"

"A bone."

"They're wonderful bones, Mama," the pups yipped. "And *he* has good smells—not like the other one."

"Assuredly, little doggie, I am not like the other one," Jack said in his fondest and most beguiling tone, holding the torch up so she could more clearly see his sweet, good-smelling, boyish face. "I love animals. Why, my own grandfather was once a bear."

"We used to hunt bears," the bitch growled, but she slunk a bit closer. Behind her, the others whined uncertainly, or at least those others without a bone did. "Long ago, my mother's littermate told of her mother, who hunted with tame men, not like that one who harmed my pup. Are you tame, boy?"

Jack wanted to stammer and delay and find some way around the question. What did she mean was HE tame? *Animals* were wild or tame, good or bad, trainable or stupid, not men, and certainly not he. But her tusk-sized teeth glistened in the dark and he said quickly, "I—yes, I am."

"Then come here, boy. Fetch me that bone you have there. Fetch it here." Jack hesitated and she whimpered cajolingly. "Come on, I won't bite you—yet. Let me sniff your hand for you. *Good* boy. Stick it out now," she sniffed and whimpered again and wagged her bristling tail encouragingly. "Good *good* boy. You may pat me now and give me that bone."

This was *not* how Jack had envisioned making friends with the hounds, but it did seem to be one way. When the bitch had enjoyed her bone for a few moments she asked, "Have you others?"

"Uh—yes. And—and there are more outside, only tell me, are we—um—are we friends now?" He was shaking and sweating despite the chill in the tunnel.

"Oh, yes. I understand men can be quite loyal once they have been taught to accept one."

"Then, will you help us? We seek a certain pomegranate."

The word was apparently unfamiliar to the dog, for she pricked her ears and whined and the others shook their own ears uncertainly and lolled their red tongues and slitted their red eyes, listening.

"It is a fruit," Jack explained. "It may be buried here, on this level. Could you sniff about, do you think, and use your paws that are—that are so superior to our weak soft hands, and help us hunt this thing? We would show our loyalty, naturally, by bringing more bones."

She growled, whined and yipped in fast succession. "Tell us more what this pomegranate is like and we shall try. But remember, more bones. These are a start but some with meat would be better."

Jack nodded and described the pomegranate as he had heard it described by the merchant. Dogs scattered in all directions.

Bronwyn grinned at him in the torchlight, and with a sigh sank to her heels, the floor being covered with dog excrement. Carole was oblivious to that, however. Sometime in the course of negotiations, she and a gray-muzzled oldster had found each other, and in an equal state of weary disregard for interspecies politics had collapsed, the dog's head in Carole's lap and hers resting on its furry back, both fast asleep.

"They are different than you would think," Jack said, telling Anastasia of the dogs. "Proud and smart, and—well, that bitch reminded me of my Grandmother, Queen Xenobia. She had them dig up the whole cellar, and they searched every crack and crevice, but no fruit. And still raisin-face will not tell us where the pomegranate is, but insists we do his gardening for him. Meanwhile, we need more bones and the bitch says they must have meat. I think perhaps I will forget training animals and learn to read the tarot."

"Well, I should think you would leap at the chance to do some gardening, though I must say," she glanced at the leaden early morning sky and at the snow-frosted weeds and rocks surrounding the castle, "it seems a bit late to start landscaping."

"It is not here in the outdoors, Loefric's garden. It is on the level below the dogs. His pleasure at seeing us alive and whole at breakfast was not keen. If I do not acquire some bones to take back with us, he will be less disappointed tonight. Bronwyn plans to garden alone until I can join her."

Bronwyn nodded gravely. "Not that we don't have all the time in the world, but I am very bored in this luxurious palace, with nothing to do."

Anastasia almost inquired what Carole intended to do while her socially superior cousin was toiling like a peasant, but Carole hung back, listless, leaning against the door frame. These low-born children seemed to have little stamina. The swan knew by looking at Jack that she would have to allow him to ride upon her back to the forest. Not only was his customary cockiness notably absent, perhaps because the idea of being a dogsbody to dogs was less than appealing to him, but like Carole, he seemed depleted.

Only Bronwyn remained herself, though an impatient and twitchy version of herself, and the enchanted Princess of the

Nonarable Lands could well imagine how trying it must be for her to play these senseless games with the malicious madman who controlled the keep while her own family and kingdom were under attack and she prevented by him from aiding them. So far she had shown great restraint in not skewering the wicked old man, which was not only honorable but wise since her tormenter was also the brother and vassal of her newly sworn ally. Anastasia saw no harm in reinforcing Bronwyn's prudence, in case the impetuous young swordswoman should be tempted to change her mind.

"My dear Bronwyn, I should like to give you a piece of advice," the swan said as she and Jack prepared to fly away.

"I'm quite sure I know all I need to and have everything under control," Bronwyn replied, a lost and rather pleading note in her voice. "But if it will make you feel better, go ahead."

"Very well, I shall. And bear in mind I say this not to hurt your feelings, but to aid you." Bronwyn nodded. Anastasia proceeded, struggling to express herself delicately. She did not wish to mention directly the possibility of Bronwyn attacking Loefric, not only to spare Bronwyn's sensibilities but to keep from giving her any bad ideas. "You are—ahem—often all too ready to rely on that sword of yours, my dear, and I believe that would be a mistake in this instance, as well as in other—shall we say—affairs of statecraft. Bear in mind that many of the Kings and Mages murdered by that scoundrel within were once great swordsmen too, and they did not prevail. It occurs to me that if the power of the fruit could be overcome by hacking, those men would still be among the living. Also, on the subject of your latest task, remember that a lady of high birth must always conduct herself in a manner befitting her station within the bounds of the situation. I would say, on the whole, that in a garden of any sort, it is always wiser to get to the root of things than to whack at them."

Bronwyn tried to befit her station as she strode past Loefric, who sat in his chair and followed her with his eyes, a wary lizard on his rock. She stomped down the stairs and stooped into the tunnel, and held out her hand for the waiting hounds to sniff. She gave as a peace offering two bones Jack had cleverly retained for that purpose. She carried a fresh torch in one hand, and her shield and sword hooked to her belt. Once past the canine welcoming committee, she stepped from the tunnel into the wide corridor of the second level, squishing her way through

198

the odiferous floor covering, past what had once been sumptuous bedrooms, and still showed rags of velvet bedhangings and drapes at blank, earth-filled windows. Torch sconces occurred at regular intervals in the wall, many of them still holding torches, giving the hall, despite its ruined condition, a semblance of everyday ordinariness, as if servants would soon emerge and light the torches, clean up the muck, and throw out the dogs.

A dark gap in the south wall indicated the descending staircase. Bronwyn noted that the dog droppings did not foul the stone stairs past the landing, and wondered at that. She wished she spoke dog, as Jack did, so she could ask them, but then, she'd probably be as bad a liar in dog as she was in Argonian.

Weeds wound up the staircase to meet her, catching in her boot heels and snagging on her ankles. Holding her torch higher, she saw that weeds grew everywhere, thicker than a forest. Somewhere too, she heard a rushing, and smelled water. She devoutly hoped Anastasia's serpents and alligators and insects hadn't sunken right along with the castle. She would not like to encounter an alligator here, or fall into quicksand, though the Mother only knew she should have no trouble, in the latter event, in locating vines with which to pull herself out.

The light from her torch fell on one wall, and she saw that here too torches were still in place. Wading through the weeds, she made her way to the wall and began lighting each torch as she came to it, devoutly hoping she would not set the place on fire and incinerate castle, dogs, herself and all in the process. In the improved light, she could see that the weeds twined through and around and even penetrated the rotting furniture that would normally adorn a great hall.

The rushing and babbling grew louder and the smell of water stronger as she edged along the wall, trying to clear weeds as she went, though they seemed to grow back twice as thick and fast as before every time she cut a swatch through them. Her feet slipped, and when she cleared the plants away momentarily she could see that mud had drifted well up the walls. The cause of this was soon apparent, when she found herself standing on the banks of a swift river, dashing its way roughly south by southwest through the great hall and into what seemed, from its high ceiling and giant iron lamps and ornate pillars, to have once been a ballroom.

If the pomegranate had been where the river now ran, she was out of luck, but at least she understood where all the dirt had come from. The river must have carried it in when it poured

199

through the walls. Any cellars or dungeons were no doubt flooded and destroyed by now, which was a blessing. Bronwyn thought that she would not like to see the dungeon of a castle in the shape of this one.

Since she couldn't go forward, she tried to start back toward the stairs. She thought she had seen another doorway, on the other side. But the weeds she had cleared had grown back thicker and stronger than before and when she raised her sword to them, they grew up to snatch it. She held on and pulled back and they tripped her feet and wound rapidly around her wrist. She stopped hacking long enough to catch her breath, and abruptly the weeds wilted back.

She didn't know what to make of that, but since she didn't wish to be trapped in this jungle for the rest of whatever life she might have left, she started hacking again, only to be re-entangled immediately. By this time she was thoroughly panicked, and hacked and whacked until she was entirely mummified in a wrapping of weeds, all save the hip that held her shield. She started to weep and curse simultaneously, furious at her own immobility, but as soon as the weeds held her immobilized and she stopped trying to wield her sword, they once again melted back.

They weren't green, these weeds—more of a pale mushroom color, and their leaves were spiky and brown, as if they were already dead, an appearance robustly and conclusively denied by their activity. These must be the plants from which the gruel was made. If so, harvest time must be rather trying. How did the Frostingdungians manage to collect a plant that fought back—but of course, that was it. The more they collected, the more this plant grew, which was why they had so much of the gruel and so little of anything else.

She stared at the weeds with new interest. What manner of plant was this, anyway? Whatever it was, she was going to have to master it if she was ever to find her way back to the surface again, let alone find the pomegranate. Stop hacking and get to the root of things, Anastasia had said. Well, then. The first part of the advice had proved sensible, perhaps the second would too.

Sheathing the sword, Bronwyn used her free hand to tug gently at the weed. At first it clung to her wrist, but as she did it no violence, it wilted back again, and she pulled further. She planned to surprise it, feeling along until she reached each root and then giving a swift merciful yank at the end. The plant would never feel a thing, she was sure, although she wasn't as

ure how the other plants would react. They all seemed to be in
sympathy.

Soon she had a sneaking suspicion she knew why. They were
either very large plants or they were all connected somehow. No
matter how many times she followed a strand to the ground,
flipping the passive excess back over her shoulder as she groped
along the vine, she never found a root. As long as she approached the task with a certain indifference, and didn't let her
urgency cause her to jerk at the plant, it acted like a proper vine
should and just lay there, but the minute she got anxious and
tried to hurry it curled tightly around her again.

Rather like her curse, in a way. The more she wanted people
to like her, the harder she tried to say something to them, the
bigger her lies got, and the less able she was to use humor and
tone of voice, the little ways she had to say something close to
what she actually meant. The harder she tried, the more her
tongue felt as tangled as this stupid vine. Did Carole ever feel
that way when she tried so hard to be beautiful that she ended up
acting as toady as Loefrig? And how about Jack, who was at his
most ridiculous when he attempted to show everybody how
brave and manly he was? But that was silly. *They* were normal.
They didn't have curses.

They also didn't have to wrestle with this clinging vine.
Stoop, bend, and pull, stoop, bend and pull. Too much effort
and it locked you in a vice. Too little and you got absolutely
nowhere, and for what? A fruit that took all the magic out of
everything, made everything ordinary and dull and monotonous.
Made her tired just to think of it. Still, the others had already
done their share. All she had to do was win a match with this
singular plant and—

It certainly was singular! Never once did she find a root
system, as she followed the vine back and forth, up and down,
over and around and back again, all through the unsubmerged
part of the ballroom on her side of the river, the great hall and on
further into the kitchen. What if the part of the plant that grew
into the river left the castle that way and wound along underground until the river surfaced, whereupon the plant too would
surface and spread its tendrils all over the land? In view of its
current hardiness, she didn't feel that was entirely impossible.
And the pasty gruel was eaten all over Frostingdung. Hmmm.

Finally, she flopped down beside an all-but-concealed fire-
place at the end of the kitchen. She would just give up and die.
The bloody plant was omnipotent. There was no fighting it, no

reason to it. And her back was permanently arched from stooping, her arm a noodle from carrying the torch aloft. If she ever did reach the surface again, she would always resemble an angry cat. Who would have anything to do with a seven-cubit tall liar who looked like an angry cat?

She sighed. Jack and Carole wouldn't even miss her, probably. They would make new lives for themselves here in Frostingdung, when Argonia had been overrun and all their parents killed. Perhaps they would not think too badly of her and would at least remember her as someone who had led them to safety, so that they weren't demolished with the rest of the country. She felt so noble about that, she started to cry, and so frustrated that, forgetting the weeds' reaction to assault, she angrily jerked on a handful lying near her right hip, beside her shield. This time the weed did not give. It pulled back, and snapped, and all around her, began to wither and die. Good. At least she'd have company.

But while she was gazing curiously at the broken end near the ground, new shoots began to sprout. She wasn't about to let it get away with that. She pulled and tugged again, as hard as before, with the same results, in a less spectacular fashion, as she'd gotten when she'd tried similar tactics in the other room. The plant was firmly embedded in the soil and didn't intend to give. Cunningly, Bronwyn drew her sword again, and used it like a spade, digging all around the plant. Since it was not directly disturbed, the weed didn't fight back or accelerate its growth, though the sprouts from her first flurry of effort had instantly grown as high as her waist.

At last she unearthed a network of roots, but instead of pulling, she felt along them until she found what seemed to be a bulb. When she could get her hand around it, she brought up bulb, roots, sprouts and all.

As she had hardly dared hope, the bulb was round, and red, and the entire root system grew from a tiny neck at the top of it. She snapped it off and watched the sprouts die. Pocketing the pomegranate, she whistled a snatch of the marching tune Carole had once used to charm her and slogged back through the muck and mire.

CHAPTER XII

"You're lying," was all Loefric had to say when confronted with the fruit, the three determined children, and a pack of contemptuous but self-controlled hounds.

"I'm not saying a word," Bronwyn denied the charge indignantly.

"She doesn't need to," Carole said. "You said we might have the pomegranate if we found it and she's found it. *And* we've done all the work you've neglected to do in this poor castle of the last umpty-ump years and made friends of your dogs as well, so stop sniveling. And do wipe your nose, won't you? You can't imagine how nasty that looks on a grown man and a prince at that!"

"Now see here, girl, I—" Loefric began sneeringly, but stopped. He had run out of anything to sneer about. The dogs snarled and snapped in his direction and he edged backwards, away from them, toward the steps. The bitch snapped suddenly and down he fled, shuffling faster than any of them would have believed he could.

Bronwyn meanwhile told an abbreviated version of how she had vanquished the fruit and its perilous porridge vine, and with a few charades and the brief help of her charm at strategic points, managed to convey to them her discoveries about the pomegranate's properties. She found talking difficult, her strength oddly sapped by her struggles, and finally, she simply pulled the red fruit from her pocket and let her friends see it for themselves. Sprouts already shot from the top. For some reason, that discouraged her more up here than it had in the depths of the cellar and she found she was almost weeping when she said, "As you can see, in spite of everything, it's quite hopeless to fight this. I don't know why I ever imagined myself a warrior. Not that it matters. We'll never be able to join Loefwin in time to help father and—"

Carole, who had been listening carefully, shook her head and said, "It's clear enough how that works. Just listen to her! Now she not only lies, she's depressing as well." She jumped up and ran to the swan bed, pulling out the hope chest. "Come on, you two, let's take this outdoors so Bronwyn can put the pomegranate in it. Well, come *on*. You wouldn't think the fruit of disenchantment would be so dangerous to someone who is enchanted in the first place, but obviously that's not so." Jack shrugged and Bronwyn shrugged back and followed him with a shamble worthy of her host.

Once outdoors, Carole wasted no time but immediately upended the box and jumped backwards as the piles and piles of treasure spilled all over the frosted heath.

"What do you think you're doing?" demanded Anastasia, who had been perching on the keep's roof all morning while waiting to learn the outcome of Bronwyn's mission. "First you gather up my things, and now you treat them as so much chaff!"

"I'm sorry, Anastasia the Alluring, but your hope chest is the only thing I can think of that can protect us from that accursed fruit. Give it here, Bronwyn."

Bronwyn sighed a world-weary sigh and dropped the sprouting pomegranate into the box. Its pale new tendrils curled as if burned the moment they touched the wood, and though the fruit's powers to disenchant kept the box's shrinking spell from affecting it, the vine nevertheless began shriveling even as Carole closed and latched the lid. "Should be safe to carry this way," she said, handing the box back to Bronwyn.

Bronwyn almost protested again that protection was pointless, and a hope chest really had no chance against disenchantment, but then, she *had* seen tendrils shrivel. And she suddenly found she was feeling a good deal better.

"That's all very well for you, my dear," Anastasia said, still flapping, "But this is my home after all. I can't stand the thought of my treasures rotting in the open."

"They're only *things*," Carole said scornfully, "But very well." And with a series of shrill blasts she whooshed everything back indoors. The last chair in nearly broke the leg of Loefric, who stumbled out the door and sank to his knees beside them.

"Please, stop—" he cried.

"But you *said*," Carole began, intending to remind him of his promise to let them leave.

"I said no one would ever make a believer of me again, but

you brats—children have," he said, blowing his nose on her hem, and gazing up at her. He was no lovelier than usual in the daylight, but she thought she saw rather more resemblance to Loefwin than she had noticed before. The face, though ugly as a hidebehind made visible, was not so wrinkled and raddled as the shadows of the keep had made it seem. "Even if you've tricked me—even if none of this is real, I—I'd rather look a fool than go on as I've been."

Carole was inclined to skepticism but the bitch sniffed at her former master's posterior and though her ears were flat, her tail twitched uncertainly. "*I* may be wrong as well, but I think the old man's trying to learn new tricks."

"I doubt that," Jack said severely. "He is a cruel man. He knew where the pomegranate was all along but he forced us to do difficult and dangerous tasks to look for it, hoping we would be slain."

"No! No, I didn't," Loefric cried. "Except for the dogs, nothing I asked you to do was really dangerous—it's just, it's just that I was so infernally tired of my own company I wanted to keep you around as long as I could and—" Tears started dribbling down the ruts in his cheeks and into his beard. "And you were so sure of yourselves, I wanted you to learn how hard it is to get what you want and find it's not worth what you paid for it, as I did. Every year I got tireder and more discouraged and I guess I've been afraid to leave the keep—afraid I'd be shunned or murdered. All those Mages and Kings I executed had quite a few relations. I've worried about it so long, it's made an old man of me. I don't even know if Fwin will have me by him any more but perhaps the thing to do after all is ask him."

Loefric's was not the only change. He had no sooner finished his speech than he was knocked off his knees by a violent quake that shook the earth.

"Run!" Anastasia cried. "All of you, run for the forest!" Since no one had any better ideas, run they did, and just in time too, for suddenly the ground split and the castle walls thrust themselves out of it like magic toadstools. Perhaps the weeds had weighted the castle down, perhaps it had been originally buoyed above the swamps by an enchantment now reinstated with the removal of the pomegranate, but at any rate the edifice rose again. Muddy, crumbling, but still mostly intact, it reared up, complete with jagged battlements and gape-roofed turrets. Stranger still, the river gushed up from its underground prison and filled its old channel, flooding the area surrounding the castle walls, so that hounds, prince, swan and children all found themselves standing on the banks of a moat. Just as they were getting used to these radical alterations, and thinking everything surely must settle down now, six giant black swans landed on the brand-new moat.

The dogs started barking but Anastasia cried out ecstatically: "They have returned! My sisters have all returned to our original nest!" And with that, she hopped into the moat and glided out to speak with them. After a brief conversation, all seven glided back to the bank, the other six fanning out behind their elder sister, who said, "Abigail, Agata, Amelia, Alastraina, Ashling and Ailis, this lady is our colleague, the Princess Bronwyn of Argonia. All except the vandalous elderly person who has so disgraced his lineage by ill-treatment of our home are in the Princess's entourage."

The swans trumpeted and gabbled and spoke some of the human words they remembered—for they had been speaking so long in the swan's tongue they had all but forgotten their human speech. While they gossiped among themselves, the air was once more filled with the beating of wings and down flew Gilles Kilgilles and Rusty Raspberry, each mounted on a magnificent steed and between them leading three others.

"Loefwin and the army have flown on ahead," Rusty reported breathlessly, pulling her bright hair up from inside her collar and flinging it back into the hood of her cloak in a dashing manner. "As soon as the Miragenians saw in their pool that you'd gained the pomegranate, they sent word that the war in Argonia is going worse than ever for us and Loefwin and his men should join the King at once. They wanted Gilles and me to swing by here and pick you up first, so here we are. But please do be quick."

Bronwyn nodded impatiently while mounting one of the extra horses.

Since Loefric pleaded to be allowed to fight honorably by his brother's side, which was all right with the others as long as he flew downwind, Anastasia offered to carry Jack upon her back so the Prince could ride one of the winged horses. Her sisters promised to gather bones and meat before night fell again in the forest, so that the hounds might eat.

They stopped only once between the monster-ridden shores of Frostingdung and the Gulf of Gremlins, and that was far out to sea. Carole suddenly hauled on the reins. Her mount obediently skimmed the surface of the vast green sea while Carole

206

pulled forth the whistle given her by Lorelei and trilled one of the songs of calling the siren had taught her.

Though the other riders were too intent on reaching their destination to notice Carole's defection and flew on without her, Bronwyn noticed at once and impatiently reined in her own horse and circled above Carole. Shortly, they were both rewarded by the sight of Ollie bumping across the sea, followed by half a hundred whales and an entire herd of seals, with a porpoise or two clowning along beside the parade. Lorelei and Cordelia, however, were the first to arrive.

"Well, sweeting, had enough of the landlings?" Lorelei asked.

"No, I—er—" Carole began. She had called thinking to ask for the help of these beings she had once so greatly admired, but at the sight of their beautiful, alien faces the memory of their disregard for human life and casual cruelty reached out to smack her as sharply as if she had been bowled over by one of their muscular tails.

"We had a piece of gossip we thought you'd enjoy, actually," Bronwyn hooted down merrily, as if they were all old chums. "My cousin has been feeling like a wretch since depriving you of that ship—"

"And well she might!" Cordelia said with a stab from her gray eyes directed at her erstwhile disciple.

"So she thought you'd enjoy a chance to meet a colleague."

"Colleague? Another siren? In these waters?" The mermaids exchanged indignant glances, replete with the promise of trouble for the interloper.

Bronwyn and Carole for their part exchanged quick, covert grins and Bronwyn continued, "No—not a siren. A man, if you can believe it, who controls sea weather like a siren—why, he's been sinking ships right and left along the Gulf of Gremlins. I hear he's done more damage in a month's time than you did during your whole life in that area, Lorelei."

"Is that so?" Lorelei demanded, slapping the water with her tail so hard she sent up a fountain of spray as high as a ship's mainmast. "We'll just see about that! Suppose you take us to this split-tailed impostor and we'll see how good he is."

"Indeed we will!" Cordelia agreed.

"Dear friends," Carole said, beaming. "I knew I could count on you."

Neither the flying horses nor Loefwin's army—or rather, air-borne cavalry, had been able to penetrate the barrier of lightning

207

bolts with which the Ablemarlonian wizard latticed the perimeter of King Roari's island shelter. The horses and their riders hung back at a safe distance, watching the exhausted men and dragons being ever more tightly enclosed by the ships remaining to harass them. The bulk of the foe's navy had already sailed for Queenston, and Loefwin was ready to give the order to his troops to fly there to defend the Argonian capitol and abandon the shipwrecked army.

Before he could give the order, five horses and a swan quietly joined his ranks, and in the sea below an incredible scene began unfolding. First the entire navy, island and all, was enveloped in a thick white mist, which the lightning bolts were impotent to pierce. Then, with a deadly gentleness that seemed slow and random but was extremely swift, the ships one by one turned their bows inward toward the island and rammed it, all but the one with the wizard, which was pulled away from the others and wrapped in the coils of a great serpent. The serpent squeezed and timbers, sails, and all disintegrated into formless flotsam. The lightning bolts died and the sea boiled with the happy activity of the sirens, and the sporting of the other creatures amid the ruins of the ships.

At Loefwin's order, as the magic mist thinned, the winged cavalry swept down upon the island and scooped up the survivors. The dragons lifted their bright heads and valiantly tried to broil what they saw as a new assault, but sank back, defeated by exhaustion. A gray-bearded man with pointed ears joyfully allowed himself to be dragged aboard Rusty's horse, whereupon the two of them told the dragons what was happening and the rescue was allowed to proceed without incident.

King Roari embraced his daughter wonderingly, before he climbed onto Carole's steed, shoving his niece ahead of him.

Bronwyn's horse heaved with relief. It was sure that the weight of both the giant King and his overgrown daughter would have broken its back.

They flew as quickly as possible for the city, but within a league of Queenston Harbor, Bronwyn heard her father groan and followed his gaze down and ahead to the dock and the city streets. The crew of one lone vessel flying a skull and crossbones tried vainly to fend off the attack of six Ablemarlonian vessels, most of which had already landed, and were belching forth enemy troops into the streets of the capital. The citizens of the city seemed to have wisely chosen to evacuate, for the landing parties met with no resistance.

None, at least, until the vanguard of the attack reached the walls of Queenston Palace, where on the battlements Aunt Maggie Brown had gathered every magician, courtier, palace guard, cook, and chambermaid to defend the townspeople crammed tightly within the walls and armed with their spindles, shovels, shepherd's crooks, and whatever other homely protection they had been able to invest themselves with.

The first assault hit the wall at about the same time the swift flying horses overtook them. Carole's horse was immediately unburdened as the King and his niece jumped down onto the wall. The first Ablemarlonian sailor who scaled the walls on his seige ladder died at the hands of King Roari, who was scrambling down it.

Carole whistled as she had never whistled before, though she would have sworn at the beginning of the day that all the music had been wrung out of her. Her mother flung her one surprised grin and resumed magically hurtling at the enemy pots, pans, crockery, paving materials, and any other household items she could muster. She also started small spontaneous fires among them.

Between her magic and Carole's, the plunder-bent attackers seemed to be having a harvest eve party, dancing spritely, purposeless steps around several cozy little campfires while missiles considerably larger than confetti were hurled at their heads, and flying horses swooped among the stars above them.

Much as Carole enjoyed watching, she hoped the slaughter would be quick, because her lips were trembling with tiredness. Suddenly, a pair of strong hands lay upon her shoulders and a rich tenor voice took up her tune. She tilted her head back and her father's beard brushed her crown. At the phrase-break, he kissed her forehead before redoubling his efforts to aid her own.

Bronwyn fought back to back with her own father, but found she had to close her eyes at crucial times and she winced every time she felt her sword slice through someone. It hardly seemed sporting at all, fighting dancers.

Another foe high-kicked and slashed in front of her and she answered with a blind swipe of her own. The man ducked and she opened her eyes defensively when she realized she had missed. She could have cut him down on the spot for he was glaring over her head to the wall upon which Jack's grandfather and father fought.

"What's 'is Worthless 'ighness doin' fighting for your side, girlie?'' The enemy demanded; pointing. '' 'E was supposed to be on the wizard's ship, keepin' that big fella behind you busy whilst we sacks the city for 'im. Lookit this, mates! The bloody King's turned coat!''

The man's angry voice carried over the songs of Carole and her father, and for a moment activity halted, while every head turned to the curly-headed old gypsy. ''Why ain't you back on the wizard's ship, where you belong, Majesty?'' the soldier demanded.

The gypsy gave him a broad smile, remarkably good-natured under the circumstances. ''Fellow countrymen,'' he said, ''I fear if my brother, King Worthyman, called the Worthless, was aboard that ship, he is dead.''

''Don't try to fool us! If you ain't the King you're—''

''His elder, if not twin, brrother?'' the gypsy roared back. ''Aye! And I'll end this battle here and now, if ye all agree and my good friend King Rrroari stops bashin' you.''

Carole and Colin had stopped singing and Maggie had stopped flinging. None of that was necessary at the moment, for the battle stilled as the foreign foe gazed awestricken at the gypsy on the walls.

''What the 'ell do ye mean by that?'' the soldier demanded, followed by grumbling agreement from his colleagues.

''I mean I'm your rightful King, ye bozo! I'm the long lost Crown Prince of Ablemarle, H. David Worthyman, eldest son of King Worthyman the Worthy and legitimate heir! Do any dare contest my claim?''

''Don't look at me!'' the soldier said. ''Just get us out of this daft country and I'll plump the cushion on your throne meself.''

Most of the Ablemarlonian nobles were on the ship lost to the mermaids and Ollie, and were presumed to have perished at sea. Those who remained rapidly acquiesced to the popular demand of their troops and waved their handkerchiefs to call a truce.

By midnight a treaty was signed, guaranteeing peace between the three countries, an indemnity to be paid in foodstuffs and magical foreign aid to help the stricken Frostingdungians through the winter and spring planting, and an alliance between Argonia and Ablemarle. Ablemarle was to be under the rule of King H. David Worthyman with guaranteed succession granted his son Davey and grandson Jacopo. Also, international traveling rights were granted in perpetuity to the tribe of gypsies known as the Xenobians, since their Queen Xenobia was now also Queen of Ablemarle.

When the treaty had been signed and the dead and wounded of both sides had been removed to the care of Argonian healers, who, with certain secret medicines, were renowned for their ability to effect an astonishing recovery rate, Maggie Brown turned her talents to their more conventional uses. After retrieving her pots and pans and persuading her militia draftees to resume their original positions as maids, table servers, cooks and scullery personnel, she whipped up a great victory feast from what was left in the royal pantry. Her husband, Colin, turned his voice from politically persuasive ditties to celebratory ones. They were all having a very pleasant time of it indeed, particularly the Frostingdungian troops, who hardly knew how to chew, so long had they been gumming gruel. At one point King Roari followed Maggie Brown from the hall and returned with Queen Amberwine in his arms. In *her* arms were Bronwyn's twin baby brothers, both as red-haired as she, and both screaming their heads off.

She was bounding across the hall to admire them and hug her mother when the front doors swung open and Mashkent and Mirza drifted impressively into the hall on a flying carpet.

Mirza bowed to her and rolled up the rug, ignoring the rest of the crowd. "Greetings, high-born. I trust you consider you have received good value for your credit?" Bronwyn nodded, and slipped on her charm. "Then may I also take the liberty of assuming you are ready to pay your bill?"

A hush fell over the hall and King Roari strode up beside her, his presence dwarfing the merchants. Jack, Carole, and Anastasia also left the table to join their friend. "See here, Bronwyn, who are these rogues and what's this about a bill?"

"I must handle this myself, Father," she said, and turned to the merchants. "Your steeds did indeed win the day for my country. Oh—Oh Prosperous ones, may your Profit increase."

"Good, good," Mashkent said, rubbing his hands together. "And we know you have the pomegranate. If you will be kind enough to turn it over, we will in turn be gracious enough to allow you a small bite of it, which will relieve you of your curse. Since this is such a festive occasion, at no extra cost we will be happy to join you and provide dancing girls—and not only that, but we will also allow your allies," he said and bowed to Prince Loefwin, who saluted him with his meat-tipped dagger, and scowled at Loefric, who avoided his gaze, "to return home on our swift and beautiful steeds."

Jack handed her the hope chest, which had been sitting beside

211

her at table. She clutched it tightly and replied, "A very generous offer. But I find that though still possessed of my curse, I am no longer bothered by it. I have grown used to it, having met so many others who seem to be similarly, if more selectively afflicted, and having also learned that it is powerless to pervert my meaning when I speak to the understanding hearts of my good friends. Seeing what the fruit did to the folk of Frostingdung, I prefer to continue struggling with being governed by my imagination rather than to be deprived of it entirely. If my family deems me unworthy to rule because of the curse, so be it."

"You are being unreasonable, Princess," Mirza said soothingly. "Surely one little bite, and then you can turn it over to us."

"I—I don't think so," Bronwyn answered as calmly as possible, her chin tremblingly undermining her attempt at dignity when she thought of the ruin of Frostingdung and the sense of loss and sadness she had felt when the fruit lay in her hand, before it was enclosed in the hope chest, "Forgive me, please, but to entrust the fruit to any private interest seems to me to be extremely—er—unwise. The fruit is just far too dangerous to continue to exist. Your country is a marvel of magic. What if the pomegranate was—uh—misused again while within your borders?" Without naming names, that was as close as she could come to telling the merchants she suspected them of wanting the pomegranate to turn the Anarchy of Miragenia into a conglomerate under the control of one firm—theirs. "No. I trust you will concur with me that the best thing to do with this fruit is to throw it into the deepest crevass of the highest, coldest glacier in the world. Fortunately, that's not far."

Mashkent evidently did not agree, for he grabbed for the box. Bronwyn dodged him and darted for the door and the winged horse tethered outside. Mirza snapped his fingers and the horse reared back and bared his teeth at her.

"Princess!" Jack shouted, "To me!" He was already astride Anastasia, and before the merchants could regain their equilibrium sufficiently to use their magic, she tossed the box to Jack, he caught it deftly, and Anastasia mowed down the merchants as she flew out the doors and into the night.

The merchants, shouting that they were being robbed, ran for the winged horses, but a shrill whistle from Carole slammed the doors in their faces, and when another whistle tune filled the air, they suddenly found they felt like dancing. They whirled and dipped for some moments until Carole judged Jack and Anastasia were well away, and she released them, a smug smile on her lips. When they regained their breath, they ranted and raved until King Roari, who was abiding—but only just—by his daughter's request to handle the situation in her own way, scowled down at them. Then, being practical men, they allowed themselves to be comforted with food and soon found themselves dickering with Emperor Loefwin over the price of a magical winter crop to relieve the food shortage, and an infusion of technical assistance to help rehabilitate the former slaves, once their bracelets were removed.

By the time dessert was served, the door opened again and a half-frozen Jack reappeared.

The Miragenian honor chose once more to be offended. "And how do you intend to pay for the horses, ungrateful woman?" Mashkent hissed at Bronwyn in a tone too low, he hoped, to be heard by her father.

"I—whatever you say," she said. Her misery was only relieved by the fact that her mother was squeezing her hand under the table and Carole patted her shoulder. "As long as it's mine to give. I cannot compromise my father's property, you understand."

"Not the kingdom then," Mirza said.

"In that case, you must give us your first-born," Mashkent declared. A gasp ran through the hall and this time the King did hear and both he and Queen started to protest, but the merchant faced those assembled and cried, "Hear me, Oh merry-makers! The heir of Argonia has profited by her business dealings with us in the form of valuable flying horses that have saved her father's country, and as you have seen, when we bill her for the humble payment we requested in our original estimate, she denies it to us. Now, when we quite fairly demand other compensation and she agrees that we may name our price, her people attempt to use force to deprive us of our Profit! What honor is there in that? How can one do business or sign treaties with—"

Bronwyn cringed but looked resigned when everyone, even her father, took their seats again. She HAD promised them whatever they asked, and they had mentioned before they might ask for her first-born, even though she didn't have one yet, and might not ever. She started to frame an answer that would make it clear to everyone that the members of the royal house of Argonia put honor above even family affection, but found words as hard to frame as she had when she first tried to tell of finding the pomegranate.

Jack saw her anguished expression and the beginnings of her

mute nod. He could not let them bully her this way, these slick experienced merchants. Princess she might be, warrior she might be, but in business matters she was as ignorant as he was of court protocol. He interrupted smoothly, the effectiveness of his wheedling gypsy horse-trading tone only slightly diminished by the noise of his still-chattering teeth, "I thought you were honest merchants and not cheats, affluent ones. The Princess but borrowed your horses and they are all being returned to you in good condition. How can you demand that she give you her unborn child in return for horses that were merely rented?"

"Very well, then." The other diners roared in approval of this speech and Mashkent waved his hand, magnanimously. "We are not monsters. We at Mukbar, Mashkent and Mirza also have mothers, and children. Therefore, we will simply borrow the child for a time."

"Five years," Jack said.

"Fifty," Mashkent returned.

"The Princess should enjoy her babe while it is yet a child. Ten, at the most," Jack protested.

"We need adult work from a bonded one, not just a child's appetite to feed with no return," Mirza pointed out.

"Thirty," Mashkent said decisively.

"Fifteen, and that is the last offer I would consider to be less than a declaration of war," Jack said firmly, crossing his goose-fleshed arms over his chest, and carefully avoiding looking at King Roari.

"Twenty-five," Mashkent replied, echoing the gesture.

"Fifteen," Jack repeated.

"Done."

When the Miragenians finally departed with their horses and the Frostingdungian allies, Bronwyn would have felt she could finally breathe again, except that now it was her father who was angry. He glared down at Jack, growling, "You've a lot of nerve, laddy, bargaining with my grandchild's future."

"Your pardon, Great King," Jack said, bowing but unhumbled. He had three cloaks wrapped around him now and a cup of warm wine had been thrust into his hand. "I meant only—"

"Don't be angry with Jack, Father," Bronwyn said quickly. "I would have given them anything they asked for. He kept me from giving in completely and bought time for all of us."

"It wasna his place t'do so!" the King frowned.

"Was it not, O King?" asked a tall, black-gowned lady with silver streaks waving majestically through her black hair. "Unless I am mistaken, according to the new treaty you have just

214

signed, Jack is heir to the Ablemarlonian throne, even as Bronwyn is heiress to yours. They have no peers that I know of in their own age group. Surely it is not unlikely that a matter concerning the future of Bronwyn's child might not someday also—''

"I catch your drift," the King admitted, though he didn't seem to know if he liked it or not yet. "But I didn't catch your name."

"I am the Princess Anastasia Ilonia Vasilia Gwendolyn Martha Nettletongue, previously a swan and presently rightful heiress to the Nonarable Lands now known as West Frostingdung, but we will discuss that later, since I am enjoying far too much my recent release from long enchantment to discuss politics."

"But how?" Bronwyn asked. "How did you change?"

"Much the same way you did, I assume, my dear. Contact with the pomegranate, I should say, though perhaps the spell was weakened when I returned home. At any rate here I am and there you are, and after all that bother I am most certainly happy we received some personal benefit."

"We did?" Bronwyn looked down, as if expecting the benefit would be in the form of new shoes.

"But of course! Bronwyn dear, has it not occurred to you that you have long ago used your three minutes' worth of charm and still appear to be speaking truthfully? I am certainly under the impression that your curse has lifted."

Bronwyn had to think only a moment before agreeing with her formerly feathered friend. But what she couldn't understand was how she could have failed to notice an important thing like that for all this time? And how had it happened? Was it the influence of the pomegranate, or perhaps her curse, with no countercurse, had worn out, as the merchants had hinted that it might. She had to test out one thing first. Taking off the charm bracelet, which might contain more power than its makers had thought, she finally shut her gaping mouth long enough to say with a sort of experimental conviction, "I believe you're right about that, Your Highness." And turning to Jack she said, "I just want to say, before you go to Ablemarle, that whatever Father says, and he will say yes, won't you, Father? I will marry no one else but you and that I will miss you terribly and I don't know how I'll stand it without you to talk to."

"My Princess," Jack bowed with a courtliness befitting his new status and kissed her hand, gazing adoringly up at her, "I would rather be lied to by you than told the greatest of truths by any other. But in the matter of this pledge you have made, I shall hold you to it."

215

"That's all very well for the two of you," Carole said in an aggrieved tone, "You're both royalty now and if you're betrothed you'll get to see each other again, but for those of us who are left without so much as a flying horse to show for their trouble, Ablemarle is a very long way away and—and I'm going to miss you too."

"And I you," he said, shifting on one knee so he was now kneeling between them and could catch one of Carole's hands in his spare one. "But do not mourn over our parting so quickly, my friend. Come spring smuggling season, you may well find me, crown and all, banging on your door to sell you your own fortune. I have been a prince only a short while but I have been a gypsy all my life and if there is one thing a gypsy knows about, it's traveling."

THE
CHRISTENING
QUEST

For David Michael Ruthstrom, Minstrel Extraordinaire and Stalwart Questing Companion, with abiding affection.

Also for my parents, Don and Betty Scarborough, my brother, Monte Scarborough, and Greg Herriford, Jeannie Jett, and Charles and Karen Parr for their help and inspiration. Special thanks to Tania Opland for listening, and to Tim Henderson, songwriter and minstrel, for his special insight into gypsies.

I would also like the acknowledge Scottish songwriter & singer Archie Fisher whose song "Witch of the Westmereland" inspired the initial meeting between Rupert and Carole.

CHAPTER I

Banshee shrieks and shuddering moans pealed from the stone walls, bouncing from buttressed arch to arrow slot, lending the whole north wing all the peaceful charm of a dungeon. Rupert Rowan, prince and diplomatic trainee, winced and recrossed his long legs, sinking back into the velvet padded chair and trying to maintain his carefully cultivated serenity despite his sister's anguished wails from the other side of the iron-hinged door. He had wearied of pacing hours ago and now had settled down to present a good example to the occasional subject who passed by him in the corridor. Most of these subjects were women, and many of them pretended not to hear Bronwyn's caterwauling, which Rupert thought very decent of them. Bronwyn was supposed to be a warrior. Why did she have to choose a time when he was in earshot to give up stoicism?

A buxom wench with a pert face and a corona of golden braids smiled warmly at him, masking the expression he frequently saw in female faces with one of sympathy. "There now, Your Highness, don't worry. The hollering relieves the pains some, see? Every woman does it in labor. She won't even remember this when she holds the little one in her arms. You'll see."

He smiled at her, a bit pitifully, striving to present a visage that would inspire her to clasp it to her bosom. "You're very kind. Will it be much longer do you think?"

She smoothed the clean, white towels over her arm with one shapely hand. "Not much, I should think. Though the first always takes longer. Is it an Argonian custom to have a male relative in attendance, Your Highness? Forgive me, but we were curious, we girls, if you were here because Prince Jack couldn't be, being in Brazoria as I'm sure it's needful he be, though very hard on our young lady, your sister, it is. We think it ever so sweet that her brother should come be near her in her husband's stead. None of *his* folk offered, not even the women." She blushed a pretty pink and covered her pretty mouth with her fingertips. "No disrespect intended, milord."

"None taken, I'm sure. We all know what gypsies are like. As a matter of fact I—"

A particularly blood-curdling bellow emanated from the royal bedchamber. The girl started, gave him an apologetic smile and a half-curtsy, and scurried off, banging through the door hip and shoulder first.

He had been about to explain to her that the last thing he intended was to be at Bronwyn's bedside for her birthing. He had, in fact, only been stopping off on the way from his fostering in Wasimarkan, where he was learning diplomacy at the behest of his Royal Mother, Queen Amberwine. The Queen had rightly pointed out that with an elder sister as Princess Consort of Ablemarle (having lost the title of Crown Princess of Argonia when her brothers were born) and elder twin brothers (one of whom, Raleigh, would be King, the other of whom, Roland, would be war leader), there was very little else for her fourth child to do that would be useful.

The Queen had declared with unusual forcefulness for a person of faery blood that she was not about to have a son of hers turn into a good-for-nothing knight errant bullying the populace and using his royal perogatives to rape and pillage. It had happened elsewhere, and Rupert was no less fond of the phenomena than his mother. He was a highly peaceable and loving sort by nature—so loving, in fact, that by the age of twenty, his frost giant ancestry caused him to be so unusually tall and well grown and his faery blood lent him such uncommon beauty and charm that he was a cause for alarm among the fathers and husbands in the Wasimarkanian Court. To the men he was called, behind his back (for it would never do to offend so powerful an ally as the Royal House of Argonia) Rowan the Rake. To the women, into whose eyes he gazed soulfully and whose hands he kissed tenderly, almost without regard for age, station, or pulchritude, he was Rowan the Romantic. He would miss those charitable and generous ladies, one and all, but his mentors, under pressure, had declared that with princesses of six major countries in a swoon for his attentions, he would need more advanced lessons in diplomacy than they had to offer. They referred him back to his own family for further instruction.

The stop in Ablemarle's capitol to visit Bronwyn had been an impulse. His ship was docking to take on cargo. He had not seen Bronwyn in several years, and she had always been his favorite in the family. She was as good a fighter if not a better one than Roland—at least on the practice field—and she had had marvelous adventures when she was still much younger than Rupert. When Rupert tired of hearing of those adventures, which he sometimes did since he always wanted to learn something new, Bronwyn was most adept at making up tales to amuse him.

He almost failed to recognize the wild-eyed creature who greeted him and clung to his hand, her face so pale that every freckle stood out like a pock, her wiry red hair loose and straggling in every direction, her belly great with child. The self-sufficient big sister of his youth all but pleaded with him to remain until her child was born, as it was to be any day. She begged him to stay since her husband, Prince Jack, could not. Rupert had failed to understand any more than the pretty lady in waiting why any masculine family member should be a comfort to Bronwyn in what was first and foremost and unarguably woman's work, but he could not deny her. He had stayed.

A long, gasping cry ended in an ear-splitting scream, and was followed closely with another cry, this time unmistakably the squall of an infant. Rupert jumped to his feet and strode to the door, leaving his rowan shield leaning against the door. All the Rowan offspring usually carried the shields made by their father as birthing gifts on their persons, for the rowan wood was proof against magic. But he was in his sister's hall and far more excited than he had thought he would be at the advent of this new relative, and three strides was hardly an incautious distance.

The door flung back against him and the girl with whom he had been speaking bustled out, brushing against him, a whimpering blanketed bundle cradled against her breast.

"Wait," he said quickly. "Can I see?"

She lifted the triangle of blanket just above the crook of her elbow and showed him a wrinkled, red little face which began to screw itself into another scream. "It's a girl," the maid informed him. "Isn't she adorable?"

"Quite," he said, trying to sound sincere. "I'll just go congratulate Bronwyn."

"Oh, not yet, milord," she said. "She's getting her bath and then she must rest a bit. I'll be bathing this child to be presented to her when she wakes."

"A bath?" he asked blankly. "Oh, of course, the baby would be needing a bath. Well, um, may I watch? I've never seen a new child bathed before."

"I don't see why not," the girl said with a saucy, calculating look from under her lashes, "But you Argonians certainly have strange ways, if you'll pardon my saying so, sir."

"I'd pardon you almost anything, my dear," he said politely, and opened the door to an adjoining chamber for her.

The baby's bath was interesting chiefly in that Rupert thought it very convenient to be able to bathe an entire human being in a wash basin that barely fit his two hands. Otherwise it was rather messy. The maid herself was far more intriguing, and he proceeded to get to know her better while his new niece slept in her cradle, carved in the shape of a swan and newly decked with pink ribbons by the lady whose ear he was nibbling.

The enormous draft that blasted open the double doors took both Rupert and his companion by surprise, as did the fact that neither of them were able to do so much as raise a finger to lift themselves from the tiled floor where they had been flung. Indeed, Rupert could not so much as twitch his knee from where it undoubtedly inconvenienced his paramour, lodged in her midsection. He watched helplessly as a rather large rug whisked in on the blast. Two gentlemen with blue robes and bandages tied round their heads with blue cords lifted the baby from her cradle and onto the rug and whisked back out again. They failed to blast the door shut behind them and Rupert could hear doors banging, presumably all the way down the corridors to the main entrance, as the rug flew through unhindered.

Sensation returned to him as the last distant door slammed back again, and he jumped up, still stunned. The whole incredible event had happened so fast he thought perhaps he had been napping in his new love's arms. But the cradle was empty and when he ran to the arrow slit in the corridor outside, he could make out the outline of a flat flying object with two figures on it. Behind him, the girl scrambled to her feet, clutching her bodice together, and scampered into his sister's chamber. Rupert sagged against the arrow slit for a moment and watched the rug disappear over the city, over the masts of the boats docked in the harbor, and far far out over the line of greenish-gray that marked the vastness of the Gulf of Gremlins.

When no outcry erupted from Bronwyn's chamber even after several moments, he cracked the door, expecting to see her in a swoon. Instead, she sat up in bed, her hair splashing like blood upon the pillow, her eyes staring straight ahead. The ladies around her started nervously, but she quieted them with one look and bade Rupert enter with another.

"Bronwyn, sister, I don't know what to say," he began. "I was helping your nurse with the baby's bath and we had only just put the dear little one to sleep and were chatting when—"

She took his hand in both of hers and pulled him down to sit

222

beside her, then wrapped her arms around him. She sobbed wearily and almost noiselessly, her face against his chest, her tears soaking his fine embroidered tunic. His own tears wet her hair, and he held her and rocked her until she was so quiet he thought her sleeping. Then she disentangled herself and lay back against her pillows, her face full of grief and something else that he could have been imagining as a reflection of his own shame at having been caught dallying when those who depended on him were threatened. The look on her face undid him, so that his own tears flowed anew. Her eyes turned outward, toward him, again and she reached up to mop his tears with the edge of her sheet.

"By the Mother, Bronwyn, I am so sorry. I had no idea—"

"I know, Ru. I know. I had no right to involve you without telling you but I thought they wouldn't strike so soon, that they'd wait until she was a little older, until after her christening—though why I imagined Miragenians respecting anything but their wretched Profit—"

"You know who they were?" he asked, incredulous.

She nodded.

"You knew this would happen?"

Another nod. "I never told you the whole end of the affair with the magic pomegranate I won from the sunken castle in Frostingdung. I had promised it to the Miragenians, in exchange for their help for our father in the Great War. They fulfilled their end of the bargain so readily I knew that the pomegranate must be of great importance. I learned that it had the power to undo all magic and sow disenchantment and despair in its stead. I could not, simply could not, place such a hideous weapon in the hands of those who care only to reap more profit than their competitors. As I told you, I disposed of it, or rather, Jack did, flinging it into the deepest crevasse of the highest glacier he could find. But the Miragenians demanded, as honorable payment of my debt to them, possession of my first-born child. Jack bargained with them until they agreed to keep her for only fifteen years—"

"*Only* fifteen years? Great Mother in the Ground, Bronwyn, how could you live with such a bargain?"

She shrugged, a mere hopeless twist of her mouth and clenching of her shoulder. "One never knows what will happen. We thought perhaps we would not marry, Jack and I, as we had planned, but even if we had not loved each other for so long, the alliance was necessary for both Argonia and Ablemarle. Then we hoped I would be barren, and tried to see that it was so but—" She rolled her eyes and sniffed, disgusted with herself for her failure to keep from her husband.

223

"I understand," Rupert said quickly.

"That's why Jack's away now, I know it. He couldn't bear to be here when they took her. He's been strange ever since I told him I'd conceived. And in truth, I don't blame him. I wouldn't be here either if I could help it. But I can't even ride after them and offer myself as my own baby's nurse. For the honor of Argonia, the bargain must be respected, hard as it is, and I cannot hope to see my child again until she's almost a woman. But, oh, Rupert, I did think they'd let me see her christened first, protected by the gifts we could give her. There wouldn't be many, of course, considering the circumstances. We've both been in secret disgrace all these years among our families because of it. The gypsies, except for his father and grandfather, are scarcely speaking to Jack—"

At that a black-haired maid who had been scrubbing the floor beside the bed slapped down the wet cloth, wiped her hands on her skirts, and with a passionate and unreadable look from coal-dark eyes fled the room.

"Oh, dear. I forgot about her. Gypsies are so sensitive." She collapsed into the pillow for a moment, then suddenly sat straight up, swinging her legs over the side of the bed.

"What are you doing?" he asked, restraining her.

"I know. I'll disguise myself as a man and go after them. I don't know if I can find Miragenia again but I did it once. I'll take the christening gifts with me so that even if I'm discovered, my daughter will have her birthright. . . ."

Her skin was hot and her breath came raggedly as she spoke.

"Bronwyn, you can't. You're not ready to be out of childbed yet. You're ill. Besides, you told me they have magic in Miragenia. You have none. You've no chance against them."

"I'll find Carole, our cousin. She'll help. She's a witch and she has magic. Besides, she's a priestess now. She can christen my child for me there. Yes. That's what I'll do. . . . She broke free of Rupert's hands and stood for a moment before blood soaked the front of her gown, turning it from white to red as she stood seeking to keep her balance. Rupert caught her as her knees buckled and tucked her in again, while her maids clucked about her.

"Where are the christening gifts you have?" he asked her, smoothing her hair back and paying no heed to the maids tending to the lower half of her body.

"Here," she said, reaching under her pillow and extracting a pitifully small packet. "They're runed spells to be burned and mixed with the christening mud. There's nothing else except . . . Take her my rowan shield, Rupert. She'll need protection."

"Hush," he said. "So do you. She'll have my shield, and I'll make myself another. Only promise me not to rise from this bed until your midwife says it's safe. I will find this cousin of ours and together we will do what may be done for your baby." He brushed his lips against her hair and rushed away to hire another ship.

Less than a month later Rupert had crossed not only the Gulf of Gremlins but Argonia, and rode across the snow-palled plains of Wormroost Valley. The shadows of the great glacial peaks reached out for him, chilling him when his path led him through them. Snow slowed his horse. It burdened the boughs of the spruces so that they drooped like old women with full aprons. The deciduous trees were reduced to bare bones. The sky was muzzy gray and wonderfully eerie. Wild animals scuttled across the snow in front of him and beside him. This was the wildest country Rupert had ever encountered. He felt certain it was every bit as dangerous as Miragenia and began to enjoy the perilousness of his mission already. Court was all very well, but a man liked action and adventure occasionally.

Now here he was, heading into this fearsome border country, accompanied only by his horse, a hawk, and hound borrowed from Roland's castle, where he had spent the night. He was readying himself to face a witch. Admittedly, she was supposed to be on his side, but nevertheless, she was a perilously powerful person. He remembered Bronwyn's tale of her quest very well, and, at the moment, the part where this particular witch had tried to drown his sister figured prominently in his recollections. Also on his mind were the opinions of his Wasimarkanian friends. Wasimarkan had little magic and less regard for it, and the attitudes of the people who had most recently raised him influenced him sufficiently that he felt he was being put on his mettle to deal with a witch.

For her part, the witch was dealing with a great many other problems of a distressingly mundane nature, and would have preferred, as she had explained to the village seamstress only the day before, to be almost anywhere else dealing with almost anything else. But she had her responsibilities. The villagers were used to a magically clean manor and common dining hall and plenty of food on the board, something Carole's mother, Maggie, with her hearth magic, had always been able to provide with what seemed to Carole unthinking efficiency. For Carole, whose own powers consisted of being able to whistle or hum objects, people, and animals into dance, maintaining the same standards as her mother took a great deal of thinking and considerably more work. She could not simply wish a thing clean, but had to whistle a broom into an appropriately useful motion, a dustcloth into yet another, and the dishcloth, ladles, spits, polishing rags, and so on, each into its own movement. Chopping knives were a nightmare, and mending had more than once produced some bizarre results when she neglected to stop the needle in time.

And unlike her mother, she could not simply expand existing supplies of food but had to locate new ones as provisions ran out. Maggie had left in such a hurry to travel to Great Aunt Sybil's bedside in the Northern Territories that she hadn't reckoned properly what would be needed for the duration of her visit, which moreover had turned into a more extended one than she had anticipated. Consequently grain, fruits, and preserved vegetables were getting low and the villagers were complaining mightily about the extra ration of fish in their diet, since Carole was totally unwilling to whistle anything less cold-eyed and more furry to its demise on a supper table. Her father, Colin Songsmith, the noted minstrel, had attended the first town council where the villagers had mentioned their dissatisfaction with the arrangements. Thereafter, he hastily recalled an important seminar at the Royal Minstrel's Academy, far to the south and safely away from the valley whose government he was supposed to administer.

Then, of course, there were her other duties, those she had taken on with her vows as priestess. There weren't too many weddings in Wormroost, for most of the inhabitants were the age of her parents or older, but many sickbeds and deathbeds to attend, and officiating at the holidays, which Mother be praised were mostly past now with no more due until surely, *surely*, her own mother, Maggie, was safely back.

Sometimes Carole had a sneaking suspicion that Aunt Sybil, who saw into other people's lives even as they were happening, had gotten sick simply to make sure Carole had enough to do to take her mind off the treacherous defection of her erstwhile suitor, Sir Brendan, formerly a knight at Castle Rowan, a week's ride from Wormroost, presently residing with his new bride in Queenston. Not that anyone cared, the witch reminded herself, hoisting her dip net and throwing on her cloak. Queenston was an overrated bore, full of lovely, costly goods and impractical

226

activities and people silly enough to spend too much money on them. She had tried it once, fostering there between her fifteenth and seventeenth years, and had found herself longing for the valley and the villagers, who were unpretentious, if demanding. And here her magic powers ran only a close second to her mother's hearth craft and her father's persuasive musicality, rather than being lost in the smoky explosion of the grandiose and exotic abilities abundant at court.

When her parents were home, there was naturally less call for whistling things about, but her priestess work was necessary. She had ample time to swim in the talkative Blabbermouth River, enchanted by a previous witch occupant of the valley for companionship. She also liked to visit Sebastian, the amiable white beast who guarded the glaciers on the far side of the valley. She had ofted explored the ruins of the ice castle, without disturbing the sleeping ice worm whose breath in winter covered the town in mist. And there had previously been occasions when she rode to Castle Rowan for a party or weekend outing with Roland and his wife, who were dull but at least close to her own age. She liked watching the unicorns when they came to bless the river with their horns, rendering it not only pure but capable of sensible conversation (otherwise it did nothing but gossip and utter trite drivel of a personal nature). She liked seeing Wulfric, the wolf who was formerly a were, lope across the valley as he sometimes did when the moon was full, pausing to howl in greeting from a safe and lonesome distance.

She could do with a bit of a howl herself, she thought, dismounting her black mare beside the loop of the Blabbermouth farthest from the village. She set her net aside while she stripped off her cloak and brown gown to reveal her bathing costume. A blue velvet, decently opaque, long of sleeve, with a divided skirt. The mermaids she had met when she was a girl would laugh at it, but her mother would settle for no less decorous attire and the villagers too were easily shocked, and certainly would have been by the standard mer costume of flashing tail and lots of hair with everything else bared to the waves. Sometimes she wished she had stayed with the mermaids, as they had desired, but though the singing was nice, she simply couldn't manage to develop a taste for drowning sailors. Besides, had she done so she would have missed out on the rest of the quest which was, except for priestess training—and she supposed she had to count Sir Brendan—the last interesting thing that had happened to her.

The hole she had hacked in the ice with a hand-ax had grown ice whiskers around the edges, but she was still able to plunge in, net and all, through the narrow opening into the chattering black waters.

Rupert, riding through the worm's-breath mist to the mumbling river, knew at once he had found the witch he sought. Who else was likely to be rising dripping wet and calm as you please from a river frozen solid? Her jet mare paced near enough for her to catch the tail of the patient beast and haul herself, whistling, from the hole. She hadn't the humanity even to shiver. Holding his rowan shield firmly before him, he flipped his hawk from his other gauntlet to circle her head, while the hound barked and whined. That should stop her from extending a witchy forcible swimming invitation to him, should she be inclined to do so. He would have had no doubt about handling an ordinary woman, but a certain nervousness around witches was, he felt, entirely justifiable.

The witch clung to the horse's tail and watched the hawk for a moment before blasting three short notes that sent the bird fluttering back toward Rupert. Its far-seeing eyes were crossed with confusion.

"Excuse me," she said, waving with her free hand, "Yoo-hoo, you there on the horse. Keep that creature on a leash, will you? Or jesses, or whatever you call them. The village won't be at all happy if I let some strange bird fly off with their supper, even if it is only fish." And she flopped a net full of them up on the ice and finished climbing out after them.

Rupert quickly swung down from his horse and gave her his hand, which she accepted in lieu of the black mare's tail.

"You were fishing?" he asked. "In there?" He looked over her dripping shoulder into the steaming hole behind her.

"Yes," she said. "Ice fishing. I realize it looks a bit peculiar, but water doesn't bother me much, even very cold water. Mer blood on my father's side, you know. But if you'll excuse me now, once outside the water I freeze as quickly as anyone, and you're between me and my cloak."

The last was punctuated with the clicking of her teeth and he snatched the cloak from her saddle, wrapped it around her, and watched as she rubbed the hood briskly against her hair and the cloak over her shoulders and arms before mounting her horse.

"I've come on an urgent mission, lady," he said, mounting his own and wishing to establish his credentials at once.

"Undoubtedly, since this is hardly the season for tourists. But excuse me, it's also urgent that I get myself and these fish to the hall." And the horse trotted smartly away. He caught up with her well before they arrived at the hall and followed her inside. "Make yourself at home for a bit while I dry off, will you?" she called back and disappeared through a side door to reappear with her brown hair sleeked back from her strong-featured and rather saturnine face. She was clad sedately in a brown tunic, skirt, and wrapped boots not half so becoming as the wet blue velvet.

"Do I have the pleasure of addressing the Honorable Lady Carole Songsmith-Brown?" he asked, knowing he did.

"I sincerely hope you'll find it pleasant," she replied. "But I suppose that depends on who you are and what it is you want."

"I was about to say that," Rupert replied, so taken aback by the witch's lack of civility as to forget his own training. "If you'd be kind enough to let me get to it."

"Sorry," she said, not sounding so.

He smiled down at her. She was probably still rattled at having such a very large stranger as he was accost her alone in the wilderness. Though he could certainly be forgiven for not noticing, since she seemed quite a lot calmer than he felt. "I am your cousin, Rupert Rowan, fourth child and third son of His Majesty and—er—also Duke of the Eastern Salt Marshes."

She blinked twice, staring, to his satisfaction, with her mouth open, and sat down, belatedly extending a hand to indicate that he do the same. "My," she said at last. "What a pleasant surprise. You're little Rupert, are you? Pardon me if I failed to recognize you. I think you were about four years old when last I saw you. You've grown."

He nodded.

"Didn't I hear that you were abroad somewhere?"

"I was. Wasimarkan. I've learned all they have to teach me now, however, and am, as I mentioned, on an urgent mission for my lady sister."

"Bronwyn? You've seen her? How is she?"

"Sick with grief," he said, and told her the story of the kidnapping, adding a few sword thrusts on his part and deleting the role of the nurse.

"Didn't waste any time, did they?" she asked with a brooding look into her mug of herb tea. She had prepared both of them a mug while Rupert spoke.

"Not even long enough to have the child christened, which seems to be what distresses Bronwyn the most. She was ready to ride over here in her nightgown to ask you to help her see that the child has full protective rites."

"But you came instead?"

He nodded.

"Let me throw together some food and get my cloak," she said, rising.

"You don't understand. They're already in Miragenia by now. It will be a long and hazardous quest."

"Oh, but I do. I'm quite prepared now, unless you're weary from your journey and want to rest a night?" Carole tried to sound merely cooperative rather than eager, but inwardly she praised the Mother for delivering her from the tedium of the past few weeks. And though the witch was sorry, in a somewhat abstract way, for the trouble that had befallen Bronwyn's household, she was not surprised and was certainly not displeased at the excitement Bronwyn's misfortune promised to generate. Not that Carole was enjoying the trouble exactly, just the opportunity to help her cousin out of it, as she had previously done when Bronwyn's curse had been a royal pain in the neck for herself and everyone else.

What marvelous timing. Just when she was about to march the entire village into the river, which no doubt would have made everyone very cross with her, Bronwyn provided her with a perfectly lovely excuse to chuck it all and venture forth to aid a beleagered baby. No, not an excuse. A sacred duty. A family trust. A dire, drastic emergency. Even if one were extremely reluctant, one would have had to respond, of course, both as priestess and family member. Anyone would understand that. On the other hand, no one, especially the Prince, was likely to take kindly Carole's unseemly delight at the prospect, so she controlled her face and modulated her voice a full three octaves below the tones of squeaky excitement she was apt to emit if she wasn't careful. "You did say it was urgent, didn't you?"

"Yes, I suppose I did. I just thought you'd need more persuading."

"Under the circumstances, I can hardly quibble. Just let me drop those fish off at a certain town councilman's cottage on the way and I'll delay you no longer."

As she was grabbing her cloak, however, the long narrow windows of the hall began rattling and the massive furniture quivered. Presently there came a great noise, a periodic booming, as of some huge drum, passing overhead and quitting just as it cleared the manor house. A horse screamed. Rupert was on his feet at once, his hand to his sword hilt. Carole touched his arm.

"It's nothing to worry about. Just one of the dragons. Since I

230

managed to persuade the council not to butcher the cow I set aside for her, she won't trouble your horse. Not unless she's unusually hungry that is.''

Unreassured, Rupert raced for the door and around the building. In the farmyard was indeed a dragon, daintily covering with a loop of her tail a charred carcass from which she was chewing a haunch. She looked up, and belched, and to Rupert's amazement, blushed. He could tell she was blushing for her color deepened so that the lightest shade of pink in her scales, which was as delicate as the inside of a seashell, turned the same deep rose as her darkest shading. Her eyes were as large as his shield and the color of lilacs. They blinked slowly and incredulously, watching him.

"Ah, Grippledice," Carole said, a pace or so behind him. "Good to see you. Meet my cousin, the Prince."

The dragon's eyes grew, if possible, larger, and then the delicately veined lids drooped shyly over them and didn't look back up again. Her head dipped toward her rosy wing. Rupert knew the look, though he had never seen it on a dragon before. He didn't pause to wonder how Carole communicated with the beast. She was a witch, after all. He assumed she used witchcraft. He bowed his most elegant and courtly bow and said, "I had no notion we bred dragons so fair in this land, cousin," and, in a quick whisper from the side of his mouth added, "You can tell her I said so. You did say it was a *lady* dragon, did you not?"

Carole nodded. "Grippledice is on mountain patrol this month. We provide her with stock in payment for her services."

Grippledice emitted a low, hoarse growl, producing a cloud of steam. Carole nodded, and turned back to Rupert with an expression of amusement and a slightly raised eyebrow. "She wants to know where you've been all her life."

"I've been—see here, I'll pay you if you'll give me that spell you're using to talk to her. I've never spoken to a dragon before."

"Sorry, but it's no spell. It's Pan-Elvin, a magical language that takes years to learn. It's all in the silent letters, you see. So when I use it, it sounds like Argonian to anyone else but the creature I'm addressing, who hears the magical silent letters in its own tongue. When the dragon replies, she uses the dragonese version."

Rupert, who hadn't quite caught all that, scratched his head and shook back the curl dangling so charmingly over his forehead. "I must get you to teach me this language then. I really have to learn to speak with dragons."

"We have unicorns hereabouts, too, but they're shy unless—I don't suppose you're . . . no, silly of me, never mind."

Rupert was about to protest that she must tell him what she meant by that, too, until it dawned on him that he knew with whom, according to legend, unicorns were most friendly. He grinned and winked at her. "No, I'm afraid I wouldn't qualify in that respect, though I'm sure I could convince a unicorn of the purity of my intentions if only you'd provide the introductions."

Grippledice, piqued at being left out of the conversation, breathed a slightly sulfurous puff in their direction. Carole made a quick reply. The dragon batted her eyes at Rupert again twice before launching herself upward, cow and all, and disappearing into the glacial peaks.

"That fish will be nasty if we don't get it delivered soon," Carole said, cheerfully linking arms with him. "And it might be wise to leave before the dragon forgets her cow and decides to take you instead. They're rather impetuous creatures, dragons."

Chapter II

The town councilman was far less pleased than Carole with her present and the knowledge that Wormroost would just have to cope without its resident witch and spiritual adviser for the time being.

"But won't that be hard on them?" Rupert asked as they left, very quickly, while the front door of the councilman's cottage slammed behind them.

Carole grinned a grin worthy of the Wasimarkanian version of a witch. "On the contrary, I think it will be very good for them. No doubt the Mother planned it that way. Still, we need to be well away from here quickly. I'm sure the stableman will be glad of the loan of a hound and bird for company and old Bernard may even remember how to hunt with them."

"Do you have the power of flight to transport us?" Rupert

asked suspiciously. He did not mind taking her along, but he didn't much care for the way she was already trying to manage things.

"No," she said, "But I do have an extra pair of skis—that is if you're interested in a shortcut?"

"Back to Queenston?"

"Through the mountain, as Bronwyn and I did when we were girls, and to the sea."

"What then? Will your skis carry us across the sea to Miragenia?"

"No, but I think the mermaids might. Or they might let us ride their sea serpent."

Rupert, who had never been on skis, through a mountain, seen mermaids, or ridden a sea serpent before, was more than eloquent at persuading the stableman that the horse, hound, and hawk he had borrowed from Roland would be a great benefit to the entire village and were deserving of his tenderest care.

The skis were too short for him and the laces had to be lengthened to fit his feet, but once mounted on the skis, he watched his cousin glide forward with a half-stepping, half-skating gait, and soldiered bravely after her. On the river, he gained confidence and skill enough to pass her, but she stopped him with a gesture, and without explanation continued at a faster pace until she came to what looked like the side of the mountain, at which point she squatted down over her skis and plunged into some dead vegetation.

In a short time her voice called to him. "Come ahead. It's safe."

He did, gliding forward, squatting about where he thought he had seen her squat, and wondering what all the fuss was about when the bottom dropped out of the river, his skis flew out from under him, and he thumped down hard on his tailbone to slide through the dead brush and down into icy darkness.

"I thought you said it was safe," he said when he had recovered his breath to find her standing above him, waiting beside the frozen waterfall down which he had just fallen. They were surrounded by cavern walls pierced with holes through which pale light glittered on a wide rink, a pool of ice.

"Don't worry," she said, "You'll get the hang of the steep places after a while. There aren't many like that one. What I meant was that the river is frozen down here, too. I wasn't sure it would be, though I suppose I could have asked it. If it hadn't been, I'd have needed you to pull me up again so we could try the other way, but I believe this is going to work."

233

Rupert finished checking and decided he was still in one piece. Carole produced a pocket torch from her bag of supplies and lit it just outside the tunnel on the opposite side of the pool.

The tunnel was long and dark, breaking off at times into channels. The first of these forks baffled Carole for a moment.

"But didn't you notice them before?" Rupert asked.

"The swan was pulling us in a boat. I suppose she just chose correctly. I haven't tried the passage since. Just a moment. I'll ask."

She knelt down and used the flame of the torch to melt a deep hole in the ice. A thin voice burbled up. "Which is the safest way to the sea for us, Blabbermouth?" she asked it.

"To the right," it said.

"Thank you," she replied.

"Don't mention it. It's lonely down here, this time of year."

The next time she asked, the river was less than polite, advising them to go, "down the center, stupid." Carole explained to Rupert that the river was changeable as it ran its course, a statement that was proved out as yet later, the voice, dulled to a sucking whisper, replied, "All ways are the same to me" and a lot more nonsense Rupert couldn't make out.

Carole knelt longer at that spot, her eyes flickering up at him in the torchlight like a wild beast who had paused to drink at the puddle in front of her. "The spell wears off here," she said. "The river doesn't talk at all on the other side of the mountain. But the right-hand passage appears widest, don't you think?"

He did and reasoned that if it was not, they could always retrace their tracks and find their way upstream again.

When at last the cave broadened onto a horizon, it was a darkened one, with an undulating ribbon of green rippling along the edge between the star-filled sky and the broad expanse of snow that was the eastern Blabbermouth.

They leaned on their poles at the mouth of the tunnel, allowing their eyes to rest on the green aurora and the stars. Abruptly, they found themselves staring instead at something quite different: All light was blocked from above when a cartsized head dipped down from the top of the cave's entrance and an upside-down muzzle emitted sulfurous gusts of welcome while great lamping eyes blinked at them.

Rupert laughed. "How very clever. She followed us."

Carole felt unaccountably annoyed at the interruption. She had been enjoying the shushed ski through the mountain and the moonlight, the prospect of adventure in the company of her handsome and amiable young cousin. Surely just because she chose to delegate her own temporary duties there was no cause for every other creature in the east of Argonia to do likewise? "Grippledice, why aren't you patrolling? You know good and well it's only us down here rather than invading armies or bandits."

The dragon did an airborne backwards somersault and landed gracefully upon her claws and tail in the riverbed ahead of them. She belched sparks at them.

"What did she say?" Rupert asked, smiling a puzzled but winning smile in the dragon's direction.

"Nothing really. She's just curious. She's a youngster yet and doesn't take her responsibilities seriously." The last came out in a somewhat self-righteous tone, considering the speaker, Carole thought, chiding herself.

"But if she's on patrol, perhaps she did think we were invaders. I had no idea dragons were so intelligent."

The object of his admiration regarded him lovingly and chirruped.

"I don't think so, Grippledice." Carole replied quickly. "It doesn't fit in with our plans. Why don't you fly away now and ter to business? Dragons do not woo princes customarily, you know. You're a separate species. It would never work out."

Grippledice hung her head sulkily. Rupert gave Carole an indignant look. "She's only trying to be friendly. You needn't hurt her feelings. Please tell her that I think she's very beautiful and that were I a dragon, I'd be sure to be smitten. As it is I hope we shall be friends."

Carole complied reluctantly. Her cousin might be a prince but he knew very little about dragons. She did know that even though her mother and father had dealt with Grippledice's parents on occasion, their dealings were cautious. Dragons might cooperate with people sometimes, but they weren't to the best of her knowledge to be trusted as friends. The sort of behavior Grippledice was displaying was so uncharacteristic as to make anyone with more brains than vanity nervous. Why, Carole and the dragon had all but grown up together and Grippledice had certainly never offered *her* a ride.

Grippledice cooed. Rupert skied ahead of Carole and reached out to pat the dragon. The beast lowered her head and nudged invitingly at him.

"Why, I think she means for me to ride her, cousin," he said, bending down to unfasten his skis.

235

"Your Highness, I don't think that's wise. No one has ever ridden Grippledice that I know of and the coast is not too far to ski. Besides, the mermaids are—"

Rupert was not to be thwarted. "Nonsense. No one has ridden her before because she has not wished them to. I'm sure that if I request it, she will carry you also. Don't be such a spoilsport. I'll need a translator. Tell her I said you must come, too, and we will only ride as far as the sea coast. I don't want to miss seeing mermaids."

The serious young man who had so movingly related to her the plight of his sister seemed now more interested in trying one new thrill after another, but that was fairly typical of the jaded sort of person one found at court, Carole thought, her good mood at winning free of the village fading into irritation.

She couldn't resist mumbling into Grippledice's ear as she climbed aboard that she hoped the dragon would be content with transporting them to the coast and then resume her more serious duties.

"Bother my duties, dearie," Grippledice said. "They include invaders and *he* is the only stranger in these parts. I see more in a single day's flight than you would see coming in a week. I can spare the time, and still leave your puny domain safe. Why are you so all-fired interested in my duties all of a sudden anyway, hot stuff? You never said much to me before except 'Your cow is over there, dragon.' Trying to get rid of me? Don't blame you. I didn't realize they made mortals like *him*!"

Carole shook her head and settled down between two spines in front of Rupert. "They don't, dragon. But he's part of my family and part of the royal family besides. I just wouldn't want you to get so carried away you . . . forget yourself and treat him like one of your cows."

The dragon snorted at that but didn't reply.

Rupert was agawk over the countryside between the tunnel and the sea, pointing out every starlit bend in the river with awe and wonder. Unfortunately, by the time Carole finished her exchange with the dragon, the beast's strong wings had already carried them to the coast. Carole dismounted and stood staring out to sea. When Rupert asked if she was calling the mermaids, she didn't answer. This caused Rupert to look all the more avidly out to sea himself, while Grippledice flapped nervously nearby. The dragon cooed inquiringly. Rupert gave her a half-impatient, half-apologetic shrug and continued his vigil. Grippledice sighed warmly and departed, sensing herself dismissed. Rupert glanced

236

quickly at his cousin, wondering when and how she was going to produce the mermaids.

Having returned to the spot where she first met the mermaids for the purpose of calling them again, the witch hesitated, recalling the less pleasant aspects of that other meeting. Weighing in her mind the merwomen's kinship with herself against their fondness for drowning anyone without mer connections, her own power against theirs, her wish to help Rupert meet the obligation he had incurred to Bronwyn against the danger, ultimately she decided that they had come this far and it would be much further to return, and not nearly so interesting. "Perhaps it would be better if you keep out of sight until I have a chance to talk to them again," she told her cousin finally. "They have a rather unusual view of . . . life, you might say, and can be dangerous to men, particularly. I would feel much better if I were able to see if I can persuade them to guarantee our passage before they meet you."

"You wouldn't just send them away before I got to meet them, would you?" he asked.

But his question was carried to sea with the same cold wind that blew the first notes of her whistled calling to the mermaids. He watched her for a while, reasoning that he would hide when he saw something coming on the distant sea, and then he paced, shivering despite his furlined cloak and gloves. He wandered in small circles, drawing patterns in the snow with the toe of his boot and still his cousin whistled. The tune was eerie and pervasive, rising and falling on the wind, but catchy, and soon he found that he too was whistling.

She batted her hand sharply at him to stop and he shrugged. "I'm not magic. Surely they can't hear me. And if they can, perhaps it helps."

"Don't—" she began but was interrupted as something large and narrow slid toward them through the waves. In the dark waters directly in front of them, two wet heads popped to the surface. Rupert was too busy staring to remember to hide, even if he still could have done so.

"Ooh, sweeting, I *love* how you modified that song of calling," said the head on the right in a sweet, piping voice. Her hair gleamed wet and faintly green around her.

"Lorelei! How good to see you again," Carole said.

"It's good to see you, too, you sly little eel, but whoever is that behind you?" she replied.

"I think Carole's going to be her same old selfish self," the

237

other mermaid said in a low and sultry voice, thick as honey. Her hair shone lavender in the starlight, and she regarded Rupert critically. "How about it, minnow? Are you keeping him for yourself or is he a present?"

"Cordelia, you haven't changed at all, have you? This is Prince Rupert, our King and Queen's son," Carole replied calmly. "Perhaps you remember his sister, Princess Bronwyn, who was with me when we met before."

"I don't remember *her,*" Lorelei gushed. "But I do remember that delicious king."

"Yesss," Cordelia hissed, flapping up for a better look and giving Rupert a good look himself at what provided mermaids with some of their frontal bouyancy and a great deal of their charm. "My, my, how much nicer the family resemblance looks on the boys." To Carole she said, "Well, are you going to tell us why you went to all the trouble to make an introduction, clamface, or are you just going to stand there on your tail and pop your eyes at us all night?"

"Cordelia, don't be such a shark. Poor Carole, do stop being so awfully dry and come out here where it's comfortable," Lorelei said. "I don't know how we're supposed to talk about anything with you towering over us like that."

"Do you mind?" Carole asked Rupert, as if excusing herself to go to the privy. "I do need to talk to them—"

"Er, no, of course not. Never mind me. I'll just stand here and bask in the charm of such lovely company." The last was almost sincere, despite the fact that he was freezing to death. The bows of both mermaids were now above water, no longer concealed by the wet and clinging hair, and the sirens smiled at him flirtatiously as he talked to little brown Carole.

While the witch was stripping to her bathing costume Lorelei winked at him. "Why don't you tell us yourself what brings you so far, sweeting?"

"Why, tales of the beauties who dwell in the sea. A sight so wondrous I had to behold it for myself, fair maiden," he replied with a wink of his own.

"Fair mai—oh, you!" Lorelei squealed, and splashed him playfully. "Wouldn't you like to come in and play, too? Isn't it awfully cold and dry out there?" Her shining eyes grew large and fascinating as the sea while her voice crooned melodiously in his ears.

"Lorelei," Carole said warningly, splashing feet first in beside her. "He is *not* for drowning. Come on. I'm counting on you to help me persuade Cordelia to take us to Frostingdung."

238

"Do *you* want to go to Frostingdung, sweeting?" Lorelei asked, still gazing up at him and rewetting her lips with the tip of her tongue.

"In your company? Any man would be a fool not to."

"And our company is the *only* reason?" Cordelia asked, the calculation in her voice coated with honey.

"Other than a small family errand that provides an excuse for the journey, yes, ma'am. A fellow can't refuse a service for his own sister, can he, especially when he's as great an admirer of womankind as I?" He leered a little to make the point, and even Cordelia fanned her tail coquettishly.

"Well, then," she said, "I do think we can help you. Ollie, accommodate the gentleman."

Carole, who had been vainly paddling around trying to catch someone's attention, watched with a rueful expression as a coil of the silver-spotted sea serpent previously lolling just beneath the surface slithered ashore. Rupert sat quickly and unceremoniously as the coil gathered him in its circumference. He straddled the slippery back, thrilling at the novelty of what he was about to do. Belatedly, he noticed Carole, still swimming, reach ashore to grab her clothing and supply pouch.

"Cousin, may I assist you?" he asked, leaning precariously toward her.

She handed up the parcel. "Thank you, no. I believe I'll swim for now." She sounded, and felt, a little helpless. She had been outmaneuvered by the mermaids and by her cousin himself at trying to obtain some guarantee of safety for him. But then, mermaids were far more experienced at luring men than she was at luring mermaids, so she supposed she would simply have to keep alert and hope for the best.

For a time it looked as if her worries were unfounded. Rupert artlessly engaged both sirens in conversation, questioning them about their domain and listening with flattering interest to their simpering replies. Before long his hair and clothing were glistening with ice formed by the freezing of droplets sprayed up on him by his excited hostesses. Most of their prey—guests—didn't care to engage them in conversation. It was fortunate for Rupert that he was inclined to do so, and restful for Carole, since talking kept the mermaids from trying out any of their siren songs on him.

Later, when they did so, they were merely showing off and he insisted on singing harmony in a competently melodious baritone.

"How nicely you sing, cousin," Carole said, when they had

239

finished, chiming in before Cordelia and Lorelei could embark upon a more lethal tune. "One would think you of mer stock yourself."

He ducked his head, boyishly pleased at the compliment. "My christening gift from your father, Minstrel Colin. The gift of song."

Even the sea serpent responded to Rupert's own odd sort of spell. The monster turned its long flat head occasionally to gaze with a sort of bemused admiration at its passenger. This caused it to forget the rhythm of its humping glide through the water and at one point threatened to dump Rupert overboard, except that Carole was watching for just such an event and spoke sharply. Ollie looked sheepish, for a sea serpent, when he wove his head back to set the proper course again.

Carole swam along to the left and a bit ahead of the mermaids, near Ollie's head. The cadence of her own stroking soothed her apprehensiveness somewhat, and the limitlessness of the sea pleased her in a way that made her wonder how she could have spent so long away from it. When she returned from the quest, perhaps she would build herself a retreat near the shore, and leave the village and her parents sometimes to go to it. Perhaps she would even live there, and people would have to come from afar to find her. If they would. She was not likely to be as sought-after as her gregarious cousin, holding court from Ollie's back. It seemed to her on one hand that everyone made a tremendous fuss over the silly young man, and she wondered why, briefly, as she looked into the sea. But when she glanced back up into the happy, enthusiastic countenance of the handsome prince, she decided that he wasn't all that silly, though the reaction of every living creature who encountered him appeared to be. She had heard of the glamor of the faeries before but this was the first time she had ever seen it in action. Her aunt, Queen Amberwine, was said to possess the quality in abundance, but was often ill or absent while Carole was at court so the witch personally had never observed her to any degree to form an opinion one way or the other. But Rupert, combining his father's imposing stature with the refinement of his mother's long and delicate bone structure, the King's bluff honesty with the Queen's charm, had some sort of magic that not even his rowan shield could subdue.

Whatever the source of his power over his fellow creatures, so far it was standing them in good stead, though in some circumstances it could forseeably be dangerous.

The mermaids' atoll was much as she remembered it, a bit higher in the water perhaps, with the fresh-water pool in the center a little deeper into the coral-rimmed circle. Carole sat on a water-smoothed ledge just above sea level hugging her knees as Rupert and Lorelei bandied further words. "Is that trove still down there?" she asked the mermaid suddenly. "The one with all the instruments you showed me when I was a girl? I'd like to dive down and see it again."

The mermaid started to nod and Rupert looked up, easily diverted from his flirtations. "A treasure trove?" he asked.

"You should see it, Your Highness," she began, but almost before the words were out of her mouth the mermaids were diving like ducks, fetching up one salt-soaked bauble after another for the prince's perusal.

He praised the gold-and-pearl harp, the ropes and garlands of gems from pirate chests, the emerald whistle, and the stringless tarnished silver lute, but it was a tiny, thin-spined comb made of a single opalescent fan-shaped shell that pleased him the most and he turned the thing, no larger than his own substantial thumbnail, over and over, stroking it. "What an exquisite piece. I can't help thinking, cousin, that if the poor child had had the usual, happy sort of birthing rites, this would have been the sort of thing she should be receiving—"

The mermaids immediately set up a sympathetic clamor, wanting to know which poor child had so aroused his interest. He told them of Bronwyn's baby, brushing a tear from the corner of his eye as he talked. Carole would have sworn, from her knowledge of the sirens, that had she pleaded for the baby on bended knee and wracked with sobs the mermaids would have responded with indifference. Rupert's account of the baby's plight instead seemed to touch their hearts, which previously had given evidence of pumping nothing but pure, cold, green seawater.

"If you think she would like the comb, you must take it to her, Prince," Cordelia said in an uncharacteristically impulsive gesture. "Let it be our birthing gift to the dear little minnow."

For once it was Lorelei who appeared mean. "*That* comb?" she asked. "Oh, Cordelia, do you think, knowing what that comb does that a split-tailed child of no mer ancestry should—"

"And who would need it more?" Cordelia replied with kindness throbbing through her until it quivered her very tail. She turned her wide, gray stare back to Rupert, who perched on an outcropping above her, looking humble and grateful and awe-stricken at the marvelous gift. "My sister refers to the magic properties of the comb, Prince Rupert. And indeed, it *has* been a while since we gifted a mortal child with anything quite so fine, but any cousin of dear Carole's is a cousin of ours, in a way," and she batted her dripping lashes at him.

Carole looked into the heavens and tapped her toe, schooling herself with priestessly patience to refrain from mentioning that the mermaids had hardly behaved as generously to their "mutual" cousin, Bronwyn.

"Magic powers?" he asked, as if unable to believe his luck. "*Real* magic powers?"

"We'd hardly give you fake ones, now would we?" Cordelia said, the edge creeping back into her voice.

"Oh, pardon me if I sounded dull, my dear lovely lady. I am just so overwhelmed already at your generous gesture of giving that unfortunate little one such a beautiful object. And to think it also carries with it wondrous power!"

"Not all *that* wondrous," Cordelia said modestly. "It will only help her grow a tail as she should have had had she not been born into deprived circumstances, and to breathe properly. It's an old device, a recruiting tool used once when our numbers were small and our power great. Now, of course, we no longer actively recruit, since Lorelei and I admirably manage this section of the sea. But if the girl should care to be schooled, we would be happy to foster her. In fact, I believe there's another of these below, dear boy, if you should care to—"

Rupert held up the flat of his hand and said in a choked voice, "Oh, no. No, gentle lady of the waves, you do me too much honor. This beautiful and powerful gift for my helpless niece I may accept for her sake, but already you have done so much, your hospitality, your transportation, your charming company, and all of the lessons you have taught me about your fabulous water world. I'm overwhelmed."

"Naturally," Cordelia said. "But that is no reason to dismiss our offer."

"I wasn't dismissing it. I simply—"

"You mortals are all alike. A person condescends to talk with you, gives you everything, and first thing you know, you're spurning the idea of even changing one little bitty thing to—"

"But wait!" Rupert cried. "I didn't."

"You didn't?" Lorelei asked. "You mean you will accept our offer and join us here in the sea? Oh, how wonderful! And don't worry about the child. Carole can easily take care of that, can't you, dear?"

242

"What I meant to say was that it was so kind of you to transport us and we're both awfully grateful and while I'd really like to come back and see you often, right now it *is* necessary that *both* my lady cousin and I find my niece and make sure she has the proper start in life."

"How well do you swim?" Cordelia asked, a definite nastiness polluting her nectared tones.

Rupert smiled innocently back at her. "Oh, I swim quite well, but not nearly so well as you or your serpent."

"Yes, Ollie is a remarkable creature. You can see why we wouldn't wish to risk him in monster-ridden waters such as those around Frostingdung. If you'll only stay a day or so more, we'll call you a ship. That would be much nicer for all of us than to risk getting eaten by monsters, wouldn't it?" Her smile left some doubt about who the monsters might be.

Carole thought that the conversation had gone quite far enough. She picked up Rupert's shield and handed it to him. "Cordelia, Lorelei, you promised the Prince you'd help us," she reminded them reasonably.

"So we promised and so we did," Cordelia said. "We brought you here to where you'll meet the very first ship passing by. But surely *you* recall how it was with those horrors created when the split-tails in Frostingdung took out their war on the sea, emptying their vile magics into our waters. I thought you *liked* Ollie. Surely you wouldn't expect us to expose him to that? So, I think since we're all getting on so well you should just do as you did before and take a ship. Or, if you prefer, if you really think it's so safe, you could swim ahead, dear, and we would send the nice young man later."

Carole gave the last suggestion the attention it deserved and ignored it. "When did the last ship come by?" she asked.

"It can't have been more than two or three years after the one you took last time, can it, Cordelia?" Lorelei said with an optimistic and encouraging smile.

"Not a bit more. We'll keep you fed on delicious seafood salad, and, meanwhile, Prince Rupert can learn to use a comb. Oh, I think you'll be ever so dashing in a tail, sweeting."

"That's a fascinating idea, ma'am," he said, "But I am bound to fulfill this quest for now. What if I couldn't change back?"

"Just think! You'd be rid of your deformity forever," Lorelei replied.

Rupert looked a little frightened, Carole thought, which showed good sense on his part. He was in over his head in more ways than one. The time seemed ripe for a threat.

"Remember the dance I taught you two?" the witch asked the mermaids, as if reminiscing again. "Perhaps you'd like to perform it for Rupert—keep your shield up, cousin—and afterwards, we could discuss this again."

The mermaids hit the water with a drenching splash and swam as if their lives depended on it. Ollie trailed in their wake, ululating inquisitively.

Rupert turned a puzzled face to Carole. "What was that all about?"

"I danced them around on the coral till the scales fell off their tails the last time they wanted to harm friends of mine," she said with deep and malicious satisfaction of a sort most common to but by no means exclusive to witches.

"Do you think they would have harmed me?" he asked.

"I think they may still, unless we're vigilant."

"I don't feel very vigilant," he said honestly. "I feel tired." Little wonder in that, since dawn had already dawned and the sun was again high in the sky. "I don't think it's wise to sleep," Carole told him. "They'll try to sing you off the island."

"But surely you can do something about that? They're afraid of you. I have to thank you for intervening. I had no idea they'd take offense so easily. But sometimes people just want me to stay somewhere with them a longer time than I want to."

She smiled ruefully and patted his dangling foot. "You were born into the wrong side of the family. People are generally more than glad to get rid of Brown witches. Even town councilmen, however useful they might find us."

"Then they're foolish," he said warmly. "I think you are a magnificent person—riding dragons and sea monsters and commanding mermaids with no more than a song. I'm very glad Bronwyn suggested that you come along."

"That's good of you, but I'm afraid I'm all out of bright ideas now, if not tunes. I'm sleepy, too, and the sirens are canny enough to know that we will be. I could try to fetch help, but the nearest coastline is Frostingdung, and Cordelia may be right about the monsters there. I had supposed they might have died off by now, but apparently not. I don't suppose you would care to change your mind and accept the mermaids' offer? I could call Lorelei back?"

He winced.

She favored him with a considering look and sighed. "Sorry,

244

but right now that seems the most practical thing. Perhaps I could manage to hijack Ollie, though the others have a much closer connection with him than I do. Without diverting them somehow I don't see how I would cope. I can always swim back to Argonia but if you have no aspirations as a merman or a drowning victim . . ."

Her voice trailed off as Rupert's gaze lifted skyward. A bright spot like a pinkish falling star sped toward them, growing more distinct as its bulk blocked the sun.

"I must remember to write Sir Cyril about this," Rupert said with a certain misplaced pride. "I don't believe there have been any other instances of princes being rescued by dragons, do you?"

"Not princes, no," she agreed. Rescue by dragon had become, for her mother and father in their early years, practically a tradition. With Bronwyn and Jack on her own youthful quest, she had helped rescue both senior dragons and Grippledice. She understandably resented the expression on the younger dragon's face when she landed. It could only be described as a dragonish smirk, as if Grippledice knew all about mermaids and had known from the first that Carole's plan wouldn't work.

CHAPTER III

The most recognizable feature of the coastline of Suleskeria oddly enough was the sea monsters Carole had not expected to see. They wallowed brazenly offshore, in greater and more unhealthy abundance than ever, snarling, mewling, drooling, attacking each other, chewing, diving, lurking, and floating like dead things on the surface of the water. The mermaids, for once, had not been merely making excuses. Even a large beast such as Ollie would have little chance of reaching shore unscathed, and then only if sea serpents were not on the menu of any of the other monsters present.

Carole worried when she saw this that there would no longer be a village at which to rest, for the monsters had menaced the town with great ferocity even when their numbers were smaller. And indeed, there was no village. There was instead a mighty city, with six buildings over two stories tall, arched gates, and domed and spired houses with gardens and fountains. There was also a covered marketplace, and everywhere people bustled, dickered, hauled bundles, rode and led horses, donkeys, cattle, sheep, pigs. Nowhere could she see any of the iron-banded buildings that had been the trademark of the Suleskeria where she had landed previously. The river was filled with barges and small boats, and the fishing industry seemed to center there. No boats at all lined the seashore. The docks were empty, the nets that had once guarded the coast now dried beside the river. Everything looked cleaner and more organized, the folk dressed in graceful flowing robes and some sort of headgear, the streets clean, the vegetation restored.

The castle on the hill had undergone structural changes, too—two new wings adorned with domes and spires, arched entrances, the whole exterior accented with mosaic-tiled decoration.

Carole whistled with unmagical amazement. "Gilles and Rusty appear to be doing very well for themselves."

The men-at-arms of Castle Killgilles were understandably startled when a dragon circled their outer bailey. They couldn't seem to decide whether to send up a volley of arrows or stare with their mouths wide open. Rupert's diplomatic training was not wasted however. Waving in a broad, friendly manner and nudging Carole to do the same he bellowed, "Yo, the castle! Greetings, friends! How is the good—"

"Baron," Carole supplied.

"Baron?" Rupert finished.

The good Baron looked considerably better than he had nearly twenty years ago, as a matter of fact. His silver-gilt hair disguised any gray strands and the new lines of authority in his face became him. Notably missing was the haunted and wine-soaked demeanor that had characterized him in times past.

His wife, the former Mistress Ruby Rose Raspberry, known to her friends as Rusty, was adept at penetrating disguises, even those caused by time and experience; she recognized Carole at once.

"My dear, you're bearing up marvelously. And where *did* you get *that* stunning creature?"

"The dragon?" Carole asked.

"Don't be coy. That utterly charming young man, of course."

"Excuse me. This is His Royal Highness, Prince Rupert

Rowan, my cousin. Your Highness, meet Baron Gilles Kill-gilles, governor of Outer Frostingdung and his wife, Baroness Ruby Rose. The Baroness is the daughter of Wizard Raspberry of Argonia. I'm sure Bronwyn will have mentioned them to you.''

"Call me Rusty, please. Everyone does," the Baroness said, permitting her hand to be kissed. It was a rather grubby hand, covered with stains and the scars of burns from experimenting with her alchemist's oven. Rupert noted that her nails, though wearing their share of stains, came to wicked points.

Everybody agreed on how charmed they all were to meet everybody else.

"You're both looking extremely well," Carole said. "Life in Frostingdung must have improved somewhat."

"In a great many ways, it definitely has," the Baron agreed. "Most importantly, it has become so newfangled—as my father put it—that he got disgusted with the whole country, decided that it would never return to the way it was when he was lord, and gave up ghosting me to venture on to whatever one does next. He haunts and nags me no longer."

"That is my job these days. Mine and the Miragenian bill collectors," his wife said with a wry twist of her thin lips. Carole noted that Rusty still avoided smiling open-mouthed in a manner that would display her rather alarmingly pointed teeth, the legacy of her ogress-descended mother. Her foxy red hair was dressed to loop over her ears, concealing their pointed tips, inherited from her half-elvin father, though the sharpness of her chin and nose, the tilt of her green eyes, and the general impression she gave of being distantly related to a vixen was unmistakable.

"Between them they are more than making up for my dear departed Dad," the Baron said, passing a wrist over his eyes in mock weariness. "You must tell Carole and His Highness the amusing tale of how you nearly burned down the west wing trying to produce simulacrums of outrageous plants to feed the populace. The Miragenians charged us extra interest on the loan for the repairs and raised our insurance on the castle another forty chests of iron pieces."

"Only because they were not pleased when they learned my experiments do work with chickweed and in time will be successful in other areas," Rusty said proudly. Behind her hand she added to Carole, "They get cranky with anyone who makes any progress with magic not in their employ. I swear they run the country with a more tyrannical hand than Loefwin at his worst."

"Oh?" Carole asked. "I thought they were only going to provide temporary aid until your own magic could be restored."

247

"My wife exaggerates," the Baron said quickly. "They simply have given such fine aid and at such reasonable rates and credit terms that even when our own practitioners developed, we found they were far more limited in scope than we remembered and the Miragenians were able to offer better and more varied services. I don't know what we'd do without the technical advisers we have staying with us at Castle Killgilles. Emperor Loefwin just appointed a Grand Wazir from among the ones he has. The Company sent him a whole case of free samples of simulated dancing girls to acknowledge the honor. Didn't go over at all well with Empress Lily Pearl, as you may well imagine."

"The Company?" Carole asked.

"Well, certainly. We deal exclusively with Mukbar, Mashkent and Mirza since they have the contract here. They have advisers in all of the former kingdoms and have done wonders. Everything has changed completely—"

"I noticed that the sea monsters are still a problem."

"Well, yes, and that is unfortunate, but as the Company explained, Miragenia is desert-based and sea-going magic isn't really in their line of products. It keeps us a bit sealed off from the rest of the world, having the monsters out there, but we really do get on so well with the Company's help these days that one hardly notices."

Rupert fell in beside the Baron, asking questions about the castle and its architecture while Rusty said in another aside to Carole, "I swear Gilles is so peace-loving now that things have improved he fails to see the danger in anything. Sometimes I think his father stopped haunting him prematurely, but I can see why the old boy couldn't take it. It's 'the Company' this and 'the Company' that and them owning the gross national product and anything else we might manage to possess from now till the end of the world."

A thin ribbon of flame shot past Carole's ear and past Rupert's ahead of her. She turned to face a glowering dragon. "If you people are quite through with my fascinating companionship, I'll just cool my heels for a while in the river. I feel the need to freshen up in case the Prince—"

The guards, meanwhile, advanced with snarls and raised spears.

"Oh, dear," Carole said. "Tell them to stop. They'll hurt her."

The Baroness gave the required command but the men-at-arms looked none too happy about obeying. "I'm afraid it won't do to have a dragon here, Carole. Are dragons the usual form of transport in Argonia these days? Father hasn't mentioned it in any of his messages."

"No. Grippledice developed a fancy for His Highness. She's actually been quite a lot of help, though I'd rather she'd leave the rest of our task to us and go back to guarding the border. I gather she's not exactly welcome. Perhaps you can convince her to go away. Your Pan-Elvin is better than mine."

Rusty walked back to Grippledice and spoke to her quietly for several moments. After a time the dragon circled the castle yard, dipped her wings once in a poignant farewell salute, and sailed off. Rusty returned grinning a rather ghastly pointed-toothed grin.

"I gave her a speech about honoring one's king and country and she told me to mind my own business and not give her any warmed-over platitudes. I do believe she's going through some sort of dragon's adolescence. But she did mind when I pulled rank on her and reminded her that there'd be no cattle forthcoming here and that not only my guardsmen but my villagers are very nervous about large beasts and inclined to kill first and question afterwards."

"Wasn't that rather harsh?" Rupert asked, blunt in his dismay at losing his voluntary transportation and most ardent admirer.

Rusty looked up her long, pointed nose at him, "Your Highness, my dear young man, you're unacquainted with the history of this country, I can see. Had the beast remained here, we would have needed to stable her indoors, I'm afraid, for it is quite true that natives of this region fear anything less domestic than a horse or a cow. It is also true that regardless of the Company's admittedly excellent precautions, we still have creatures even larger and more dangerous than a dragon roaming the wilderness areas by night."

"Not hidebehinds anymore, however," Gilles said with a fond look at his wife. "Not around here. They disappeared forever, shortly after Rusty and I married. I do see why the royal family has associated itself with ogresses in the past. Pointed-toothed beauties have abilities not commonly credited to them by most men."

Rusty blushed. "Gilles, not here."

A gaggle of stylishly clad ladies appeared at the doorway, ostensibly at the Baroness's command. They covertly in some cases and not-so-covertly in others, watched Rupert with a certain hungry wistfulness.

249

"How perceptive of you, girls," Rusty said to them. "I was about to summon you to show our guests to their rooms."

"It was the dragon, mum," said the boldest one, with the squat build and wolverine-translated-into-human face, Frostingdung stock bred true and homely. Her eyes were bright and cunning, flickering from her mistress to Rupert, who acknowledged the attention with one of his more vacant smiles. "We thought it might harm you and—"

"The dragon was in more danger from us than the other way around, as I explained to her."

A slender young thing with fragile white-gold curls peeking out from a lot of pale blue wisps of veil favored Rupert with a seemingly shy glance made bold only by her kindhearted concern, which made her eyes larger and bluer than should have been humanly possible. "The poor thing. I just love animals. I would hate to see one mistreated. You must have been very worried about her."

"He'll survive, I'm sure," Rusty said with an amused twitch of one red eyebrow. Carole began to wonder if the dragon was the only one to be endangered by predatory Frostingdungians. Her doubts were confirmed when Rusty suggested the time had come for the guests to freshen for dinner. As one unit, the ladies closed in on Rupert. Carole was escorted to her chamber by the slowest of these, who spent the whole time asking impertinent personal questions about the Prince.

The feast was something of a surprise, too, like nothing Carole had previously experienced in Frostingdung, or in Queenston. The gown the impertinent maid brought her should have been a clue that there would be something unusual about the evening. It folded almost square, with the deep rectangular sleeves extending only slightly beyond the edges of the skirt. The material was blue-green silk so fine Carole's mind boggled to think how many threads must have gone into the warp to produce so sheer a fabric. The whole dress centered on the square-yoked neck, embroidered heavily with gold-and-silver metallic thread—as were hem, sleeves, and scattered clusters of birds and lily-like flowers. A hair veil accompanied it, in the same richly embroidered fabric, and Carole couldn't help hoping, it would add some warmth. Though Frostingdung's climate was warmer than Argonia's, the drafty stone halls were still drafty stone halls, and chilly despite their cheerful tiled mosaic inlays. She slipped into the gown, shivering, and briefly considered wearing her customary woolen garb underneath, but her image in the looking glass warmed her considerably.

The banquet hall was not at all cold, lit with silver braziers and hundreds of wax candles, with fresh blossoms and trays heaped with various foods, nuts, fruits, vegetables, and a great many sorts of meat chopped into pieces and served on mounds of rice. The floors were piled with rugs and the ceiling and walls hung with silken hangings and more rugs. Shields and weapons anchored them at strategic points.

Rusty wore an olive-and-gold garment similar to her own, while Gilles sported sapphire trousers of a full cut, a handsome silver jacket that matched his hair, and a scarlet sash. Rupert was clad all in dark blue satin, with only a strip of white embroidery trimming his jacket. His modest apparel did not keep the eyes of the ladies from him. The guests were seated on cushions opposite their hosts, facing a long, low table on which the food had been arranged.

Rupert was seated on Carole's right, while on her left sat a swarthy man with black eyes and beard, wearing a robe and headwrap of emerald-and-white-striped wool. Apparently the inappropriately flimsy Miragenian dress was adopted only by the foreigners. The Miragenians still had sense enough to wear the winter versions of their own traditional garb. On Rupert's other side sat the blond beauty of the morning, who, as it turned out, was a fostering noblewoman from one of the further-flung Frostingdung affiliates. To the lady's disappointment, Rupert addressed most of his conversation to the Miragenian on Rusty's left. Pointing with his dagger to the crested shields decorating the hall, he asked, "I note that all seven Frostingdungian states are represented, but I'm not familiar with Miragenia's shield. Is it among them?"

The Miragenian shook his head and smiled a very white and toothy smile, reminding Carole of a gypsy conducting a horse trade. "No, Your Highness. We have no shield because we are an anarchy, you see, a collection of independent businessmen specializing in the magical, miraculous, and marvelous. We have no central government to boast a crest. Our own company naturally has a trademark, but this is more suitable for our products than for military paraphernalia."

Rupert nodded wisely. When the man's attention was diverted by the lady on his other side, the prince turned to Carole and asked, "Where *is* the place, anyway?"

"From what Bronwyn said, I got the distinct impression that it moves," she told him. "I don't suppose your new acquaintance would volunteer the information?"

For once Rupert's diplomatic training came to the fore, countering what she had come to think of as his characteristic naivete. "I don't suppose so," he agreed. "And I also don't suppose it would be a good idea to speak of our mission in front of them. What do you think?"

The Miragenian on her other side leaned forward to proffer a remark so she nodded and returned her attention to him.

"His Highness and Lady Carole have been expressing interest in the way your company's products have changed life here in Suleskeria, Samir," the Baron said to the man beside Carole.

"Truly? Perhaps you would be needing some of the same commodities in your country, Your Highness?" the merchant said.

"Perhaps. I was just wondering what . . . form your products take."

"Ah. Many forms. We specialize in spells and potions of all sorts, curses, charms, amulets, talismans, magical beasts, transport, and servants—though the latter items are, as you may guess, rare and costly, and available only to our wealthier clientele."

The prince gestured in a grand and worldly manner, and said, "Naturally. But could you give us an example say, of something in this room for which your . . . merchandise is responsible?"

"Why, the feast you see spread before you. Begging the charming Baroness's pardon, but no lady could prepare such a banquet on such short notice without our help." (Carole scoffed to herself. He had obviously never seen her hearth-witch mother in action.) "The fresh fruits and vegetables were procured by our excellent magical servants, who helped speed the preparation as well, using magic of time and distance available only to such entities as they are."

"How clever," Carole said. "Can we meet one of them?"

"Alas, no. They have all been returned to their containers to await further service and they are most retiring by nature. But there would be little to see in any event. They are not particularly intriguing visually. My deepest regrets that that which I control can be of no profit to you in that regard, dear lady."

"Sir Ahmed and Sir Samir have been doing the most wonderful rehabilitation work with the river monsters, Your Highness," the blond girl exclaimed in a blushing gush.

"Rehabilitation?" Carole said. "That should please your sister, Princess Daisy Esmeralda, Rusty."

When Rupert looked puzzled another lady leapt into the breach

252

and elucidated. "The Baroness's elder sister, Empress Lily Pearl, is married to our Emperor Loefwin, Your Highness. Her other sister, Princess Daisy Esmeralda, is married to our Prince Loefrig, the Emperor's younger brother. Princess Daisy Esmeralda loves animals—as I do myself, dear little things. Except monsters, of course."

The blond girl, not to be outdone, butted in, "She means those these wonderful gentlemen haven't helped with their re-structuring potion. They've made many of the nastiest monsters absolutely adorable."

"And very tasty," the animal-loving lady added with a smile that showed a pointedness of tooth more pronounced than Baroness's. The lady quickly hid her smile behind a lace handkerchief and batted her lashes over the edge.

"I seem to have heard that you are acquainted with our homeland, Lady Carole," Ahmed remarked.

"Now where would you have heard that, I wonder?" Carole said, deliberately fluttering, something she had learned to do watching the seamstress's sister, a former dairy maid who now fancied herself a milliner. "A relative of mine once visited your land. Perhaps that's what you heard. I understand that it was very . . . exotic."

"Ah, a relative value, dear lady," Ahmed replied. "But the exotic is highly esteemed by both Samir and myself as well. That is why we prefer field work as technical representatives to remaining in the Company headquarters."

Rupert proceeded to question them at length about their work, questions which they answered vaguely and with a hint of condescension.

After the feast, when the gentlemen retired to the library for port and pipes, and the ladies, at least Carole and the Baroness, retired to the newly restored alchemy laboratory to watch the retorts bubble with the results of the Baroness's latest experiment, Carole was able to tell her old friend the real reason for her visit.

"We dare stop only long enough to get a good night's sleep but I had hoped you might have some clear-cut notion of how we could locate Miragenia."

"I don't. But I would very much like to give you a present to take with you for the child. Bronwyn is absolutely correct in assuming her baby will need all the protection she can get. The Miragenians are interested in little but power and profit, from what I can see. Why they should want a child is beyond me, but I'm very glad it isn't *my* child."

253

Carole nodded gravely and waited.

"The only question now is what it shall be. What would be appropriate, I wonder? I've never been good at this sort of thing. What are you giving her?"

"I haven't decided, to tell you the truth. I thought of giving her that invisibility pill you once made out of hidebehinds when we tried to escape Loefwin's castle, but the child might swallow it accidentally before she had real need of it and on someone that small, who knows what the proper dosage would be? She might well be lost until she's fifteen or twenty years old."

"My dear, if you believe that, your experience of babies is even more limited than mine. They howl most alarmingly if their needs are not attended to. Whether she could be seen or not, if the child was deprived of food or a diaper change for any length of time, she'd make herself highly visible. If I were you, I'd save that capsule for myself. Miragenians are sneaky in the extreme. It won't hurt to have something on hand that can help you be sneakier. Which gives me an idea. Hand me that parchment over there, will you?"

She sat at a counter for a quarter of an hour, carefully lettering runes onto the parchment with special ink, tossing sand over it to dry it, though it still smeared somewhat, and rolling it up to present to Carole. "There now. That should stand her in good stead."

"What did you decide on?"

"A hunger for knowledge, a sharp eye for detail, and an avid taste for trouble. Not the usual precious baby gifts, I know, but they're traits sufficiently related to me that I can pass them on with my blessings. She should give the Miragenians a run for their money, growing up endowed with such a gift. I also added a rudimentary knowledge of Pan-Elvin. Coupled with the other, she should have several dialects mastered by the time she's six or seven. Children tend to be fond of animals; if the people are beastly to her, the company of real beasts may give her some comfort."

They departed the next morning amid general consternation and a few tears from an uncommonly drowsy-looking lot of lady's maids, who were not used to arising quite so early but who refused to miss the opportunity to catch Rupert's eye a final time during his leave-taking. The baronial carriage took the cousins as far as the river, where they boarded a sleek, private sailboat with magic wind, courtesy of the Miragenians.

"Damned decent of them," Rupert said. "I begin to admire

these people, for all their haste in running off with the children of others. Baron Gilles told me some of the most amazing facts concerning their participation in the rebuilding of Frostingdungian magic."

"Their replacement of it with their own, from what Rusty told me," Carole replied. "I just hope there's not a time limit on this wind. The Emperor's castle is a good long way from here and I know of no place closer where we might rest for the night."

Carole found the riverbanks were more densely populated than they had been on her previous visit, and the boat traffic much heavier, but by mid-day their boat had passed beyond those powered by more prosaic means of propulsion and had likewise left behind all but the thinnest habitation.

Alone with none but his cousin to impress, Rupert was quiet and placid, staring contentedly at the shadows of the bare trees striping the sluggish gray-green river, watching the banks for animals, replying to Carole's occasional sally with a vague smile or a monosyllable. The magic wind ruffled his buttery curls and the sunlight glinted heroic bronze from his face and hands. Carole, to whom the sort of country through which they were passing was no novelty, felt restless, and inclined to be pettish that the youth so full of charming conversation for other females had little to offer her when they were alone. Perhaps his tongue was tired, as well it could be. From what Rusty reported, the Prince had continued to hold forth among the admiring throng long after she had retired.

The sun sank ahead of them, directly in their line of vision, bouncing blindingly off the river. Carole thought they must be approaching a town again, for she heard hoofbeats through the woods on the left bank and the rustle of someone or something plowing through foliage closer at hand. Rupert stared straight ahead, into the brilliant light, and seemed not to hear the noises. Though Carole twisted to try to see what was making them, her eyes were too full of spots from peering into the brightness to be able to clearly make anything out. She thought she saw a rapid movement and a wisp of green before Rupert gave a strangled cry and sat bolt upright.

The green wisp transformed itself just in front of the bow, outlining a cool, slender shape against the glare of the sun. The shape undulated seductively before him, beckoning him closer with a wink of a rounded green ray here, a come-hither twitch there, a blink of incandescence, and a wonderful rhythmic crackling of exuberant energy.

To Carole the light was different—green with black bars, the crackle menacing, surrounding her, imprisoning her, threatening her with an overwhelmingly searing jolt if she so much as leaned forward to touch Rupert.

Rupert could see nothing to one side or the other, but could only stare straight ahead at the ladies of light, who were cajoling and beckoning him, whispering promises of secret tales more intriguing than any he had ever heard, of perfections beyond what he had thought possible, of sensations of softness and comfort and ease not dared dreamed, of grace and voluptuous warmth coupled with wild excitement. He rose slowly, intently, to his feet and stepped forward.

Carole cried out as the boat dipped toward the bow and the sail slackened. No sooner did she cry than from somewhere beside her, another angrier cry broke through the crackling. The foliage rattled again, and the green lights flamed up with a whoosh and blurred off the way they had come, leaving only the dazzing sunlight.

Rupert half-fell back into the boat with the recoil from the release of the spell. The rowan shield he wore at his back clacked against the boat's hull. Simultaneously, in the brush along the river, another rustling of leaves was followed by hoofbeats and the patter of running feet. A tag-end of green curled and disappeared behind a tree root and Carole, watching intently, grabbed an oar and turned the boat, paddling for shore. The magic wind deserted the sails and they hung slack and unresisting as she altered the course. Rupert recovered rapidly, and helped her paddle. They put ashore near the tree where the last of the green vanished. Carole climbed out and scanned the area. The crystal bottle was shaded by the tree root, all but one edge, which glittered like a peridot in the sun's rapidly dying light.

A silver-inscribed stopper dangled from the bottle's neck by a silver chain. Carole stuck it rapidly into the mouth of the container. Something about the bottle felt unsavory, disquietingly sly and somehow unnatural, tricky.

Once the bottle was sealed she held it to the sun, trying to look through the green-tinted glass to see what swirled murkily within.

"What is it?" Rupert asked.

A pair of eyes opened abruptly inside the bottle, staring out accusingly at them. "Take out the stopper," a voice commanded silently.

"Oh, no, you don't, my dear," Carole said. "In you went and in you're going to stay."

"Who are you to keep me here? You aren't one of the masters." The voice was huffy.

"No, but neither am I someone you can order about," Carole said. "If you didn't wish to stay there, why did you return?"

"It's . . . my place, of course. The only place since . . . since I've been in service. But without the stopper, I am free. You are not a master. You can't keep me." The voice wavered from sounding as if there were a blank space in what it knew of itself to a belligerent determination to cover up that lack of knowledge.

Carole was not fooled. "No. But if you want out of there, you'll need to answer a question or two. You're one of the Miragenian servants I take it?"

"Fancy that! So much power over the helpless and clever, too! How did you figure that one out? Let me guess, the bottle—"

"The spell you cast on us, for starters," Carole said. "Who put you up to it?"

"What? That little love charm? Surely you're not miffed about that? Obviously some lady wanting to impress that large fellow looming over your shoulder."

"You nearly killed him."

"It's not my fault if he's clumsy enough to fall in. She just wanted him back. The masters hire us out for profit, you know. The results are not always guaranteeable. Don't hold me responsible. Let me go and I promise never to do it again. How's that?"

"I'll let you go when you tell us where Miragenia is and how we can get there."

The eyes closed and opened again. "Why?"

"Why what?"

"Why do you want to go there? Big contract for the masters, eh? More profit to their coffers?" The voice seethed with a stew of hostile emotions and the eyes all but burned a hole in the crystal bottle.

"Hardly," Carole answered. "And why is none of your business. Keep that attitude up and I can assure you you may stay stoppered in there for good. Frostingdung has quite enough monsters loose already."

The eyes blinked again, wetly this time, and were half-veiled, but the voice was stubborn. "Are you bringing them more business?"

"We can't say," Carole replied.

"Then I can't tell you," the voice said, choked to a near-whisper.

"No," Rupert said from hehind her. "Not to do business. Not exactly."

"Ah!" the voice said, brightening. "Make trouble then?"

"I wouldn't say that," he said.

"What would you say?"

"We need to tend to something they have that belongs to us," he answered cagily.

"There's a smart lad. If they have something that belongs to you, you'll be lucky to see it again."

"Then you'll tell us?" Rupert asked, encouraged by the voice's obvious lack of good will toward Miragenia and Miragenians.

"I'm thinking about it."

"I have ways of making you talk," Carole warned. She would feel no sillier making a bottle dance than she did having an argument with one.

"You've bullied me into it," the voice said cheerfully. "I hope you feel better. Like heroes, eh? Pushing mists around. Don't think you're forcing me, either. Anything that will cause the masters trouble is fine with me. To get to Miragenia, you need only cross into the desert, and if they want to see you, they'll arrange to come to you."

"But they don't," Rupert said. "We already told you that."

"There are magic words, in that case, but you mustn't let it get out. I only know because you overhear a lot of things sitting in a shop window. To make them think they want to find you, you have only to keep repeating the motto of the profitable client—"

"Which is?"

" 'I want to get rich quick—' " The voice broke off with a screech as a snakelike flash of black wrapped around it three times, missing Carole's fingers altogether and snatching it deftly from them. A glowering rider mounted on a froth-flecked black steed glared at them from dark eyes burning out above a black face covering. He drew his saber and bore down on them, driving them towards the water. Only the fact that his attention was divided while he stuffed the bottle into a bag slung across the horse's back saved them. For as Rupert stepped backwards, drenching himself to the knees in the river, the sky suddenly darkened, the rider's horse shied, and the rider, not giving full attention to his mount, slipped sideways and threatened to lose his seat.

Grippledice's front claws grazed the part in Carole's hair as

258

the dragon overflew the cousins and landed in front of them, flaming. The horse reared, screaming, and bolted, rider clinging desperately to its mane, streaming cloak trailing smoke and sparks as the terrified mount galloped heedlessly off down the trail.

Grippledice beat her wings once and started to take off after the horse, but Rupert cried out. Carole stopped the dragon with a word.

"Tell her we need to find that desert as quickly as possible now," Rupert told Carole. "We have no way of knowing how long the Miragenian was listening, or when or if he will compel the bottle to tell him of our conversation. We must reach the desert and use the magic words before they discover we know them. Otherwise, I fear we will never find Miragenia or the child."

CHAPTER IV

Carole deeply regretted the haste, for she had looked forward to visiting the Imperial Palace again and seeing for herself the changes wrought by Miragenian decadence. She had also hoped to visit Princess Anastasia and her sisters in their castle in the Nonarable Lands. Both places might have yielded some very useful christening gift for the child. She and Rupert needed to find Miragenia and use the magic words before they were altered or in some other fashion the cursed place managed to elude them. They couldn't expect to find so many neglected bottles that they could afford to waste the information they had gleaned from the first.

They flew several hours before the desert appeared as a beige sea on the far side of low, rugged foothills. The heat reached out and grabbed for them even before they cleared the hills, and the dragon relaxed, flexing her wings more fully, luxuriating in the sensation.

"Let's see now," Carole said. "The magic words were what? 'Now to get rich quick . . . how to get rich quick' . . . ?"

"I want to get rich quick," Rupert said. "I want to get rich quick."

"I want to get rich quick," Carole chanted. "Fine. I don't see anything yet, do you?"

The desert was closer, but just as empty as before.

Rupert shook his head. "Neither do I. Perhaps we're not saying it correctly. Tell me, have you ever wanted to be rich?"

She glanced back at him, her hair whipping in front of her eyes, "Why?"

"Well, I just thought if we could really say the words with conviction we'd be more likely to succeed. So I wondered . . . I wondered if you ever wanted to be rich. I mean, I believe I should enjoy it."

"But you're a prince. You *are* rich."

"Not exactly. I can't just suit myself. I must dress just so for each occasion, my spending is controlled by the exchequer, I go where I am sent. I never go hungry, true, but my choices are dictated for me by whatever someone else thinks is the good of the realm. Actually, I'm finding this journey more interesting than anything I've done in recent years. But back to my original question, cousin. How about you? What would you do if you were rich? What would you buy? Dresses, jewels?"

She considered. "That would be very nice but I actually haven't anywhere to wear such things. I would like a house facing the sea for myself, perhaps, and a lot of conch shells to keep songs and stories in, like Sir Cyril Perchingbird has in the Archives at Queenston. I would like to be able to come and go as I wish, and perhaps to buy one of those carpets or flying horses the Miragenians have, since dragons don't ordinarily find me to their liking."

"How about a dowry?" he asked slyly. "You're not too old to think of marrying yet—"

"Bite your tongue," she said crisply and finally.

"Well, pardon me."

"It's under consideration. If I choose to marry it won't be to someone who wants my dowry. Or anything or anyone else but me. In fact, it would be very nice to get rich quick simply so I would be wealthy and powerful enough that no one, not even princes, would feel free to ask impudent questions. Yes, indeed, I can see that as a very valid reason. With that in mind, I can say decidedly that I want to get rich quick."

Rupert was wondering whether to respond with a tart rejoiner or freeze her with silence when the dragon abruptly began downflapping and the heat shimmering above the surface of the sand suddenly coalesced into walls, spires, and gates rising from them, a city with the same architectural accouterments within its walls as those so recently grafted on to Suleskeria. "It worked," Rupert said, gaping.

"Magic words generally do," she said with somewhat contemptuous smugness, still smarting from his unintentional probing of her old wound.

A cloud of dust billowed around the walls, dancing motes on the heat waves.

If the elusive illusory city had any intention of scurrying away into the concealment of heat and dust, Grippledice quickly foiled it for she flew so swiftly over the wall that she stampeded a herd of flying horses grazing on several of the flat rooftops. She landed on the largest of these rooftops, one covering a building large enough to be the great hall of some palace. It turned out to be a warehouse. This they learned when, dismounting Grippledice, they saw a train of mules back a wagon up to the front of the building. The mules strained their harnesses upwards, shaking their heads and stamping, their eyes rolling as they tried to see the dragon they smelled above them.

The warehouseman, arriving at the door to inspect the cargo carried by the mules, followed their gaze and saw the dragon, who could not restrain her curiosity and looked back down at the man. Carole groped in her medicine pouch. Her fingers closed on the hidebehind capsule. Knowing that she was probably sacrificing it prematurely, but unable to think of any other way to avoid drawing further attention to themselves, she popped the capsule far back into the dragon's gaping jaws. Grippledice, startled, turned from the edge of the roof to see what had occasioned the small interruption in her surveillance of the warehouseman, then vanished. Rupert and Carole stepped quickly away toward the center of the roof.

"What did you do to me?" the dragon demanded, shooting a warming blast of fire over Carole's head.

Carole ducked behind Rupert, knowing the dragon would hesitate to harm him, and quickly whispered her reply. "I gave you a pill that will make you invisible for a while. You'll recover. But meanwhile, it would be very helpful to what we have to do here if you'd find something to occupy yourself elsewhere. Two people can disguise themselves sufficiently to infiltrate Miragenia long enough to locate and christen a child. Two people and dragon are a bit more conspicuous."

261

"That is true," Rupert whispered. "Say that I wish her to leave now as well, that we appreciate—"

"Yes, yes," the dragon grumbled. "I can see I'm not wanted. Nevertheless, dear Prince, just holler if you're in hot water again. I'll understand and come. The language of love speaks with equal warmth to all creatures." And with a rush of hot wind she was gone, once more stampeding a herd of horses flying overhead.

The warehouseman and his helpers unloaded the cargo and carted it inside the building, no doubt assuming the dragon was just another transitory spell conjured on the roof by some competitor, or perhaps an advertising gimmick. Before anyone could change his mind and investigate further, Rupert hopped nimbly to an adjoining rooftop and urged Carole to do the same, springing from one of the closely packed structures to another until they were a good distance away from where they first arrived.

They had flown all night and found the desert in late morning. Now the day grew so hot that Carole found it difficult to stand, much less jump. Below them, the streets were quiet. People napped or ate inside their houses or under the awnings where they did their business. She could hardly believe her own eyes when Rupert, spotting several robes spread drying on a rooftop, scooped up two and began to don the larger, handing her the smaller.

The idea of tormenting her overheated, sweating, heat-drenched body with another layer of clothing horrified her. Her expression must have showed it.

Rupert turned to her cheerily, tugging at the robe's sleeves, which refused to cover him below the middle of his forearm. He pulled the hood up over his golden hair and lowered his burnished lashes, letting his chin touch his chest. "If we wear these robes like this, you see," he said, his words getting somewhat lost in fabric and the dust skimming the heights on a simmering breeze, "no one will ever recognize us for anything other than Miragenians."

"As soon as we've captured him, I want him measured for a proper robe," the chairperson of the board of Mukbar, Mashkent, and Mirza proclaimed. "Such an ill-fitting costume makes a joke of our corporate dignity."

"On an Argonian, mademoiselle?" the old man, Mashkent, asked with a sly twinkle in his eye. "What possible difference could it make to our corporate dignity what an Argonian wears?"

262

The board members were seated on deep cushions surrounding a circular pool of visions, and had just been entertained by watching the dragon land and disappear and the Prince and his companion deck themselves ludicrously in borrowed robes.

Mlle. Mukbar, heiress to old Mukbar's controlling interest in the firm, head of the household composed of herself and nine younger sisters, lifted her raven tresses with a langorous arm. Her eyelids, heavy with their fringes of curling black lash, veiled her almond eyes and her full, carmined lips pouted at her old uncle. "Naturally we'll assume control of such an outstanding asset as His Highness. Or weren't you watching? He is a fine figure of a man of wealth, power, position and family connection. Just the husband my sisters and I need. With his past training, he'll make an excellent sales representative, once he gets used to us."

"And how do you propose to make that happen?" Mirza, sharp-faced and nervous in middle-age, his black hair threaded with gray, challenged her. He had rather fancied himself as husband to the Mukbar heiresses. Keeping the wealth in the family was not a bad idea in Miragenia. "He has come for the brat, of that you may be sure, and will neither leave nor stay and certainly will not do your bidding willingly until he has done what he came for. And that, as you know, is not possible. Are you so desirous of him as to use spells on him, mademoiselle? That would be damaging to the dignity of the firm also, I would think."

She laughed an earthy laugh from deep in her memorable bosom. "Nonsense, my dear Mirza. It is standard operating procedure among women of choice to use all manner of spells to procure the proper mate. My scruples will give my dignity no trouble whatsoever. Besides, he will be safest there, among my sisters and myself. He must be kept from the child until her destiny has taken its course."

Mashkent, ancient now, his whiskers wispy, his eyes sparkling with a certain magically induced artifice from behind clouded lenses, shifted on his bony shanks and cleared his throat. "You're your father's daughter, Alireza, to speak so. What are we to tell the parents when they demand their child back when the fifteen years allotment has passed? Will you have your pet diplomat make them some pretty speech about how she chose to remain in our service, only without her body?"

A golden-skinned, round-faced man with a thatch of black hair and a smug expression tapped the edge of the pool in front of him. "You grow addled in your old age, Illustrious One. You do recall my prophecy, do you not, that that child will bring certain ruin of the balance of trade? She is a liability, which the dear lady has in her infinite cleverness managed to turn into an asset, even while ridding us of the danger."

"Had we waited until the mother had performed her sentimental rites over this babe, we would not have had to deal with this princeling at all. He increases our danger a hundredfold, he and the witch."

"It all depends on your point of view, Uncle," Alireza Mukbar said, stretching blissfully. "The man's presence here is to my mind an unexpected bonus. We have not only profited from the brat, but I, at least, intend to profit from him as well."

"Greater profit might be obtained from our creditors by allowing him to find the child," Mashkent pointed out slyly. "He would be of great interest to them, you may be sure."

Alireza scoffed. "He'd never make it. The valley's guardian would intercept and spoil him, as she does all good things, and we would have no profit from him at all. Besides, isn't there a prophecy about that somewhere, too, Ali?"

"Assuredly, First Sale of the New Day," he said, using one of the Miragenians' most flattering terms for a beautiful woman. "If this prince becomes the prey of the valley's guardian, the profit-and-loss ledger will look even worse, for the woman will gain undue influence. Much as I would hate for you and your charming sisters to be no longer available for wooing, lady, I agree that, other than having him eliminated or transformed into some innocuous beast, allowing the prince to fall into your loving arms would be the safest thing to do with him."

"And his companion?" Mashkent asked. "The witch?"

"Surely a profit may be made from her also," Mirza said.

"What magic does she possess?" Alireza asked.

"Nothing of great note: a minor variation on the siren song plus an occasional borrowed trick like the one she did with the dragon. Still, she may cause disruption of trade if not handled properly."

"Neutralize her ahead of time?" Mashkent asked, pulling his beard. "We can safely do nothing to quell her power without further study of it. We can arm the security forces with wards against her, however, and distract her so that her power is concentrated elsewhere when we apprehend her."

"The competition won't interfere?" Mirza asked sharply. "We can't risk allowing anyone else to become involved in this. If our

Gorequartz creditors learn of the presence of this pair from anyone other than ourselves, we may have a great deal of difficulty. I still think perhaps the best thing would be to send the man as a gift, disguised, up the Cashflow, avoiding the guardian, and let the Gorequartz priests do with him as they will.''

"You're too cautious," Alireza chimed in, undulating her slender fingers at him in breezy dismissal. "Giving away assets before learning their full advantage to us is not like you, Mirza. I fear your little brush with the Guardian when you tried to obtain some of that cheap love potion to win my sisters and me undid you. The Gorequartz priests already have what they desire and if they know nothing of this prince, they will not miss him. I, on the other hand most certainly will. Nor is the witch going to appeal to our competition. Especially not if we surround her with a pall of bewilderment and strangeness. She will appear unprofitable, and none will wish to deal with her. Now then, my dear fellow board members, if I have eased your trepidations sufficiently, I will excuse myself while you deal with the witch. I must make my own simple preparations for acquiring her companion.''

CHAPTER V

The first order of business was to locate Mukbar, Mashkent, and Mirza. Since the firm was large and influential, the cousins had anticipated no difficulty in learning its whereabouts. But each person they approached together turned from them to another task or customer.

"This will take all day at this rate," Carole said, shifting miserably inside her overabundance of clothing.

Her awkward fumbling was accentuated by a woman bargaining at the stall ahead of them. The other woman's movements were like a dancer's, fluid and graceful, golden bracelets clinking on smooth rounded arms as she gestured, fingers flying like doves, enhancing every softly articulated word. Rupert sighed as her beautifully formed head turned ever so slightly, the waterfall of black waving hair shifting beneath a sheer emerald veil, hooded dark eyes taking him in, nostrils flaring beneath the coin-rimmed veil, sweet flicker of tongue darting out to dampen lips suddenly in need of softening. He held her gaze for no more than a moment before she swirled, a fragrant, heady cloud wafting from her veils. She beckoned with a slim finger, her eyes darting back for another tantalizing glance.

"What did you say?" Rupert asked Carole, keeping one eye on her and the other on the swaying veils sauntering just ahead on the dusty street. Carole repeated herself snappishly, but he replied with a blitheness born of relief. "Why, certainly it will take all day. This town is little used to strangers, since so few can find it, and two of us together bewilder them. We'll alarm them less if we split up," he said. "I'll do this side of the street, you do the other." And so saying, he trotted briskly after the departing green-clad figure.

Carole watched him, and hoped that the woman was as friendly as she looked. Perhaps their hunt would be over as soon as he caught her. Just so he proceeded directly with business instead of dallying about while his suffering cousin baked in the street. She watched the preoccupied merchants and approached the first. Tension and dread knotted her stomach. She suddenly longed for her recalcitrant villagers at Wormroost, lazy and spoiled and expecting her to take care of them. At least there she had some worth. Here people dismissed her and went coldly about their business as if she had never made a purchase in her life and wasn't about to start with them. She felt tempted to give them all dancing lessons, but it sickened her to think she had to dance people around just to get a little decent human cooperation from them.

A large animal with a hump in its middle, ridiculously attired in tapestry, tassles, and bells, brushed against her, nearly stepping on her foot. It gave her a supercilious look, very much like the one she and Rupert had gotten from the last vendor. She started to laugh, thinking that if even the animals in this place were unfriendly, she was being a ninny to allow the attitude of the people to cow her. The beast continued to glower at her, worked its jaws, and spat. She sidestepped the gob just in time, and ducked straight into the path of an enormous lumbering mud-colored animal with wrinkled skin and a nose that resembled a front-end tail. The beast was heavily laden. It was ridden by a small nut-brown man who threatened Carole with a riding crop. She wasn't too concerned about the riding crop, but the animal had a pair of horns situated on either side of its prodigious nose, each of them larger than four unicorn horns put together. She ducked again, tripping over a little brown hairy beast standing on its hands and juggling balls, which it dropped when she tripped over it. It jumped to its feet chattering and grimacing at her furiously. When she tried to retrieve the balls, it threw them at her. She longed for the animals of her home, work-hungry beavers, opinionated moose, dim-brained bears, rare and magical unicorns and even love-sick dragons.

In front of Carole a woman squatted beside a pile of glittering objects: mirrors with mother-of-pearl frames. The sun flashed from their surfaces. The woman eyed Carole suspiciously over a length of black veil much mended with inept embroidery.

"Mirrors for sale," she said dully. "You want to buy one?"

"Well, no. That is, I don't think I need a mirror."

"You think wrong then, girlie. I never saw one who could use it more. Take a look."

She thrust the mirror into Carole's face and Carole thought at first that a mistake had been made. This was no mirror but a moving portrait of a face that was beautiful, fine of feature, with milky skin rather than her own sallow complexion. The mirrored face was crowned with lustrous black waves, not with strawlike hair slicked back into a single brown braid. The nose was straight and patrician, lacking the Brown hook.

"Your mirror's defective," she told the merchant, handing the object back to her. "That's not me."

"It's what you ought to be. What you should look like if you was to do your duty and beautify the streets instead of being just another dowdy body taking up air. If you buy this mirror, see, you'll have the model before you, so you'll know what to strive for. With the proper accompanying spells and potions and maybe a judicious application of virgin's blood now and then to keep you young, you may come close."

"Thank you, but I think I'll pass," Carole said. "I was just going to ask if you could direct me to the firm of Mukbar, Mashkent, and Mirza."

"I could, but may I run at a loss if I will. I have business to do. If you want information, I suggest you go to them as sell it and let a poor woman earn her living."

She got a similar reception from everyone else on the street, even at a place where she parted with two of her small store of coppers to purchase an inedible pastry. Everywhere she was regarded with distaste and indifference.

She stumbled along, suffering with the heat, while trying to avoid the animal dung thick and steaming in the streets, she bumped straight into another vendor, who held her at arm's length. He brushed her off, and with a crazed expression lurched into his sales pitch. "You look like a lady who's going places. With my wares, you can so do pleasantly, safely, quickly, expeditiously, and without the need for such a fierce frown."

"Stop," she said. "I don't want to hear another word unless you can tell me where I'll find the firm of Mukbar, Mashkent, and Mirza. No one else will tell me and I'm not about to waste my time listening to someone who's going to be insolent when he's done with his own business."

"Ah, I can do better than that!" he said. "Though I have only myself just arrived here today. How, you may ask, did I manage to arrive so opportunely for yourself, just at the time when you most need aid. Why, by means of my wondrous wares, I answer. With the help of this marvelous item you too can be on hand for significant occurences among those who need you—even two during the same day. *And* have all of your adventures narrated to you in thrilling detail at no extra charge—"

"*What* are you talking about?" Carole asked, fanning herself with her hand and trying to stay patient. Crazed this character might be, but he was the only one so far who had heard her request and retained his eagerness to speak to her.

"Why, thissss—" he said, gesturing to the side of the road where a hollow stump lay and inviting her to follow him. "My magical, mystical travel log. I would be only too happy to give you a free demonstration."

"Sitting down on the log will be plenty for now," she said wearily. Before he could say more, a little round woman turned from the cartload of scrolls she was unloading and rushed to Carole, putting a restraining hand on her arm.

"No, no, my dear. Pay no attention to this man. He is a charlatan. I've been watching him and he's sat here all day. You're the first customer he approached. He may be a slaver. A young lady like you should be more cautious."

The man backed hastily away as the little woman glared at him. Picking his log up under his arm, he made a swift departure down the street.

Carole stared after him, stricken. "It's very good of you to be concerned for me," she said, "But he promised to help me find the firm of Mukbar, Mashkent, and Mirza. No one else will. I can't afford to buy anything."

268

"That is very plain. I just didn't want you to come to any harm. You may not buy today and still be a good customer in the future. You have the look of one seeking employment to me. I'd offer you a job if I could, but my business is run on the good will of my customers and I'm afraid you would not engender good will, no offense. Still, if you promise to keep away from slavers, I'll tell you where you can find the competition, and perhaps they'll be able to hire you so that you can someday come and look at my wares with a more positive eye, poor girl."

Toward evening, following the woman's directions, Carole stood before a shop front remarkable only in that it boasted a permanent awning and a recess in the wall, unlike the barrows and tables and spread-cloths of the other vendors. In front of a collection of pots, an elderly man sat on one rug while weaving another.

Carole was about to speak to him when two men sneaked up behind her, grabbing her arms in tight grips. They panted through guilty grins at the old man. "Here she is, Illustrious Employer. The witch you sought."

"Indeed," the weaver grumbled. "Very brave of you, capturing her just as she was about to introduce herself." The rug upon which he was seated rose high with his indignation. It plopped abruptly to the ground as the weaver said, "Stand by, but unhand her."

He spun around as the guards obeyed, the rug turning with him, and regarded her through rheumy eyes alight with some uncanny glow that made her think he might have fireflies behind his milky-white lenses. He beckoned her to come closer, and shook the clawed end of his weaving comb under her nose. "So you came to find us, did you? I thought you might. But I'll tell you it will do you no good. A bargain is a bargain, and you were present when it was made, even if you were too young then to have better sense than to do commerce with that redhaired liar girl and the cheat of a gypsy boy. You heard the deal as it was signed and sealed, and we have taken delivery, to the Profit of the righteous. If those who welsh on deals are not happy, let them think again before depriving their buyers of prepurchased goods."

Carole sank to the ground, crossing her legs, and facing him tiredly. She watched his righteous wrath rise and fall with his breath and decided that behind his eyes the fireflies were laughing at her. His pretension to an ethical argument was a sham. He had merely assumed a bargaining position, in quite the same way as the seamstress did when a lady from Rowan Castle was negotiating the amount of embroidery embellishing a new gown. "I'm glad to hear that you don't deny taking the child," she replied at last. "And there's really no need to be unpleasant about all this. As you say, I was there. I'm not challenging your basic position, just your timing."

"I see." Mashkent slitted his eyes and folded his hands, regarding her impassively, waiting for her to say more.

"In your haste to collect your debt from Bronwyn, you spirited the child away before she could be christened. I don't know how familiar you are with the ceremony, but it will add inestimably to her value to you."

"How good of you to be concerned for our investment," he said. "Perhaps you would care to enter my home in order to estimate for us somewhat closer the inestimable value of this ceremony of which you speak?"

"That would be very nice," she said demurely, thinking thirstily of long drinks of water. Also, now that she and Mashkent had found each other, there would be no further need for her cumbersome, suffocating disguise.

"No sooner said than done," Mashkent said, inclining his head and smiling a sweet old man's smile full of fatherly kindliness and consideration. He clapped his hands once, resoundingly.

Tendrils of varicolored smoke slithered forth from the shop, curling toward her. The tendrils were very like the ones she had seen enter the bottle on the river bank. She watched them so intently she missed the disappearance of the old man. The tendrils wrapped themselves around her arms and legs and bore her gently aloft, so that she rested as if on a down mattress, very comfortably on her lower side. Nevertheless she had to duck her head to avoid injury as her translucent guides transported her through the low doorway leading from the cluttered shop to the garden that was the heart of Mashkent's home.

At the heart of the garden was a magnificent pool, surrounded by many peripheral pools. The group was connected with a web of blue-green tiled gutters with what seemed to be overflow rippling between them. Mashkent sat near the largest pool. It contained no fewer than thirty-five fluting fountains, showering the pool on seven different levels. The whole thing was larger than the finest, biggest mill pond in the east of Argonia, the new one just constructed at Little Darlingham.

Carole's vaporous guides deposited her on a silken cushion, wisped away momentarily, and wisped back with silver trays full of cut up bits of fruit, nuts, smelly cheeses, dates, and a sweating silver goblet of a tart fruit drink that was more thirst quenching than the water she had hoped for. She ate and drank as daintily as possible. Her host did not join her, but studied her with every evidence of benign pleasure in her pleasure. He made occasional friendly remarks about the garden, the varieties of flowers growing therein, which bird was singing at any given moment—they were all larks or nightingales or doves or something melodious and romantic, it seemed.

When Carole was quite finished her host clapped again and the vapors deftly removed the trays. Swishing around Carole like the ghosts of silken cloths, they wiped her hands and mouth.

Belatedly, Carole thought of Rupert. "Perhaps, actually, I should wait until Prince Rupert finds us to discuss this matter. He was . . . detained."

"Ah. Was he? But surely you need not delay your mission. You are in accord on this matter, I take it?"

"Yes, but, well, I—"

"You are distressed on his account, no doubt fearing in your womanly fashion that he has no place to dine and rest as you do. That is commendable, but a misplaced concern, I assure you."

"Nevertheless—" she said, fluttering her hand in an imitation of the gesture she'd seen Miragenians use, the one that meant "I need not explain the rest to you."

The old man's smile tightened momentarily, his patience strained, then he clapped his hands again, saying to her, "I shall undertake to settle your mind in this matter." To a solid and refreshingly human-looking minion, a boy of about eight, he said, "Check the pool and report to me if Prince Rupert is safely settled for the rest of the day, if he is comfortable and in amiable company, and has dined."

The boy bowed low and scuttled to an adjoining pool, over which he leaned low.

Carole sat erect, straining to see beyond the child into the pool. She recalled Bronwyn saying something about these pools that acted as crystal balls. She supposed that was what this was all about. She caught vague billowings of curtain-like draperies, soft, dappling light, and a bare glimpse of a familiar tawny head, eyes closed, breath sifting through the hairs of his mustache.

Mashkent laid his hand on her arm, restraining her from rising to see more of the picture. "I consult the pool as a courtesy to a guest. If you wish to consult it yourself, there will be the standard fee, of course." He accepted the boy's report that the

271

Prince looked very comfortable indeed. He settled back onto his own cushion, calling for a pipe attached by a long tube to an ornate bottle filled with colored water. "Now then, perhaps you had better tell me of this matter which weighs so heavily on your mind. Tell me of your part in this—and of what you intend to do. Thus I can better determine what terms we might negotiate between us."

Carole shifted, the backs of her legs and her sweat-soaked gown sticking to the silken cushion. Now what? It was all very well for Rupert to be peacefully napping, but he was the trained diplomat, not she. Setting terms and negotiating was supposed to be his bailiwick. "First," she said, "I would like to see the baby."

"No doubt," he replied. "But I am afraid that is quite out of the question."

"There was nothing in the agreement forbidding visiting rights," she pointed out, "and we have come a very long way."

"You should have made an appointment," he said, and she sensed beneath his firmness a certain squirming. "Many regrettable matters could have been avoided had you not failed to do so."

"The same could be said of your firm," she replied calmly. "The question of timing I referred to revolves around just such an omission of securing a convenient time for all concerned. My cousin says you took the baby without announcing your intention to do so. Whatever your opinion of Bronwyn, your methods strike me as a singularly callous way to treat a new mother and child. I would think that even your people share with us certain human feelings that would—"

"Even my people? You have an unfortunate way of expressing yourself. Naturally we have a high regard for human sentiments of all varieties—births, deaths, marriages, love affairs. All of these experiences not only affect us in the usual personal aspects of our lives but are also sacred to us for reasons far deeper than your own. All such happenings are highly profitable. People lose their senses under the influence of strong emotion. They throw caution to the wind. They would do anything to gain this or that. So yes, assuredly we share those human feelings of which you are so fond and revere them, but in the case of your cousin, a deal is, you understand, a deal." He shrugged. "Surely as a fellow vendor of magic, you can see that. Among my people, it is written, 'He who fails to collect a debt shall himself soon be a debtor.' It is one of the most fundamental laws of the Profit.'"

272

"I wouldn't know about that," Carole said. "I don't consider myself a vendor of magic at all. I use my magic to help others. They pay me only by providing me with things I haven't the time or skill to provide for myself."

"Even if you believe such drivel as you are telling me, it is fundamentally the same thing," he said.

"It is not. I'd never demand someone's baby, even on loan. But if I did I would certainly give them a chance to practice their own birthing rites on it first, so they'd be sure it was safe and protected from harm, and wouldn't worry themselves sick over it."

"I thought you said this rite would enhance the value of the child. Now you tell me its function is protective. And you have yet to mention what your role in the affair is."

"Very well," she said. "The rite would enhance the child's value by providing her with protective personal attributes, but it is difficult to explain to an outsider. I was depending on my cousin for that. He is representing the child's parents. I am a priestess of the Mother, authorized to perform the rite."

"Ah, a functionary of your faith, rather like our own accountants?"

"Rather like an . . . uh, well, I suppose you could put it that way." She didn't wish to demur on what would be a minor point to the old man and thereby break the fragile thread of understanding so perilously spun between them. "Truly, I think I've said enough that you can understand why Rupert should be fetched and we should be allowed to see the baby. Christening is very important for Argonian children."

"All Argonian children?"

"Yes, but particularly those of royal or magical lineage. It is the chief source of influence in early life, affecting personality, physical development, interests in matters both mundane and magical, skills, character, and the Mother only knows what else. If the child is properly christened, she will be much more valuable to you. From the family's standpoint, she will have the protection of the gifts presented to her by her kinsmen and their allies. There are so many forces automatically aligned against a child born to power, you see, that protection is a matter of primary importance."

"I find this difficult to comprehend. Can you give me examples of these valuable gifts? What were your own, for instance, and how do they affect you today? And which are you bringing for the child?"

273

The fireflies in Mashkent's eyes danced anxiously and Carole flinched from them.

"I'm afraid I can't, actually. I will not learn what the baby's gifts are until I perform the ceremony. As for my own gifts, why, that was very long ago. Perhaps by the time my cousin can be fetched I'll think of some to discuss with you. I can tell you, however, that the gifts are so important to our lives that if the child is not christened, you may find that inadvertently it will be you and your firm who violate the terms of the agreement. For without the protection of the gifts and the rite, the child may not survive her fifteen years with you to return to her parents."

If she had hoped this was a clinching argument, she was disappointed, for he waved the last statement away as if it nullified the parts to which he had been listening so avidly. "That would be sad for your cousin Bronwyn," he said. "She owes us fifteen years of the service of her child. If this one does not fulfill the requirement, we will be forced to collect her next one. Now then, I think it is time you retired to a place conducive to your meditations."

So saying, he clapped his hands and the two guards reappeared beside her. "Do not waste your breath on these employees of mine, my dear," Mashkent cautioned. "They have been given protection against your charms. We can arrange for them to place you in irons if you prove uncooperative, but that seems so inhospitable. I trust you'll find your quarters comfortable."

Alireza Mukbar's spells went for naught with Rupert, who had strapped his rowan shield around his chest to ward off any possible blows or spells from the hostile Miragenian populace. Instead, it was primarily prosaic if pleasant occurences that brought about his captivity.

He had followed Alireza's green hem through a rabbit warren of alleys until she passed through a gate. He thought it would not amaze her greatly that he followed. He was surprised, however, when a young girl locked the gate fast behind him and thrust the key deep into the bodice of her gown. Then she giggled. Her giggle was echoed by seven or eight others as a vast array of black-haired girls poured into the garden and arranged themselves around him, laughing and talking and—as they grew accustomed to him—touching.

When his green-gowned beauty reappeared with a goblet of wine for him and one for herself, and looked deeply into his eyes as they drank, he thought perhaps he had done something to transfer him prematurely into that happy land where the Mother sent all of her best children upon their demise. As the ladies pressed closer, touching, tittering, and gazing moonily up at him from big dewy eyes, he decided, on the basis of some of the touching, that he was far from deceased. Besides, he couldn't recall anything that might have put him in such a sadly permanent condition.

He accepted the wine. The women spoke to each other in a language different from that of the marketplace, one he found impossible to understand, although when his original prize addressed him, her purring voice was in a language he could follow, little more than a variation on Argonian, spoken with a slight accent, which he found utterly charming.

They settled him in a cool, breezy room, with a fountain singing in the middle and delicious things to eat and drink. Then they began haggling over him, sending daggered looks and shrill exclamations over his person, while pinching and patting him for emphasis. Even in his wine-soaked haze he began to grow alarmed. His green-gowned temptress returned just as he was about to rise to his noodle-like legs and bolt. She no longer wore a green gown or much of anything else except two long narrow handkerchiefs of sheer pink fabrics suspended from a golden belt, covering the center of her buttocks in the back and shifting alluringly from one thigh, to the other. A lacy vest of gold cloth might have been made for her when she was eight years old, now totally inadequate for its task, strained to cover her gleaming cleavage, which gleamed all the more fascinatingly when she clapped her hands, sending the other girls scurrying from the room. She lowered herself beside him.

"Do not think too harshly of my sisters," she said. "They are passionate and hungry for affection. They find you pleasing as I knew they would." Her silken fingers slid beneath the strap of the rowan shield planted awkwardly in the middle of his chest. She felt for the buckle, tickling, so that he involuntarily pulled her hand back.

"Very nice girls," he agreed. "As you say, affectionate. I'm glad they like me."

"I don't know why they were so greedy tonight. We will have to make out a schedule." She licked her lips appreciatively and ran her eyes from his own, down across his torso, lingeringly, to his toes and back up again. "I am sure there is enough of you to go around."

"Enough to . . .?" His tongue was thick. Speech was made

more difficult as she sought to impede his tongue with her own. She succeeded, for quite some time. "Enough to go around? I'm sorry. I don't quite understand. I believe we need to talk about this . . . ahhh, yes—well, then—perhaps not. . . ." and forgot to protest again for a dangerously long time. Nonetheless, he lacked neither honor nor will to such an extent that he failed to intervene when her nimble fingers, seeking to encounter something else altogether, closed on the mermaid's comb hanging inside his belt. He clasped her slender arm from wrist to elbow in his large hand and with the fingers of the other hand gently removed the comb from her grasp. "I'm sorry, but I'm afraid your family wouldn't like what might happen to you if you handle this comb. Perhaps we should talk, after all."

Her sweet musky perfume grew a tinge more heady, her skin under his hand a touch more velvety, and her voice purred more compellingly than ever, punctuated by moist flickers of her tongue tip against his earlobe. "You will be my family. My love. My husband. Our husband." Her fingers curled toward the comb again playfully. "Now. That's settled. Since it's all in the family, what is that? A gift for some other sweetheart? You'll find enough here to keep you busy, my darling. Give it to me instead and I promise you'll need none of the others to make you forget her."

He moaned.

"Don't you trust me to keep my promise?" she said, pouting.

"It's not . . . that," he said thickly, trying to unwind his tongue from the roof of his mouth where it seemed wont to curl from sheer ecstasy. He continued manfully. "It's just that the fact is, now that you mention promise, I have one to keep."

"Forget her," she breathed huskily into his ear.

"I can't."

"I will make you do so," she threatened, tickling the hairs beneath the rowan shield.

"You will not, for I can tell that you are a tender and loving lady. You would not wish me to forsake the poor little infant whose protector I am to, um, that is . . ." His tongue was cleaving to the roof of his mouth again and his diplomatic training was as if it had never been.

"For the sake of a dalliance? But a dalliance is hardly what we—I—have in mind. You are a splendid man, my love, a superb man, a man who, with a little work, will be worthy of me, of my dear little sisters. You must stay and be ours. . . ."

"Nothing would make me happier, I assure you," he said, his

276

tongue coming unstuck the moment she reintroduced the subject of himself at the mercy of her voracious sisters—plus the little work and worthiness business. "But I must do so with a heart and mind free of distractions."

"Your heart and mind may do as they please," she said, laughing, gleaming again. "But the rest of you must remain here with us."

"Yes, but you don't understand. I must see to the safety of my infant niece, only child of my sister Bronwyn, to whom I have sworn a vow."

"Silly boy. You must not let your concern for some child prevent you from following your more adult inclinations. I happen to know that the child is quite safe and is being spoiled and pampered in accordance with her station."

"You know where she is? You can take me to her?"

"No, I cannnot. She is no longer here and we emphatically desire that you be."

"Where is she? What has become of her?"

"Don't bellow so, darling, they'll think we're quarreling. Why, the little dear is being a first-born royal highness, as she was meant to be. Oh, my love, must we talk business?" She ruffled his hair and favored him with a petulant expression. "I know so many more interesting things to do."

He lay motionless, though it was a challenge worthy of a religious hero on the rack, and stared coldly at her until she continued. He decided that later perhaps he would discuss this incident with Sir Cyril Perchingbird and see if inaction under duress did not sometimes constitute sufficient merit to qualify one for a medal of some sort.

"But it's so dull, really. A barren queen wanted a baby and since the Company *had* a perfectly good new baby owed to them, with no one able to tell the difference if quick action were taken, it was a simple matter of transferring the child from the debtor to the client, who took it from there."

"But the child has a family. She was only to stay here fifteen years."

"The clients who asked us—I mean, the Company—to procure the child are renting her services. So you see, it's nothing for you to get tense about. It's not as if she's a slave or anything dismal like that which might have occurred if with my tender heart, I hadn't searched and searched to find just the right opening. I'm very good at my work. Gore . . . the country where the child now lives in splendor and luxury is a very

277

affluent one, one of our chief exporters of magical goods, and the King and Queen will spoil the brat rotten." She flopped herself down, folding her arms under her breasts and pouting in earnest.

He turned and stroked her hair. "You have relieved my mind considerably," he told her, then added casually, "What was the name of this place again? It must be close by."

She was very good at her work; it took him a long time to learn the rest of what he wanted to know from her, and a great deal of effort, which was how he came to be sleeping so soundly when Mashkent's servant saw him in the pool of visions.

Carole found one commendable aspect of the Miragenian way of life: It apparently excluded the idea of dungeons. She was locked in a room that must have been no less luxurious than Mashkent's own quarters, and perhaps more so. Looking it over, she decided that it might be a showroom for the firm's products. This she deduced by the way the mattress floated in midair, lying upon a rug hovering above the multitude of jewel-bright carpets strewn one atop the other in colorful profusion on the patterned floor. A small cascade of colored water spilled down one wall. The soft light of the waxen tapers shining from various nooks and crannies in the carved recesses of the walls reflected from the satiny tumult quick glimpses of faces and figures, people, animals, and landscapes. The falls formed a pretty stream bisecting the room. The stream was bridged at intervals by steps or little arches with golden rails, in which the reflected candle flames danced with their own shadows. Huge windows in ornamental shapes faced the garden in which Carole had spoken to Mashkent, but the view could only be seen through a deeply carved lattice. In every row of lattices sat a row of colored bottles, each row a different hue, each bottle the prismlike crystal of the peridot-colored one from the river near outer Frostingdung.

A young woman, veiled and obsequious, bowed her way into the room just as Carole dropped onto one of the cushions.

"If madam does not wish to retire at once, perhaps I could explain a few of the distinctive features of this chamber," the young woman said, and, without waiting for an answer, continued in a persuasive voice undertoned with what seemed to be great excitement at the opportunity of sharing the information with Carole. Either she had not been informed that Carole was other than a rich customer or else she was so used to giving this

278

particular pitch that she was unable to vary the routine to suit the circumstances.

"The bed will lull madam to sleep with a gentle rocking motion once madam has mounted it by means of uttering a simple command that will cause it to sweep you off your feet and onto your back as smoothly as the most adroit lover."

Oh. Marvelous. Just what she needed. An amorous inanimate object. Silently, Carole vowed to remain on the cushions for the brief time she intended to rest before deciding how best to find Rupert, grab the child (for if the Miragenians didn't care whether or not the baby survived her first fifteen years, it was quite out of the question to leave her with them), and go.

"In the window," the maid continued, "you will notice the display of finely-crafted Gorequartzian vessels. These vessels will explode into flames and poisonous gases the moment they are touched by unauthorized hands, instantly immolating the intruder in the most painful fashion."

Ah, so the maid did know Carole was a prisoner. And the bottles were there to detain her. Not the same as the ones in the river then?

"Lastly," the woman continued, "I am required to explain to you that the firm disclaims any responsibility for damage to yourself or your property if you fail to heed our warning and will also hold you responsible for any damages occurring to company holdings resulting from said failure. Peaceful sleep, madam." She finished, and bowed out.

Carole sat tapping her fingertips against her cheek for a time after the maid left. The bottles might or might not be dangerous. At the present time, she was inclined to think that they were. Otherwise, why leave a lot of valuable and potent magic lying around free for the taking? Not that under ordinary circumstances she was one to appropriate random bits of other people's magic, but if the bottles were like the one by the river, perhaps they were just what she needed to execute her task. On the other hand, they might be just what the Miragenians needed to execute her. If the bottles did contain entities such as the one she had previously encountered, they had no doubt been set to watch her, to prevent her escape, even if they wouldn't actually explode. The maid's warning was clearly aimed at making the firm's involuntary guest reluctant to experiment. Nor did Carole merely wish to escape. Not without Rupert and the child. She stared into the waterfall, considering.

As she stared, she noted that some of the faces floating past were familiar ones. Surely that was the woman in the marketplace appearing briefly in a widening of the water's spill over an ornamental stone, only to narrow back into nothingness as the strand of water containing her thinned and dropped into the stream. And there, on the other side, wasn't that Mashkent himself? And the woman with the mirrors? Yes, no mistaking that dull countenance so badly in need of help from its own merchandise. When Rupert's dreaming visage tumbled over the artfully carved rocks, she had all the confirmation she needed.

She whistled a long, low note and held it. Rupert hung there for a moment, suspended with his chin in the narrow part of the rivulet, his dozing eyes and peaceful brow with the yellow curls broadening out over the rock. As she lost the note he drained away.

Having spotted him once, she recognized glimpses of his face at other points in the waterfall and tried to whistle them to a stop. If she aimed badly, she stopped another face. That of the old merchant, she noticed during one such mishap, was still awake, and contained a thoughtful expression that made her wish she knew what was behind it. Trying to outguess strands of water was slippery going, and she found she had trouble puckering fast enough to stop the one she wanted, tending instead to be in the middle of inhaling just as Rupert slid down the wall.

How was she to slow down the images in the stream long enough to sort them out? Perhaps if she could think of a tune that would call to Rupert's image particularly. . . . Her magic supplied it from a snatch of a love song she had heard him sing for the entertainment of the ladies at Castle Killgilles. She hummed it slowly, like a dirge. The water backed up, as if dammed, flooding the tiled banks from where she sat back to the waterfall, water lapping the edges of the costly rugs before she could find what she sought in its depths. That wouldn't do. Water gushing out the door would attract the Miragenians' notice. She stopped humming and the water flowed back into its course.

Taking one of the candles in hand, she examined the pool at the foot of the waterfall. The sides of it were built up slightly so that one might sit beside it. If she didn't hum quite so slowly, perhaps they'd contain the initial flow of water long enough for her to locate what she needed. She hummed a bit of a lullabye at what she hoped was an appropriate speed. The waters slowed and an infant appeared: a child crowned with dark red ringlets outlined against water. A tall, glittering structure rose in the background like a huge pile of coins, mist encircling its base.

The child was wrapped in the arms of a girl whose hair was straight and light brown. They seemed to be sitting in a boat of some sort, and the baby was bawling lustily. The scene flowed past. Carole allowed the water to resume its original level before she hummed the love song again.

Rupert's image dutifully slowed down to where she could observe it in all its slumbering glory. Why in the Mother's name was he sleeping his life away when for all he knew she was still alone in the Miragenian marketplace and the baby still remained missing?

Maybe the Miragenians with whom he was staying had looked into a similar pool to assure him that both cousin and baby were well. Maybe. But did they have such pools elsewhere? It occurred to her that perhaps the water with which she was presently dealing was the runoff of the pools in the courtyard, carrying the visions, which continued to flow even when they were no longer being examined. It made sense to her. Time and events flowed on no matter who was watching, so why not the images? Anyone lacking Carole's talent would have been unable to understand what the waterfall and stream contained, so it probably seemed to the Miragenians perfectly safe to have the water running free for anyone occupying the room to observe if only they could look quickly enough.

Old Mashkent flashed by again and Carole whistled him to a dribble with a song that resembled not so much a song as a chant of the back-and-forth bicker of the marketplace, the buy-and-sell, too-high-too-low cadence she had been hearing all afternoon, unaware until her magic plucked it from her memory. The old merchant climbed onto a hovering rug that rose above the shop to soar across the city. As soon as the image died she caught another, and kept track of the rooftops the rug passed, feeling sure that his trip was somehow connected with her own.

The rug approached a dome composed of stone carved so intricately it resembled heavily starched lace. At its base, the dome's skirt scalloped up in curving arcs above a garden. In this garden, the merchant was met by a lady swathed in a pink-and-gold gown like the one Carole had worn at Castle Killgilles. Though the gown was a different color, the luxuriant hair and the set of the head made Carole certain that this was the same woman Rupert had pursued from the marketplace.

The merchant asked a sharp question. The lady gave him a quick answer that failed to satisfy him. He scowled and asked another question. The lady shrugged, looking smug, and pillowed her cheek on her hands, eyes closed.

So. Now Carole knew where Rupert was. She had only to find the house with the carved dome. Simple enough, if she could first free herself from Mashkent's hospitality.

She eyed the bottle-decked lattices thoughtfully. If she could not touch the bottles, perhaps she could dance them from their niches. If she stood on the far side of the room while doing so and the bottles exploded, so much the better. They would open the windows for her. Otherwise, she would have to hope a piece of the lattice was loose enough that she could jiggle it out, making a space large enough for her to fit through. Fortunately, years of walking and swimming the Blabbermouth had kept her somewhat on the stringy side of the usual sturdy Brownwitch build.

She danced the first three rows of bottles out with the first bar of her song, but as she took a breath, she heard them clamoring. Even though her song was now directed at their counterparts remaining in the lattices, they continued to bounce about on the thick layers of carpet on which she had been careful to land them. The lot on the floor were colored violet, periwinkle, and fuschia, and from them arose a collective whimper when she whistled them to stop. As she returned her attention to the deep ruby row still lining the next row of lattices, one of the ruby bottles cried out. Carole cast a furtive glance at the door. She was trying to whistle loudly enough to move bottles from across the room but not so loudly as to disturb guards posted by her door.

"Shhh," she hissed at the ruby bottle. "Stop complaining. No one's hurting you." As the bottle danced down, it twisted. Within, she saw the glitter of accusing eyes.

"Not hurt us, indeed? What do you call keeping us locked up in here while you jounce us around as if you were trying to make butter if you don't call it being hurt?"

"Confined," Carole said reasonably, allowing the troublesome object to drop beside its fellows on the carpet.

"How would you like being confined then?" asked another protestor, this one from the jade row beneath the ruby one.

"I am, you know, and I don't care for it at all," she replied when that bottle, too, rolled onto the carpet.

"Is that why you're taking it out on us?" whined the ruby complainer on the floor.

"I'm doing nothing of the sort," Carole hissed back. "I'm just trying to . . . none of your business."

Finishing the jade row, she started the row of robin's-egg

282

blue. "We could do business together," the first of these whee-dled, winking at her. "You won't get through the window without my help, you know. I propose a fair deal. You get me out and I get you out."

"Don't listen to that one!" the ruby vessel cried. "If you free *me* I won't cheat you out of the other two miraculous wishes you're entitled to by terms of the oral contract."

Carole danced the last robin's-egg blue bottle down and frowned at the crystal-strewn carpet.

"Look who's calling who a cheat," the robin's-egg blue vessel scoffed. "Maybe it is three wishes, but I naturally assumed that this honest and warmhearted lady would not insist on more than a simple trade, since she shares our predicament. Of course, if she's going to be as greedy as our present masters, I suppose there's no—"

"Listen," Carole said, "I am absolutely not interested in your wishes right now. I have plenty of other trouble on my hands without the kind that would come from your magic. If the maid wasn't making the whole thing up about fiery explosions. Neither do I want to be accused of theft."

"Just what do you want?" the ruby bottle asked. "If you free us all, you're entitled to three wishes from each of us. I wouldn't dismiss it so lightly if I were you."

"I don't, but I certainly haven't the time to sit around thinking of wishes all night, nor do I have the pocket space to carry all of you or even one of you. If I open one, can't that one free the others?"

"If that is your wish."

"That's one of them. The others are to get me out of this room and to help me free Prince Rupert and the baby." So saying, she approached the bottles, took a deep breath, pulled the stopper on the ruby one and waited for it to explode.

"That was four wishes," the ruby one said. "I'll give you the first three."

The room exploded in a mass of popping stoppers and spraying colored mist, through which Carole hurtled, covering her head as she reached the window, only to find herself passing harmlessly through it as though it were no more than illusion. The world blurred around her, a spinning confusion of garden and crescent moon, stars, and spires, streets with closed stalls, and arched doorways, all stirred with ruby mist, until she sat down sharply in front of an elegant edifice topped with the intricately carved stone dome. In less than a heartbeat, a ruby dust devil swirled from above, bearing something large and solid, which thumped down beside her.

"I wish you had been a little more patient," Rupert complained, rubbing his backside. "I was going to come for you as soon as I had all the information."

Morning was breaking and Carole and Rupert fled Mlle. Mukbar's mansion for the cover of a ruined wall, behind which they hid, watching the marketplace come to life. In a very short time, the shops were besieged by blue-corded agents of Mukbar, Mashkent, and Mirza. Rupert, watching through a peephole as the guards briskly searched the street, shook his head, smiling with a hint of pride. "Those Mukbar girls have taken quite a fancy to me," he said. When Carole looked puzzled, he gave her a carefully worded explanation of how he had fared since he left her.

His cousin took her turn at the peephole as he talked and now stepped aside, pointing, so that he could look.

"I wouldn't like to undermine your self-confidence, Your Highness," she said, "but I think those colored clouds might have more to do with the abundance of the Company's minions than does the devotion of your fiancees."

In the street, four guards were now running headlong through the piles of fruit being thrown at them as they were chased by streaks of violet, ruby, and jade. Evidently, the protection they had been given against magic was only proof against Carole's own or else had worn off after a short time and had not been renewed, because after a spirited melee in which the guards definitely came out the losers, the street in front of the ruined wall was clear of both guards and colored streaks. Angry fruit vendors cursed and gesticulated graphically to the departing disruption before stooping to retrieve their bruised goods.

"Were those bright streaks what I think they were?" Rupert asked Carole. She nodded.

He groaned. "How could you? I thought you were going to make things easier here. Instead, the moment I trust you by yourself while I attend to more urgent business, you run off with the private property of the very people with whom we need to negotiate, thereby managing with considerable imagination to violate the only sort of violatable law in this entire anarchy, making us fugitives, no doubt with a price on our heads."

"I didn't run off with anything," she said. "They ran off by themselves, and I can't say that I blame them. They're some sort

284

of intelligent magical creatures with minds of their own. From what I can tell, no one has any business claiming them as property.''

"That's your opinion and according to your customs, not theirs," Rupert said stubbornly.

"It is also my opinion that you've little room to criticize when you've done nothing more constructive than sleep through my efforts to help the child after you abandoned me to—''

"I wasn't abandoning you. I was researching.'' Witches! Pah! They were more trouble than their so-called powers were worth. His rear still smarted from his cousin's idea of rescuing him from a danger that was far preferable to the conditions he now endured. "It may interest you to know that the child is not here in Miragenia, but in a land called Gorequartz. Had you not put us in a position requiring us to hide ourselves, we would need only to stand out in the open long enough for the dragon to find us and we could have her take us there.''

Carole was watching the peephole again and made a gratified sound. "There's the scrollseller again. Perhaps she can tell us how to get to this Gorequartz place.''

She quickly rounded the edge of the ruined wall, Rupert right behind her.

"No," she said, fixing him with a stare that promised him a dancing lesson if he didn't cooperate. "You're too noticeable. She knows me. I'll be right back.'' With that, she darted out into the street. She crossed quickly, holding her borrowed veil close to her face as she dodged horses and dromedaries to reach the scrollseller. The woman spoke a few words with her, nodded to the northwest corner of the street, and shrugged.

A sudden flash, farther down the street, caught Rupert's eye. A hag hunched over a pile of shining mirrors beckoned to a newly arrived blue-corded company agent. She pointed in Carole's direction. The agent tossed a coin in the air, where it caught the reflected glimmer of a mirror before landing in the woman's hand, from there going straight to her teeth. The mercenary turned backwards and called to someone behind him.

Rupert bounded around the wall and into the street, promptly tripping on an overturned barrow formerly containing melons. When he lifted his face from the street, three blue-corded guards swept past him to close on Carole. She trilled once, tentatively, and again, confidently. When he stood the mercenaries were reeling backwards, cursing their masters for the unprofitable planned obsolescence of their protective spells. Their curses were to no avail. They danced helplessly an arm's length or so away from Rupert, whirling slowly at times or kicking out with little hopping leaps, but basically doing a two-step that kept them well out of reach of his cousin, who was whistling for all she was worth. Rupert held his rowan shield before him as he walked around the dancers to Carole's side. He used his shield gallantly to protect both himself and the poor friendly merchant woman, who had been gracefully two-stepping all over her spilled scrolls.

The dance company grew larger as curious merchants from adjoining booths edged forward to see what was happening and were caught by Carole's whistle. The street resembled a somewhat sedate block party. Many of the merchants trampled their own wares or those of their immediate neighbors. No doubt the loss of the trampled goods would be another crime to be balanced against his and Carole's account, Rupert thought grimly. Nonetheless, the sight of the merrily dancing feet of the merchants topped by their fiercely scowling faces was so humorous he couldn't help grinning.

His grin died as a street musician arrived playing a set of pipes with a high skirling tone that totally drowned out Carole's song, setting everyone free. Rupert drew her back behind his shield as the crowd closed in on them. An almond flew through the air and struck him a blow on the left shoulder. It was followed immediately by a clay pot, smashing against his exposed elbow, causing the shield arm to drop numbly to his side. He collapsed against the wall.

Carole fell on top of him. The merchant woman behind them shrieked. Rupert hitched himself up, spilling his cousin into the crook of his knee as he used his right arm to support his lifeless left arm. No sooner had he raised the shield than a sword crashed down on it. The blade banged off the wood, rebounding to its owner, one of the blue-corded mercenaries, who jumped backwards to avoid its bite.

The shield would protect them as long as he had the strength to maneuver it, for it would repulse any magic and surely, in a magic-proud land such as Miragenia, most of the blades would have some little cheap enchantment on them.

Suddenly a violet haze shimmered above him, causing him momentarily to imagine he had been hit harder than he had first thought. Then the haze was joined by a ruby one and a jade, and the three colors gathered into a malignant rainbow, attacking the merchants with their own wares, the mercenaries with their own weapons.

The shield before them, Rupert and Carole ran down the street, dodging missiles, merchants, and mists. Rupert's long legs fairly flew over the pavement. Carole trailed him at an ever-increasing distance until he reached back with his large paw to catch her up and jerk her forward at arm's length. She was still a good five paces behind him. He dragged her around a corner and almost collided with a raggedy figure who suavely blocked their path.

"Good morning, gentlefolk. I see you are traveling, and traveling is what I am about. Ah, who's this? Why, if it isn't the young woman from yesterday! Having once availed yourself of the services of my splendid travel log, madam, wouldn't you like to try it again? Picture yourself and your companion journeying swiftly up the headwaters of the Cashflow River to the ancient scenic city of Gorequartz. See the sparkling rivers cut through the mysterious magical valley, feared by the most acquisitive of merchants. See the shining sacred temples of many-hued glasses. See the priests float in stately procession down flower-strewn canals in the glamorous barges of the rainbow god, following their quaint, centuries-old custom of parading through the city before presenting to the massive godhead guarding their harbor the human sacrifices that have made Gorequartz a byword to those trafficking in raw magical force and power."

Carole missed part of the speech, for her heart was still beating a hard tattoo in her ears, but she recognized the speaker. "Rupert, the woman in the marketplace said this man might be a slaver—"

"Nonsense, lady. I am a freeborn man, a traveler, and a slaver of no man as I am slave to none. Indeed, you should know as much and so should the woman of whom you speak, for you did no more than gaze at my travel log before it caused the women to provide you with that which I promised it would deliver: the best route, the most scenic and expeditious mode of travel to your destination. If you will but mount upon my travel log once more, this time while it lies atop other materials awaiting us in yonder river, you will once more experience the wonderful convenience and economy of my marvelous device."

Rupert looked down at Carole, dismayed. "Human sacrifice? But Alireza said it was such a *nice* place. . . ."

The travel log rolled back and forth in the bottom of a small boat. The boat also boasted a pair of sturdy oars to augment the log's magic, but despite Rupert's most powerful efforts, progress was slow. The boat kept drifting back toward the grated gate regulating river traffic in and out of the city.

"I thought the log was going to spirit us away," Carole complained, squirming.

"And so it shall," the merchant said, "just as soon as you start singing to the boat and dance it up river for us." And he lay back nonchalantly against the bow—or perhaps it was the stern. They both looked the same since the boat was sideways in the water.

Carole complied, but crossly. Her whistle was whistled out from the long night of herding watery images. Her lips still tingled from orchestrating the dance in the marketplace.

Rupert was no more pleased than she. "It was ill of you, sir, to offer desperate folk magical aid where you had none to give."

"Ah, but you're wrong. I had it, of course. I knew where the river was, which was more than you did, and between my log and this boat, I had all that we needed, save one missing ingredient. The power of my log attracted it—or her, as you see. The rest of what I promised, the so-charming detailing of the wonders of the journey, I shall be happy to personally, enchantingly provide."

"You've been this way before then?" Rupert asked.

"Would I offer you such expert guidance if I had not?" the man asked, sounding both wounded and distinctly evasive. By way of diversion, he launched into his narrative at once. "You have here, for instance, some very fine banks," he began expansively, throwing his arms out to embrace each side of the river.

"Let's forget the banks for a moment," Rupert interrupted. "Tell us more about this place we're heading, this Gorequartz, and why anyone would want to practice human sacrifice."

"As to the last question, my dear fellow, you seem to have me confused with a theologian. If you want me to give you proper guidance, you must let me do so in my own inimitable way, to describe for you each noteworthy landmark in its time, to give it full glory—"

Carole stopped, gasping, her cheeks aching with whistling, her lips buzzing from humming. "Who said we wanted such useless services? The boat would move upstream far more quickly if it had less to carry. It's in my mind that unless you prove very valuable very soon you would be of far more use to us dancing back to shore with your log in your pocket."

The man's eyes widened with terror, but not at her threat. Pointing behind her left shoulder, he gulped and asked, "How valuable would you consider it, madam, if I were to point out that at this very moment your lamentably neglected spell is singing us into the path of another very large craft?''

Carole followed the pointing finger of their self-proclaimed guide to see a huge, bulge-sided boat bearing down on them. "Oh, Mother," she groaned, but wasted no other useless words before breaking into a shrill if exhausted whistle at a fast clip. Her song was copied from that of wild running rapids, though she was fairly certain rapids never ran upstream.

No sooner had she begun to sing their craft away from the big boat than a squad of mercenaries burst through the town gate and onto the left bank of the river. They brandished spears, bows, and in some instances, lightning bolts, which they hurtled at the smaller boat. This seemingly uncalled-for belligerence did not please the occupants of the larger boat, which had so far failed to notice the true target of the aggression. Archers on the deck of the big craft fired back. Unfortunately for Carole, Rupert, and their guide, their own small boat was far more susceptible to the rain of arrows than were the attackers on the river bank.

Carole dipped and dodged, ducking arrows so vigorously that breathing was chancy and whistling nearly impossible. Meanwhile the bow of the greater vessel loomed ever nearer, while the smaller boat wallowed from side to side as its occupants sought to evade the variety of missiles hailing down upon them.

Rupert threw up his shield, but Carole could make no use of it while trying to sing her spell, however erratically. Just as she thought she could not tweet another note, the little boat shuttled like a water spider to the lee of the larger craft, which began crawling past, its bulk protecting the smaller vessel from the attackers landside. This left the mercenaries to concentrate their fire on their unintentional targets in the large boat while their original quarry crept upstream.

Carole heaved a deep sigh, rolling her eyes upward in time to see yet another feature of the Miragenian landscape so far unheralded by their guide. The underbellies, necks, pluming tails, and beating wings of a herd of flying horses swooped overhead. Every horse was mounted and every rider armed. These airborne assailants were not deceived by the cover of the larger boat and began chucking spears at the smaller boat with aim sufficiently accurate to pin Carole's skirt to the deck, through which the haft sank to half its length.

Another spear chunked past Carole's nose. As she lunged

violently sideways, so did the boat, which flipped over. She splashed into the water and kicked free. The spear held the stout wool of her skirt and jerked her back. The last thing she saw before her head slammed against the side was Rupert and the merchant tumbling toward the bottom in a haystack of plunging spears and arrows.

CHAPTER VI

Rupert found that although his arms were very long, suddenly he hadn't enough of them. The shield broke his fall when he plummeted into the water, but the travel log seller had grabbed onto him while still clutching the allegedly magic log. Since the panic-stricken merchant held the log against his body with his arm instead of using it to help him float on the surface, the combined weight of water-logged log and water-logged merchant threatened to sink Rupert, merchant, log, and all.

Carole's skirts and hair canopied over them like a large jellyfish, the woman attached to them floating flacidly in their folds, alarmingly unlively. Rupert stopped his plummet with a hard kick toward the surface. He was very strong and it cost him little effort to move. To his surprise, he found holding his breath under water no strain at all. It felt almost natural.

He grabbed Carole's skirt, jerking. She bounced upward and he kicked after her, releasing the hold on her skirt to gain a hold on her waist while angling up between the shadows cast by the boats. The arrows still hissed into the water on all sides of him as he raised his face to breathe. Carole drifted listlessly, supported by one of Rupert's arms, but the log-laden merchant climbed Rupert's other arm, dragging Rupert lower and lower, while he tried with decreasing success to continue kicking to stay afloat. If only the merchant would unhand his arm, he could raise the shield and use it to buoy them up, but the merchant continued to claw at Rupert. Fingernails and logbark bit through Rupert's tunic sleeve, pulling him off balance.

An arrow whizzed by Rupert's ear and the merchant howled

into the same ear. In that instant, the iron grip on Rupert's arm loosened, replaced by a clawed hand groping for his eyes and nose. Rupert ducked backwards. The hand grasped his throat in a stranglehold.

His breath was knocked from him and he stared upward at the circling wings of the flying horses, the great vessel looming over him, the arrows plunging toward him. Rupert knotted his muscles, bracing them against each other to shrug off the merchant with a heave of his shoulders, but he waited, for he wanted to give the travel-logger as long as possible to come to his senses and allow Rupert to help him in a way that wouldn't get them both killed. Closing his eyes tightly, Rupert entreated the Mother to take literally his prayer to deliver him from fools, and heaved. Whether it was the heaving or the praying that did it, at that moment the hand at his throat relaxed.

He opened his eyes, shut them, and reopened them, for a rosy glow pulsed toward him, thrumming in a familiar way, the glow dissipating as the thrumming grew louder.

The arrows turned magically aside as a strong wind chilled the Prince's wet hide to the bone. Against him the merchant shook convulsively.

Suddenly, the water exploded upward behind them as if something large had dropped into it. Rupert felt teeth graze the skin of his back and buttocks as warm breath and cold water touched his bare skin at once. He was hoisted by the seat of his pants into the air, through the arrows, through the horses, the merchant still clawing at one arm while Carole hung from the other. The leather belt with which he had closed his robe cut deep into his middle where the dragon's teeth pulled it tight, away from his back. He felt the material of his britches strain treacherously. It was sturdy cloth, but not that sturdy.

As if things weren't bad enough, Carole struggled to wakefulness just as the dragon lifted them up through the herd of hostile horsemen. His pants loosened another fraction as he adjusted his grip to hold onto Carole while she squirmed. He thought his arms would burst from their sockets, for he was already overburdened without her making matters worse.

Fortunately, she quieted quickly, most intelligently taking in the situation almost as soon as she woke. She moved not at all except to shake her head, spraying water, and twist it slightly as if to listen to something. She adjusted her grip so that she clung more securely but with less encumbrance, tight against Rupert's chest and shoulders.

The merchant fought Carole's hands and she batted at him, causing the wind to increase at Rupert's backside, the belt to tighten so that, breathless, the Prince issued a whuffing grunt.

"Be still, you cheesehead, and cooperate," Carole told the merchant. "If you keep causing my lord cousin to make such pitiful noises, the dragon will burn us both from the sky to save him further discomfort."

The wings beat her voice away from their hearing, but the merchant reared attentively and painfully against Rupert's arm. "Eh? Dragon?" he shouted into Rupert's ear.

The Prince groaned again and the muzzle pressed against his hindquarters trembled with a deep ominous rumble.

In his other ear, Carole shouted, "Grippledice wants to know if you're safe and shall she set us down somewhere?"

Rupert nodded with a necessary economy of motion that nevertheless contained an abundance of passionate enthusiasm for the dragon's proposal.

The three of them dropped sickeningly as the dragon swooped low, skimming the water quickly. The line of scrubby greenery separating desert and river blurred past them. Ahead the desert floor dropped and rocky hills rose sharply from the flatlands, breaking into austere red-striped rock slabs, backed by higher slopes sparsely dotted with dark green, followed by wave upon wave of misted blue mountains with white ridges bleeding down into spiderleg veins.

Into this landscape Grippledice carried her live cargo. For a time she still followed the river, which narrowed somewhat beyond the first few mountains where various streams fed into it. Past the second set of slopes, she veered abruptly away from the river and down a long narrow valley, walled on both sides by heavily forested slopes. All of this speed and motion did Rupert's britches and his sense of security no good whatsoever and he rapidly decided that he couldn't be responsible for everyone's welfare. When Grippledice passed the next particularly abundantly leafed tree, he would drop the merchant into it and relieve some of the strain on his own midsection and trouser seat. The merchant would simply have to hope for the best.

He did not give up, after all, however, for his pants beat him to it. He cried out as he felt rather than heard the rip as cold air rushed against tender parts. The three of them dropped, dizzyingly, for half a heartbeat before dangling by the remaining strip of his belt. The invisible dragon sought to reduce altitude and potential injuries with all possible haste. When the belt gave way and the three of them were pitched to earth, it was blessedly not too far down and they rolled harmlessly onto the grass.

Rupert, having made sure that he rolled onto his back before collapsing, gave in to the searing pain in his arms and middle and to the generalized aching of his entire body. He sobbed.

Carole sat up and rubbed her head, a luxury she had had to forego while hanging on for dear life and being carried aloft. The ground cover between Rupert and her suddenly crushed itself flat and a piece of ragged double-woven woolen cloth spewed out of nowhere, drifting gently to cover one of Rupert's ankles.

"Ptui," the dragon said in Pan-Elvin, then, more elegantly, "Will he live, the one who warms my heart?"

Carole examined the heartwarming party in question critically. "Barely, I think. He'll need some mending."

"Hist!" the dragon said. "Something's cooking."

The horse's wingbeats seemed light as a bird's after listening to the heavy drumming of the dragon's flight. High overhead it soared as its rider cautiously patrolled the valley, slowly circling, scouting. The merchant rolled his eyes back in his head and covered them with an arm. Rupert looked past caring. The horse was far beyond them when suddenly it reared, whinnying, and galloped upward, wings and hooves working double time to gain altitude. The rider hung on for dear life. Clearly the animal was running away from him. As the horse sailed over their heads, a curse echoed downward from the rider and a thunderbolt streaked from his hand into a low-hanging cloud, the impact crackling through the treetops.

Ominous rumbling followed close on the initial crack, clouds obediently gathered, the wind freshened and whipped the trees, the sky darkened even further, and soon icy rain slanted through the pervasive shadows.

"That is just what I dislike about Miragenians," the merchant complained. "No sense of fair play. His miserable companions could not find us, he could not find us, but does he give up and go away peacefully? No, he has to make things miserable for this whole valley, whether he thinks we're in it or not."

"We are, though," Carole grumbled argumentatively, not because she didn't agree with him but because being knocked out and dragged through the air was not the sort of thing that brought out the good side of her naturally uneven temperament.

"We might not have been," the merchant said stubbornly.

Carole sighed and stretched with her hands on the small of her aching back. Rupert groaned and she abruptly felt ashamed of herself and began to wonder if there wasn't something she could do about him. He was writhing, arching his spine and trying to rub it. Judging from her own soreness, which did not compel her to contort herself in nearly so extreme a fashion, Rupert's must be nearly unendurable. She turned to the merchant. "See if you can get that log of yours out of the rain and dry the river water off it somewhat, will you? As soon as the weather clears a little, we'll need to build a fire, which should be easy enough with Grippledice here. I'll try to find some kindling."

She gathered the kindling by hand, trying to move quickly enough to keep warm, a process hindered by her protesting muscles. Ordinarily, had she been feeling lazy, she might have used her magic to save herself the physical effort but her music was spent from her efforts of the day and previous night. She shivered with the dank drizzle and marveled at the abrupt transition from searing Miragenian sunlight to this dim chill, but reminded herself that part of the abruptness was magically induced by the thunderbolt. The spell would probably wear off soon.

While she searched for kindling, she kept her eyes open for a certain flower from which a painkilling tea could be brewed for Rupert. She had had her doubts about him from time to time, true, but he quite literally hadn't let her down when she most needed him and clearly needed help in return now. She spied a cluster of the helpful bell-shaped white blossoms a ways further through the trees and started picking her way toward them.

The sticks she carried snagged in the trees as she passed, breaking and tumbling from her arms, scattering on the ground. Bending her aching back again to collect them, she felt like lying down beside them and crying. Slowly, she retrieved the wood, but decided emphatically that she could not juggle two things at once and returned to the spot where she had left her companions.

Rupert huddled into himself, shivering. The merchant, to Carole's surprise, was finally showing some concern for someone other than himself and was piling bits of his own sodden tatters on top of the moaning prince. Carole stashed her kindling with the log under a protecting bush and retraced her steps to find the flowers again.

They weren't there. The spot was the same one she had seen before. The trees were identical—a large elm with dead vine stalks weaving up the side opposite a shaggy-barked hickory with a broken branch hanging from its top creaking back and forth at right angles. But the little pool of blossoms that had nested between them was missing. Kneeling with less grace and agility than her Great-granny Brown, Carole examined the place where the flowers had been. Broken stems pricked up among the moss-beared tree roots, and one or two leaves remained to reassure her that indeed these were the remains of the flowers she sought.

She shivered and looked quickly around her, searching the gloom. She saw no one, either friend or foe, and half-shrugged, half-flexed her stiff shoulders. At any rate, she was fairly certain that the armed mercenaries on their winged steeds were unlikely to be her rival posy pickers. As her eyes scanned the trees, however, they lit on a refreshing patch of white. This time her effort was rewarded with success and she returned to her companions with her skirt cradling enough flowers to brew the tea.

The enchanted rain was short-lived, but so was the sunlight in the steep-sided valley, and by the time the one left, so had the other. Grippledice lit a fire with only a minimum of delay caused by the need to dry the travel log. Rupert and the merchant huddled so near that their clothing smoldered. The dragon stayed close, her invisible tail whipping like a gale across the grass as she thrashed it anxiously, rumbling concern for her Prince.

Though Grippledice had not had the foresight to drop them conveniently near a stream, every curled leaf and every knot hold on every fallen tree in the forest held water, so that was no impediment to making the tea. The dragon stopped rumbling concern for Rupert and started bellowing on her own behalf, however, when Carole said that all they needed was an implement in which to brew the tea and suggested to Grippledice the only item she could think of with which they could improvise such an implement.

"One of my scales? That is not one of your hotter ideas, witch."

"Perhaps not, but there's nothing else available that's fire resistant. Don't be so selfish. Look at poor Rupert. He needs that tea."

A long silence. Rupert remained huddled, but looked up at his name and attempted a valiant smile, which didn't work out at all.

Near Carole's face a curl of smoke blossomed, a long sigh smelling of rotten eggs escaping with it. "I'm sure it will hurt quite a lot," the dragon said.

"I thought you said you loved him," Carole chided shamelessly. "What about all those noble deeds one hears involving great pain and sacrifice for love between dragons and knights?"

"Is that what they were about?" Grippledice brightened a little. "I somehow never thought they went that way from the snatches I heard. Mummy said I was too young yet to be told. Do you know any?''

"I'm not much good at telling stories, but once the Prince is feeling better, no doubt he'll recall some he learned from the Archives when he was a boy. I'll be happy to translate.''

"Well . . . oh, holy smokes, I suppose so. It won't have to be a very large scale though, will it?''

"Large enough for at least one cup of tea. I can reuse it to make enough for that other man and me.''

The dragon snuffled and smoke boiled forth with enough volume to cause Carole to step backwards.

"This *is* an emergency, you know. I do wish you wouldn't be such a baby.''

"I know, and I'm trying to be brave, but I *am* a baby,'' the dragon protested. "I'm still not quite a half a century old. That's extremely young for a dragon.'' She snuffled again. "Very well. You may take a scale. But try to take one of the ones low on my side, near my belly, where the ground and the air currents loosen them anyway.''

Carole reached toward the voice till she touched the dragon, who guided her with rather finicky instructions until she worked her way down the invisible side to a scale sufficiently loose to suit its owner and sufficiently large for her own purposes. Gently but firmly, the witch gave a sharp tug and dislodged the scale. The dragon almost forgot herself and burned down the forest.

Rupert and the merchant found that in spite of their infirmities they could move with amazing speed when necessary. Carole hugged the ground with the scale shielding her head until Grippledice regained her composure.

The three humans sat side by side on a fallen log, any garments that could be spared draped over twigs by the fire. Until the Prince was sufficiently convalescent to deliver the promised tales of love and valor about dragons and princes, the merchant regaled Grippledice with an account of a journey he had once guided into the realm of the Queen of Dragons, with whom he claimed to be well acquainted. Carole applied a bone needle and a bit of yarn she had unwoven from Rupert's trouser leg to the seat of his pants while he sat bare-legged, his Miragenian robe wrapped demurely across his lap. He made ungrateful faces while sipping the first infusion of the hard-won tea.

Suddenly the wind whipped viciously across their fire, bending it low, whipping loose the twigs serving as clothes hangers and singeing the hem of Carole's cloak. A shadow fell across the crushed brush where Grippledice invisibly curled. Behind it, shrouded in deeper shadow, something stood, eyes mirroring the flames.

"Interloper," it accused in a low, slightly nasal feminine voice throbbing with anger. "Defilers of magic. Ghouls who drink the very blood of universal wisdom—"

"You got us wrong, lady," the merchant said. "This is not blood, just a little herb tea. We are not what you say. These two are Argonians and me, I'm a traveling man."

"You are interlopers!" the voice said, its source shifting forward. The outline might have belonged to a smallish woman wearing a cloak with a stylish puffy hood, but Carole couldn't make out the details clearly.

"Just who do you think you are to come barging in as if you owned the place, calling people names?" Carole demanded. Rupert freed a hand from balancing the scale at his lips long enough to touch her arm restrainingly. Without thinking, he shifted the fingers of his left hand to support the rest of the puddle of tea suspended seemingly in midair above it.

"I am Effluvia, guardian of the valley, protectress of this sacred place and these sacred plants and their proper usage. I alone know how each magical aspect of this valley must be treated, nurtured, and cultivated to produce a power for wisdom and glory in its truest and purest form. You have dared to trample this ground, to ravish this valley for your own selfish ends. For that I will punish you, summoning the concentrated power of my own divine essence, loosing it upon you so that—" The voice stopped and focused on Rupert, who still sat with his head lowered, sipping, trying to pretend he wasn't present. "You. Man. Dast you continue to commit your crime even as I confront you with its enormity?"

"Lady," Carole said wearily, hoping that her whistle had been restored enough by now to allow her to deal with this creature. "My cousin has had a very hard day. If you'll be so kind as to excuse us?"

The creature—for as it stepped forward into the firelight Carole could see it was not entirely a woman—did not respond well to firm courtesy. With a nasty snarl she stretched out her clawed hand and hurled a spell, something like a thunderbolt but smaller and more to the point. The spell knocked the tea-filled invisible scale from Rupert's lips. Almost in the same motion the creature spun around in the light, so that her victims got a good look at what they were dealing with. Her face was long and pointed in the middle, her chin receding, her forehead and nose prominent, eyes small and shining hard and bright as arrowheads in the rain.

Her waist-length hair was unbound and blacker than the shadows except for two broad white streaks like parallel lightning bolts shooting from her widow's peak to the beginning of what Carole had mistaken for a cloak. This last item had been curled around Effluvia's head and as it unfurled was revealed as a long, luxuriant tail of black fur. This she brandished at them like a banner, except of course that she had had to turn herself around backwards to do so.

"If you would smell my flowers, interlopers, smell this as well!" the Effluvia creature cried, and her tail tip jerked.

At the same time the brush between merchant and cousins and their assailant sprang up. "Knock my friends around and attack an unarmed injured man, will you? I'll cook your goose, skunk!" Grippledice roared in Pan-Elvin. Her three former passengers were knocked off the log by her strong tail even as that other tail jerked and a dreadful stink of dragon-sized proportions assaulted the air from around an invisible but equally dragon-sized space in front of them.

Grippledice roared and the woman shrieked, suddenly aware that these were not just any dragonless wayfarers she was tormenting. She spun back around, caught some of her own essence reflected from the invisible scales, and reeled backwards in a swoon. A great gust of wind swept between her and her intended victims as first the grass, then the tree tops flattened with the dragon's passing. A most unsavory odor floated back to settle over the spectators as the tree tops lashed back into place again.

The merchant was laughing, his eyes and nose running in unseemly chorus. Carole fanned the air rapidly with both hands while holding her breath and wondering if her magic could come up with a fume-dissipating song. Rupert struggled to his feet and approached the fallen skunk-woman, who had recovered enough to cough, a feat complicated by her attempts to hold her nose at the same time.

"Madam, I fear there has been some terrible mistake that has caused distress to us all. Pray let us help you clean yourself and we'll discuss this like civilized creatures," Rupert offered gallantly, though nasally, for he too was of necessity holding his nose.

She said nothing, too busy coughing to speak or even to hear him, and he turned, walked away a short distance, sighed deeply, squatted down, and very carefully began to pick up a handful of large wet leaves, with which he proceeded to wipe all exposed surfaces, save the fur of her tail, which he left strictly alone for reasons of prudence as well as propriety.

"Watch that tail or she'll have you for sure this time," Carole cautioned, but he shook his head.

"I don't think she's able. She's quite debilitated by her own—er—essence. But see here, cousin, her tail has caught most of the stink and she is a *lady* whatever. I don't suppose you would mind, uh . . . ?"

She rolled her eyes but obligingly gathered a fresh batch of leaves and, with Rupert supporting Effluvia's front end, brushed the fur of the creature's tail with them until she was unable to hold her breath any longer. She staggered away, breathed deeply for a moment, gathered fresh leaves, and started over again.

Effluvia still could barely speak. She looked up at Rupert wonderingly, blinking rapidly as the tears coursed down her cheeks. Rupert patted her shoulder. "Maybe you can make magic with some of the other flowers you have here to improve the atmosphere."

Effluvia's lips moved, murmuring, "My God," it sounded like then, pettishly, "I have been shamed. You're trying to rub it in."

"We're trying to rub it off," Carole corrected her with exaggerated patience. "If you hadn't been so possessive about a few little flowers . . ."

"But I am the guardian of magic in this valley and the custodian of its use."

"Unless I missed something, those flowers were just flowers," Carole scolded. "They're not magic at all until you use them and anyone has a right to use wildflowers, for pity's sake. I've heard of game preserves where you can't chop wood or kill animals, but plucking wildflowers?"

"Standards must be maintained," the skunk-woman said, her long nose twitching but her beady eyes looking pleadingly at Rupert.

"In that case, lady, why did you not ask to taste my tea?" Rupert asked gently. "You could have told in that way that my cousin upholds the highest standards in her brewing. She sought only to ease my pain so that we might continue our quest to find my infant niece, who has been ruthlessly abducted."

"But surely *you* must understand that no one knows how to truly use the magic of this sacred valley but myself," Effluvia continued to plead, now whining slightly as she brushed the moisture from her pointed face with two hands still odiferous enough to cause her snoutish nose to wrinkle. "I must protect the wonders of this place against those who ride the flying

299

horses. Those pimps of magic dwelling in Miragenia are not fit to step foot in this valley."

"I do understand," Prince Rupert said quickly, "and we couldn't agree with you more, could we, Lady Carole? As our—er—native guide mentioned, we are Argonian ourselves, not Miragenian at all. He is, but—"

"I've been meaning to talk to you about that, Prince," the merchant said, raising a finger to draw attention to himself. He was standing as far from them as he could while still remaining as close to the ruined embers of the fire as possible.

"Later," the Prince said firmly.

"As His Highness pointed out, I think we've had a misunderstanding here, Effluvia," Carole said just as firmly. "I take it that you are a sorceress or a priestess of some sort, charged with protecting this valley. Yet we saw no signs posted, no wards against entering, no medicine bags in the trees, no guardian beasts. We had no way of knowing we were trespassing on your realm. I occupy a similar position to yours myself in my own village, so you see if anyone can understand your position, I can. And while I must say I still maintain that wildflowers are wild and should be free to anyone, we had no mind to offend you. Had you spoken to us first before just wading in and attacking Rupert, this could have all been settled without so much fuss. As it is, you made the dragon angry, spilt the tea and didn't do yourself any good either."

"Oh, I do see your point, and while I was only doing my appointed sacred duty to the greater glory of the Grand Prismatic, as I'm sure you'll understand"—this with an almost coy look at Rupert—"I accept your apology and ask you all to be my guests. You must tell me of your travail and let me show you the compassion and hospitality the valley can offer to those who would honor rather than defile it."

"We do appreciate that," Rupert said humbly.

"I must ask, of course, that you leave your own guardian beast outside," Effluvia said. "Whatever it was."

"A dragon," Carole enlightened her quickly. "A very protective and jealous dragon."

300

CHAPTER VII

By the time the group reached Effluvia's den, Effluvia had gone from trying to run them off to being effusively thrilled that they were honoring her humble hut with their presence—"they" meaning Rupert, of course.

Her den burrowed into a mountainside, with a front of slim branches and packed mud fronting on a shallow cave. A curtain of furs hung over the doorway. Their suddenly solicitous hostess wrapped everyone in furs from a pile that smelled faintly of skunk and poorly tanned hides.

To Rupert she said, "Your Highness, if you and your companions will divest yourselves of your wet and soiled garments, I will take them outside and wash them in a bath of herbs that will leave them clean and sweet-smelling."

As she expected, everyone was too stunned by her graciousness to object, and she gathered the clothing and departed with it without interference. Once outside her muzzle split in a wide toothy version of the human grin she had once been capable of displaying, her little eyes dancing with blissful wonder at the gift that the god had bestowed upon her in the guise of the Prince. After hugging his clothing to her until she reached a semblance of calmness, she dumped the entire pile in the hollowed log that served as a rain barrel. She was thankful that the magic many-hued tulip, whose mate bloomed within the great temple, was some distance away from her hut. If the Prince knew of the power of his sacred face, he was being very cagey about it. But he was not the only one who could be cagey. Though she had known him at once when he bent over her after what had seemed her ignominious defeat, she had kept her peace, waiting for a sign. When he maintained his pose of humility and ignorance, she maintained hers of loyal guardian who had to be won over by unintentional interlopers. But all the while, the knowledge burst in her breast that the god had jested with her. While pretending to send an opponent to defeat and disgrace her, the

Great Polyhued had manifested himself in this amazing show of grace. She could hardly wait to tell His Brilliance. She would, though. The blessing was hers alone, and she of all of the god's servants knew best bow to use it to its fullest advantage. Kneeling, she whispered the briefest possible message into the tulip's petals.

Rupert was nodding when she returned, without the clothing and with a smug expression on her snout. Effluvia brushed his face with the end of her tail, newly and more pleasantly scented. She was not prepared for them to sleep. Rupert, gratified by her apparent change of heart and curious to learn what caused it, was content to loll against the wall, a roll of skins supporting his bare back while the fur robe covered him from mid-chest to mid-shin. His lower legs and feet hung out. Effluvia tapped them with her tail from time to time, to emphasize certain things she had to say. This made him smile no matter how serious the subject. Fur tickled.

He told her without embellishment of unnecessary explanation why he and Carole sought Gorequartz. In her present friendly mood, perhaps she could help. On the other hand, he did not yet trust her and disliked volunteering any more information than absolutely essential to elicit a sympathetic response.

"I think what you wish to do is very noble," Effluvia gushed when Rupert had finished. "But I doubt if the evil King will allow it. You'll need the help of the priests."

"You seem to know a great deal, madam, for a woman who sports a tail and lives in the woods," the merchant observed slyly from his cozy nest of skins.

"You seem to speak freely for one who has not even given his name," she countered.

"I am Timoteo, adventurer, raconteur, and traveler of great renown. I seek not to be rude, dear lady, merely to comment that your degree of erudition about matters in Gorequartz seems unusual for a person of such a rustic background."

"I have not always lived here nor have I always appeared as I do now. In part my current condition is due to that same evil King of whom I speak, he who holds your niece, my dear Prince." She paused dramatically. "For you see, your niece could not possibly be the firstborn daughter of this King. He had a daughter by his first wife, the true Queen of Gorequartz. I am that child."

"What race did you say these people *are?*" Carole whispered to the merchant.

"A superior and magical one," Effluvia said in a voice that overrode her.

"They would be," Carole muttered to herself.

"They slew the sorceress who ruled there, gave the backward denizens of the land productive employment in the crystal mines, and avenged the Rainbow God, the Grand Prismatic, the Many-Hued, serving him with devotion and sacrifice which he has handsomely repaid over the years by granting his favorites great prosperity and an elevated form of civilization."

"About your tail, though," Rupert prompted. "What about that? Do all of your people possess tails?"

"Of course not. No one else is so honored because no one else is guardian of this valley and particular handmaiden of the god. The tail is part of my present form, a gift spell placed upon me by my benefactor, the High priest of the Grand Prismatic. My father would have had me slain but the High Priest, an admirer of my late mother, preserved me from death and gave me this form that I might serve the god with my life and essence until such a time that he called me to a higher, more public sort of task, fitted to the wisdom and grace I have obtained while performing my humble duty in exile."

"That was very decent of the High Priest," Rupert said, "But I don't understand why he needed to save you. If you're the King's daughter, and he wanted a daughter badly enough to convince the Miragenians it would be profitable to have my niece passed off for his own child, why did he try to kill you? Didn't your mother have anything to say about that?"

"She would have had, but, alas, for her, she did not say so quickly enough. The King is desperate for a male heir, someone suitable to take his place so that a secular person may sit upon the throne of Gorequartz, disputing the judgment of the divinely inspired priests. As the King has the army, the situation is very difficult for those who serve the god truly and lovingly. When my mother bore me, my father was greatly disappointed, and when by the time I was seven years of age she had no other issue, he was beside himself with rage. I was playing innocently in the garden one day when I overheard him telling his steward that he would either have to offer my mother up to the god, making it possible for him to take a new wife, or else my mother would have to agree to follow an old custom of my people, sacrificing the child of unsuitable sex so that the divine would know they had made a mistake and supply a more appropriate offspring.

303

"Naturally, this shattered my young life. I couldn't think what to do. I could not go to my mother, for surely my father would be there, speaking to her, and I was afraid for him. Mother and I had made many pleasant trips through a secret passage to the temple, however, where I played with the crystal prisms and blew bubbles on the rainbow pipes while Mother confided with the High Priest in his chambers. The High Priest had always been kind and good to me, more like a father than the King. In my distress, I ran through the secret passage and found the good man. I told him what my father had said, and that I knew my mother would want me to have his protection. He kept me hidden there in the temple until the day when he was called upon by the King to send Mother to join the god. Tender of my youthful sensibilities, he told me he had an important task for me and that he would use great magic to make me fit for it, child though I was. Thereafter he sent me here in this shape to guard this valley and here I have remained."

"But if the King doesn't want a girl baby, why didn't the new Queen import a son?" Rupert asked.

"I suppose none were available—especially none that look like the King. He's the kind of man who notices those things. If the new Queen is barren, someone else's daughter will at least give her a few years to bargain with until she can conceive a son—"

"Or sacrifice my niece to save her own life," Rupert said, shaking his head in disbelief at such barbarism.

"Unless your niece is as fast with her feet and tongue and as well-connected as Lady Effluvia here," the merchant said with admiration.

Carole said nothing, but stood, grasping her fur robe around her, and hobbled toward the door.

When she had been gone for some time, Rupert wrapped his own robe about him and ducked outside to look for her. She had found her still-damp clothing drying beside the hut and was pulling on her leggings.

"Where do you think you're going?" he asked in a low voice he hoped would not penetrate the skin hanging over the door.

"Anywhere, as long as it's away from here. Effluvia's furry tail isn't the only one she has that stinks. Do you really think she'd help Bronwyn's child when she's as good as admitted she's already sacrificed her own mother?"

The skin slipped aside and Effluvia's snout poked out, sniffing. "That's easy enough for you to say. You obviously have no concept of higher responsibilities than mere family loyalty. I have my own destiny to fulfill, my own obligation to the god. Even at an early age I knew it transcended being a mere brood mare for the royal line, as my mother was, poor thing. And I do wish to help this niece of yours, dear Prince. I wish very much to help her escape the fate I almost fell prey to. Tomorrow I shall personally guide you all through my valley and to the temple where my benefactor, I'm sure, will aid you even as he has me.''

On that note, she popped back inside, leaving Carole fuming and Rupert staring thoughtfully off into space. Carole couldn't tell whether or not he believed in Effluvia's self-proclaimed compassion, but she did not. It was out of character.

''That creature burns me up,'' a familiar voice said from atop a rocky ledge just above the roof of Effluvia's hut. ''Who does she think she's fooling?'' Carole looked up, hoping to see Grippledice, since by now the hidebehind pill should have started to wear off. Instead the dragon, after her thorough bath in the river, resembled nothing more than a rain shower as her run-off pattered on the roof.

''Ah, Grippledice,'' Rupert said cheerfully, speaking to the dripping ledge.

A stream of steam mixed with flames warmed his left side, boiling the vegetation behind him. ''What's the matter with her?'' Rupert asked, rubbing his face. The air was redolent of hot skunk.

''She's jealous and angry,'' Carole answered, ''and tired of being invisible, no doubt.'' She scratched her head and regarded the ledge, frowning. ''You don't suppose that hidebehind pill might have fermented after all these years and gotten stronger instead of weaker, do you? Surely not. Still, I must ask Rusty—''

''What's she jealous about?'' Rupert asked, a hint of satisfaction marring the tone of innocent concern he strove to project.

''What? Why, that you've taken up with and—as nearly as I can tell—been taken in by Effluvia. Don't ask me to intervene, either. I agree with Grippledice.''

''I can explain it all, I promise you,'' he said, and gazed up at the dripping wind steaming and streaming around them in its aggrieved fashion. ''But please tell my dragon everything is all right and that, if only she'll be patient and help us a while longer, we should be in Gorequartz tomorrow.''

Carole translated, then shook her head. ''She says not if Effluvia is going with us. Grippledice will have nothing to do with that woman. You'll have to choose between them.''

305

"Can't you reason with her?"

Carole shrugged. "I'd rather reason with you, since personally I feel that Grippledice is the one showing sound judgment. You may not have noticed but those are skunk skins wrapped around you in such profusion. That woman has no compunctions about betraying anyone and has as good as bragged about it. What makes you think she's not going to buy her way back into her father's favor by seeing to it that if he sacrifices Bronwyn's baby, he can include us and make a family affair of it?"

"I think you're exaggerating," Rupert said stubbornly. "It doesn't sound to me as if he'd have her back on any terms. I agree that she may have something up her sleeve but if we keep our wits about us . . ." His voice trailed off, giving way to a discreet and supposedly crafty look.

"That's what I like. A definite plan," Carole said.

"Have you a better one?"

"Certainly. Let's climb aboard Grippledice right now and have her take us to Gorequartz."

"I can't think how that would help, except to shorten the journey and to soothe Grippledice's feelings. If Effluvia has the influence she claims, she can help us. If not, we will be in no worse straits in her company than we would be going as uninvited strangers into what I can only presume from its customs must be a rather hostile culture. If the priests oppose the King and realize that an impostor child has been substituted, it may well be to their benefit to help us, to let the baby return with us."

"I can't believe Effluvia is interested in helping anyone but herself."

"No, perhaps not, but, on the other hand, it probably matters little to her if, while helping herself, she helps someone else in the process. That, my dear cousin, is what diplomacy is all about. To convince the other party that one's own best interests serve them even better than oneself."

"Very well then. I'll let you explain that to the dragon," Carole said, and returned inside.

Without the dragon's cooperation, the walk through the valley took most of the next day, and Carole's spine itched every step of the way. She wished Grippledice had remained in sight. The dragon's protective presence would have been a practical sort of comfort, but the beast had clearly departed ahead of them. Very sensible of her. Any witch with a modicum of self-respect would

306

have done the same thing. Or better yet, persuaded the beast to take her aboard as a lone passenger and gone to fetch the baby without the rest of the tiresome party. Of course, Rupert *could* be right in his wishful thinking that Effluvia would somehow prove herself more help than hindrance, but, oddly, it was less the Prince's optimism than Carole's own dead-certain conviction that the skunk-woman was going to betray them that kept the witch pacing behind the others, starting at rustlings in the trees, peering into shadows, and listening closely to every change in conversational timbre that might indicate the moment had arrived to muster her own magic to their defense.

Because however muddle-headed her royal cousin might be at the moment, he was family and he had saved her life. He was, on the whole, a very decent young man. She was growing quite fond of him. Nevertheless, she felt he needed the benefit of a more suspicious nature to keep him from falling prey to wistful thinking and misplaced idealism. The merchant definitely had a suspicious nature, but would hardly fill the bill, since he was one of the very persons Carole felt Rupert needed to be suspicious of. Therefore, she could no more leave him to the mercies of the various unscrupulous parties with whom he was choosing to involve himself in this escapade than she could leave Bronwyn's baby to the tender mercies of her infanticide-prone foster parents.

Her resolve wavered badly at times, however, for the going was rough. The merchant insisted on rattling off lurid descriptions of the countryside at every other tree. She reminded him that he no longer had the so-called travel log and didn't need to keep up the accompanying prattle, but he shrugged and grinned at her infuriatingly and said he had gotten into the habit and who knew but what he might not find another log? He wouldn't want to be ill-prepared. But the worst thing was that Effluvia led them on a circuitous path through the valley, "protecting" various sites along the way with her nauseating scent.

The first of these was another innocent patch of the painkilling flowers.

Rupert stepped gently over them but Effluvia made a disgusted sound in her throat. "Too bad that by the time I return they'll have died. I gathered for drying that other batch your little friend would have defiled yesterday, Prince, but I have no use for any more now. Oh well. The worst thing is that the Miragenian pigs should have them." And with that, before the merchant and Carole could step around the flowers, Effluvia imperiously held her hand aloft, waved them aside, raised her tail, and proceeded

307

to make it most expedient for them to circumvent the patch by a field's length. The flowers wilted on their stalks with barely a whisper of protest.

They were dead before Rupert could so much as open his mouth, but he looked back at the flowers with a stricken expression. "If you weren't going to use them, I don't see what difference it would have made to let them live a day or so more," he said.

"You have no idea how depraved some people are. They use such magic to relieve them of pain they've obviously brought on themselves. The most disgusting thing about the Miragenians is that they use absolutely no sense of discernment about their clientele. They'll sell to anyone who pays them, regardless of worth or station in life."

"I see," Rupert said politely, but he walked half a pace ahead of her and said little until they reached a rocky cliff. Here, too, Effluvia raised her tail.

"You will note on our immediate left and for some distance above us rock of the finest kind, with its stunning blue-gray striping casting long and sturdy shadows onto the leafy forest floor."

"Phew!" the merchant finished unceremoniously. He had failed to notice that the rock was about to be protected. When he could breathe again he asked, "Your pardon, lady, but why do you think anyone would want to steal any of this stupid rock, with or without your stinking it up?"

"Stinking it up, indeed! A lot you know," Effluvia told him. "That rock *you* so stupidly refer to as stupid will be chiseled into an entirely different formation by the time I return if I don't properly safeguard it. A small fragment of it in the pocket of a delegate to the god is enough to send the most cowardly and whining sacrifice staunchly to his death. Before I came to this valley there was a heavy black-market trade in pieces from this stone. I am proud to say I have successfully put an end to that. This cliff has not lost one chip since I arrived."

"It seems to me people who . . . practice a religion involving human—er—delegates to the gods . . . would prefer to have those delegates go calmly," Rupert said. He was trying very hard to be, or at least sound, broad-minded.

Effluvia gave him a small, knowing smile having all the charm of green mold on his breakfast toast. "You know nothing of our magic. True, the priests keep some few pieces of the rock on hand for specially favored prisoners. My mother may have been granted it as a boon in honor of her long friendship with the High Priest, for instance. But a sacrifice without fear and pain is really only half a sacrifice. To extract the most benefit, the delegate should feel the maximum amount of fear and mental chaos before the god sunders his body from his spirit. Fear and pain have great power, as does the fascination and dread they arouse in onlookers. Our priests are able to condense and use that power to the greater glory of the god and the magic of Gorequartz.''

She spoke with a faraway look in her eye, her head tilted, the small smile growing vaguer, softer, as if she were remembering a particularly entertaining ball she had once attended, or an athletic event of some sort. Rupert shuddered.

Later that afternoon, Effluvia protected a spring whose water could inspire love, and the gemstones in it, which could ease grief. A mountain pasture, whose grasses could guarantee inner peace for as long as a blade could be chewed, was her next target. By the time she finished with the pasture, chewing its grasses would ease nothing but the necessity to chew anything the rest of one's life. By evening, the magical and wondrous places in the forest were cloaked in a miasma of bad odor. Effluvia looked heartily pleased with herself.

She graciously extended her protective powers to include them when they camped that night, halfway up a mountain pass. Before any of them could utter a word of protest, the skunk-woman paced around them, enclosing them in a circle of stench. Carole scooted closer to the clean smell of the campfire and tried not to inhale. Rupert hunkered beside her, making himself as small as he could. He shivered slightly in the cold, thin air. His nose twitched uncontrollably and he looked miserable.

"Enough to choke a horse, isn't it?" he asked.

"You'll notice we saw only magic things. No magic beasts," Carole replied with as little movement of her mouth as possible. "If she tried her nasty business on a unicorn, she'd be punctured in a thrice. Mum's friend Moonshine would never stand for her polluting any of the streams he cleanses with his horn. And you know what Grippledice thinks of her.''

"Yes," the Prince said. "Of course, she did have a hard childhood, still . . .''

The merchant Timoteo, already curled by the fire for sleep, opened his eyes long enough to look imploringly heavenward and then back to Carole, who nodded slightly, patted Rupert's forearm, and assumed her own sleeping position. Little space remained between her and Timoteo but Rupert squeezed himself into it, something Carole did not appreciate since he left no place for Effluvia but next to her, where the skunk-woman's unfragrant tail twitched ticklingly near the witch's nose all night.

Effluvia proved a more helpful companion the following day. They reached the bottom of the pass by noon, the river less than an hour later. They followed the river upstream around a sharp bend, beyond which it spilled from a sizable tunnel carved into the mountainside. A long, wooden boat was tied near the tunnel's entrance. Effluvia immediately climbed into it.

The merchant was the first to follow her, eyeing the length of the vessel warily. How very convenient that Effluvia should have a boat here just when she needed one. Even more convenient that it should be just the right size. But then, she did possess a certain magic—most of it less helpful than this. He shrugged.

Rupert followed him, looking upward one last time before boarding.

Once they entered the first tunnel, they were underground most of the way. Now and then the river slipped out of one hole and into the open before slipping into another, but mostly they rowed upstream in darkness. Rupert and the merchant took turns at the oars. Even when they had been rowing for some time, neither of them suggested aloud that Carole use her magic. Nonetheless, Carole hummed a soft song to the boat to ease its glide and let it cut through the water with minimal effort on the part of the oarsmen. This much she could do without Effluvia's knowledge, for the river roared in all their ears and no one could be heard without shouting.

All the rest of that day the men rowed, the river roared, and Carole sat in the dark humming. When they saw light again, it was twilight.

The boat bumped gently against a dock leading from the water into the nothingness of a thick mist. Behind them the tunnel was no longer a natural indentation in rock but a carefully carved arch over a long stretch of increasingly calm water. Ahead of them, boats and barges of all descriptions plied the smooth, shining expanse daubed pink with the setting sun. Above them rose an incredible edifice, the same Carole had seen in the stream in Mashkent's house, a conical tower of rising domes, walled with gold and roofed with clearest crystal, surrounded at the base by a bank of silvery mist.

"How strange," Effluvia mused as two massive men with

310

manes of golden hair and arms as big around as Carole's thighs tugged the little boat to a mooring. "I grew up in the palace amidst wealth and luxury, it is true, but somehow it is only here in this simple holy place that I truly feel at home."

"My dear, I do understand," Carole could not resist saying. "I feel the same way every time I leave my father's hall to visit the seamstress's cousin, Sean the Shepherd, in his little hut in the hills."

CHAPTER VIII

The High Priest appeared nonplussed when Effluvia had herself announced and then pushed her way in before the lay brother guarding the door had time to finish the announcement.

"My . . . my dear, how you've changed," the man on the crystal throne said, his golden beard dropping an inch lower on the V of tanned chest bared by his suit woven of every shade, tint, and primary color in the spectrum.

"Oh, yes, Your Brilliance. I have. How long has it been, ten years? But the god blessed my vigil with success at last and I think that you will find that not only have I grown in stature but also that I have been transfigured by the experience of living in the woods, by the grace and wisdom of the god, protecting the tranquility and order of the growing things."

"You certainly have," the High Priest said. "Brother Bullcow, will you be so good as to swing that incense a bit closer? Ah, there, thank you."

"Furthermore, Your Brilliance, I think that you will agree that the fact that I have been chosen to be the custodian of the marvel I bring to you will demonstrate beyond my own admittedly ample abilities that the time has come when you should reverse the spell upon me, allow me to resume my residence and rightful place here, along with my more standard female appearance, and use this person I present to you as an instrument to forever bring Gorequartz under the sway of those of us who are holier than the rest."

311

"No doubt I will agree, my dear child, but I think it necessary that first you show me this person."

She had been blocking the doorway, much to the annoyance of the brother serving as herald. Now she turned and, with a clash and a tinkle of crystal on crystal, swept aside the curtain of colored, tear-shaped beads which shielded the High Priest, even when the gilded wooden door was open, from the view of the secular not specifically admitted to his presence. Carole and the merchant sauntered in blinking at the sudden flood of light pouring down from the transparent ceiling and bouncing from the solid gold walls. Rupert, to Effluvia's annoyance, insisted on finishing explaining to the lay brother guarding the outer door what the device on his rowan shield meant. It took a cross look and an ominous hist from Effluvia to capture his attention.

Rupert ducked through the door to avoid bumping his head on the golden curlicues protruding from the arch. The High Priest's expression spawned a thin squirm of a smile on Effluvia's ungenerous mouth. His Brilliance was obviously trying very hard not to look startled, and was failing miserably. Nor did Carole feel that His Brilliance was simply unused to extremely tall people. He stared at Rupert's face in a fashion bordering on fascination.

Everyone continued to either stare at Rupert or stare at everyone else staring at Rupert for several moments.

"You see, Your Brilliance, that in no way did I misrepresent the importance of my blessing," Effluvia said, talking slowly, sure that she would not be interrupted by the High Priest, who sat with a smile dawning on his face, beaming rays of approval in her direction. "This gentleman is known as Rupert Rowan, a Prince of Argonia."

His Brilliance kept nodding but did so in Rupert's specific direction now, still smiling and staring.

Rupert, after a polite interval, said, "I take it then that you are the gentleman of whom Lady Effluvia has spoken? Very pleased to make your acquaintance, I'm sure. Perhaps I should explain why I asked this lady to escort us here. As a member of the Argonian Royal House, I have been designated diplomatic representative of my sister, Princess Consort of Ablemarle. These folk accompanying me are my staff, my cousin, the Honorable Lady Goodwitch Carole Songsmith Brown, a theologian like yourself, and Mr. . . . Timoteo, who has helped with our travel arrangements. We have come in regard to a misunderstanding which has occurred and with which the Lady Effluvia seems to feel you

312

might be able to help us. We are quite willing to negotiate. I am widely known in my own lands as Rowan the Rational."

The High Priest continued to nod, evidently enjoying himself immensely.

Rupert smiled, too, and nodded. "I'm so glad you see it that way. Perhaps if I outline the problem for you. It goes back many years, to a time when the Miragenian firm of Mukbar, Mashkent, and Mirza had occasion to assist Princess Bronwyn and Lady Carole on a mission."

"Your Highness, please, I'm sure as you say that we can work out some arrangement which will be mutually satisfactory," the High Priest said, beaming at Rupert, something like awe still making his eyes round under his bushy dark gold brows. "You have traveled long, I know, and little of daylight remains, but there is something I would like to show you before darkness settles on us completely. Please, if you and your party will accompany Brother Bullcow, I will just arrange to have a little supper prepared for us to take aboard the barge while you are freshening up."

Brother Bullcow headed for the door, incense swinging. They all turned to follow him when the High Priest added, "Oh, Your Highness, our people are not used to visitors. It would be provident therefore if you and your staff would don the robes worn by our lay brothers prior to leaving the temple. Just for discretion's sake, you understand."

Rupert nodded gravely.

Effluvia stood by the High Priest's throne, looking after the others with a triumphant smile.

"My darling child," the High Priest said, "you showed great promise as a youngster, but you have now quite outdone yourself. Where did you find him?"

Effluvia lowered her eyes modestly, "It is as I told you, Father. The god sent him to me as a mark of favor. He literally fell from the sky. What do you suppose it means, Father? There I am, all alone in the valley, the outcast child of the secular Queen and the god's representative on earth, and all at once *he* drops from the sky?"

The High Priest frowned for a moment, then tenderly stroked the black crown of the skunk-woman's head. "Always plotting, eh, my dear? Even now. Well, it may very well be true, what you're thinking. It may indeed be the only way to use this miraculous gift." He shook his head, laughing silently. "The resemblance is absolutely astounding."

Two pikemen and five full-fledged priests herded Carole, Rupert, and Timoteo down several winding flights of stairs, across a floor larger than most of the village of Wormhaven, and down more steps. All three looked a great deal like the common conception of a spectre—dressed in long, white robes of loose and gauzy material complete with deep hoods that shadowed their faces. Underneath, they wore their original clothing. Each robe was ample enough to cover a very large person in full court costume under winter gear. Rupert's robe hit him at knee level, while Carole's and the merchant's dragged the ground.

The foot of the last staircase was swallowed by boiling silver mist. The priests walked through it as if it didn't exist and urged their guests to do the same. Carole kept expecting a trick, a hole to open under her feet, a monster to coil around an ankle. Instead, after a brief thickening, the mist parted to reveal a somewhat larger dock than the one at which they had landed, surrounded in deepening gloom relieved by a row of torches set in brackets along its length. At the end of the long wooden ramp, a barge awaited them.

On its open deck three golden steps led to a long couch upholstered in cloth of gold. The hull rose at either end in a graceful curl. Four men, two at each end, stood with long paddles, the blades shaped like a sun with waving rays. The priests surrounded Rupert and Timoteo as they seated themselves. Rupert slid four of them aside to make room for Carole between them. The High Priest himself boarded last. Hampers smelling of hot spices, bread, and chicken were placed on the deck beside the golden steps. To Carole's relief, Effluvia did not join them.

The river lay calm as glass between its banks. One of the priests explained that farther ahead, a special barrier called a lock had been built to regulate the flow of water, so that the traffic of large vessels to and from the sea could be restricted. Lining the banks on each side were buildings rivaling the temple in magnificence. Each of the buildings was long and low, with a courtyard looking onto the river and steps leading to the water. Spires were set on either side of the steps and the openings were the by-now predictable pointed arches. What was not predictable, however, was the building material. For each edifice was constructed entirely of small squares of colored crystal, each square a different hue from the ones adjoining it. The dying light of day washed through these panes onto the water, giving it the appearance of one enormous, multi-faceted rainbow. Her face and those of her companions bathed in particolored light, Carole watched the buildings slip behind, while the long rainbow of river rinsed away beneath her. She was aware of an odd feeling of recognition that puzzled her until she realized that the buildings reminded her very much of the merchant's showroom window before she had removed the bottles containing the mists.

Several barges passed them farther down the river, many more opulent and elaborate than the barge on which they traveled. The helmsmen of the richer vessels nonetheless bowed as they passed. From curtained alcoves, fingers swept dense velvets aside. Eyes peered out with bright curiosity. Where the passengers rode open to the air, they bowed low to the priests, eyeing the guests only covertly. Lay brother garb did not entirely conceal Rupert's unusual stature, and he kept pushing the hood back and twisting to see his surroundings.

"Perhaps we should have brought the screens, Your Brilliance," one of the priests suggested with a shrewd look at Rupert.

"Not at all. We may stimulate a few exciting rumors before our disclosure is made public, but no one except those we wish to know will be aware that our guests are other than newly appointed lay brothers. Relax, my child."

Carole watched her hosts warily and wished they would stop their mysterious chitchat. It made her nervous. For all of his apparent amiability, the High Priest did not strike her as being anyone who was going to be terribly interested in the plight of Bronwyn's baby—or her relatives for that matter. And no doubt it was easy to be pleasant when one knew that one had enough power to do whatever one chose whenever one got around to it.

The river looped to the right. Suddenly, dead ahead loomed a castle. Carole was sure it was a castle rather than a temple this time for the design was dedicated to fortification, with the proper towers and battlements she was used to seeing in Argonia. They were, however, gorgeous turrets and towers and battlements, all in rough stone through which glimmered raw crystals of amethyst, agate, garnet, and sapphire. Not a good defensive design, of course. Far too easy to scale such walls even without a ladder. But awe-inspiring nonetheless.

The river turned left at the castle after filling a loop of moat separated from the main body of water by earthworks reinforced with stone topped with a wide paved footpath. Armed guards stood at either end of the path, and greeted the priests with deference.

The High Priest muttered something to a lesser priest, who muttered something in turn to a boatman, who whispered to a guard. The guard spun a tidy about-face, unhooked a horn from his belt and blew a long, lowing note. A general scurrying ensued from the wall facing the moat. A short time later the chain clanked and weathered wood creaked and the huge slab of a drawbridge lowered ponderously into its slot on the far side of the footpath. Two other guards strolled forward, received and departed with a message, and in a short time a harried-looking herald issued forth, bowed low before the junior priest, nodded sharply three times and scuttled back across the bridge.

The High Priest nodded. His minions began arranging the hampers of food on the path, brilliant cloths spread upon the ground first, followed by the golden cushions from the divan on the barge, followed by an array of fruit, chicken, bread, and sweets, as well as crystal decanters of wine. The dishes were of etched gold. Carole was very glad she would not be responsible for cleaning them. She also wished they might have been able to have some of the chicken while it was hot, for the chill as the sun went down was seeping through her layers of clothing. Hot food would have helped.

Soon a great clamor arose from beyond the drawbridge, a horn blared, and a matched set of heralds announced, "All hail King Yagthra, Lion of Gorequartz, and Queen Egelina the Fair."

Carole did not believe she had ever seen a Queen look as twitchy as Egelina the Fair. Not even Amberwine when Bronwyn was married. Egelina, like almost everyone else in Gorequartz, was indeed fair, with a tumbling corona of golden curls under her lacy crystal circlet, and blue eyes large and frightened. The rest of her was also large, the reason evident, for her eyes kept darting to the food throughout the conversation. The rest of the time they were fastened on Rupert, now and then jumping apprehensively to the snoozing bronzehaired infant carried by the third unliveried adult who trailed behind both King and Queen. This person kept her eyes modestly lowered, ostensibly observing her charge much more closely than babies really need to be observed, while casting quick, melancholy glances toward Rupert. Never once did the woman look at the High Priest, and only when she was addressed did she make eye contact with His or Her Majesty. Rupert, for his part, spent a great deal of time watching her and the baby, who could only be the kidnapped heiress to the Ablemarlonian throne.

King Yagthra might once have been handsome, but his face

316

bore the ruddy sheen of someone who had been drinking far too much wine for far too long. His pores were large and coarse, his nose bulbous, his eyes veined and teary-looking. His aroma made Carole think that perhaps he had served as the inspiration for the High Priest when that individual had decided on the particular spell he used to "enhance" Effluvia's personal power. The High Priest did not stand when greeting Yagthra and Yagthra did not so much as incline his head to see what was on the menu.

"Greetings, Your Majesty," His Brilliance said, indicating the spread. "We have guests to honor and thought, who but the sovereigns of the city are worthy to make these particular people welcome? Therefore we had this repast made ready and sent forth the invitation to you and your lady and daughter to join us." Now he rose, offering his own cushion to the King, who, spotting Rupert, suddenly seemed barely able to stand. The High Priest nodded toward the nurse and child standing behind the Queen. "My, your new daughter is large for her age. And red of hair also. How very unusual."

The Queen sat down abruptly and began munching a plum. Rupert joined her immediately, to cover her breach of manners, and the High Priest, with some amusement, seated himself beside her, speared a chicken leg and used it to gesture with, saying, "Your Majesties, allow me to present our guests, Lady Carole, her cousin and guardian in our land, Prince Rupert, and their servant. Perhaps we could all dispense with our hoods now, Prince Rupert. It is the custom—"

"Of course," Rupert said, and tugged his down around his neck. The Queen gagged on her plum, the King turned redder, and the baby began to squall. The High Priest appeared vastly amused.

"Is this some sort of priest's trick, Jasper?"

"You wound me, brother," His Brilliance replied. "I merely wanted to share with you the special properties of these guests of ours. I wanted your opinion on how to best utilize their unique contributions in the upcoming festivities. Or perhaps your lady would be so kind as to give us her opinion. She seems to have a few tricks of her own," and he looked unmistakably, pointedly at the baby. Yagthra glared at the High Priest. Now that it had been mentioned, Carole could discern a family resemblance in the set of their jowls, the knobs on the ends of their noses. The King was not presently overcome with family feeling, however, and jerked his wife unceremoniously to her feet, while the nurse scurried ahead of them, throwing only a single last wondering glance back at Rupert.

317

His point made, the High Priest seemed to lose sight of the fact that his guests had still not actually had time to eat, and ordered the feast taken up again. Carole quickly snagged a chicken breast, a half loaf of bread, and a bunch of grapes, and climbed back on the boat. Regardless of whatever other dramas were taking place, there was really nothing so sordid as family jealousies.

Rupert chewed thoughtfully on a chicken bone as he boarded the barge, and paused before he sat down to stare after the departing royalty. Timoteo and Carole were behind him and the lesser priests, followed by the High Priest, who motioned them all ahead. Suddenly, Rupert let out a "whoof" and fell into his seat coughing and thumping his chest while everyone else strove to keep their balance. One of the priests pitched overboard and had to be plucked from the river. The High Priest took the disturbance placidly, boarding the boat only after it had ceased rocking maniacally to and fro. Not until he was comfortably settled and the boat was proceeding down river did they notice the missing place on the couch.

"Where is the scruffy fellow? What's his name? What became of him?" he asked. One of the priests made as if to look under a cushion but thought better of it.

The wet priest, now encased in one of the picnic cloths, said, "I didn't see him, Your Brilliance, but perhaps he, too, was thrown overboard."

"Find him," the High Priest commanded with much authority but little interest in the subject.

The boatmen poked along both sides of the canal with their oars and the priest who was already wet was lowered again on a rope to search but no trace of the merchant was found. Carole thought of diving to fetch him, but something held her back. The merchant had always been a noisy fellow when in jeopardy. If he was so quiet now, either he had reason to be or he was past reasoning. She had been watching the King's departure and the High Priest's preparations for leaving when Rupert overbalanced the boat, and had not actually noticed the merchant falling overboard. But it seemed to her that she did recall a release of pressure on the cushions beside her. She had heard not a splash, but a careful plop, as of something sliding deliberately into the water.

After their perfunctory initial search, the priests made no further effort to locate the merchant's body and at the High Priest's insistence continued instead past the palace, down the river, and through the lock.

The lock was well-named, resembling nothing so much as a giant door bar. Earth and stone jutted into the river for a cart length or so on either side, while between stretched a sheet of solid iron. Torchlight from the little hut atop the earthworks bounced off the iron, and the water slapped powerlessly against it. A man emerged from the hut, bowed, and at the High Priest's direction gave orders to one of the great, gray beasts Carole had seen in Miragenia. The beast lumbered forward, dragging a chain which powered a cogged wheel, thereby sliding the iron barrier back into the cliff rising on the eastern side of the lock. On the earthworks sheltered by the cliffs on the western side another beast rocked back and forth, dragging its chain, no doubt waiting orders to drag the barrier back into place. In fact, there were two of the barriers, with a little valley of water trapped between them. When those slid aside, the priests' barge rose on the flow of newly freed water and floated easily through the locks.

They saw no more palaces, temples, or even houses for the remainder of the short distance between the locks and the harbor. Craggy cliffs soared above them on either side, studded at regular intervals by torches whose light reached the water as little more than candle flame. Nevertheless, when they gained the bay, between the three-quarter moon and the torchlight Rupert and Carole were able to view clearly the thing they had been brought to see.

The sight of it wiped all thoughts of the priests, Effluvia, even Bronwyn's baby from Rupert's mind as he stared, his eyes rising slowly to take in the whole object. Carole whistled a low, unmagical exclamation of surprise. The priests looked from Rupert to the object, nodding and murmuring excitedly, and the High Priest looked even more pleased than he had when he first saw Rupert. And no wonder. There was more of Rupert to be pleased with—or at least, there was a larger edition of him. Rising from the waters was a duplicate of Rupert's head and face, about twice as large as the drawbridge at the castle and seemingly carved completely out of crystal. The sea lapped around its chin and earlobes, wetting the curls twining toward the throat. The expression was the same one Rupert wore when he concentrated hard on some knotty problem or the other. Except that when Rupert wore that look, it made one want to pat him like a puppy and tell him not to fret. Blown up, with its crystalline angles basking in moonlight and torchlight, the same expression on the image was stern and forbidding.

319

"So," Rupert said. "I'll be blessed. Now at last we know what became of Rowan the Recreant. How reassuring. I never did believe what they said about him."

"Who?" Carole asked. "What did they say about him?"

"It is appropriate to genuflect before the Rainbow God, woman," one of the junior priests told her, and pushed her firmly to the floor, forcing her to kneel, halfway facing Rupert, halfway facing the statue.

She started to whistle the clod into the sea but Rupert knelt rapidly beside her. "Never mind, cousin. It isn't important. I'll tell you later." He had scarcely bent his knee, however, when the High Priest caught his elbow and motioned him back onto his seat on the couch.

"Not you, dear boy," His Brilliance said. "You're the god reincarnate. Hereafter you do not bow, you are bowed to."

CHAPTER IX

"*There* you are," the furious collection of flying draperies accused the boatload of priests, witch, and newly appointed God as if they were a cart full of hoodlums. "Rupert, darling, will you be so kind as to tell these provincials who I am and what would become of their teeny little economy without the buying power of my firm?"

Rupert, who had been uncommonly quiet all the way back to the temple, still bore a stunned look, as if someone had separated his brains from his face by means of a hearty blow from a mace. He stared rather stupidly for a moment at the raven-haired lady clad in scarlet and silver, hands on hips and arms akimbo, clearly waiting for something. The witch at his side elbowed him in the waist.

"Isn't that the Mukbar woman? What in the name of the Mother's sweet earth is she doing here?"

The High Priest overheard and swept in front of Rupert. "Illustrious mademoiselle, to what do we owe the honor of this unusual, and may I say unprecedented, visit?"

"I have come to reclaim company assets," she replied, looking straight at Rupert.

"Could this not have been handled in some other fashion? Our agreement with your firm, mademoiselle, is that all transactions are to take place in Miragenia."

"And who are you to quote me trade agreements?" she asked.

The brother in charge of patrolling the mist ended his measured rounds in a skittering run. "Your Brilliance, forgive me. This accursed woman has been braying at the door all evening. I told her to go away, and tried to force her to depart, but she flew out of reach on her wretched rug."

"I want that man fired for incompetence, and his pay docked," Alireza demanded, pointing a dramatic, long, carmined fingernail at the offending person. "I did not fly through duststorms and rain, pursued by your inadequately controlled demons, to endure idiots when I've come to speak with someone in authority. I take it, sir, that you *are* someone in authority?"

The High Priest flushed; he momentarily bore a striking resemblance to his brother. "You might say that. I am Jaspar the Deep-Veined, High Priest of the Grand Prismatic, Spiritual Father of Gorequartz."

Alireza took in the title with a satisfied gleam under her curling lashes and a little lick at her full upper lip before saying, "Ah, forgive me, Your Brilliance. I had no idea . . ."

His Brilliance took in the seductive look and savored it, forgetting the less savory insult. "Of course not. We have never met. I last visited Miragenia before your dear, departed father joined his gods. Though I must say, I recognized you at once. The legends of your beauty and business acumen rampant among those of us who trade with your firm have not been exaggerated. We are honored. Please, please, come inside."

Effluvia was much less charmed by the new visitor, and didn't hesitate to say so. Her tail rose to half mast almost involuntarily, and the High Priest, standing beside her, stroked her back quickly in an attempt to soothe her. When Carole left Rupert to the mercy of the embattled women and the priests, he was looking rather dazed. For once she was more than happy to be overlooked.

The room in which she had been installed was grand and spacious, with the moon shining in from the crystal dome as well as a bed with an optional canopy to shield those who preferred the security of a properly enclosed sleeping space to the grandeur of the natural spectacle above them.

She did not mind that her magic was so little regarded that the lock which snapped shut behind her as she entered was neither

321

iron nor apparently warded against her, but the absence of wash water and a bit of stiff grass with which to clean her teeth did impress her as sloppy. Perhaps while everybody was entertaining themselves watching the High Priest and his powerful female associates torment poor Rupert, she could slip out and find some, and lock her door back behind her with no one the wiser. Later that night she intended to slip out again and find a clear spot from which she would be visible. There she hoped to be spotted by Grippledice. She would feel much better about the whole situation once the dragon knew where they were.

The lock gave easily after she hummed two bars. She peered out into the hall, wondering where the water containers were kept. In the kitchen, no doubt, but where was that? She watched for wandering members of the household, glad for the protective coloring of the hooded robe. Rounding a corner, she saw a flash of white as a lay brother slapped barefooted down the hall ahead of her. He left behind him an open door and she walked toward it, praying he had been returning from a late snack.

He had not. Reaching the room's open door, she saw that it was another bedroom, but an extremely luxurious one, with crystal bedposts and a canopy colored like the rainbow, golden walls, and a fountain, which at least solved the water problem. Then she spied Rupert's cloak draped over a chest in the corner and realized the brother had been readying the room for the temple's most illustrious guest. Well, Rupert wouldn't mind if she washed up and borrowed a bit of water. She would do her washing here and tote a basinful back to her own room for use in the morning. She would need to look fresh if she spent most of the night waiting for the dragon to appear.

She washed quickly in Rupert's basin, dumped the water back in the pool, and held the bowl under the fountain. That was when the quartz-studded wall behind the pool creaked open and a woman peeked around the corner. Seeing Carole she started to retreat again, but Carole whistled her to a shrill stop and slowly jigged her forward.

When the woman had done a little bransle step around the edge of the fountain and was standing in the center of the room, the witch confronted her.

"I beg your pardon, mistress," the girl said, her feet still shuffling in the dance and her face full of guilty confusion. "I knew not that this was your place. I was looking for the god."

"The god is out right now," Carole said, patiently. "Perhaps I could take a message?"

"That won't be necessary," the girl said, drawing herself up a little and trying unsuccessfully to stare Carole in the eye. "The god is all-knowing."

"In that case I don't see why you need to be sneaking around through fountains to find him." The girl lowered her eyes, more confused than ever, and Carole recognized her. "You're the nurse to the Queen's daughter, aren't you?"

"I—no, I mean—who are you? You were with him and the priests, weren't you?"

"I hardly thought you noticed."

"Are you his handmaiden?"

"Not if I can help it," Carole muttered.

"What?"

"Nothing. I said, I suppose you could say that I am. Are you quite sure I can't help you?"

"Perhaps. It's about the Princess."

Carole kept quiet and tried not to appear to be holding her breath.

"Well," the girl said, shifting her weight from one foot to the other. "It's just not fair. I know the god is all-knowing but probably he wouldn't even think to question Her Majesty if she chooses to claim a baby is hers. But the Princess isn't, you know. She's not even from Gorequartz."

"No!" Carole said. "You don't say."

"Oh, yes," the girl said. "You see, the Queen sent me to fetch her from the Miragenians."

"All alone?"

"One of the priests went with me."

"Really? Then they knew about the exchange."

"Certainly. There's nothing goes on in this city they don't know about—and arrange."

"But the High Priest seemed only to be suspicious of the Queen this evening—"

"He was just twisting the knife," the girl said. "I wish you would speak to the god about him. He's not a nice man at all and I don't think he's truly dedicated. When the Queen first married His Majesty, His Brilliance sent for her. I know. She had me come with her, through the secret passages, which is how I learned of them. His Brilliance doesn't know I know because I stayed hidden. But I heard him propose that she betray the King with him. She never really refused him but after that she started eating heavily and not letting her hair be brushed except once a day. I think she was just frightened. If she betrayed the King and he found out, she was doomed, and if she didn't accept the High Priest, she was also doomed; she made herself undesirable so she

323

would not need to choose. It worked well except that she never conceived a child. His Brilliance proposed the plan to her, told her that there would soon be a baby available.''

"And she accepted?" Carole asked, her anger rising. "Knowing that the baby would eventually be killed?"

"Not necessarily," the girl defended her mistress. "Normally she would have until the girl is seven years old to bear the King a boy. Should that happen, she and both children would be safe. However, I fear His Brilliance only proposed the plot to expose it, to get revenge on her for depriving him of enjoying her beauty.'' Even with such a euphemistic finish, the girl lowered her lashes again, no doubt blushing, if only the light were sufficient to register it.

"Well, it seems she fell for it, didn't she? I still don't understand your part in all this however. Why should you care what happens to the child?"

"Oh, mistress, I am her nurse. She feeds at my breast. How can I not care? Perhaps it is wrong of me, but I feel that the god sent her to me for taking my own little one, the one I lost these three months past at the summer's-end sacrifice, when my beloved Selig was mur . . . was chosen as delegate to the god. Seeing the god today, I knew I must be right, for he is not so stern as his image, but kindly in appearance, and caring. I know now that my Selig is eternally happy with him, that he has had compassion for my loss and will help me to preserve the little one he sent to comfort me.''

"My, you do have a lot of faith, don't you?" Carole said.

"I never did before I saw him today with my own eyes. I thought he was as hard and cruel as his priests but—''

Her worshipful look as her eyes lingered on her memory of Rupert was almost embarrassing. "I do see," Carole said quickly. "And you are absolutely right. The god is a very pleasant sort of deity and I am positive he'll be glad to help you with this matter but—''

A scuffling noise overrode her voice from the hallway beyond, followed by the slapping of feet.

"Is there room in there for me, too?" Carole asked.

"It's very narrow here, I—'' the girl began.

"Never mind then. Back in you go, quickly.'' She had long since released the spell, but the girl's movements were swifter than any dance step as she disappeared back into the wall. Just in time, too, for the slapping footsteps reached the room and a lay brother scowled at Carole from the doorway.

"What are you doing here?"

"Looking for my cousin," she said innocently.

"He's still with His Brilliance," the brother said. "And I think it would be a good idea if you were, too." With that, he waited with stiff spine and stern countenance until she meekly stepped around him and allowed him to forcibly escort her where she wished to go anyway.

Rupert almost wished he were the god everybody felt he resembled. Then he could smite the lot of them and be done with it. Both of the women seemed to feel that they had some claim to him. In the case of Alireza Mukbar, he was not surprised, since he had allowed her to seduce him and believe that he endorsed her plans for their so-called future together in order to extract necessary information from her. But Effluvia's counterclaim both baffled and repulsed him. The High Priest's proud look in the skunk-woman's direction bothered him even more.

Moreover, the High Priest positively gloated over the venomous darts shooting between the women and the outrageous things they said to each other. He stroked Effluvia as if she were a house cat, only partially to keep her tail under control. The rest of the motivation for the petting seemed to Rupert rather unwholesome. Meanwhile, the High Priest's eyes drank in Alireza's heaving bosom and gesticulating limbs, his fingers fondling Effluvia's hair.

Rupert did have to admire one thing about Alireza, however. Impassioned as her speech and gestures were, she was not totally out of control. She pointed out that Rupert had a prior commitment to her and her firm and that arrangements could still be made for the people of Gorequartz to lease his services. She also pointed out that any attempt to try to retain him would cancel out a rather large debt still owed by the Miragenians for the last shipment of crystal bottles.

"Speaking of the bottles, your quality control is way out of line these days. That abominable witch who attached herself to my fiance was able to loosen practically the entire last shipment. The bazaar is still in an uproar and my uncle has taken to his bed. If the *creature* who has the audacity to claim that she is entitled to any consideration where His Highness is concerned had been doing her proper job as a guardian, the witch would never have escaped us. I demand her return."

"My dear, dear young lady," the High Priest said, droplets of spittle forming at the sides of his mouth with the strength of his sincerity. "We can do better than that. We will use her in the dedication ceremony, two days hence. Several significant delegates will be sent forth. I am sure the recent conversation we had with Her Majesty may bring some bearing on her decision of what gesture is needed to provide her with more appropriate offspring—''

Rupert again forgot his diplomatic training in the face of his moral outrage. "See here, Your Brilliance. If you have any notion of indiscriminately disposing of a member of my staff and an innocent infant in your vile rites of human sacrifice—''

"My dear young man, what utter nonsense! Indiscriminate? Vile rites? Wherever did you get such an idea?''

"Is it not true then?'' Rupert asked hopefully, the heat and color draining a bit from his face.

"Certainly not.''

"I am so pleased to hear it. Of course, I felt all along that it was rubbish to suppose that one of the world's greatest exporters of magic practiced human sacrifice. . . .''

"Now that part *is* true,'' His Brilliance admitted as if modestly acknowledging a compliment. "How could it be otherwise? All greatness among men is the result of human sacrifice of one sort or the other—for one to gain, another must be deprived. It's only natural—or, as in the case of the Great Polyhued—supernatural. But I can assure you that there is nothing vile or indiscriminate about our rites. They are exceedingly tasteful and have a wealth of socially significant factors surrounding them and are celebrated most discriminatingly at specific times of the year.''

"Ah,'' Rupert said. "And what times are those?''

"Oh, there are a great many. I'll be happy to see that you are provided with a calendar to memorize. All that need concern you right now is the one taking place just before sundown tomorrow. Right now the preparations are being made for the ceremony later tonight at which we will arrange for the appropriate conditions. I wish I could invite you to witness it, but that really would spoil the surprise.''

"Naturally, we can't have the surprise spoiled,'' Rupert said, barely keeping the sarcasm out of his voice. "Tell me, who else do you intend to kill this time?''

"Kill? We kill no one. We send our delegates living into the mouth of the god, who regurgitates them as magical entities, empowered to serve in a far more fascinating and useful fashion than they did formerly. You understand that unlike many of the more primitive peoples who pathetically ape our worship, we do not generally sacrifice our best contributing members: beautiful

326

virgins, good-looking heroes, those sorts of people. Only in extraordinary circumstances, and extenuating ones at that, does an unusually able and attractive individual go to the god. No, we send those who are in some way unable in their present form to make their greatest contribution: thieves, you see, dissidents, unfit spouses, children of the wrong sex—"

"You mean daughters," Carole said from the doorway, through which she preceded her keeper, her entrance sudden and dramatic amid the chiming of crystal beads. Effluvia and Alireza, who had stopped their wrangling long enough to listen to the man they were fighting over gain instruction from the one able to grant him to either female contestant, glared in unison at the outside interruption.

"Of course," His Brilliance replied, beckoning the two newcomers in without missing a beat. "What else would I mean? Though you understand, not only the children but all of the delegates are marked by the god for his transformation by their very unsuitability to move among the rest of our people. As for the transformation itself, the god in his glory manifests that. We priests are merely donors of the delegates, and are personally responsible for nothing save donating, and collecting the resulting product, and seeing that it is properly packaged and utilized. Other than that, we serve only to distribute the credits due from the sacrifice to the proper sources and thereby increase the gross national magical byproduct."

"Hmm," Carole said. "I wonder if my great-grandmother who enhanced her magic by eating children looked at it that way."

"That's something else entirely!" the lay brother beside her said, making a determined effort to tower menacingly above her.

Effluvia spoke up, her tail rising behind her more ominously than ever. "Was there some reason for this impertinent interruption? I was under the impression the underlings had been secured already, Your Brilliance."

"I found her in the god's room," the burly lay brother explained to the High Priest. "And that after I saw Brother Bullcow lock her in her room as sure as I see her standing here now."

"I needed to have a private word with His Highness," Carole explained with smiling patience, quite enjoying the discomfiture of the others.

"I'm afraid that's impossible," Alireza said, linking her arm in Rupert's. "His Highness is vital to this discussion."

Rupert's chin firmed and his eyes flashed for a moment, as he firmly and with very deliberate gentleness disentangled himself.

"Surely you can spare me a moment to consult with my staff," he said.

The High Priest intervened. "A moment only, Your Highness. There is much you need to understand, much to learn, and much to settle among us before your introduction to our people, and precious little time. That must take up all of tomorrow. You must be well rested so that you thoroughly comprehend what you are told. I can spare only a moment more in clarifying this situation for Mademoiselle Mukbar and then I must hasten to perform my offices at tonight's ceremony. The only thing of interest your staff member can possibly add to this discussion is an explanation of how she came to be here. All guest quarters are locked automatically. Is this in some way connected with her magic power?"

"You might say that," Rupert replied quickly.

"Indeed I might. I just did as a matter of fact. Please do me the favor of elucidating. Outside magic is always of great interest. One learns even from the humblest of sources."

"Ah, yes. Well, you see, my cousin just happens to be a very special sort of witch. She is a great sorceress of doors. They find her powers irresistible."

"Remarkable," the High Priest said. "Just how does this power work?"

"Goodness knows," Rupert said, smiling innocently. When the High Priest began tapping his nails on the arm of his crystal throne, the Prince added quickly and in what he hoped was an erudite and knowledgeable tone, "You see, magical power is, for the Argonian witch, frequently a matter of ancestral inheritance. My cousin was related to a wood nymph on her father's side. The wood in the doors still recognizes her as a relative. Because of that bond it refuses to bind her in other, more customary manners, or to cooperate with others who would do so."

"My, that *is* remarkable," Alireza said, fanning her eyelashes up at him. "I don't believe I've ever heard that particular type of power explained so well before."

Brother Bullcow rushed in before Rupert succumbed to the temptation to make the explanation yet more interesting. The brother's spindly legs pumped beneath his gold-colored, diaper-like temple garment. His lofty forehead was dotted with sweat. "Your Brilliance, your indulgence please, but I must interrupt. A messenger has just arrived from the palace. The Queen says—"

"Not in public, you fool," His Brilliance snapped. "Gentle ladies, Your Highness, I fear we must delay this discussion until later. Brother Erng, please see that Lady Carole is placed behind her friendly door once more, only this time please add a lay brother to keep the door from being so easily swayed by her charms. Mademoiselle Mukbar, it grieves me to leave you but—''

"I do understand.''

"Effluvia, my dear, if you would linger for a moment. Remember, Your Highness, your instruction begins early.''

Rupert gave him a curt nod and followed Carole and Brother Erng, who closed the door on Carole and posted the guard before Rupert was able to learn what had caused her to seek him out. Behind the door to his own pleasant quarters, he paced for a moment, worrying a thumbnail and staring distractedly at the fountain. Presently he heard a faint creaking. Something in the fountain stared shyly back.

He circled the fountain slowly. Just as slowly she stepped out, still staring, taking him in with eyelids still half lowered, long hair, not the yellow-blond shade common in Gorequartz but a pale caramel strung with gold shadowing her face. He gave her his hand to guide her around the fountain. She amazed him by falling to her knees, hair sweeping over her head as she pressed face and arms to the floor.

"My dear lady,'' he said, kneeling beside her, "are you ill?''

"No, Precious Polyhued. I come in worship and supplication. I bespoke your handmaiden and pray you will be merciful and grant my plea.''

"Yes, and what was that?'' Rupert asked. "My . . . hand-maiden was unavoidably detained before she could discuss this with me.''

"My Lord, I ask that you spare my little Princess, my baby. Take me instead if you must, but spare her. She is so small and helpless and she is not truly the daughter of the Queen.''

"Sweet lady, no project could be dearer to my heart. But how can I do so?''

She was taken aback. "How can you? But . . . ah, I see. This is a test, isn't it? You're testing my faith. But I do believe in you, which you must understand, even though you may see into my heart and know that I find your priests abominably cruel, your image forbidding. Your person, on the other hand, is all I could wish for in a god.'' She gazed wonderingly into his eyes as she said this, and he found he was stroking her cheek and brushing back her hair as she spoke. "You are so warm, and I know you are kind—you are the god. You have only to spare her, do you not?''

He stopped stroking and looked at the floor.

"Well, do you not? Oh, no, was I wrong? Is your gentle countenance a jest crueller than the fists of your priests?"

"Believe me, I'm not jesting," he replied, looking up quickly and gaining courage from her desperation, her very helplessness. "I want to help the child but to do so I must thwart those very evil priests you so bravely denounce in your adorably valiant way."

She sighed and smiled slightly, the suspicion abating from her expression. "But could you not deny them the rainbows they seek tonight, and thereby thwart them?"

"It isn't that easy," he said. He wanted badly to tell her that he wasn't a god, but doubted she would believe him. Besides, it was as the god she wanted his help for Bronwyn's child. "You see, in this incarnation, a lot of my powers have been hidden from me. My cousin, the one you call my handmaiden, knows a great deal. She's sort of a minor goddess herself." He was rather proud of that. Why should he bear the burden of deification alone after all? And Carole was better equipped to play the part than he. "Give me a chance to talk to her."

"When?"

"I'm afraid it can't be until tomorrow. She's locked in her room again and this time with a guard."

"But that is no problem for you, Grand Prismatic!"

"Isn't it?" he asked.

"No, for you have shown *me* the way to help you. You need only use the secret passage and guide her through it."

"Now why didn't I think of that? So I have. And the guards will probably be distracted anyway, what with the ceremony and the hoopla at the palace Brother Bullcow came rushing into the audience chamber about."

"At the palace?" she asked suddenly, springing to her feet. "There is trouble at the palace? What sort of trouble?"

"I don't know. The Queen wanted to send a message to the priest about something—"

"Oh, no. I should not have stayed so long. They will discover I am gone and have left my child alone. Oh, please, grant my wish. Deliver my child."

"I have a better idea," he said. "Why don't you deliver the child to me? Then my handmaiden and I can take you both somewhere safe. To tell you the truth, that is why I've come among your people this time."

"Truly?" Her voice was so faint he thought she would drop to the floor before he could help her back into the passage.

"Truly. But you must help us. We can't have you bringing the baby here. Where is a safe place?"

"Until tomorrow night, the safest place in all Gorequartz is that most sacred to you, most taboo to all others. Your image in the harbor."

"Wonderful. You fetch the baby. I'll fetch Carole and we'll meet there and—I'm sorry, I'm afraid I don't even know your name."

"Jushia," she said.

"Oh, yes. Jushia, of course. It would be," he said, remembering belatedly that he was supposed to be omnipotent. "Jushia, don't worry."

"Oh, no, my lord. With you on my side, never. To do so would be heresy."

"There's my girl," he beamed, and patted her fanny as she fled ahead of him into the passage.

He had one foot on the threshold when there was the slightest of taps on his door; a scraping as someone pushed it open. He shut the secret door on his sleeve and was still trying to extricate it when Alireza Mukbar slithered into the room.

"Rupert, darling. I'm here. Sorry I'm late but it took me a little time to bribe the wretched guards. I *told* them their god would be ever so disappointed, but the fellows haven't a jot of romance in their souls. Come to me, my lo . . . just what is it that you're doing there?"

"Washing a spot from my coat," he said, splashing a little in the fountain while still furtively tugging to loose the sleeve without tearing it.

"With you still in it? Silly boy. Men are such babies. What do you think servants are for?" She undulated toward him and as he turned to shield the door from her view, his sleeve, or most of it, pulled free.

"Ah, that's better," he said, tucking the telltale arm behind his back. "Now then, what can I do for you?"

"What can *you* do for *me*? Darling, don't be ridiculous. When you know you've been dying to see me. Rupert, you *have* been dying to see me, haven't you? Surely you can't be taking that hideous skunk creature seriously?"

Her delectable lower lip trembled, but Rupert was too distracted to be interested. What if she heard the scraping noises issuing from the walls.

"Alireza, you are an extremely beautiful and desirable woman," he said in a voice a bit too loud to be intimate.

"Yes, of course," she said, her eyes widening, startled.

331

"Well, I think I have been taking advantage of you. No, no, don't protest so sweetly. I'm very smooth when I want to be. You probably just haven't caught on yet."

"Not caught on? Do you think I'm a fool? I knew you would come here. I—"

"Yes, but did you know I'd release those smoky things? Eh? I doubt that occurred to you."

"Really, Rupert, that *was* inconsiderate of you. Why, they've done three times your weight in gold pieces in damage to the city. Not even the shrewdest of Profit prophets can foresee what will happen if they decide to wreak their vengeance elsewhere. Don't you care that they might have hurt *me*? They chased my carpet until I cleared the city walls."

"One can't blame them really," he said. "I would have chased you myself."

"You're too gallant," she said, giving him a look as hot as the desert from which her power base sprang.

"No, that's not what I mean. I simply can't blame the bottled things for being angry about being kept slaves."

"Darling, you're a bit confused. *People* are slaves. Magical entities are just there. If they're a useful commodity, one uses them but—"

"Without their consent?"

"I admit one never thinks to ask them."

"There, you see. You admit it."

"Admit what? Why are you trying to tell me how to run my business all of a sudden? I came here to—"

"Shhh," he said, muffling her face against his chest before shoving her towards the door. "You've had a long trip and you're becoming overwrought. I think we should talk about this later. Goodnight now. I'll see you tomorrow."

She had unlocked his door upon entering and as he pushed her out, he fastened the bar that locked it from the inside.

He was allowing himself a sigh of relief that diplomatic training included how to start a fight as well as prevent one. A resounding clamor echoed from within the walls and the passage door popped open again, spilling Carole into the fountain.

She sputtered and dripped as she climbed out onto the carpet while Rupert looked on with a mixture of consternation and wonder. "I knew that opening had to be around here somewhere," she said, nodding at it in an emphatic and victorious gesture. "But where is that woman? Did she find you?"

"Which woman?" he asked a little plaintively. "You're the third who's been here since I left the audience chamber."

"Poor thing. I mean the baby's nurse. Or was she among your admirers tonight?"

"Cousin, sarcasm ill befits your role as priestess."

"Perhaps you'd rather I'd sacrifice people instead?"

"Never mind. In answer to your question, yes, Jushia found me. If you'll just pop back into that passage before we're detained again, I'll tell you all about it as we go."

Timoteo the travel logger shivered in his soaked robes and wished his accomplices had thought to leave him a change of clothes. He felt like a fish baking in wet leaves as he huddled in the tiny secret room beneath the footpath separating the moat from the canal. He would have to dry off before he executed his plan or he would leave big muddy footprints all over the palace floors.

He thought weeks had passed instead of only hours since the priests stopped splashing around looking for him and the drawbridge was finally raised. He was glad the entrance had been where his accomplices said it would be, and well marked with the shell-tied ribbon he pulled inside after him. He had always been a bit squeamish about jumping into rivers, though the terror with which he had so thoroughly impressed the Prince and the witch in preparation for this moment had been more or less feigned. They were both, he could be sure, thoroughly convinced that he had drowned, and since they were convinced, the priests would also be convinced. His hiding place would remain a secret, as it had been since it was clandestinely built into the footpath by the ancestors of his friends when their slave labor constructed the path. Its admittedly modest secret was passed from father to son, mother to daughter, and had proved useful for slipping past the guards at either end of the footpath and onto the drawbridge when lowered for heavy traffic. The use of the little room provided his friends with a way to evade inconvenient questions, prevented them from having to construct untruthful excuses for their comings and goings when truthful explanations would assuredly have pleased neither the guards nor Their Majesties.

He heard the groan of iron and timbers and the stone-enforced walls of the little chamber quivered slightly as the drawbridge thunked down onto the path above him. He did not use the entrance through which he had come. Instead, he used the one on the opposite side of the path. It opened under the bridge, just above water level in the moat, which was lower than that of the canal. The guards customarily faced out, his allies assured him, and with the ponderous bridge in position, his exit would be unobserved.

Footsteps were overlayed by the low murmur of voices soberly conversing in tones suitable to the religious occasion drawing them forth. When the clamor overhead reached what Timoteo judged a prudently crowded level, he swung himself up onto the bridge, landing acrobatically upright. Most of the traffic was concentrated near the center of the bridge, but enough people strayed near the edges to conceal him. No one gave him a second glance, each person intent upon his own business which, judging from the expressions on their faces, was not cheerful.

Timoteo scowled and marched briskly against the tide of people, his expression arranged to say to all who saw him that he was a busy, important man who had been accidentally drenched and who needed urgently to return to his chambers in the palace for a change of clothing before rejoining the crowd bustling off to the ceremony. He kept within the throng until he was inside the palace. His allies had drawn him a floor plan, which he had memorized, and now he had no trouble locating the privy tower, where he secreted himself in darkness almost as overpoweringly smelly as the skunkwoman. To pass the time until the castle would be clear enough of inhabitants, he recalled his recent travels in four different countries and went back over the instructions he had received from the relatives of the allies he had met in one of them. He hoped his contacts had stayed on friendly terms with their kin, and that the prearranged signal would have indeed been prearranged on this end as well. If not . . .

With that foray into futile worry, he decided that the atmosphere of his hiding place was depressing him. Slipping out into the torchlit hall, he turned left at one of the bedchambers, dried his feet and legs, and regretted that he could not borrow an item or two of dry clothing without providing clues to his identity. He used the front staircase to reach the second floor, and the main hallways rather than the back ways, reasoning that for the ceremony of which he had been told, a lesser servant or two was more likely than his or her betters to be running loose, unconsoled by religion. He fully expected, on reaching the nursery, that the nurse and her charge would both be absent, tending to their spiritual needs.

He opened the door to the nursery as if he had come bearing a message for the nurse. As he expected, however, she was not there. The room was dark and gently redolent of baby oil, powder, and the faintest lingering scent of soiled diaper. The nurse's cot was flat and tidy, the blanket pulled up over the pillow. Outside the narrow window thunder crashed and lightning crackled across the pane. From the cradle beside the window a thin and plaintive cry arose. Smiling, Timoteo knelt and scooped up his quarry, quieting her with the extravagant promises he made to all females of any age.

Now came the difficult part, the part with which he needed help. Suddenly he felt sure that it would not be there, that his allies in the city would not be alert for his signal. Though the plans had been set for the night of the ceremony from the beginning, he had not had time to contact anyone after his arrival and make them aware of his presence. The barge's proximity to the little room had been a fortunate happenstance that was supposed to take place in a more deliberate fashion, and would have, had he not been under guard with the witch and Prince. Still, his allies were exceptionally well-informed of activities in and around both temple and palace. He had to trust that his predicament had been noted. If so, they should be watching.

He lifted a torch from its sconce outside the doorway and carried it back into the darkened room. With the baby snuggled in the crook of one arm, he carried the torch to the window, raising and lowering it in a deliberate pattern, slowly and precisely, so that it would not be confused with lightning.

The baby slept against his chest and he folded his wet robe over her blanket as he carried her through the hallways and down the steps to the delivery entrance. No sooner had he reached the door than another lightning flash revealed a rope writhing down across the wall, atop which a man stood with outstretched arms.

Timoteo handed him the child and scaled the rope without further encouragement. Vast relief expanded within him as the man handed the child to a woman standing in a small craft on the other side of the wall. The woman cradled the baby against her breast. The men joined her, and silently they rowed across to the opposite shore.

Timoteo had to hand it to these Gorequartz kinfolk of his friends. They knew how to steal a child. There was still much more to be done, of course, but the hard part was over. They could work the rest of it out later, when it was safe to talk.

CHAPTER X

Rupert would have liked to lead the way, but was daunted despite all of his best intentions. The passage, just large enough for any average-to-smallish size person, took considerable contortions and acrobatics on his part to accommodate his great stature. These were made no easier by the inflexibility of the rowan shield still strapped to his back. It insisted on catching on the walls at every twist and turn, but he dare not leave it behind. The explanations and instructions he had planned to issue had to wait until he and Carole entered a wide spot, a central downward staircase with the narrower corridors branching off of it in two directions at each level.

He told her the bare bones of Jushia's message, ending with the caution that they would be making their way to the godhead in the midst of what had been referred to as the Ceremony of the Midnight Rainbow.

"Hmph," Carole said. "Sounds like a lodge meeting for old trappers' wives or something to me. Still, I suppose it will keep everyone too preoccupied to follow us for a while."

"I suggest we keep moving unless you wish to return to languish in your dungeon again. I can handle this alone, you know."

"I wouldn't dream of it. Once we have the child, I see nothing to stop us from just continuing on until we're back in Argonia. And I'm afraid if we're caught again I'll have to languish somewhere other than the very nice room I have so cleverly escaped this time. One gets awfully good service associating with a God."

"I'm not a God," he said testily.

"Yes, well, I think we should both try to bear that in mind, eh?" They were descending the staircase as they talked and suddenly found it ended in a blank wall. Although they felt along it and Rupert went so far as to put his shoulder to it, it offered no egress. Carole softly hummed several religious-sounding hymns before recalling that the chief function of the passage seemed to be to expedite trysts. Thereafter she hummed one of her father's favorite ballads about illicit love, cuckholded husbands, and indiscreet horse grooms who came to especially gruesome ends. The wall swung inward with barely a whisper, nearly knocking them both flat before they could scramble around it and out into the mist.

The mist had changed. Instead of the dense, obscuring silver-white of earlier in the evening, it now surrounded them in a glowing kaleidoscope of pearlized color, lit from without and dancing with shadows. They walked cautiously through it, listening for the pacing of the sentry, the slish of canal water against the banks. They heard nothing but a vague disturbance, then, as they stepped forward, a subdued chanting rising on the swirls of color, falling in a hushed murmur to the docks where it hissed like the inhalation of some great monster, muffled by mist and distance.

Carole sidled forward and Rupert lost sight of the tail of her skirt in the mist until her hand reached back for him, fingers wiggling at him to follow. He did. He didn't need the warning gesture of those same fingers at her lips. He stayed perfectly quiet of his own volition, his breath deserting him as he surveyed the scene before him.

The lights of moon, stars, torches and candles shone through the crystal panes of the shrines lining the banks. Bubbles of irridescence skimmed the breeze across the canal, illuminating the water, collecting the reflections from the brightly lit shrines and casting them into the canal as dark, moist replicas of their daylight manifestations. Elongated shadows swayed somewhere in the midst of the light behind the dazzling panes, intoning a song as regular and monotonous as a drumbeat. The river nearest the temple dock, shadowed by the great edifice, was dark. With a meaningful glance back at Rupert, Carole lowered herself carefully into the river. Rupert paused long enough to adjust the strap of the shield so it wouldn't unduly hinder his movements then pulled off his boots and let them fill with water and sink before joining Carole. The water was warm and fragrant with the freshness of a storm-bearing wind.

"Are you a strong enough swimmer to reach the harbor?" she asked.

"I was strong enough to save you," he reminded her.

"I know, but that was a short ways. This is quite long."

"Yes, in fact, you know, I believe that perhaps while I wear the comb it may give me a certain advantage in the water. I seemed to have no problem breathing that other time—"

"Fine. We can swim above water most of the time so that we'll spot the nurse, should we pass her, but we may need to stay submerged for some time to hide."

He nodded and they set out, Carole leading, side-stroking with their faces to the shrines illuminating one bank.

During their previous twilit ride, they had failed to notice the rectangular pools connecting the shrines along each bank to each other. But now the beaming colors danced off the pools and the water cast bright snakes of light and shadow across the countenances of those who chanted beside the pools, staring upward with eyes full of prayer and terror. Very far away, thunder boomed. The moon and stars simmered in a cloudy stew.

Carole and Rupert stroked past three more of the shrines. The same scene was repeated over and over, as if they kept swimming past the same place. Far away, lightning first blanketed the sky with light, then pierced it through with blazing forks.

As the lightning sizzled closer, the chanting increased in volume, the swaying of the worshippers echoed in the clawing limbs and whipping trunks of the trees framing the shrines and pools. Carole stopped stroking and rested, floating with her hands grasping the bank, her chin on her knuckles, watching. Rupert had been watching her rather than the shrine, so when the first bolt actually struck the spires, he missed all but the flash. Beside him, Carole's breath stopped sharply and her eyelids flew wide.

"Wha—" he began. She lay a finger on his hand and pointed.

In Gorequartz, lightning was not only striking twice in the same place, it was striking repeatedly through the spires and into the shrine pools, the forks aiming themselves with the accuracy of catspaws. In the pool they faced, the High Priest stood ankle deep, clad now in a black-cowled robe with a multicolored hem that stretched above him in a semicircle as he lifted his arms to pray. Upon his chest was a long prismatic stone that sang with a light of its own. When the lightning struck the spires, it channeled through the pool and into the stone, which gathered the light in a great shining star and dispersed it through the High Priest, who jerked spasmodically. Then, his rigid form bowed backward, and all of him disappeared—cowl, robe, flesh, muscle, tissue, and organs snuffed out by pulsing jolts. Only the bones were left, spine arched, jawbone rising and falling with the chant, empty eye sockets beseeching the sky.

The lightning died. Once more the High Priest stood whole, clothed in his robes, his arms still raised, prayers interrupted. Rupert shivered, neck hairs bristling. He watched fascinated

338

while the chanting priest was flayed twice more by the lightning and reclothed in flesh and vestments as the spires collected and transmitted the deadly light. Then Carole tugged at Rupert's hand and they swam again, now carefully avoiding catching sight of the spires.

They had all but lingered too long. As the lightning receded, the chanting dribbled to a mournful thread. The worshippers filed away, one by one, from the river back to the secular reaches of the city. The swimmers reached the castle just as several richly clad folk arrived, dripping water from elaborate headgear that kept most of the precipitation from their fine garments. They hurried across the lowered drawbridge back into the palace. A fleeting, graceful shape, bareheaded, with hair dark and shining, caught Rupert's eye and he nodded silently to his cousin.

Carole pitched her hum deep and made it slow enough that the girl did a gentle two-step toward them that looked rather as if she was undecided between returning to bed or singing in the rain.

Seeing Rupert, albeit a bedraggled and drenched Rupert, the girl's face suffused with alarm. "Grand Prismatic! Forgive me but I was delayed. The Midnight Rainbow began before I reached the castle. I could not but stay."

"Perfectly all right," Rupert reassured her. "We just wanted to be sure everything was well with you and the baby—"

Jushia bit her lip and her feet kept wanting to two-step back toward the drawbridge. "I don't know yet, Precious Polyhued. But I shall know more when I can row her to you at dawn, when the locks open."

"Fair enough," Rupert said, "We'll be waiting." And as she left he said to Carole, "Sorry, old girl, but it looks as if we're in for a damp night." But the mer-descended witch was already stroking ahead of him, into the concealing shadows and away from the torch glare of the lights left burning on the castle walls for returning worshippers.

Around the bend the locks loomed, outlined by shimmies of dimming sheet lightning. The great beasts stood at either end, heads lowered, extra tails swinging gently. The hut was alight with the flicker of a single candle. An occasional snort of laughter or a quarrelsome burst of conversation carried across the water.

"We must go over, for we can't go through. Unless you can whistle the locks open, that is?" Rupert's voice was half-mocking, half-hopeful.

Carole shook the water from her hair and blew her nose clear.

"You may not have noticed but the locks are made of iron. My magic won't budge them."

"Then over it is. I'd like it better if those chaps up there were sleeping on the job, I must admit. Why is it only in repressive societies that one can get decent help?"

"Perhaps they'll be too taken with their own pastimes to notice us. After all, they're just supposed to accommodate night-time barges and things. I don't imagine they're used to guarding *against* anyone. We'll see soon enough, I suppose."

The stones embedded in the earthen portion of the locks were slick with water and weed and deadly cold, but they were also irregular and provided good handholds and footholds. Carole's feet were small enough that she was easily able to haul herself belly down onto the flat cottage-wide surface atop the lock. Rupert's much larger foot slipped, skinning his bare toes and instep. He bellowed—not a very intelligible or human sounding bellow, but a definite noise. The chatter inside the hut silenced abruptly. The whites of Rupert's eyes looked big as hen's eggs. Carole swallowed. The great beast on the end of the lock nearest them rocked restlessly against the chain confining one of its heavy, wrinkled legs and turned its head almost fearfully in the direction of the newcomers.

Carole took a deep breath and hummed quietly to the beast, but in a compelling, forcefully driving rhythm that set it rocking harder, straining the clanking chain, then tearing the stake from the ground before trudging tunefully toward the hut.

The swimmers dashed for the other side of the lock while the occupants of the hut dashed away from it. The clamor they made stampeding to the opposite end of the lock while the beast trampled their hut and its counterpart across the river cheered it on, trumpeting from its front tail, was quite enough to conceal any slight sound Carole and Rupert made scrambling down the far wall and back into the river.

The torches on the ridge top flickered in the rain, many of them darkened and half-hidden by the smoke of the others. The swimmers steered away from the stripes of light cast by the torches, clinging instead to the darkness near the cliff walls. Swimming was rougher where the river dumped into a sea whipped into waves by the last of the storm winds. Rupert had to abandon the side stroke and swim as strongly as he could to keep from being swamped. The comb might be protecting him and it might not, but he would prefer to test it at some later time, when he—or it—could afford to fail.

The godhead was unguarded and unlighted, alone, frowning

sternly in the middle of the harbor. Carole made a sudden porpoise-like leap and grabbed the lower lip with both hands, hoisting herself easily onto the shelf between lip and teeth. Rupert jumped up after her, his extra height helping him achieve what his lesser buoyancy would not.

The mouth was open to form a quizzical snarl, the tongue a wide, curving platform where the sacrifices were dashed to death. Rupert couldn't see how at first, but holding on to the roof of the mouth he made his way carefully to the back of the tongue. A tentative hello fell endlessly down the throat and echoed back to him.

"I don't like it here," he said. "One . . . one can't see clearly from here, and it's the first place the priests will look. They make their sacrifices here, you know."

"I didn't," Carole said. "I wish you hadn't told me." She leaned backwards across the teeth, bracing herself with her hands, and stared up the nostrils. "I can't believe the detail in this thing. Will you look at those little crystal hairs? They've gone to incredible trouble to make this idol look like a real person."

"Oh, I doubt very much that anyone made him look like anything," Rupert replied somewhat absently, for he was studying the distance between the corner of the mouth and the earlobe and wondering if the dimple in between would provide sufficient handhold until he could set foot on the end of the curl jutting out along the chin. "The family resemblance is proof enough to me that they left him entirely authentic."

"Left him? Whatever are you talking about?"

"Rowan the Recreant, of course. This poor fellow we're standing in. Mother help him, I always had a feeling that the stories were wrong. Cowardliness just isn't a family trait. I had supposed they just made him up as a cautionary tale, but apparently not." Carole continued to look puzzled and a shade annoyed. "He was one of my ancestors—one of the great frost giants from before we Rowans came to Argonia. Father told me about all of them, way back, as soon as I was able to recite the family chain. Not much about him, you understand, because he was a disgrace, left Great-great-etc-grandmother Adelheit alone with a whole passle of gigantic Rowans. But Sir Cyril took an interest in him and did a bit of research among other tellers of tales for the archives, to add to the chronicles of the Royal Family. I used to spend a great deal of time with Sir Cyril before I was sent to Wasimarkan. Splendid fellow. It must have been that shape-shifting enchantress who did him in."

341

"Sir Cyril?"

"Rowan the Recreant. There are stories about the enchantress elsewhere in the family chronicles, and a descendant or two later in the lines who supposedly was attributable to her. She was very powerful—much more powerful than anyone we know today. She was thought to be immortal, though since she's not around now she couldn't have been, could she? And she could change her size at will, which was the aspect that I imagine attracted the forefathers. Ladies of their own stature in foreign lands must have been hard to come by for a fellow as big as this one." He patted Rowan the Recreant's upper lip sympathetically.

"I suppose it's not unlikely, considering that she was able to shift her own shape and also considering the wealth of crystal in this country, that she might have been able to change him into crystal, too. The way I would reconstruct the story, going on what was told to me already, was that after that first fling—the one that's in the family chronicles—where he outsmarted the enchantress and escaped her land with all those jewels that he took back to give to Adelheit's father to win her hand, he must have had second thoughts. The next time the ship was passing by, he decided to give the enchantress another lookover. Perhaps Grandmother Adelheit wasn't that easy to live with. Perhaps the enchantress had more to offer than jewels. Who knows? But apparently she was not the sort of lady who took kindly to being left to pursue her own career while her lover ran off with the proceeds. Perhaps, who knows, those descendants that were hers were also his, unbeknownst to Grandmother Adelheit. At any rate, I think this is absolute proof that when he jumped that ship, he never intended to desert his lord, but was merely taking a little detour to see an old friend who proved not so friendly. Clearly, he was never again able to leave this harbor."

"Uck," Carole said, "You mean to say that we're *in* him?"

"Yes, isn't it intriguing? I shall have to speak to Father and to Sir Cyril about clearing up his reputation when we return home."

"Do that," Carole said, "I'm sure they'll be relieved to hear that he's come up in the world from being a berserking coward to being worshipped as a god." She yawned and shivered in her wet clothing.

"Well, yes, I suppose legend might choose to see it that way. I hope you won't make too much of the resemblance though, when we tell them about it. I confess I find it rather embarrassing."

"Convenient though."

Rupert couldn't argue that, but nevertheless he felt a twinge of guilt for making use of the situation. He wondered what he would do if they were somehow unable to make good their escape and he was forced to continue in the role in which the priests had cast him.

"Rupert?" Carole asked.

"Yes?" He was busy inspecting the ear again.

"What do you suppose that Midnight Rainbow ceremony really does? Besides scare everyone with the power of the priests?"

"Eh? What? Oh, I haven't the foggiest idea about that. You're the magician here. Look, I'm going to climb to the top of Grandpa's curls and keep a lookout, what do you think?"

"You could stay here and rest where it's dry, but I agree that one of us should go up there. That way if Grippledice passes by she'll be sure to see us. It would be wonderful to have her on hand as soon as the nurse and the baby arrive. But we could always take turns. Dawn is still a long time off."

"I know," he said, "But I'm so tired that if I fall asleep here I probably won't wake in time to relieve you. Up there the light will waken me."

"Suit yourself," she said. "But I could go as easily."

He shook her shoulder in a friendly grasp, like a mother dog mouthing a pup. "I have a better disguise than you do in this situation, cousin. If I am spotted, nothing very dire will happen to me. What could be more natural than a god perching on his own likeness? I'd be able to warn you, so you could jump into the sea. The other way wouldn't work nearly as well. Wait. Here. . . ." With a certain amount of fumbling and genteel cursing, he unslung the shield from his back and handed it to her. Shortly thereafter the mer comb clattered down upon it. "The christening gifts should all be in one place, with you, where they can be bestowed as soon as possible. Even though we'll have to carry the gifts for her later, the bestowing will give her some protection. Now you stay here and rest up so your magic will be ready to use when we need it."

With that he hooked his fingers over the sharp crystalline edge of the famous Rowan dimple, crawled along the Rowan cheek until he could place a large foot on the tip of the Rowan curl, and grasped the Rowan earlobe to pull himself up into the ear. He had little problem maintaining a grip on the slippery crystal surface—Rowan the Recreant had large pores. The giant's stony curls proved easy to climb. Rupert found a flattened place at the crown, probably where the giant's helmet usually rested, since Rowans had never had to worry about baldness.

For her part, Carole made herself as comfortable as possible, curled up against the giant's gums, her head resting on the curve

343

of the shield. The comb she tucked safely in her medicine pouch. She knew, despite Rupert's gallantry, that she would never be able to manage sleep under such circumstances, but she did.

Rupert slept sitting up amidst the crystal curls, his head drooping against his chest. The scrape of wood on stone just before dawn was not as loud as the pounding of the waves, but it was a different sound, and woke him at once. It came from behind him instead of in front of him, however, and he peered over the back of the giant's head to see the nurse sitting in her little boat, wringing hands stung red and raw by the salt water. Naturally, he realized, she would bring the boat in at the idol's rear, where she would not be so easily observed. Utilizing the many good gripping places offered by the giant's coiffure, he scrambled down to meet her.

Though Jushia looked as charmingly fragile as ever, with a hint of wildness added by her blowing hair and red-rimmed eyes, Rupert noted at once that something was conspicuously missing. "Where's the child?" he asked, lowering himself into the boat beside her while keeping it moored with a grip on one of Rowan the Recreant's stray tendrils.

She apparently noticed the same thing about him that he had noticed about her at about the same time. "You don't know?" she said, wailing slightly, which was fortunate for he could barely hear her over the pounding of the surf.

"Of course not. You were going to bring her here, remember?"

She pressed her face into her hands before looking up at him again, eyes wet with more than sea water. "Oh, dear. I thought perhaps you were testing me after all and had transported her here in some divine fashion." Her head craned slightly sideways, as if he might be concealing a child behind his back. "You really don't have her?" She saw without a reply that he did not.

He touched her shoulder reassuringly. "Maybe she woke up crying while you were gone and one of the other ladies fetched her to give her something to eat. Have you asked?"

"I looked in the quarters of Lady Fanya and Lady Aseneth. Both were alone and sleeping. I was afraid to raise a general alarm for fear you were testing me, you see. Now I must. Be gentle when they sacrifice me tomorrow."

"Now, now. Let's not be hasty. The child has to be around somewhere. There are only so many things you can do—er—" He stopped, deciding not to go into what things could be done with a helpless baby. "We'll return to the castle and search it as well as we can without rousing anyone before you raise the general alarm. I'm sure that we'll probably find the baby tucked away in the corner of the kitchen in the care of a kindly maid or something. You'll see.''

He took the oars and pushed off with a kick from his large bare foot, cutting it slightly on the sharp-edged hair of his forebearer. His feet were so numb with cold that he hardly noticed. It occurred to him that perhaps he should wake Carole and apprise her of the new developments, but there was little she could actually do until they had found the child. She was much safer staying where she was and guarding the christening gifts. And should he and Jushia not find the baby, he would need to return through the secret passage to the temple. If the child caught between the powers that ruled Gorequartz was not with the King and Queen there was only one other logical place she might be—with the priests.

CHAPTER XI

Carole dozed off with the pounding of the surf vibrating against the giant's teeth, shaking her and, at the same time, lulling her with its rhythm. She became aware that the sound had quieted in the middle of a dream. She rolled fitfully over, so that her other cheek would rest against the carved rowan leaf on the shield. Her body had been clenched tight as a fist. She ached all over from cold, even as she slept. She heard the familiar Rowan rumble as she turned in her sleep. Rupert stood over her. His voice came and went with the waves and he gazed down at her, his face curiously altered. While she somehow did not find it strange that he should be glowing with his own light, she did wonder that he should have found a change of clothing: sandals of a design she had never seen and a sort of breechclout made of bearskin, which would have made her a very welcome blanket. Furthermore, the whole ensemble—bearskin, sandals, glow and all— was distinctly see-throughish. Rupert's expression was anguished and vaguely hostile as he looked down at her.

She raised herself on one elbow to ask what he wanted, but sank back down again as if her limbs were made of noodles.

"Morag, how come ye back?" the voice asked. It was at once softer and deeper than Rupert's. It gonged in the back of her mind rather than falling on her ears. He continued to look at her. She realized he had mistaken her for someone else.

"Come, lass, would ye mock me, to lay here in your small size upon the rowan shield and look as innocent as if you had never doomed me to this?" He flung his arms up and shook his head helplessly at the crystal interior of his own mouth. Carole was not unacquainted with ghosts. Argonia was lousy with them. She just hadn't been prepared for this one in this place. She could not quite wake up but she did manage to gather her thoughts, to pull them in from the woolly world of other dreams so that she could focus. Someone needed to have their wits about them. The giant's ghost had obviously mistaken her for his old mistress and nemesis, the shape-shifting enchantress. Did she, Carole, resemble this Morag then? Perhaps the woman was an ancient Brown ancestress . . . but surely not. The giant was far older than Argonia and the whole line of Browns.

"Did you know what you did to me, Morag? Did you know it all? That I would stand here forever and never feeling with my body but feeling all the same? That I would stand for years in the sea, looking for you, that I would watch you die at the hands of the newcomers and never be able to save you any more than I could slay you?" He sighed and looked at her with infinite sadness. "Oh, girl, if you had to die, why did you not join me? I could have done you as I've learned to do those other poor sods those crazy religious fanatics stuff down me throat. Oh, Morag, I only wanted to see you again. Was this any way to treat the man you loved?"

He turned his face to the side where the tears slid off his nose while his shoulders and chest heaved and collapsed like the waves rolling against his stone body. Carole pitied him and also hoped he didn't grow so distraught he stepped on her. While in one sense she felt he was no larger than Rupert, in another she felt herself to be very much smaller. The matter of size seemed rather confused. Now, for instance, his face hung very high above her and his tears splashed toward her like washtubs full of water that never quite hit.

Carole sighed softly and somewhere inside of her another Carole stood to meet the giant. "Brace up," the dream self said, slapping the giant encouragingly on the ankle, which was all the farther she could reach. "Just look at you. You're a mess. What sort of God blubbers like this? Hundreds of people are sacrificed in your name and you stand about feeling sorry for yourself?

What would your worshippers think? Aren't you supposed to be setting an example?''

"How can you speak to me so, Morag?''

"Not Morag, just a simple village witch and a priestess who knows good and well the responsibilities a deity has to its followers. And speaking of your followers, what do you *mean* allowing people to be sacrificed to you? That's the most repulsive, tyrannical, barbaric thing I've ever heard of, even from a giant barbarian!''

The giant mopped his eyes with one hairy arm and blew his nose rather disgustingly, but the danger of enormous hysterics or a towering rage resulting in rampage and destruction to Carole's sleeping person seemed delayed if not permanently abated. He bent and lifted the Carole dream-self in one hand, eyeing her suspiciously. "You're not Morag, eh? You do sound like her.''

She assured him she was not, nevertheless. "Morag is long dead as you yourself just told me. What I'd like to know is why you aren't. Do the sacrifices your priests bring you give their lives to sustain yours?''

He snuffled and mumbled. She looked up at him sharply. Like a child guilty of overturning the milk pail he looked quickly down at her with his eyes the size of a cart and away again. "I said no. It's not like that. Not like you think. I've no wish for what those fanatics do to folk hereabouts in my name. Twas a fine thing to slay in the heat of battle with the blood rising in me, but to stand here forever cold and forever wet and forever alone, and have fools push people to death down my throat as if I were a man-eater of some kind, arragh, no. I never wished it. I would die and crumble and line the sea with these clear stone bones of mine if I could, but the stone preserves what was me, you see. I watch and listen and feel and never am able to stay a hand to those who would murder and cast the blame on me. I do all I can. When the bodies break inside me like cracked nuts I save the part that was human, the part that was that person, and before they can be trapped as I am, I belch 'em out quick as I can, and that much I can save. There are advantages for the disembodied who are not bound as I am, you know. A body who knows how can trick time and space, can enjoy anything. If only I were free of this crystal prison, I could do that.''

"Just be careful if you ever leave *this* crystal prison that your faithful devotees don't snap you up as they do those poor souls you belch and put you and all of your wonderful otherworldly advantages in a shiny new crystal bottle to sell to anyone who wants to enjoy the benefits of both worlds.''

"They do so? In truth?" His voice swelled like the tide and his right fist clenched and unclenched. Suddenly Carole saw the dream-self fall, but she couldn't tell if the height was great or small, or whether the moaning giant was growing or diminishing or if she was. In the middle of pondering the question she found that it wasn't the least bit important, since she was quite alone after all.

When Rupert joined Jushia in embarking upon the search of the castle for Bronwyn's baby on what would later be referred to as the Morning of the Divine Visitation, he learned one thing that had not previously impressed him about castles: Quite a few infants dwelt in one and each of those infants was prone to crying long before any sensible adult would consider arising.

He and Jushia separated to save time, she taking the west wing occupied by the royal family and the central portion containing the offices, meeting and court halls, and the kitchen. Rupert took the east wing, containing the quarters for the other nobles and the seaward extension that housed the servants. He realized almost at once that the search would have worked better the other way around. Jushia would have been far less conspicuous than he amidst the families and servants, he far more at home among the castle's administrative offices. He prided himself on his regal appearance, even in bare feet and wet trouser legs.

He did not search every room, of course, only the ones where he heard babies crying. That accounted for approximately every other room. Rupert was not shy about popping his head in, holding aloft the one of a series of guttering torches he borrowed from the hall sconces long enough to ascertain if the child in the room was the one he sought, which it invariably was not. Where the crying child was already tended by a woman or girl, he simply smiled and nodded amiably, checked the child, and headed for the next room emitting youthful howling. With babes in arms, some of the women followed him to the door and into the hallway, while others sank to their knees in awe and terror. Still others continued their tasks and wondered if the nice-looking, tallish fellow ever found his way to the privy tower after all.

It was not until Rupert left, disappointed in his quest and having seen a good many more of the offspring of Gorequartz than he cared to, that the women in the hall consulted with the women praying in their rooms and those gawking at the doorways and concluded that they and their children had been specially blessed by the God that morning. They then proceeded to

348

try to decide what, if anything, the visit portended. Vociferous interpretations quite drowned out the cries of the babies.

Jushia was not in the linen storeroom where she had promised to meet him. With the castle stirring, he grew nervous waiting, twice having to hide behind bales of sheets and diapers to avoid detection when the maids and other nurses arrived to gather their supplies for the morning.

When the first of the bustle was over, Rupert peeked out. Finding the corridor temporarily clear, he left his sanctuary and strode importantly into the great hall, as if he belonged there. He hoped to find Jushia consulting with someone on the problem of the missing child, if indeed she hadn't already recovered the baby and was delayed by the need to fuss over it. He didn't seriously think anything was very wrong. Except for the theft of Bronwyn's child, which had given him an excellent excuse to have an adventure, nothing had ever gone very wrong in Rupert's life. His rank and personal charm, while not causing him to be unduly spoiled or callous, had nonetheless isolated him from the worst rigors of the lives of those less amply blessed.

So when he saw the priests proceeding from the King's audience chamber, he was not overly alarmed, but nonetheless took the reasonable precaution of stepping back into the shadows and watching.

Unfortunately, one of the passing court ladies had spent the wee hours of the morning nursing her sick child and spotted at once the god who had, as she later claimed, miraculously cured her little one just by looking in on him, showing a love and concern hitherto not identified with the Grand Prismatic.

"He's here! The Precious Polyhued is here, descended to join us!" she cried, and from all over the palace other worshippers began to flock, babbling supplication and adoration and a lot of other things impossible to make out.

The priests, who disliked the idea of anyone overwhelming the populace without their supervision, dispersed the worshippers by swinging the incense holder like a sling and uttering threats and imprecations. Rupert found to his surprise that he was almost glad to see them, particularly when he recognized one of the prostrate worshippers as the Queen, asking him to send her a son quickly, and offering up her person as an implement to be used for divine inspiration if he chose. Feeling a little queasy, Rupert patted her on the crown as he joined the priests.

The High Priest waited until they were all discreetly behind temple walls again to remonstrate with his god. Alireza Mashkent lounged possessively near the crystal throne and burly lay brothers guarded the exit through the beaded curtain.

"Now then," the High Priest said, "Suppose you explain to us, Your Highness, just what you were doing in the palace alone and without our per . . . protection."

"Since when does a god need protection?" Rupert asked innocently.

"You never know when some crazed iconoclast who lost a relative as last ceremony's delegate might try to test your divinity," the High Priest said. "It could even be arranged that one would do so."

Rupert nodded and stared, waiting. The High Priest stared back. Rupert was a good starer but the High Priest was better. He had had more experience, besides which his control of his followers was subtly magically enhanced. While in possession of the shield, Rupert had not felt the High Priest's power. Whether it was that power or his sleepless night that made the Prince feel slightly dizzy, he couldn't say. He *did* know that if he stood for a moment longer silent and stiff-kneed he was likely to keel over.

"So," he said coolly, "no doubt you were wondering why I was in the palace. I was searching for my niece."

"Your niece? The young woman with you? I thought she was your cousin," His Brilliance said. "I'm afraid I must have missed something vital in this conversation."

"Then perhaps Mlle. Mukbar can enlighten you. The Miragenians have lent my niece, the Crown Princess of Wasimarkan, tentatively named Magda Xenobia Amberwine Ethel Ermintrude the First, Duchess of Millpond, Countess of Cedar Grove, Marquisa of three prime blocks of real estate in Queenston, Lady of Unicorn Bayou and Honorary City Assemblywoman of Fort Iceworm, Northern Territories, to your monarch's wife to impersonate her firstborn child until such time as she can produce one. The Miragenians are obligated to return the child to her parents in its fifteenth year under the terms of an agreement forged by Queen Bronwyn and themselves in the Year of the Great War in Argonia. If you sacrifice the baby first, it is clearly a breach of all agreements."

"*Fas*cinating," His Brilliance said, steepling his fingers in a judicious manner. "Well, then, if this is all done by some agreement or other I see no harm in accommodating you, though I must say it's highly irregular. An agreement is—"

"We've been told," the Prince said drily. "But Mlle. Mukbar's firm was a bit hasty in removing the child from her home and

350

birthright—and her birth rite for that matter. They took the child before she could be christened. Therefore, I shall not only need to see her, but to see to it that she is christened in the religion of our native land by my cousin, who is a duly qualified representative of our faith."

"Christened?" His Brilliance asked as if Rupert had said "cooked."

"It's a name day and much more," Rupert said.

"It sounded to me from your recitation as if the child had quite enough names. I fail to see why she needs a special ceremony."

"The names aren't actually hers unless given to her at the ceremony along with the gifts and blessings of her people and the Mother—"

"These gifts, are they valuable?" Alireza asked.

"Only to the child. In a royal child especially, they form the basis for the character and personality of the adult."

"I see. Yours must have been extremely interesting."

Rupert ignored the lascivious smile accompanying the Miragenian woman's last remark and waited for the High Priest to say something.

His Brilliance shrugged. "I see no reason why she shouldn't have this christening then, if it pleases you. You are the God reincarnate after all. But we could have had the child brought here. There was no need for you to roam about the palace alone, spoiling the impact of your appearance at the ceremony this evening."

"I beg your pardon," Rupert said. "But I believe it was necessary. As it happened, I did not find the child. Perhaps you will tell me where she is?"

"Alas, I fear we are unable to do that, though if you wish we can put her abductor to the question. So near to a ceremony, the usual procedure with any criminal is to sacrifice them, but I think we could make an exception if—"

"Excuse me," Rupert interrupted. "What abductor?"

"Her nurse was captured this morning trying to escape after having collaborated in the child's kidnapping. We were consoling and consulting with the parents—or should I say the foster parents—of the baby when we encountered you."

The beaded curtain tinkled and Brother Bullcow entered at a gallop, slid to a halt, and genuflected. "Your Brilliance, I beg your indulgence for interrupting, but I must report to you that the foreign witch is missing from her quarters again, despite the guard on the door."

"How sad," the High Priest said, his cold blue eyes on Rupert's face. "My, what a lot of disappearances there are today. Your Highness, do you know anything of this?"

"Nothing. I'm sure it is coincidence that two people you only casually mentioned you intended to honor so murderously on my behalf should disappear before you have the opportunity to do so."

"Heroically spoken," Alireza said. She descended from her place beside His Brilliance to twine herself around Rupert's arm. Rupert did not shake her off but neither did he change his posture except to stiffen slightly. "I think, Your Brilliance, that you should give your god a theology lesson. He's a nobleman, a diplomat. Surely he can be made to understand the interdependence of economy and religion, and why at times paltry personal considerations must be secondary to the good of government."

"Strange that *you* should be the one to make such a statement," Effluvia said, making a grand entrance by sweeping aside the curtain with a flash of her tail, "for I have come to report that by making such a fool of yourself as to follow the god from Miragenia, you have led the unbound entities here. They descended upon the quarrymen last evening. The miserable fellows fled for their lives, the oxen drawing the carts bolted, and the entire load of crystal for that day was lost."

"How very costly for you," Alireza said in a civilized tone.

The High Priest brushed his hand across his eyes and for the first time Rupert noticed that the man looked tired and ill. His skin bore a waxen sheen and his teeth were accompanied by more pale gum than usual. His voice lost its bantering superior quality as he spoke this time. "Enough of this infernal bickering. Mlle. Mukbar, you have foolishly blundred, as Princess Effluvia so aptly pointed out, and thereby have canceled any claim you may have on my sympathy in your cause. Your company must decide to do without you, I'm afraid."

"This is outrageous! I demand a better deal! His Highness is mine."

"Not at all. His Highness is the very image of our god and more valuable to us than your entire firm. The Princess Effluvia is widely known as the daughter of the King. Their marriage will once and for all unite Gorequartz under a single holy figurehead, though I, of course, will continue to supervise until I expire. By that time, the union should have produced offspring: a boy fit to be my successor."

Rupert was stunned. He hardly approved of having his future disposed of in such a manner, but schooled himself to proffer

352

only the mild comment that a youthful-looking man such as His Brilliance surely should not need to think of succession for some time, but could reign himself if he so desired without the help of Rupert, Effluvia, or any child of theirs—perish the thought, the Prince added to himself. He cringed at the idea of a fair-haired and dimpled daughter with a long black tail. He cringed even more at the thought of what would be required of him in the begetting of such a child.

The High Priest sighed deeply and pinched his nose between his thumb and forefinger. On some people it would have looked noble. "In that I fear you are wrong. You are still unfamiliar with our ceremony of the Midnight Rainbow, but it is my duty, as your earthly representative, to prepare for the sacrifices and the bounty collected thereafter. Look upward and tell me what you see."

Rupert looked. Above the crystal dome the iron-gray clouds tumbled, some of them edged with the pulsating bronze of lightning.

"To sacrifice to the god, to collect that which we require from the sacrifice, it is necessary to first draw upon the power of the storm. To do this I must wear the sacred pendant that directs the lightning through me, making of me a fit vessel for the work of the god. But vessels break with much use, you see, and more's the pity, so shall I. The High Priest traditionally lives but half a hundred years. That is one reason the central power of rulership has been vested in a secular King. If the King and High Priest were one man, himself of divine descent, there would be no need for him to personally undergo the rigors of the ceremony to maintain control. Lesser brothers could perform the more rigorous rites without loss of prestige to the ruler."

"I can see why you would find it of great Profit to thus thwart me, Your Brilliance," Alireza said with a confident sweep of her thick, dark lashes that in no way betrayed she was worried about being flung down the throat of a crystal idol. "His Highness is indeed worth a great deal to you. However, I am not without value. If harm befalls me, the firm of Mukbar, Mashkent, and Mirza will never buy another piece of goods from you."

"Madam, it is precisely for the commission of such follies as the trade agreement that commits Gorequartz to dealing exclusively with your firm that the present King should be deposed. Our wares are truly priceless. We should not be restricted to selling them at your price. And I think that you may be able to observe from your bottle later that your uncles will be no less eager to serve their Profit without you than they were under your directorship.''

''If I agree to this plan,'' Rupert said, ''you must allow my niece, my cousin, and Mlle. Mukbar to return to their homes. I will not play your part otherwise.''

''No?'' the High Priest smiled a weary and almost tender smile and snapped his fingers. Before Rupert understood quite what was happening, Brother Merryhue lit a candle from an assortment on a tray beside the wall and stuck it under the Prince's nose. Rupert suddenly realized that his own attitude was highly unreasonable. The High Priest naturally had the best interests of all concerned at heart. Having borne the rowan shield his whole life, Rupert had seldom been victimized by magic. The experience was novel. He was without resistance to it. He gazed at the priest with more trust than he had ever bestowed upon his own father, and, when Effluvia glided forward to take his hand, he beamed at her. Alireza Mukbar made choking sounds as the brothers hauled her away.

CHAPTER XII

Carole woke steaming. Her woolen clothing smoldered smotheringly against her sweating flesh, while beneath her head the smell of kindling ready to ignite rose from the rowan shield. She felt these changes but saw none of them, for when she tried to open her eyes, they were assailed by light of searing brilliance. She squeezed them tightly shut again and hoped she was not already blinded. While she lay still, the crystal beneath her, shadowed by her body, was bearable, but when she flung out her arm it burned. She allowed herself one or two heat-accelerated heartbeats to wonder what had happened and what to do about it before humping herself, hands and knees together, onto the shield.

Tugging the sleeves of her tunic down to cover her knuckles, she used them to push her and the shield forward, until she could peer out across the giant's teeth. Above a pounding sea, a hot wind seethed through turgid clouds, which in no way diminished the blaze of an oppressive orange sun dominating a full third of the eastern sky. Its fire flashed off every facet of Rowan the Recreant's face. Carole thought that on truly sunny days the frost giant must provide a traffic hazard quite as dangerous as mermaids to passing ships, if indeed any ships ever passed.

Balancing the shield on the Recreant's left molar, Carole flung herself over the tooth and lip and into the cool blue-green sea. The water was warm. When her hands and shoulders broke the surface, the saltiness was soothing as an herb bath to her lightly broiled skin. She dove deep, opening her eyes gratefully to an undersea terrain far more brightly lit than any place she had seen in the company of Cordelia and Lorelei. Still, the ferocious light was softened by the shadows of fish and seaweed and skipping waves. Long, green tendrils furled from the enormous bulk of the giant's submerged body. Carole swam in a tight, brief circle, orienting herself, noting the giant's position so that she wouldn't inadvertently swim headlong into his outstretched arm, half raised as if to protect himself. Rowans must have been less wary in those days, it occurred to her, for surely the famous shield would have protected the giant from the fatally magical aspects of the enchantress's wrath.

Thinking of Rowans and wrathful women reminded her that Rupert would still be waiting for her. He must still be asleep. How was he managing not to fry atop the head of his ancestor? Kicking upward, she saw Rupert's own shield bobbing just below the cleft in the giant's chin and she surfaced beneath it and tucked it under her arm.

With her hand shadowing her eyes, she searched the great head for her cousin. Pure and brilliant slabs of dancing light sculpted the nose and brow while the blinded eyes stared disbelievingly toward the cliffs, shadowed deeply in places while in others it was lit with rainbows on the sea and in the air and reflecting from the cliffsides, which winked with mirrored veins of icy-bright stone. No wonder the place was sacred and the hapless Rowan the Recreant had been named God of Rainbows. His former lady friend had certainly dressed him in the part.

All of that Carole saw clearly. What she did not see was Rupert, either perched or poached on the giant's pate, nor did she see boat, nurse, or child. She thought perhaps Rupert might have taken a swim but saw him nowhere near, and, besides, he was keeping lookout. Surely he would not have abandoned his post without alerting her. Several other possibilities presented themselves. Having examined and abandoned them all, Carole next dove to the bottom to satisfy herself that the most immediately dire fate she could imagine had not yet befallen him. While there were a few bones clothed in seaweed and barnacles instead of flesh, they were too old. Carole didn't bother to prod them. Instead, she swam upward again, under the giant's arm, toward the cliffs.

The cliff wall rose sheer and sharp. Any seaward invader would have to have good scaling ladders and tough boots. As she had neither, Carole dove again and surveyed the bottom, the topography of which was largely defined by the giant's huge feet, which met the cliffside on either side of the harbor. The right foot disappeared as far as the arch into the hill. Rowan the Recreant must have given a great kick, she thought, trying to get a leg up before the sorceress stiffened him for good. Fish swam in and out under his heel, toward and away from the toes, which made her curious. She dove a bit deeper and peered under his heel. The cliffside had crumbled away under his toe, forming a small cave. She wriggled closer, tucking her wet skirts up to free her legs and keep the cloth from tangling in the crystal.

The cave was not as dark as it appeared from the outside. She pushed her arms against her sides and bobbed up, seeking its roof. Her head broke water, and salty, wet, but perfectly breathable air filled her mouth and nostrils. She was in a grotto, pillared with crystal, dappled with wavery light. A beach of sharp quartz and clear white sand surrounded the pool. She scrambled up onto it, scratching herself on the sand. Beyond the pillars the grotto opened into narrow rooms, and she pressed back toward one of them.

Having seen nothing but temple, shrines, and castle, Carole had no idea where she was in relation to other areas of Gorequartz. When she heard the mumble of voices and the ring of metal on stone coming from somewhere above and in front of her, she was relieved to know she was near something that presumably had a landward exit. The only question was how would she get past the people behind the voices to reach it. Her wet clothing and the direction from which she came would, at the very least, present her with a somewhat unconventional appearance. The only way to avoid answering awkward questions would be to avoid the people who might ask them, so she was cautious as she felt her way upward, keeping to the wall and listening, trying to place where the voices were.

What she *heard* did not ultimately help as much as what fell on her. When a shower of sharp and shining sand spattered down on her scalp and shoulders, she realized that the voices, and the feet responsible for loosening the sand, were directly above her. The floor of the tunnel soon confirmed this when it took a goat-challenging slant upwards. She hoped the noise the workers were making would disguise the rattling of sand and the rasp of her breathing as she climbed. She had to sling the shield across her back to free her hands. The crystal pushed through the earth here, cool but cutting, and the sand stuck miserably to her wet skin. She slipped repeatedly, coating herself in grit. When her hands found a spot that no longer sloped away from her, she dragged the rest of herself up and stared blindly into the space before her while her breath evened and her pulse slowed. The pinpoints of light in the gloom ahead of her failed at first to register as anything but part of the random pattern of stars dancing inside her own eyes.

By the time her eyes had adjusted so that she was aware that the lights were moving, the men behind them had spotted her.

"See there! See there!" an excited voice hissed. A finger pointed past the light, eerily disembodied and importantly accusing. "I told you! Ears like a pachyderm's I've got and I told you there was someone back here but—"

"Hush. You'll bring the hill down on our ears. You there, come out here." He crunched towards her and she saw his white and shining face, lit from below, great holes around his eyes, which looked both frightened and belligerent about being frightened.

"Oh, Riz, it ain't a person," the other voice breathed.

Riz looked back into the darkness, then at Carole again. "It is so. What else would it be?"

"*Her*. The old one from before. Maybe a statue of her, put back here. What would an ordinary lady be doing in these caves?"

"No good, I say. And statues don't move."

"No one saw any woman before. And this section was blocked off till this morning. Mark me. This is *their* doings, them from before."

"You're daft, Ancher. That's superstition. Don't let the priests hear you."

Unable to impersonate a statue any longer, Carole very slowly raised a spectrally white arm and glided forward, as much as one could glide on sand.

One of the lights jumped backwards. "Oh, I told you, I told

357

you. We'll be paying now for taking the crystal. The ghosts of them old ones is back. Them colored things that got the evening shift . . . ghosts, I tell you, and this is—''

"That's heresy, man. Do you fancy gagging the giant your own self?''

"Hey there!'' a voice hailed from the back. "Riz! Ancher! What's going on back there?''

"Ancher's seen a ghost.''

"What? Another one? What color?''

"White and shiny, like us.''

"Ghosts ain't white and shiny they're—'' A third light joined the first two. "My-dear-old-mother-in-law-gone-to-give-the-god-the-bellyache, who the thunder is she?''

More lights confronted Carole, casting a sinister pattern of light and shadow on the staring faces. Carole had rather fancied having her turn at playing goddess, but couldn't wait for them to talk each other out of or into the notion. She started to whistle them a jig to dance them from her path.

"Who ever heard of a whistling ghost?'' Riz asked. "Take her!''

She was still struggling for the strap that bound the rowan shield to her back when they seized her and dragged her out of the mine.

Their overseer didn't seem to be under any delusions about her mortality or lack of it, but was nonetheless delighted to see her for reasons of his own. With the shield strapped to her, she could whistle and hum all day to no particular effect, so she stood quietly while the man inspected her.

"Anyone know who she is?''

"Ancher'n Riz say a spook.''

"She will be soon if she ain't already. I reckon the warder at the dungeon will be agreeable to taking her for the ceremony instead of my ma. That damned pious brother-in-law of mine thought he'd get rid of her, but the priests'll take a substitute. You three bring her along and keep her quiet. I want no husband or father come looking for her before she's locked away safe and ready to be decked with pretty posies.''

They loaded her in an ore cart with a freshly mended side and wheel.

"Ooo, didn't they do a lovely job?'' Riz asked. "I saw this last night, after the oxen wrecked it, and I never thought to see it roll again.''

Though not so influential with priests as his brother-in-law, the overseer was a man of no mean influence himself, and the gold pieces he slipped the warder readily persuaded the official to bring forth the missing mother and take Carole in her stead. All of this was done with the nonchalance of an everyday business transaction. Carole could see where it might be. The edicts and rites of officialdom often needed to be modified by ordinary people and the bureaucrats responsible for carrying out the attendant procedures. One man's detested and expendable mother-in-law was another's beloved mother, after all. The position of warder must be a coveted one. The man was plump and affluent-looking with a magnificent silver beard and a number of gold and crystal rings augmenting his spotless black uniform.

"Well now," he said when the miners and the overseer's mother had left. "You'll need a bath. Can't have you going dirty like that to the god, now can we? Makes a poor appearance. Spoils the ceremony and musses the flowers. You're in luck, my girl. We have plenty of water around here and one of your fellow delegates is a real ladies' maid formerly in the employ of the Princess herself. Boys, take this woman to the holding tank for the delegates, will you?" Meaty hands clamped on her arms and led her firmly away before she could extricate herself from the shield's restraining influence. If only they had been efficient at their jobs instead of so lazy and corrupt they would have had the sense to take a shield from her at least long enough to see if she had a weapon. They did not, however, and when she was able to take it off, she saw that it was so crusted with crystal sand they probably had simply failed to notice that it wasn't part of her clothing.

The holding tank was not a dingy cell but a room with a view of the moat—through iron bars—a southern exposure, and comfortable low couches. The floor was of scrubbed wood. The walls were painted with inspirational pictures of the temple and the godhead. Three other people occupied the room.

"That water's coming right up, miss, and a spot of lunch as well," the guard said, sounding more like an innkeeper. "Two of the ladies ate before they arrived but the King's chef sent down some very tasty victuals for the other young lady on nonvolunteer status." He indicated a woman huddled in a cloak that looked smothering, then shoved Carole almost gently down beside her, saying, "I heard the conversation out there and I just want you to know that we custodians of the delegates here at the dungeon don't think less of you for being an exchange. Your sacrifice is greatly appreciated by us, I can say for me and all the

359

others, and I don't want you to be concerned about being pleasing to the god. I'm sure you'll wash up fine."

She stared after him for a moment.

"Don't look so stunned, my dear," said the comfortable-looking matron sitting across from her. "Naturally he's grateful. Those of us making the ultimate sacrifice enrich our land and loved ones by doing so."

"Not to mention that if we go, he doesn't have to, nor any of his relatives," a thin, dark man added, smiling wolfishly.

Carole shook her head back and forth once and began skinning out of the rowan shield. The strap caught on her elbow. She cursed and turned her back to the cloaked figure next to her. "D'you mind?" she asked. Trembling fingers complied. Divested of the object, Carole turned to thank the woman, and the nurse Jushia's face looked miserably up at her.

"What are you doing here?" Carole asked. "Where's Rupert?"

"I beg your pardon?" the girl said, dusting off the sand Carole shed with every movement.

"Rupert. Where is he? Did he meet you?"

By that time enough sand had fallen from her face that the girl blinked with recognition and gasped slightly. "Milady, your pardon. I didn't realize it was you. As to the God, I know not. I left him searching the halls for the Princess." She explained about the Princess's disappearance and her subsequent meeting with Rupert and added sadly, "He didn't even materialize to vent his wrath on those who persecuted me. Do you suppose I proved unworthy?"

"I doubt it," Carole said, brushing the worst of the sand from her, liberally sprinkling the floor and the nurse in the process. She wished she could stay for the bath the warder had promised her, but she needed to pounce with an appropriate song the minute the iron-bound door opened again. "I could use your help," she told Jushia.

"Anything, milady. Though as handmaiden to the god you—"

"Do forget that for now, won't you? It's a misunderstanding. Rupert—the god—isn't free to do as he chooses."

"He explained all that," the girl said. "About how he was reincarnated without the powers befitting his station. And how his evil advisers seek to take advantage of him."

"Good. Then you'll help?"

The girl nodded, although she looked almost as frightened of Carole as she was of imminent death.

"It's very easy. All you have to do is hold onto this shield and

360

follow me carrying it. You will find it quite serviceable in case matters should become complicated, and, in addition, it will protect you from spells.''

Though their conversation was carried on in murmurs, the other occupants of the room watched them closely. The matron pursed her lips and whuffed with disapproval. The thin, dark man uncurled himself, stretched, and sauntered over to them.

"You breaking out of here, are you?" he asked Carole. "I am better help than she is.''

Jushia hugged the god's shield and stared balkily up at him.

"You're free to come along if you like," Carole said. "But don't get in the way.''

"Who, me? Get in the way? Lady, had I not been fingered by jealous rivals I would still be the slickest thief in Gorequartz. I disappear like a shadow in the night, you mark me. Just get the door open.''

That was done for them in short order by the sympathetic guard, who found himself engaged in the acrobatic chore of doing a series of high-speed pirouettes away from the door while twirling the water basin above his head. Carole whistled until the others, safely lined up behind the rowan shield, filed out behind her. Only the matron remained.

"Fancy not wanting to do your part," the woman said. "It'll go hard on you for your selfishness.'' What could be harder than being sacrificed to a crystal idol she didn't get a chance to explain, for they quickly left her alone with her good opinion of herself.

The warder soon joined his men in the dance. Carole stopped whistling when the escapees reached the courtyard. The others scattered while she and Jushia followed the thief. Carole was rather hoping that in this backward part of the world they might not have heard of a portcullis yet, but her hopes were in vain. The thief ran straight up to the portcullis and stopped, looking momentarily puzzled before snapping his fingers, dodging across the portcullis to dash up the steps leading to the castle wall, and plunging himself into the moat. The nurse hesitated only a moment before diving in after him and Carole followed.

By the time the pair of guards stationed on either side of the drawbridge ran to investigate all the splashing, the thief had led the other two back of the crystal shrines, into a warren of houses and small tributary ditches leading to the central canal. He slunk like an eel along the pathways and alleys, leading them at last to a street where people sat earnestly weaving flowers into garlands

361

and swags, across a tributary that smelled like a sewer, and through a crack in the far wall, to a rickety ladder that dropped into a dark hole smelling of urine, mold, and stale smoke.

A torch flared as they descended. A grizzled face examined them, and questioned the thief sharply. The thief's reply must have been satisfactory. Other torches flared up and revealed a group of raggedy people lounging beside racks of dusty bottles. All but three of the group were men. From the corner a child cried. Jushia sprang down the last rung, dropped the shield, and leaped forward, to be hauled back by the laughing thief.

From the shadows behind a rack of bottles stepped a familiar figure, smoking a thin roll of weeds stuck in the side of his mouth, while with a certain competent grace that was not at all unmasculine he bounced a redhaired baby over one shoulder. Pulling the roll from his lips with his free hand, he nodded approval to the thief. "Excellent, my friend, excellent."

The thief took a flourishing bow then broke into a wide, foolish grin. "We pulled it off, Timoteo! We did well, eh?" The thief said this with such joy that it was evident his ventures did not always go so smoothly.

The man Carole had known as a merchant did not indulge in such a crude display of pleasure but allowed himself instead a small, restrained smile, its effect spoiled only slightly when he chucked the baby under the chin before turning her to face Carole. Despite the chucking, the royal chin trembled with impending howls.

Carole felt a rush of absolutely maternal affection for this small relative. Despite all the trouble she had been through on behalf of the little scamp, she had been thinking of her as more of a goal than a person. The sight of the largish human infant with the chubby wet fingers and dissatisfied pout, lying absolutely trustingly, if not happily, in the arms of the disreputable Timoteo, made the witch feel that even if she had not been bored out of her mind at Wormroost she would willingly undertake the quest again. Between the Miragenians, the Gorequartz throne, the priests, and now Timoteo, the child was being tossed around as if she was a ball.

"Priestess, I believe your side of the family delegated you to christen this child. Please do so now. Our side of the family will stand witness. It is too bad Prince Rupert cannot be with us on this occasion, since I am sure he believes this whole snatch to be of his devising. Still, he will have the satisfaction, should he survive the devotion of his worshippers, of knowing he has created a most excellent diversion."

"Master Timoteo, excuse me if I seem a little puzzled. Are you claiming kinship with this child? There is no Miragenian blood in her lineage of which I am aware."

The merchant smiled sweetly at her. "Cute," he said and to the motley group behind him, "Isn't she cute? I never knew witches were so cute. I always thought they were serious, dour women. You mean to say you did not realize by this time, seeing us all together here, that we are gypsies, the family of Xenobia and Prince Jack? Kinswoman-much-removed, you wound me. I am Timoteo, also grandson of Xenobia, she who is twice a Queen. She regrets that she cannot be here herself, that my grandfather, my Uncle Davey, and my cousin Jack could not personally attend this important event, but that would appear too outwardly a breach of the famous deal, would it not? That so stupid deal made by my cousin, who can hardly call himself a gypsy now, without the consent of his Queen, the great-grandmother of this child. Unfortunately, she is not only Queen of the Gypsies but also Queen of Wasimarkan, so matters had to be handled delicately. But I assure you, never once from the time this baby was taken by those dogs of merchants, did we intend to tolerate it. No one, but no one, steals a child from the gypsies. It is always and has always been quite the other way around. A matter of honor, you see?"

Carole couldn't decide whether to dance or faint. What with talking to long-dead giant gods, fretting over the absence of princes who weren't gods, being captured and imprisoned for sacrifice and just as precipitously escaping, she had had rather a lot to take in that day. To find the baby safe with the paternal side of the family, the quest all but over, was a bit more than she could assimilate. So, as the representative of the maternal side of the family, she merely nodded. Actually, she only caught snatches of what Timoteo was saying. The baby had not been considerate enough to wait until her rescuer finished his speech but had commenced howling in the middle of it. Carole jerked a thumb in the direction of the nurse and covered an ear with her free hand. The gypsy took the hint and unceremoniously deposited the child in her nurse's arms. The nurse repaired to the corner occupied by two of the gypsy women.

Carole sighed with relief at the reduction in the noise level and at the fortuitous turn of events. She smiled at Timoteo with deliberately open admiration. "I must say your disguise was worthy of the famous Wizard Raspberry. I never guessed you were other than a real Miragenian merchant and I could have

363

sworn all along there was no band of gypsies accompanying you."

"Oh, as to that: I was always alone but wore the disguise so that I would not be so obvious as your very large cousin, the Prince. One can be more useful that way. In fact, I found it possible to be of aid to you before I met you in Miragenia—there on the river bank in Frostingdung, where I frightened away the Miragenian who set his mist upon you. These people here had nothing to do with that. They are relatives of a tribe allied to us by marriage and other little favors, and they have traveled all through these lands and worked the Gorequartz area extensively, though very carefully. We gypsies are widely connected. They were honor bound to help us, for it is not possible for any gypsy to tolerate the insult of outsiders stealing a gypsy child."

Carole scanned the swarthy faces. None of them was as well-to-do as the gypsies she had seen, certainly none as well-fed as Jack had been in his boyhood. As she watched them, their eyes slipped from hers. They did not trust her and did not like her presence. Gypsy honor or no, their cooperation in Timoteo's scheme could cost them dearly.

"We'll need mud," she told Timoteo. "And I'm afraid the mud of this city won't do. It's tainted and unsuitable. I suppose it's not possible to get good Argonian soil already consecrated, but soil from the farmlands here would be close enough."

The thief spread his hands expansively. "But that is very easy. The flowers were carted in this morning from the country in their own dirt to keep them fresh. There are barrows of leftover dirt sitting nearby. The garland makers will be only too happy to have us remove it. Choomia, you go," he said to one of the women. "Miri, help her. It's honest work. Not fit for a man."

The women returned in a short time, the topmost of the several tattered skirts each wore bulging from the arms of its wearer with a load of rich brown dirt.

"And water," Carole said apologetically. "River water is best. The sea water is too polluted for our purposes by being dedicated, however mistakenly, to that crystallized frost giant in the bay, and the canal is as bad."

"Fortunately, lady, the highborns agree with you, though for different reasons. They import river water for washing and drinking," the thief said. "This is work more to my taste." And he swung gaily up the ladder, to return shortly bearing the water in a pitcher of silver set with cut gems. No one had said that he should be the only one in Gorequartz not to profit from a religious occasion.

They poured the dirt into a pile which Carole then spread out on the top of a splintered piece of an old door. She blessed it, strewed it with cleansing herbs, and added to it the ashes from the small parchment rolls bearing the gifts of distant well-wishers, Rusty Killgilles and those early donors whose gifts Bronwyn had entrusted to Rupert earlier and which he had in turn entrusted to Carole shortly after she agreed to accompany him. All of these she had kept dry, rolling them in fish bladders. The bladders fit readily in her pouch for just such purposes—they also made excellent balloons should an occasion turn festive.

One by one she burned the rune-covered bits of parchment, letting the ashes mingle freely with the dirt. The runes endowed clear-sightedness from her seeress Aunt Sybil, a good ear from her own father, Colin Songsmith, and a few other gifts that were more on the order of well wishes than magical bestowments. Wasimarkan was too far to send anything very potent. It was a good thing for this child that a few extra things had been added between home and here.

Using the special priestess grip she had learned at the seminar in Little Darlingham, she smeared the baby totally with mud while getting practically none of it on herself. When the child resembled a mud pie, Carole held her aloft, saying, as Rupert had instructed her, "In the name of the Mother we who are gathered today name you Magda Xenobia Amberwine Ethel Ermintrude the—!"

"Wait," Timoteo said. "She cannot be called that. There are already people in her family with those names."

"That is the idea," Carole said. "To honor those people—"

"It is not a good idea. We cannot have two Xenobias. One is quite enough. You must give her her own name. A name suitable for a gypsy girl. Call her Romany also."

The interruption in the ceremony and last-minute addition of a name was highly irregular, of course, and Carole gave Timoteo a stern look to let him know she knew. On the other hand, the whole situation was highly irregular, and what difference could one name more or less possibly make? "Very well," she said, "Magda Xenobia Amberwine Ethel Ermintrude Romany it is. So you are christened. So shall you be called—though not all of it all of the time, of course."

She used the remainder of the river water to wipe off the mud before handing the child back to Jushia.

"Good," Timoteo said. "Now we feast."

Carole was mildly surprised at that, but Timoteo drew forth a dagger and someone else pulled a loaf of bread from the belly of his tunic. There were even a few berries and a great deal of wine, which had been stored in the dusty crystal bottles.

The gypsies were universally drunk by the time Carole decided that if she was going to give the child the remaining gifts, she had better do so while they were only seeing one child. Retrieving the baby from Jushia, she pressed the mermaid's comb into the little fist. She explained to the gypsies and the nurse what the gifts were for, since they might need to help her use them. The comb she tied around the baby's neck with a sandal lace. Jushia regarded it with frightened eyes but cocked her head at it attentively, as if its magic were speaking to her.

The shield was used as a cradle, the child deposited in the middle of it while Jushia rocked it back and forth with her thumb. Then, one by one, the gypsies stepped forward to bestow their own gifts: a ring to give the child lightness of finger, a pair of ankle bracelets to bestow fleetness of foot for dancing and running, a colorful flowered scarf to wrap around her head and conceal her true thoughts from her enemies, an embroidered sash to tighten around her middle so her belly wouldn't hurt when it was empty, a pair of earrings that would enable her always to hear what was to her advantage, the promise of a tamborine to fill with music and money. Timoteo presented her with the last gift: a twig, he said, from the travel log, which would always show her the surest and most interesting ways to wander.

The gypsies toasted solemnly if not soberly, then Timoteo stepped forward and picked up shield, baby and all. "I will keep these things for her, priestess. Romany will live with us."

"Nonsense," Carole said. "If we can get her out of this alive she will be returned to her parents."

"They do not deserve her. Besides, the Miragenians would be able to steal her from you again and send her back. How would you prevent that, eh? With us she will be disguised and safe. I want your word as a priestess you will tell no one and will not try to find the child."

"I can't promise that. Rupert and the baby's parents will be frantic about her. Don't be unreasonable. There's no longer any question of a 'deal' since the Miragenians have negated it by sending her somewhere to be killed. They're not entitled to her so-called services any longer, and we can make war on them if they try to take her now."

366

"Ah, a very sensible solution. Why do we simple gypsies never think with such admirable clarity? Nevertheless, the baby goes with us. Your word, priestess. You may let the relatives know she is safe. We will give you escort back to your land."

"And that's all?"

"There is nothing else."

"What of Prince Rupert? He saved your life as well as mine. Are we to leave him here?"

"Why not? He is a god here. You can send the dragon back for him later, perhaps, but he may not wish to go."

"I fail to believe that. If the priests start demanding that he allow people to be sacrificed to him, I imagine he will place himself in danger in short order."

The gypsy shook his head sadly and placed his hand on Carole's shoulder. "You are a nice lady, witch, but you don't understand noblemen as I do. My own kinsman, once he became noble, conspired with your kinswoman to sacrifice this child before she was born. It is the way of noblemen to sacrifice people for their own safety, the way of the rich to sacrifice the poor, the way of the poor to sacrifice each other not to be poor any more. In this place they take it to extremes, it is true, but I think the adjustment will be less for your prince than you imagine. Come with us, or you may make all of our cleverness on your behalf come to nothing."

"That was clever? That your friend would have been slaughtered if I hadn't happened to be captured and managed to free him?"

"We knew you would show up at the dungeon eventually. Your guide was a plant, he was waiting for you. I know your true powers, and knew also that you would free him when you freed yourself. We had, of course, an alternate plan if you did not."

"Which was?"

"Once you had christened the child, trade you back for him. What else?" He grinned broadly at her. "But I knew you would save him. You're a nice lady."

"Your confidence in me is touching," she replied. "But if I'm to maintain your high opinion of me, not to mention mine, I simply must find a way to desanctify Prince Rupert so we can both be quit of this Mother-forsaken place. I'm very happy that you'll be taking the child now. But can't someone please stay here just a while longer to lead us to the rest of you? I know a secret passage. I should be able to bring him straight back, or perhaps meet you somewhere safer."

367

The gypsy shook his head again, this time fiercely, all trace of tolerance or humor purged from his face. "Too dangerous."

She glared at him, then spun on her heel and headed for the ladder. "Thank you for helping me escape. Good luck"

The kindness was back in his face, along with a hint of reluctant shame as he said, "Murdo, Pietro, blindfold her and lead her to the alley near the shrines, where she can see the temple without attracting the priests' guards. You know the way, so that she won't find this place again." She drew back and pursed her lips to whistle, but he leaned forward and clamped his hand over her mouth, his other hand against the back of her head while his companions did as they were bid. "You don't understand, nice lady. You are not a gypsy able to find your way to us without giving us away. Anyone sent to meet you would be likely to end up making nasty little clouds for the priests to put in bottles and sell to the merchants. Probably along with the rest of us. Gypsies do many things better than other people, but being killed is not one of them. That is why we know so well how not to get caught. And why we trust no one but our own. And please do not worry if they manage to make you tell how you were brought here. You would never possibly find it again. But just in case you do, try to avoid getting recaptured as long as possible, eh?"

He released her and she resisted a childish impulse to spit at him, and said instead, as she was being led away, "Noblemen aren't the only ones who sacrifice other people to their own ends, are they?"

"Stop right there." He jerked the blindfold loose and stared her in the eye. "Priestess, witch lady, what are you doing? You trying to appeal to a gypsy's chivalry? Because if you are, dear lady, I can tell you, we don't have anything like that. We can't afford it. I want it very clear in your mind that you are going out there, probably to die, because you are being stubborn about a fellow who is having a very nice time and probably even now does not care about you or me at all. I appreciate that he saved my skin when he thought I was a worthless merchant. And I am saving him the aggravation of doing what he set out to do and saving the child for him so he can continue to have a very nice time. You could come, too, but you won't. So no more back talk, eh?"

A very weak cough broke the tension between them. Jushia stepped timidly forward, her chin extended a little as if waiting for a blow. "Excuse me, but I must know: Rupert, the Prince, is he not truly the god?"

368

"Having just seen me consecrate a child to the Mother of all creation, how do you suppose I'm going to answer that?" Carole snapped, as angry at the interruption as she was at the gypsy.

"He is a minor nobleman with a fortunate face that will provide for him the rest of his life," Timoteo answered more politely.

"However long that is," Carole added.

Jushia looked as if she might cry. She reached across Timoteo to stroke the baby's red curls and stood staring at the child rather than at either of them as she said, "If he is not a god, then he is a very good man who has willingly endangered himself on behalf of my little one. Your Choomia has milk enough for two, she says, Master Timoteo, and I feel sure you will get my Princess away if anyone can. So blindfold me, too. I know things that may help this lady save her kinsman."

Timoteo signaled and the nurse was blindfolded along with Carole. The two of them were led away.

When they were gone he turned abruptly from the ladder and bounced the baby so fiercely she started crying. "Women," he spat.

When at last their guides deserted them, Carole and Jushia tugged off their blindfolds and gratefully leaned against the nearest building. The streets were noisy and teaming with shouting, screaming people and the crash of things breaking, the scent of flowers and dung. The gypsies had not led them through the throngs, but along the byways. Nevertheless, the agitation and the smell of fear was as tangible as the rain that drizzled steadily down all day. The atmosphere felt shrill and jumpy. The gypsies had whispered agitatedly between themselves and stopped and backtracked along another route two or three times, and on several occasions someone had bolted past them running in the opposite direction.

As promised, their guides had left the women within a quick sprint of the mist at the temple's base. The guard's sandals smacking the wooden dock on the far side of the temple reassured them that they still had time to locate the secret passage. Jushia groped for the passage for a time, unable to locate it. Carole softly hummed the ribald ballad, and the door wall slid away two handspans down from her. Both women stole quickly inside, leaning upon the wall until it closed. Carole found to her surprise that the inside was not so dark in the daytime as she had imagined it would be. Where the crystal dome met the inner wall, a thin strip of light brightened the passage. Jushia led her directly to the central staircase, and proceeded to climb. Carole followed her up two twisting flights, to the level of the audience chamber and the rooms where she and Rupert had been kept.

Carole hesitated, but Jushia touched her arm and gestured upward. Down one of the narrow passages, Carole thought she heard Rupert's familiar rumbling voice, but Jushia was already three steps ahead of her so she followed. They reached the top of the stairs only to face a blank wall.

"Now what?" Carole asked, but Jushia was already fumbling with the wall. When she had fumbled for several moments, Carole grew impatient and hummed the song that had opened the lower door. Nothing happened.

"Why are we here?" she asked.

"The pendant," Jushia said. "The pendant of the Midnight Rainbow, the one that empowers the priests to collect spirits in bottles. It is kept here. If we take that, if we can destroy it, the priests will be unable to make a profit from the sacrifices, to give lives to the god only to rob him again."

"Good thinking," Carole said, and began humming what she could recall of the chant from the ceremony. The door swung open almost at once.

Jushia made no move to enter, but looked at Carole expectantly. "Do you think you can conjure the guardian of the pendant as you did the door?" she asked.

"What guardian? You didn't mention a guardian."

"There. See, beneath the altar. That must be it. I've heard tales." As Jushia spoke the molding beneath the altar, which was the only furnishing of the small, crystal-domed room, raised all seven of its heads and hissed at them. Carole hummed to it softly and skirted the altar to one side. The heads followed her movement. Jushia, her face white and her hands trembling, circled around to the other side and snatched the treasure from its pedestal. A brief flash in the sunlight and it disappeared in Jushia's mouth while the snake swayed to Carole's tune.

The nurse backed out into the passage again. Carole followed, still humming. Once through she tugged at the door with all her might to close it behind her.

The two of them fled back down the stairs to the level Carole had wanted to stop at originally. Carole panted for a moment, looking back up behind her. "That was very easy," she said. "You'd think they'd have more of a guard."

"That serpent would be a deadly guard to anyone else," Jushia remarked, when she had spit the pendant into the palm of her hand. "The priests are unused to anyone else possessing magic here, and have guarded only against their own sort of powers. I suppose they protect against the regular kind of heroes, warriors, you know. No doubt the snake has the power to grow three heads for every one cleaved from it."

"How about that? Good for me," Carole said. "And if we have that pendant the priests can't perform the ceremony?"

"Not the ceremony of the Midnight Rainbow, which empowers them to collect the spirits after the sacrifice. But I'm afraid they have already performed it this time. They will be able to take ours. But perhaps with this we can bargain. Otherwise, I intend to take it to my death, if need be."

"Let's hope that won't be necessary."

Another rumbling query from Rupert lured them down the side passage. The tone of his voice was aggrieved. The women rushed as quickly and quietly as they could. They were not so quiet, however, that they failed to mask the swish and thump of a seven-headed body negotiating the staircase above them.

Two crystal goblets stood on a quartz table between Rupert and the High Priest. The table was a huge slab of stone, rough rock on the outside, clear crystal with hints of purple in the center.

His Brilliance held a crystal decanter, from which he poured each of them another draught of honey-colored fluid. Lifting a goblet by its stem, he proposed a toast. "To the growth of your faith in you."

Rupert smiled, both to be courteous and because he was in a pleasantly mellow frame of mind. "As you say. But what is this drink? It's excellent."

"Elixir of the gods, shall we say?" His Brilliance chuckled benignly. "You qualify. Enjoy it."

It was sweet and rather oily and went down smoothly. "Nice," Rupert said. "Lovely goblets. Lots of nice glasswork in this region." He had dozed fitfully for three hours in this room waiting for the High Priest. During that time, Brother Merryhuc had kept the incense burning near his couch, which helped him relax, feel less upset about the situation, more willing to see the viewpoint of his hosts. He realized he had been rather selfish previously, insisting on having his own way. If it helped these people to worship him, who was he to deny them? On the other hand, part of him wasn't willing to make any such concessions but wanted only to demand, "Just who and how many of your devotees am I supposed to sacrifice to myself?"

"Crystal," His Brilliance was saying. "We don't make glass. We mine and carve crystal. It is useful for . . . holding things. And amplifying them."

"Amplifying?" Rupert asked, sipping.

The High Priest shifted slightly in his seat, his half smile deepening into a sort of patriarchal contentment at being the holder and dispenser of wisdom. "How much magic have you practiced, my son?" he asked. It was neither an accusation nor an expression of awe, doubt, or fear. It was asked more in the tone of an innkeeper inquiring of another how many customers he had served.

"Very little," Rupert said. "My family has not, at least on my father's side, bred magicians."

That caused the High Priest's smile to deepen even more, which suited Rupert, who was beginning to think ever more highly of the man, of what an attractive person he was, of how comfortable this room was, this temple. All those nice little arched windows with the breeze from the river, the tinkle of chimes, the coolness of uncarpeted stone, the quartz tables, all very gracious, very distinctive.

"You mustn't apologize," His Brilliance said. Rupert hadn't realized he sounded apologetic. He hadn't intended to. "I ask only to point out to you that you needn't be anything more than you are to practice almost any sort of magic worth doing. Why, you could enchant rings around that slovenly girl you brought with you using the proper incantations, mordants, and agents."

Rupert's head buzzed. He took another draught of the liquid to clear it. "Wait now. Incantations I've heard of. But mordants? Agents?"

"You've encountered the agents already. They are the entities we will collect at the ceremony tonight for exportation. But first, in a separate set of bottles, we siphon the energy of the crowd— the fear, the anger, the blood lust, all of those wonderfully powerful feelings that, when bottled, add power to any incantation, any spell, making even the most minor of magicians able to work truly potent magic. Yes, indeed, it is the mordants and agents provided for us by the god you represent that bring us the prosperity and plenty we here in Gorequartz enjoy for the very nominal sacrifice of a few misfits and malcontents."

"Ah, prosperity and plenty. That is why the people don't mind, eh?" Rupert slid down in his chair, most of him contented and wanting to smother with sleep the part that clamored against the inertia of his body, the lethargy of his spirit that made him listen so contentedly.

"Why, they more than tolerate it, my son. They embrace it! My children love their God of Rainbows, his bounteous gifts of rain and sunlight that make the food grow, the mining easy, and the gold flow in from afar. The sacrifices add a little zest to life. Enjoy it while you can, you might be next, you see? And our system of selection does get rid of all of the scolds and rebels, the officious but inefficient official, the extra daughter, the unwanted relative. What other system does so much? Our ancestors, having a smaller population, were able to utilize the inferior folk they conquered in this region. Can you imagine a people so ignorant that they ignored the god in the bay, did not go near him? Instead, they worshipped some dingy woods goddess, a deity totally inappropriate to the climate and terrain, whom they credited with creating the crystal. The fools never even connected the rainbows or the crystal with the god, who was after all *made* of the stuff.

"But we, who had for ages sacrificed to our battle god, Utur, saw him at once in the head in the harbor and embraced him. We decked him with flowers and fed him our enemies. He rewarded us, when we had discovered the secret of the pendant captured from the heathen witch, not only with victory, as your ordinary battle god might, but with an ongoing means of establishing a solid and flourishing economy, which is much rarer. No, no, my son, these people are not apt to return to the ways of darkness and dissidence for the sake of an unwanted relative or two. And the ceremonies themselves are such marvelous affairs. With your presence they'll be that much more so. Why, using our enlightened process of collecting that wondrous energy obtainable only from those who die, not in battle or honorably or of old age, but deliberately, helplessly at the hands of their leaders under the eyes of their fellows, makes our ceremonies so much more fulfilling than they were. They were not so exciting before we discovered the use of the pendant and how it can be used to gather power in the person of the priest by channeling the storm's power into him that he in turn may use it to set up the proper vibration in the bottles for sucking the spirits from the air, that he may meld them shut and seal them with the seal that binds them to service.

"Now we can capture the screams, the pure elemental terror of the sacrificial delegate and use it productively to facilitate all manner of curses, spells, and enchantments, lending them power and weight not to be obtained in other times. I used just such a mordant to effect the spell on my dear Effluvia. I will use a similar mordant to release it, restoring her to her former beauty and grace. But you can see, it is a process to be proud of and one you may well feel privileged to be a part of. Why, the survivors of the delegates have often remarked to me what a comfort it is to know that no tiny portion of their contributing member's Ultimate Ecstasy is going to waste.''

Overhead the clouds had turned black and suddenly a bolt of lightning cracked against the dome, flashing through the chamber with pure dazzling light before sheets of rain began rolling off the dome. The small part of Rupert that was not trained, not ensorcelled, not drunk, and no longer shielded from the force of the evil around him, stopped cowering for that flashing instant and cried out in protest, overturning the table and sending Rupert lurching for the door. At that moment, someone called his name and a piece of the wall swung forward.

The High Priest lunged for the door ahead of Rupert, but it opened before he reached it, and three lay brothers tumbled in. "Your pardon, Your Brilliance, but we had to report—''

Carole and Jushia crowded at the entrance in the wall, beckoning frantically to Rupert, who tried to reverse course and stumble toward them.

"We had to report that while trying to contain an outbreak of the marauding entities on the edge of the city, a group of palace guardsmen captured a band of thieves with the Princess in their possession. They have been taken to the holding tank for—''

Carole ran into the room and grabbed Rupert's arm, dragging him toward the secret exit while whistling a dance tune at the guards and the High Priest. Jushia pranced in the entrance, unable to resist the song. She dare not enter the room or be trapped but she was able to turn to try to set her dancing feet in the direction they wanted to go, to take herself out of Carole's and Rupert's way. She screamed, the pendant falling from her mouth to lodge in the scooped neckline of her gown.

Carole and Rupert reached the exit just in time for Carole to switch her whistle back to the one that had tamed the monster originally. Slowly it uncoiled, swayed, and slithered back up the passageway. But too late. The High Priest and the lay brothers had freed themselves of the spell. It took only two of the brothers to subdue the drunkenly befuddled Rupert, while the High Priest sagely clapped a hand over Carole's mouth, and the remaining brother caught Jushia with an arm around her neck.

CHAPTER XIII

The High Priest was aglow with the satisfaction of a day well spent. Despite the sloppy job that had been done of garlanding the barges due to the interference of the escaped entities, this was sure to be one of the finest sacrificial ceremonies he had ever conducted. True, he would not be as prominent a figure as he usually was, but he felt that the splendor of the occasion was not entirely due to the presence of the young buffoon who so resembled the god. Effluvia cut a wonderfully awe-inspiring figure with the black cloak covering her hair and tail, blood-red roses crowning her as she stood beside the white and gold figure of the living god, who was duly propped up with an oar at his back.

Though these two made a splendid spectacle, they were scarcely the most spectacular part of the ceremony. What the people who lined the rain-drenched rock of the cliffs had come to see was the parade of delegates, more than had ever been sent to the god at once since ancient times, when Gorequartz first was conquered. The bay was choked with boats and barges filled to the danger point with the privileged who paid for the honor of contributing to the mordant. Four barges besides the one containing the High Priest, Effluvia, the god, and the three women prisoners were filled with priests. Three more barges were crammed with delegates. The captive thieves alone filled two barges. The King and Queen rode in yet another, the baby cradled in the Queen's plump arms. Overhead, the angry skies had given way—as the High Priest had compelled them to do when his magically charged presence passed between the spires and pools of the shrines—to dark blue sky, a brilliant if waning sun, and a rainbow of unsurpassed vibrance and clarity. In the bay, the rainbow crowned the crystal head with a halo of color reflected in every facet of the huge frowning face. The rainbow's beauty was echoed in the barge filled with crystal bottles ready to collect the rich mordant that would come of this ceremony, much enhanced by the gang of thieves who would multiply the benefits of each death with a multitude of grieving. Another barge contained the bottles for collecting the agents that would be belched forth by the god.

The crowds were gabbling with excitement and fear, for the escaped entities had been hard at work, systematically wrecking house after house, concentrating on only the nicest places. They were unable to touch the crystal, of course, but there were many fine articles made of other substances that had been lost forever. The High Priest had little fear that the entities would disrupt the ceremony itself, although the Mukbar bitch watched the occasional explosions of color spiraling above the rooftops with a smirk, her eyes narrowing vindictively at him if he caught her at it. Actually, he wished there were some way to lure the apparitions close enough. He knew they could be recaptured, if only they were not so afraid of being swallowed again by the god.

While the lay brothers, clad in their golden ceremonial robes, rowed forward in their barge full of mordanting bottles and carefully began placing them on all but three of the god's lower teeth and inside his mouth, between his tongue and teeth, His Brilliance debated about the order of sacrifices. In his sure-handed way, he decided after only brief deliberation that the witch should go first. For one thing, her own contribution to the mordanting would be small, since she was gagged and the only person who might presumably care about her was well-nigh oblivious to everything. Besides, who knew the full extent of her powers? Best dispose of her quickly, before she could cause more trouble.

And though it was usual to take the men first, since they generally died less sensationally and without that lovely surge of lust that added such a fine edge to the mordant, he thought the Mukbar woman should go next. What if her relatives came sailing in on rugs to rescue her and spoil the story he planned that she had in fact never reached Gorequartz. After her, the male thieves. Sometime in the interim the Queen would respond to the bait in his opening speech by offering up the baby and he would expose her and break up the monotony of the long string of males by sending the god that particularly fat and regal morsel. Then the nurse and baby, perhaps. When the sacrifices were done, the Prince could make another little speech thanking everyone on behalf of the god. Now then, if only he would look properly impressive while His Brilliance introduced him to the buzzing populace, along with Effluvia, just to get people used to them as a pair, Gorequartz would have a rite unlike any it had ever seen before.

Rupert felt violently ill. What in the name of the Mother's

right nipple had they given him to drink anyway? Whatever it was, it was wearing off at just the wrong time, while he was being rocked into queasiness in the middle of the bay. No doubt the effects were meant to last longer, but His Brilliance had not reckoned with Rupert's sheer size—or maybe the High Priest just hadn't had time to get enough of the cursed stuff down him before all the interruptions. It took a bit more than that to fell a Rowan, as a rule.

As Rupert tried desperately to keep from embarrassing himself in front of all of Gorequartz, his relative sobriety was a mixed blessing. With no sword or shield or magical talent, what could he do to help anyone amidst this mass of hostile humanity? He wasn't yet sure he could stand up properly. Still, he knew he would have to die trying. The entreaty in Jushia's dark eyes unnerved him completely, as did the utter dejection in Carole's when he caught her looking at him over the puffiness of cheeks constricted by the gag, her flower garland slipping down over her angry eyes. On the barge adjoining theirs sat that merchant who was supposed to be dead, and the fellow all but snarled at him.

Inside the stone-bound body of his ancestor, the priests finished arranging the bottles, and Carole was plucked from the boat, hauled up to the giant mouth, and marched to the back of the tongue. The High Priest nodded. He and Effluvia took hold of Rupert on either side and helped him mount the wide ladder extending from the bow of the barge to the lower half of the crystal jaw. Rupert wobbled more than necessary, deciding it would not hurt to allow them to think him still under the influence of the drugged drink.

As he faced the crowd, the chant which had begun in the background rose to a crescendo, mingled with gasps and an occasional cheer. He felt their fear and anger, their pulsing excitement as if it were his own. It surged through him, and past, stirring some deep response within him he could have done without just then. He felt naked without his shield. Where was it now? Not doing the child any good, that was for sure. The poor little tyke writhed below in her false mother's arms. But he failed to see the shield.

The crowd blurred before him. He turned to look at Carole. She was on her knees, looking down the giant's throat. Already he felt her fear coursing toward him, passing him, through the High Priest, toward the bottles. Funny. He had not gained the impression that the mordanting emotions were so tangible, but he felt each of them, strong as his own pulse, Carole's the strongest now. Fear, yes, and dread, but dismay and regret at her failure to save anything, to spare even the child, her despair at having to die so futilely after so much effort. On all sides, the crowd throbbed with movement, the bay brimmed with chanting bodies.

The High Priest held his hand straight up, and stillness dropped over the crowd. "My children, the god has come among us again. He has been attended by enemies and ill-wishers and these he would have slain to his glory. He has been attended by liars, imposters so evil they lie even before they can speak, by women so debased as to pass off the get of foreigners for their own royal children, by witches and by thieves, but all of these shall be purified and utilized in his name to the greater prosperity of his people."

Though this was meant to be but a preview of events to come, it was spoiled by the King, who was gray with nervousness, and shoved the Queen and her baby forward, where they were handed along from man to man to the foot of the ladder as if they were no more than a child's ball. "Hear me, Grand Prismatic!" the King cried. "The faithless woman was my wife, the brat no kin to me. Take them both and use them, for they are worthless as they are."

The Queen shrieked as she was hauled aloft and almost dropped the baby. "It was that wretched nurse! I am innocent! She took my son because I sent her lover to the god and she gave me this girl-child instead. I am innocent!"

That gave the crowd something else to chant about, and Jushia was pushed forward, too. Rupert groaned as she was roughly hauled up the ladder and pushed down beside Carole. The High Priest groaned also. His predetermined order was being rent asunder by the untidy demands of the crowd. Still, they were generating the sort of excitement necessary for proper mordanting. He gestured. The tops of the giant's teeth and the cavity between teeth and tongue where the first row of bottles sat was filled with water. He stepped into the mouth with his bare feet. The Queen was being bound hand and foot by one of the priests, the baby thrust into the arms of Effluvia, who held it out from her as if it were a snake.

The High Priest would commence the mordant transferral at once, which would bind the crowd to his will again. He stood in the water, raised both hands and chanted, feeling the energy he had gathered join with that still flooding his veins from the ritual of the previous night. All before his eyes faded into one glorious prism of color and light and in his ears was a single roaring until

378

everything had drained from him, into the bottle. But where was the rest of it? More of the raw mordanting emotion should be bleeding from the delegates, filling him from the crowd, but it was not. He opened his eyes and saw that the rainbow above him was hidden, the sky boiling with flashing clouds again. The crowd stirred and murmured as lightning forked closer.

The King was the first to pick up on the disturbance. "Is something amiss, Your Brilliance? Have your incantations gone wrong? Or perhaps they displease the living God?"

"Your Brilliance!" the lay brother whose duty it was to shove the delegates to their destiny cried. "Your Brilliance! The royal nurse—she has the pendant in her teeth."

At that the priest hopped, dripping from the water. Effluvia and Rupert were ahead of him, Effluvia holding onto the baby with one hand while clutching at the stone with the other. The nurse hung precariously over the back of the tongue, the chain of the pendant in her teeth, the long stone shimmering with movement and whining slightly. The High Priest felt his own excitement flow out of him and into the stone. The nurse's face was grim, her teeth clenched, eyes shut, sweat standing out on her brow as the pendant swung back and forth over the dark hole.

"Evil, vengeful woman," His Brilliance cried in a voice that echoed off the back of the giant's throat. "It will do you no good to destroy the sacred stone. You are doomed and all who are with you are doomed." But the time for threats or bargaining had passed. Effluvia grabbed for the stone. Rupert grabbed for the child with one arm, for Jushia's foot with the other. Jushia dropped the pendant.

It swung wide and shattered on the far side of the giant's throat, its shards like shooting stars. The baby squirmed against Rupert's elbow and let out a great squalling cry as its blood spurted onto his hand. He saw that one of the shards had hit the baby's forehead, lodging just above her nose, but even as he looked the wound sealed and the bleeding stopped. Behind him he felt the crowd pushing forward, thrusting through the sea and over the boats, into the mouth of the giant. It would soon push them all into the gaping throat.

But the excitement was too much for Effluvia. For so many years, she had had but one response to threats of any kind that it was automatic now. Her tail flew up, her essence striking His Brilliance squarely on the belly of his rainbow-hued robe, filling the mouth of the giant with a cloud of putrid noxiousness and driving the crowd back into the sea, driving His Brilliance, the

379

priests, and Rupert—still holding onto Jushia and the crying child—back toward the giant's teeth, panting for air.

The mordanting bottles were overturned, and many were broken. In the bay, people coughed spasmodically, some hanging onto the sides of boats where they had been knocked in the scuffle. His Brilliance, himself wracked with coughing, gave the sign that the mordanting bottles were to be disposed of, the agent-collecting ones set up.

The priests in charge of this procedure stalled a little, taking their time gathering the bottles together, hoping the brisk wind that had risen would cleanse some of the stink from the giant's mouth.

"NOW!" His Brilliance roared, and the bottles were set in place in the giant's mouth so fast none of the priests had need to draw breath again until safely back in the empty barge.

"Get that slut of a nurse off the God and throw her down the hole!" the High Priest commanded, turning away from the mob of worshippers. The words were not out of his mouth before a scream erupted from the bay. More screams were followed by thrashing, splashing, and the splintering of wood as boats wrecked upon each other in their haste to escape the streaking bands of color descending vengefully upon the crowd.

"That's my property!" Alireza screeched, her voice roaring over the tumult of the crowd. She realized her mistake almost at once as the bands of light converged upon her in a single whirling mass. She dove overboard.

Everywhere people followed her example. Rupert thrust the baby into Jushia's arms, pulled Carole away from the hole, and began untying her hands.

In the bay Timoteo leapt from boat to boat, shield in one hand, knife in the other, cutting the bonds of his fellow gypsies and sending them into the sea. He somehow managed to avoid the streaking entities. He was scaling the ladder to the lower lip when the High Priest regained control, arms lifting, body swaying, chant rising high as the rainbow streaks abandoned their assault on Alireza Mukbar and whirled angrily toward the mouth of the giant.

The High Priest exalted as the entities flew toward him, but his exaltation wavered and died as they converged—he was not drawing them, they were attacking. He fell upon the bottles in the gutter of the giant's mouth and was enveloped in a buzzing blizzard of color. Another blizzard knocked Effluvia against the teeth. Still others went for the minor priests and the prisoners.

Carole jerked the gag from her mouth and blew a piercing

whistle that escalated into a wild reeling song. Timoteo landed in front of Jushia and the child before the first note, covering them with the shield. The entities gathered themselves into an angry cloud, leaving behind the prostrate bodies of the priests and Effluvia, and danced out to sea just beyond range of the whistle, where they hovered like a cloud of wasps. The High Priest crawled to his feet, unharmed and infuriated. The priests from the boats swarmed up the ladder, pikes at the ready. Timoteo struggled with the first one, but his knife was knocked from his hand with the pikestaff.

The High Priest seized the baby away from Jushia again and held it aloft. To Carole he said, "You may live if you keep the wild agents away from us. But the sacrifice must go on. This child has caused much trouble. She shall be the first."

Carole wasn't listening. Her whistle had died on her lips even before the entities had departed. She turned to look at Rupert. Unshielded, he nevertheless was not dancing. Instead he stood near the back of the mouth where he had rushed to save her. He alone remained still in the midst of the turmoil. A glow emanated from his body. It brightened the longer he stood there.

Her first thought was that one of the entities had harmed him in some way, but when the High Priest carried the child Romany to the back of the cave, Rupert spread his arms and walked forward, driving the High Priest before him.

"What are you doing to me, man?" Rupert demanded in a voice as great as if it indeed came from the crystal head his own calm face resembled. "Go away. Send these people home. Give that baby back to its mother. Do you think I want you to murder little children? Fah! You don't think me a god, you think me a monster. Leave off then and be gone with you. You're giving me a headache."

"The Grand Prismatic has spoken!" the crowd cried. But while he was speaking, Carole was not whistling, and the streaking entities attacked again, flying toward the giant's nostrils this time. Carole tried to pucker, but the giant's tongue slipped out from under her and she fell. The crystal head quivered, as if in pain, and a long crack opened in one cheek.

"Quickly, go," Timoteo said, handing Jushia down to Murdo, who waited with a boat whose former occupants now inhabited the sea.

"The Princess!" she cried, but the colored streaks dived at them, knocking her to the deck and Timoteo into the sea. Carole grabbed for him, but the head quaked again and a cavern split it from chin to nostril. Carole rolled to avoid it. Rupert grabbed the

381

baby from the High Priest just as the entities shoved him off the back of the tongue, to fall screaming down the giant's craw. Another rent and the skull cracked apart. The entities did a jackknife turn in midair and swooped down upon Rupert. He dropped the baby into Carole's arms. "Swim!" he yelled.

She stayed for a moment and tried to whistle them away again, but by now the din was too loud for her to be heard. Before the crack that split the crystal head ear to ear and dumped her into the sea, she saw the jewel embedded in the child's forehead, as harmless-seeming as a pasted ornament. Taking up the shell comb, she managed to comb the fine red locks just two short strokes before they were forced to dive.

They had to dive deep because wreckage and bodies were everywhere, but finally Carole found a place to surface: near the boat containing Timoteo, Jushia, Murdo, and several other bedraggled gypsies. She tried to hand the baby to Jushia but the child flipped her tail and jumped like a porpoise from between Carole's hands. Jushia squealed and fished for her. Romany leapt up into her lap. Carole caught the glitter of the crystal above the baby's nose once more before diving again.

The giant calved like a glacier, pieces of his crystal shell crashing into the sea, exploding tons of water upon the remainder of his hapless worshippers. On a portion of lower jaw, Rupert fought the entities, flailing at them while his own mighty blows threatened to unbalance him as they struck through nothingness.

Damn, Carole thought. She should have taken the rowan shield from Timoteo. She tried to swim and whistle at the same time, but the water was boiling now. The rest of the giant began disintegrating. The part beneath Rupert trembled. The colored rainbows regrouped for a final assault.

A wave threw Carole backwards and swept over her. When she looked up, the sky was black, with something shooting down from it. At first she thought it was another bolt of lightning, but then she heard the roar of the dragon, mightier than all other sounds, and saw that it was Grippledice, who knocked the entities aside.

"Desist, nasty things!" she cried, "I told you to find him, not kill him. Haven't you any manners? Now depart before I turn you all into steam!" And with that she swooped down to retrieve Rupert, who flung himself gratefully onto her neck just as the last piece of Rowan the Recreant crumbled away beneath him.

In the dragon's wake, a great streak of white light rose from the sea, to join the scattering entities. Winding around them like a ribbon, it gathered them together and rose with them toward the clouds. Thunder rolled a black cloud across them and when the lightning next flashed, they were gone.

The storm cleared remarkably soon. From Grippledice's back, Rupert and Carole hunted among those still left in the bay, searching for some sign of the gypsies, Jushia, and their small charge. Overhead a brilliant rainbow decorated the sky as if a disaster had not just occurred within its arch.

Carole dived repeatedly but was unable to go near the center of the bay because of the vast disturbance created by the destruction of the giant.

The rainbow had fled by the time Carole slung herself across the back of the floating dragon one last time. Rupert reached down and finished hauling her upright. She collapsed with her back against his chest and he almost collapsed under her weight. He was not in appreciably better shape than she was. Both were exhausted, shaken, and bitterly disappointed at having come so far and undergone so much for the sake of the child only to lose her again. Grippledice alone was cheerful. She growled at them in what was meant to be a comforting fashion and rose, circling the bay again.

From the rocky precipice where hundreds of spectators had stood a single arm waved slowly back and forth. Grippledice swooped towards it.

Timoteo basked in twilight as if it were the sun of noon and smiled at them. "Welcome, friends. I trust you had a pleasant swim."

"Where's the child?" Carole asked. "Where's Romany?"

"Safe," he said. "At her nurse's breast and well away from this wretched country under the protection of many fine fellows almost as splendid as me."

Rupert snorted most undiplomatically.

"Prince!" Timoteo sounded wounded. "Was that nice? You doubt I am a splendid fellow? I am such a splendid fellow I came back to let you and the witch lady know the little baby Romany is safe, so you should not worry, so her mama should not worry. And this is the thanks I get?"

"Timoteo, we're really not very concerned with your feelings right now, if you'll pardon me for saying so," Carole told him. "The child was wearing a fish tail and had a head wound when I entrusted her to you. It's a bit difficult for me to blandly accept your assurance that she is safe."

"You will take us to her now," Rupert said bluntly, "or I will instruct this dragon to burn you to a crisp."

Timoteo bobbed his head and scratched his whiskers in a meditative manner. "Yes, I thought of that. I said to myself, 'Timoteo, if you are a good fellow and go back there, that royal gentleman is apt to set his dragon on you. But then, if he does, he will have lost himself a very good friend, the only person in all the tribes who might let him know something about the child from time to time.' I would feel so sorry for you if that happened, Prince. And then, I am a brave kind of man, you know, so I decide to risk your dragon."

"You can't mean to keep her," Carole said flatly. "She's a Princess, entitled to a good education, a permanent home, good food—"

"Ah, lady, there is no education as good as the road. Nothing so enlightening as lacking occasionally for good food. As for a permanent home, have I not been telling you that travel is broadening?"

"She was wounded," Carole insisted. "And half fish."

"Lady, you told us yourself that the comb only makes her a fish while she is in water. As soon as she dried off, two little pink girl legs again, poof, just like that. As for the piece of crystal in her head, it doesn't seem to be hurting her. She acts no different than she did before. And it's kind of pretty. Gypsy girls like jewelry."

"That particular piece of jewelry was the one that the priests used to attract lightning to them, to harness its power for trapping souls," she said. "I have a hard time believing that it hasn't harmed her in some way."

Rupert kneaded her shoulder in a restraining way and said, "At any rate, she'll need special watching during thunderstorms. The piece that hit her is only a fragment of the original crystal, but who knows how much power may still be in it, or how it may have changed? She really should be back with her family where it can be studied and she can be properly protected."

"Protected as she was protected when the Miragenian soul-slavers stole her right out from under your nose, Prince? She is safe with her family now, with the part of her family who saved her. And that piece of stuff in her head is better hidden by her kerchief when among nobility than studied and prodded. Your nobility, Prince, would make her feel like a freak, a bear to be baited. With us she will be raised as one of our own, her little extra eye of no more interest than a cauliflower ear or a gold tooth."

"Timoteo," Carole said, her voice grating with reluctant men-

384

ace, "I don't want to have to give you dancing lessons. Tell us where the child is."

"Witch, I love to dance, especially with such a pretty lady to call the tune. I will not tell you. If I tell you you will use your dancing and your dragon and take her away from us. That would not be good for her and probably not so good for us either. You I will not tell at all because always you will have the unfair advantage of your magic power and could steal her away while making us all look like fools. The Prince here, though, he and I might work out a deal."

"What sort of deal?" Rupert asked. "The right is clearly on our side. The child belongs with her mother. Her mother wants her back."

"Her mother agreed to give her away for fifteen years to people who weren't even related to her. You weren't even supposed to get her back, just to get her christened. She's christened, she's with family. Her mother can pretend she's fostering. At least she will know little Romany is not being a slave."

"And just how is she supposed to know that?" Carole asked. "We have only your word and pardon me but—"

"Don't be insulting, lady. My word is good enough. But I know mothers. I know how difficult married sisters are. I know you and the Prince are going to have some time explaining this, that it may cause you trouble. And you are good people. So I tell you what. You don't talk to me any more about having dragons burn me up or dancing me into the ground and I promise, once a year, on the baby's birthday, I'll let you, Prince, see the child. You can visit her, see that she's safe. Tell her mama she's safe. But you must let us come for you. You must come blindfolded and not try to find us again. And you can't confuse the girl by telling her about her mama and papa or about being a princess. She'll be happier just thinking she's a gypsy girl. When she's fifteen and old enough to decide for herself what she wants, then she can know, she can choose. Fair enough?"

"I have no more right to make that kind of deal with you than you say Bronwyn and Jack did to deal with the Miragenians in the first place."

"You also have no choice. It's the best offer you've had so far. What do you say?"

"Bronwyn will send armies, spies."

"She would be foolish to do so. Xenobia will explain it to her. But she can do whatever she likes. The deal is between you and me. You may act as her emissary to the baby as long as you don't interfere and meet my terms. Answer me now, give me your word, or nobody's going to see her or hear from her again until we're good and ready. And we may not ever *be* good and ready. She's a very nice little girl."

Rupert deliberated for a moment. If the gypsies were so confident they could keep the baby secreted from her mother and all the might of the combined Wasimarkanian and Argonian thrones, then perhaps she truly would be safer from the Miragenians with them. He stared into the gypsy's shrewd brown eyes, which met his steadily. And slowly he knew. The man was telling the truth. He was overextending himself in fact, going beyond the bounds of what the tribe wanted, risking his own prestige, despite his nonchalant air, to ensure that the child would have her heritage when it was safe for her to do so. The Prince was shocked to realize also that the gypsy man, for all his mocking ways, admired Rupert more than he envied him, had been surprised at a nobleman who declined to be a god, and felt that perhaps such a man could be trusted even by a gypsy.

"Very well. I accept your terms," Rupert said.

"Good. Then give me a ride on your dragon to the skunk-woman's woods and I will contact you in a year."

Bronwyn's reaction to their news, while less violent than some might have expected, was hardly calm. Still bedfast, she blanched even whiter than the knuckles of her clenched fists, then turned red as her hair, her blue eyes snapping as if about to explode from her face. To the maid who fidgeted beside her pillow she said, "Send me the captain of the guard, the commander of the army, and Her Majesty Queen Xenobia at once."

The maid tripped over her curtsy and escaped as quickly as possible, leaving Carole and Rupert to face her mistress's wrath alone.

"Now then," Bronwyn said, "let me get this straight. You found my baby, you christened her, you delivered her from murdering priests to whom the Miragenians sold her, thereby breaking our agreement—"

"The gypsies saved her, actually," Carole corrected, somewhat timidly in the face of Bronwyn's anger. "I only christened her as you requested."

"And you left her with them? And agreed that Rupert should see her once a year while I cannot? What sort of an agreement is that? Who gave you the right—"

"They're good people, Bronwyn, really. They'll look after her," Carole said placatingly.

"I know they're good people, you double-crossing witch! I married one of them, didn't I? But she's *my* daughter, and, since the Miragenians have broken their word—"

Rupert did not respond to her words, but held her hand tightly, feeling the guilt behind them as well as the anger, the fear and the anguish and the disappointment. Bronwyn tried to break away from him and slapped at him, but his arms were long enough. He easily kept well out of her reach while still retaining her hand. Finally she let out a huge breath, leaned back against her pillow, and stared at them. A single forlorn tear slid unnoticed through the freckles on her cheek.

"She had a fish tail when you saw her," Bronwyn continued bitterly. "And a piece of glass in her head. How safe can she be?"

"I know you don't like the mermaids, Bronwyn, but the ability to turn mer when necessary is a very practical gift in any circumstances. Timoteo said she was perfectly normal again as soon as she was dry," Carole said.

"Timoteo! Timoteo! He'll taste my blade if I ever find him, this Timoteo! He's stolen my little girl. And she's injured. That piece of glass—"

Rupert stroked her hand with his thumb and after a moment said, "It was crystal, Bronwyn. Magic crystal. And I don't feel that it was an accident that it struck the baby where and when it did. The giant—our ancestor—I think he meant it as his christening gift. It has powers that may protect her. He was so sorry for all the horror committed in his name, so appalled. I think the crystal shard embedding itself in her forehead was not a chance injury at all, but a deliberate benediction, a mark of favor to guard her. She'll need guarding, Bronwyn. The gypsies are right about that."

"That we are," Xenobia said, sweeping majestically into the room and facing her grandson's wife with the same imperial air with which she had always faced everything. "You think you can keep her safe? How well have you done so far, eh?"

"You had no right—" Bronwyn began, trying to climb out of bed. Rupert used his great strength as gently as possible to keep her there.

"And you had no right to put her in jeopardy in the first place, giving her to strangers as if she was a stray dog."

Rupert faced the gypsy woman angrily. "Have you learned nothing as Queen? Do you think she wanted to let the Miragenians have her baby? I was there. We had no choice. Their magic was powerful. Even if they had never made a bargain with Bronwyn, the Miragenians could have taken that child at any time.''

Xenobia looked long into his face. Then, surprisingly, she dropped her gaze. Her elbows, crooked aggressively at her sides, relaxed. ''I know. I know. That is why I sent Timoteo. That is why the child must not come back here.'' Her eyes met Bronwyn's and held them. ''Forgive me. I have blamed you for the child's destiny. I do not read the crystal ball, but I think that this child is no ordinary baby, no ordinary princess. My people are good at hiding, good at lying, good at what it takes to survive the treachery of others. Not that some royal people are not also good at those things, but not you, Bronwyn. You, who were the greatest liar in all Argonia, are too honest for the people who would harm your child. Let us help you, eh?''

Bronwyn bristled, her back braced. Rupert continued to stroke her hand. Suddenly she turned and burrowed into the pillow, her head bubbing up and down. Then as quickly, she turned back.

''But why can Rupert see her and I can't?''

''Because you would lead her enemies to her. Because, again, you are no longer a good liar. You see?''

Bronwyn glared at her, but nodded sharply. Xenobia left, looking troubled, and neither so pleased nor so sure of herself as she had looked when she entered the room.

They were interrupted again when the captain of the guard and the commander of the army arrived, but Bronwyn apologized curtly and told them to wait outside before returning her attention to Carole and Rupert.

''What of these enemies of ours? The priests, that skunk thing, and the Mukbar woman?'' Bronwyn asked.

''We should cut off trade agreements immediately, of course,'' Rupert said. ''Miragenia has held Frostingdung in an economic stranglehold of dependency ever since they began commerce. There may be some difficulty, but I think with the problems Mukbar, Mashkent, and Mirza will be undergoing with the loss of their chairman and the trade with Gorequartz, they'll be much more amenable to reason than before.''

''The Mukbar woman is dead then?'' Bronwyn asked.

Rupert shrugged. Carole said cautiously, ''I can only say I never saw her come up.''

''And the skunk thing?''

Carole shook her head.

''We'll have them searched for then. And any remaining priests. If it isn't safe for my daughter for me to find her, I'll find her enemies and deal with them instead. I'm sorry I can't

388

thank you properly for your trouble right now, Rupert, Carole. I know you did a great deal and . . . well, but I have to *do* something now, you see, before I go mad. Ask Captain Ironbow and General Gristlebone to come in as you leave, will you?''

Grippledice waited for them in the courtyard. Her scales gleamed with an artfully limited range of color both Rupert and Carole found restful.

Rupert was more than glad to have the interview over, its outcome more successful than he had anticipated. The sunshine warmed him to his very bones. ''Would you tell my dragon she is looking more beautiful than ever?'' he asked.

Carole did so, and gladly, adding her own greetings to Grippledice to his. ''It is so nice to talk with you when I can see you again.''

''No thanks to you,'' the dragon said. ''You almost turned me into one of those hidebehind things with your blasted pill. I had to fly all the way back to Wizard Raspberry's castle in Argonia to get the damned thing removed. That's what took me so long. I figured when my Prince wanted to take up with that skunk creature that my being invisible must be leaving him cold. Once the spell was off, I ran into those flying refugees from a dyepot. They had no quarrel with dragons, so they agreed to be on the lookout for you. I had no idea the sight of my sweet Prince's face would inflame them with rage that way. I circled the city several times, but I wasn't even warm. Just couldn't find you, since I couldn't see you anywhere. Those things broke into houses saying they were looking, too, but they had fish of their own to fry, I can see now. I had to stop to feed yesterday, and so I found a cozy place in the woods to nap, but when I heard my Prince speaking in that big, booming voice, I fairly smoked out of there. So how about it? Ask him if he'll come up to my cave sometime.''

She set them down in the courtyard of Queenston Castle, where they barely drew a glance. Queenston was long since used to the dragons.

Rupert bowed low to Grippledice when her question was relayed to him. ''Tell her I'll be delighted to do so when duty permits. Right now, I'm on my way to the Royal Archives to see Sir Cyril. There's a little matter of a Rowan's reputation that needs to be rectified.''

''I have something to add that may interest you,'' Carole said, and told him of her dream conversation with Rowan the Recreant.

Rupert stood scratching his head for a moment, his frown

389

uncannily like that of his much-enlarged ancestor. "Oddly enough, I seem to have known that already. Carole, I think I shall forego making myself another rowan shield after all. If I had worn it when poor old Rowan the Recreant wanted to speak through me, I doubt he could have. I *knew* what he had to say, you see. That's why I feel that the crystal was a gift. And I seem to know a great many other things about people now—about Timoteo, and Bronwyn, and Xenobia, for instance. Do you understand what I mean? When you were back there in Gorequartz about to be sacrificed, gagged so you couldn't speak, I felt as if I were you, that I could have spoken almost in your voice and told what you were going through, because I knew. You're a witch, a priestess. Now you tell me. Is that magic?"

She considered for a moment and nodded. "The bit with Rowan the Recreant certainly was. The other could be, I think."

"Then that settles it. We Rowans have never been known as particularly magical fellows, but I can't help wondering if it's not because we're always shielded against it. I think I shall be the first to do without and perhaps I may find others who would not ordinarily be able to speak who can do so through me."

Carole squeezed his arm and said, "Come along then, and tell Sir Cyril the Recreant's side of things. I'll join you. I have a christening to record."

Grippledice blew a warm little gust of steam. Rupert turned back to scratch her between the eyes. As he did, he felt a warm rush of affection and admiration for himself wash through him. He stared at Grippledice for a moment and grinned, then hugged her scaley neck. Perhaps it would not be necessary to learn Pan-Elvin after all.

ABOUT THE AUTHOR

Elizabeth Scarborough was born in Kansas City, KS. She served as a nurse in the U.S. Army for five years, including a year in Viet Nam. Her interests include weaving and spinning, and playing the guitar and dulcimer. She has previously published light verse as well as seven Bantam novels, *Song of Sorcery, The Unicorn Creed, Bronwyn's Bane, The Harem of Aman Akbar, The Christening Quest, The Drastic Dragon of Draco, Texas,* and *The Goldcamp Vampire.* She is presently at work on a fantasy trilogy as well as a novel about the war in Viet Nam. She makes her home in Seattle, Washington.

Special Offer
Buy a Bantam Book
for only 50¢.

Now you can have Bantam's catalog filled with hundreds of titles plus take advantage of our unique and exciting bonus book offer. A special offer which gives you the opportunity to purchase a Bantam book for only 50¢. Here's how!

By ordering any five books at the regular price per order, you can also choose any other single book listed (up to a $5.95 value) for just 50¢. Some restrictions do apply, but for further details why not send for Bantam's catalog of titles today!

Just send us your name and address and we will send you a catalog!
